RED
BRIDE

CHRISTOPHER FOWLER

RED BRIDE

LITTLE, BROWN AND COMPANY

A *Warner* Book

First published in Great Britain in 1992 by
Little, Brown and Company
This edition published by Warner Books in 1993

Copyright © Christopher Fowler 1992

The moral right of the author has been asserted.

A CIP catalogue record for this book
is available from the British Library.

ISBN 0 7515 0159 X

Printed in England by Clays Ltd, St Ives plc

Warner Books
A Division of
Little, Brown and Company (UK) Limited
165 Great Dover Street
London SE1 4YA

For the heartbreakers —
Charlotte and Claire, Poppy and Amber.

Acknowledgements

Love goes to all those who have borne the brunt of my brusque telephone manner during the writing of this novel.

On the research front, special thanks to movie PR hotshot Alex Ritchie, and to Carol Foster for her advice on death and divorce. Thanks to Richard Woolf for coming up with a highly gruesome murder, and to Jim Sturgeon for his endlessly loyal support. Encouragement for writers is now available in the handy form of John Jarrold, whose enthusiasm for the printed word amazes me. Ann Suster managed to advise and edit me while actually having a baby (don't try this at home), for which I thank her. Thanks also to Jenny Luithlen for taking me beyond the language barrier.

Although the characters in this novel are fictitious, Andy's Barber Shop opposite Chalk Farm tube is real, and the only place in London to visit for a superb No.2 Flat Top.

Finally, ultraspecial thanks go to my agent Serafina Clarke, for supporting the idea while others wondered what on earth I was on about.

Trust must prevail
And in our hearts' confusion
Whatever love we give
It's better far that we should learn to live
Without illusion.

Noel Coward

Prologue

The rain has finally ceased.

The storm has abated. Electricity still charges the acrid air. Uprooted plants and palm leaves wash lightly at the shore. The settling sky, which moments ago had possessed the sealed lustre of chalced onyx, has added streaks of burgundy at its horizon.

From a glass-smooth sea of bitter crimson she rises, barely causing the warm water to stir about her. As she walks, the ocean bares her shoulders, then her arms. It is as if heaven has reached down and coupled with the brine itself; as though the furious spume of the waves has erupted into laden clouds to produce a golden union of sea and sky. The woman appears as a miraculous mirage, a phantasm, high and clear-complexioned, the planes of her face reflecting the pearl light of the tide. She is youthful, tall and loosely limbed, yet already in possession of a formal grace.

She turns her face to the penumbral globe which slowly sets behind her, her skin strangely pale in this savage climate. Her glossed black hair is twisted along her neck like the mane of a thoroughbred racehorse. Her slim dark eyes are as unfathomable as the ocean from which she rises.

As her feet find purchase on the seabed she ascends, the water returning in rivulets along her thighs and calves. Her naked body reflects the dying sun and the wine-dark colour of the sea, the colour of blood. The sanguine droplets glisten like rubies at her breast. Across her pale throat is tied a single rope of pure white pearls.

She pauses for a moment, filled with wonder. Then she closes her eyes and draws a breath. The air is spiced with lemon and brine, nutmeg and cinnamon. Her lips part in a moment of bitter exhilaration. Yet within the air she detects a loamy stench of corruption, as if the storm winds have exposed rotten roots within the freshly sundered vegetation. Soon will come remembrance, the unbearable pain brought on by loss, and the knowledge of something worse.

But for now, all is calm. The danger has passed. In the dying light she fills her lungs and slowly strides towards the waiting shore.

SUMMER

CHAPTER

1

John Chapel

A sea of heat swelled against the buildings in Shaftesbury Avenue. Lurid, unnatural light flooded across the sticky pavements, lengthening the first cool shadows across ochre brickwork. It was far hotter inside the club, but nobody minded. A pair of drunken insurance executives were attempting to remember the words to 'My Way'. They leaned on each other for support, slurring and hissing into the microphone as they watched the playback phrases of the song overtake them on the video screen. Their colleagues were wedged into a semi-circle of cane chairs near the bar, their jackets removed, their shirt collars loosened. They whistled and applauded each half-remembered lyric, stamping their feet as the end of a verse was reached. The waitress who removed the mounting Sapporo cans from the table between them had her thigh stroked for the second time by a balding young man with sad eyes and sloping shoulders. As she returned to the till she made a mental note to add a fictitious round of drinks to his bill.

The song had long reached its conclusion by the time the insurance men had pulled each other back into the audience. The sweating compère, a man dressed in a pale blue evening suit more suited to a Florida wedding than a Karaoke club, unclipped the microphone from its stand. He thanked the performers and welcomed a newcomer to the stage. Her name was Linda, she was a personnel officer for — he consulted his notes — Webber-Goldtrott Merchandising — a cheer went up from a table near the bar, and she was going to sing 'We've Only Just Begun'.

The basement room was stratified into distinct groups: hard-drinking executives straight from their offices, a shrieking hen party, several rowdy birthday celebrations. Briefcases formed a leather mountain at the coatcheck. At the table near the bar, a half-stripped girl in a nurse's uniform stood beside the balding young man from the Webber-Goldtrott party. As she encouraged him to remove her blouse, a chorus of clapping began to grow faster.

'She's already paid for,' the young executive shouted in his colleague's ear. 'I prebooked her on Visa. Can I claim the cost, or should we split it between us?' He passed his group director a crumpled slip of paper.

'I hope you're joking, Caverett,' bellowed the director, glancing down at the slip, a bill for over ninety pounds. 'I'm not passing your expenses unless you give me an account to lose it on.' Lee Caverett looked crestfallen. His entire career was predicated on his ability to falsify expenses. He returned his attention to the gyrating stripper while Linda from Personnel sidestepped harmonies at the microphone.

'She's very attractive,' he pointed out. 'Makes you wonder why she has to take her clothes off for a living.'

The director was a pragmatic man. 'Because blokes like you are prepared to book her,' he replied. The stripper was now standing astride Caverett's left leg, swinging her pelvis along his thigh. She unclamped the beer from his hand and poured a little of it inside his shirt, reaching in to massage his chest. The audience's attention had now shifted from the singer to the scene unfolding at the rear of the room. The director pushed back his chair to provide more space for the off-stage entertainment. As Caverett buried his face between the stripper's breasts, the hen party released a shriek of delight. Unnoticed at the bar, two waiters were attempting to wedge a plastic bucket beneath a leaking waste-pipe.

'Where the hell is John?' asked Caverett, unable to tear his eyes from the stripper's arching back. 'Everyone else is here. I can't believe he hasn't turned up for his own leaving party.'

'You know what John's like,' said the director. 'Did you honestly expect him to show? He's not exactly gregarious by nature.'

'I don't trust people who can't relax. I've never even seen him without a tie.' Caverett drained his beer can. 'He's certainly picked the wrong job to transfer to.'

'Perhaps,' said the director. 'His honesty is going to prove a liability. People like John are pleasantly predictable. You always know where they are. At the office, at home, or travelling between the two.' He held his palm out flat. 'Straight arrows.'

'Sanctimonious bastard,' said Caverett, tearing the lid from another can. 'Good riddance. He never liked me much, anyway.'

'I don't suppose he did. You were probably too devious for him.' The director tipped his watchface to the light. 'I bet you, at this very moment John Chapel will be on Waterloo Bridge. About halfway across.'

The temperate evening currents twisted along the glowing surface of the river to rise about the cantilevered concrete girders of the bridge. John Chapel stood in the centre of the stone balustrade looking back towards the Houses of Parliament, his arms outstretched at right angles to his torso. The warm breeze embraced his cruciform body. As he shifted his feet further apart on the rough stone, he felt completely alone. A woman passing on the opposite pavement paused to watch him.

Looking up, he saw a thin parabola of cloud dipping over Westminster, one end sheened in fading sunlight, the other lost in a haze of smog. A train pulled out of Charing Cross Station, thumping between the blackened steel struts of Hungerford Bridge. Shards of shadow split the faceless buildings of the South Bank. A group of concert-goers had gathered outside the Festival Hall in a disorderly queue. He could almost hear their conversation drifting across the river.

The moment he had stepped up onto the balustrade, he had felt the sweat fade from his shoulderblades, leaving his body cool and dry. Now, perched in the middle of the bridge, he lifted his head and allowed the passing air to brush his neck, to ruffle his hair. Free from the constricting architecture of the West End, the city opened out to touch the world at its riverbanks, and the sky reached down to examine its passing sepia reflection. Watching the distant activities of other people, he felt the cramping thoughts of daily routine fall from his mind like brittle flakes of paint, returning strength to his sagging spirit.

During the recent heatwave he had stopped here every night, preparing himself for the train journey ahead. He had never felt the urge to climb the wall until this afternoon. The drop to the water was a considerable one. Reluctantly, he lowered himself back onto the pavement, dusting his knees and stooping to collect his briefcase.

Tomorrow the fine weather was supposed to break, segueing to a weekend of rain. He checked his watch, noted the remaining nine minutes before the departure of his train, and set off to the station.

Helen looked up in surprise when he entered the lounge. She was standing on the patio before an unlit barbeque stove, repeatedly jabbing at a pile of sausages. As John passed on his way to the bedroom she tapped at the glass with her fork, an irritating staccato sound. He turned and slid back the door, knowing that she was about to continue their conversation from this morning.

'I thought you'd spend half an hour with them, at least. I haven't even had time to put the meat on.'

'It's too hot. They're in a basement somewhere. They booked a stripper. They're going to get very drunk. Your basic nightmare.' He dropped his briefcase. 'I don't suppose they'll even remember whether I turned up.'

'John, it's a matter of social etiquette, that's all. It's what people do when they leave a job.' She brushed a twist of ginger hair back from her eyes. 'It would have been a goodwill gesture.'

'Forget it.'

He walked back into the bedroom and began to remove his shirt, which was once more stuck to his body after three quarters of an hour spent standing in a railway carriage. As he sat on the bed to remove his shoes he caught sight of his stomach forming a fleshy concertina over his belt buckle. He tried to recall how other men appeared approaching thirty, and realised that he had no exact knowledge of his colleagues' ages. He had rarely socialised with people from the office. On the occasions that he and Helen had arranged to dine with Howard Dickson and his wife, the conversation had always revolved around company business. Discussions at home were no less consistent, rarely moving beyond the price of Josh's new school blazer, or arrangements for the weekend shopping. There were no surprises between Helen and himself. They knew where they stood with each other. He liked that.

He carefully adjusted the shower temperature before stepping into the cubicle. 'Clean towel just outside the door.' Helen had heard the taps being turned on. She was never very far away. Whenever he received a telephone call, she had the habit of replying to John's comments as if the caller was speaking to her as well. Lately he had noticed that much of their dialogue took place without the benefit of eye contact. They held mundane conversations through a variety of barriers — across rooms, between doorways, through their son. The familiarity of home life, reassuring and comfortable. He soaped his chest, leaning back against the wall of the shower to let the water run through the curly black hair covering his pectorals. Somewhere outside he could hear birdsong calling in the dusk.

In the steamheat of the cubicle, with the water beating against his face and throat, the familiar unresolved questions about their life together began to surface in his mind.

'Save me some water, won't you.' Helen was peering over the top of the shower door, watching him.

'Christ, Helen.' He sighed and closed off the taps, irrationally annoyed with her for breaking his train of thought.

The entire neighbourhood seemed to be barbequeing tonight. The air in the garden was acrid with smoke. They ate on the patio, as they had every night for a week, enjoying the last of the fine August weather. 'I assumed that we'd be together for the entire evening,' said Helen, lowering her fork to her plate and studying her husband's face. Between them sat Josh, oblivious to everything except the mound of food before him.

'We will be,' he agreed, knowing she would be upset if he worked. 'It's just that I have some studying to do before Monday.'

'There's the whole weekend ahead, John. I have a church meeting on Sunday afternoon. The house will be quiet then.'

'I won't be here either, Dad.' Josh distastefully scraped the herb seasoning from his sausage. 'I'm going over to Cesar's.'

'There you are, you'll have all the peace and quiet you need.'

'It's not as simple as that.' Sometimes he found it hard to explain his thought processes to her. 'I can't leave it to the last minute. There are dozens of clients' case-histories to read. This is a whole new field for me.'

The tip of Helen's tongue protruded between her teeth, a habit she had developed to indicate annoyance. 'John, they worked you right up to your departure date. I've hardly seen you at all in the last month. Now you want to get straight into the new job without a break?'

'It's not that.'

'Your son has started to forget what you look like. Haven't you, Joshua?'

The boy studied him thoughtfully. 'I don't have a father. I'm a half-orphan.'

'You see what I mean?'

'I know, and I'm sorry.'

'Don't be sorry, just be aware of it.' She leaned forward across her plate, searching his eyes. Her unruly red hair was still wet from her shower. 'It's no big deal. We missed you, but now you're back. We're still together, aren't we?'

'Yes,' said John, 'we're still together.'

He was searching his briefcase when Helen entered the study.

'It's just started raining. The weather wasn't supposed to break until tomorrow. What are you looking for?'

He pushed the case aside and began to search his desk. He couldn't remember picking up the company report Howard Dickson had lent him to study. The others had been fooling around, trying to get him to have a drink while he was clearing his desk.

'If you tell me what you're looking for, perhaps I can help you.'

He glanced up at Helen. She was standing before him in a pale cream dress, her freckled forearms folded across her breasts. He smiled. 'You're not going to like it.'

'Tell me quickly.'

'I have to go back to Webber-Goldtrott tonight.'

'Oh, John …'

'Howard gave me a report on the agency, its history, finances, that sort of thing. I'm supposed to study it and make notes. I know exactly where it is.' He could see the damned thing on the window ledge in his office, just where he had left it.

'Can't you get it tomorrow?'

'I've surrendered my keys. Tonight's my last chance until Monday, and then it'll be too late.'

'John, this is *exactly* what I'm talking about.'

He slammed the case shut and turned to face her. Beyond the open window rain began to patter heavily into the garden. 'What do you want me to do?'

'I don't know. There's a part of you that's never here with me.'

'It's eight o'clock. I'll be an hour and a half at the most.'

The look on Helen's face was indecipherable. She appeared hurt, scared of being excluded. He reached forward and kissed her lightly on the lips before she pulled away.

'Sometimes, when you leave ...'

'What now?'

'I think you're not going to come back. That you're just going to disappear.'

'Don't be silly. Why would I do that?'

'I don't know. Because of what happened with us. Because you feel ... buried.'

'You're wrong, Helen. After eleven years, I don't feel buried. Or anything else.' He edged her towards the door. 'I have to go.'

'Then you'd better take this.' She held the umbrella before her, a peace offering.

'Thanks. I really won't be long.' He paused in the doorway. 'Stop worrying so much.'

The sky had lowered now, the dark full-bellied clouds scratching the tops of the buildings in the Strand, heavy enough to deliver a full night of rain. He found the report lying on the sill in his overheated office, exactly where he had set it down. The building was virtually deserted. The elderly doorman called him back as he was leaving. 'Are you not going to the party, Mr Chapel?'

'No, Frank. Thank everyone for me, will you?'

'I will. And good luck in your new job. Films, isn't it? I haven't seen a film since my Edith was alive. *The Prisoner Of Zenda*, I think it was. Sounds very glamorous, anyway.'

'I don't suppose it will be.' He hovered on the step. 'It's a PR company. I'll be handling movie publicity.'

'I s'pose you'll be wining an' dining all them film stars,' called the old man. 'We'll be reading about you an' Ava Gardner in the *News Of The World*.'

'I don't think so somehow, seeing as she's dead,' muttered John to himself. Still, he wondered what his new position would involve. The salary was excellent, but Howard had been typically vague about his duties, and his hours. Whatever the job entailed, he had a disturbing suspicion that it would affect his family adversely.

He had no idea how much.

CHAPTER
2
Waterloo Station

Setting off in the direction of the station, he once more found himself heading for Waterloo on foot. There were no taxis to be seen in any direction. The bridge now presented itself as an inhospitable concrete arc, rainswept and dismal.

The station itself covered an entire city block with its crescent-shaped concourse and twenty-one platforms. The main entrance was a memorial constructed to the memory of those members of staff who had died in the First World War. Above its doors a great gold clock was set into the stone, wreathed in red ironwork. This was topped by a statue commemorating the glorious dead, surrounded by shields of the war's great battles. It had always struck him as an absurdly grand entrance for a mere railway station, more suited in an operatic setting as a portal for the dead.

Later he tried to remember the sequence of events, but never seemed able to account for every moment. The approach was deserted as he crossed the road before the worn steps which fanned up to the concourse. To the left, the angled glass roof of the curving sliproad protected a handful of passengers searching for taxis. Opposite, a battery of mounted floodlights bathed the ornate entrance in sharp white light. He remembered waiting to cross the road as a taxi approached, looking up at the battleshields and reading the names through phosphorescent needles of rain — Mesopotamia, Dardanelles, Egypt. He remembered seeing the deserted entrance lined with the roll-calls of deceased employees, the distant blur of travellers on the concourse beyond. He remembered hearing the slams of taxi doors and the crunch of gears as drivers pulled away into the sliproad. It was then that he saw her, darting through the rain, one red high-heeled shoe touching the ground, then the other, and he wondered how it was that she did not slip over. The dead white light seemed to trap time itself as she ran, freezing her from one second to the next in a series of surreal tableaux, a knee raised, then falling, the other leg outstretched.

Then she turned. Her hair swung from her neck in a glossy black scythe. Her slim dark eyes narrowed beneath an ebony fringe. Around her long pale neck was a single strand of white pearls. The rain sheened her figure in misty light.

John stood transfixed as she reached the steps. He had a fleeting impression of the look on her face, earnest and determined, late for her train. She wore a low strapless dress of sparkling red sequins that reached halfway to her knees. A tiny crimson evening bag glittered at her waist. Her polka-dot shoes sported improbably high heels. And yet the sophistication of her attire ill fitted the feral, flowing movements of her body. She raised a hand to her lips, as if she had forgotten something, lingering for a moment at the top of the steps — and then she was gone. John stepped from the kerb, his eyes still focused on the doorway ahead.

This sprite of a woman, the lightness of her body, the plucking of her balletic limbs touched something deep within him. From her entrance into the blazing curtain of rain which hung between himself and the station to her disappearance within the darkened vestibule of the terminal, the passing moments — and they could only have been moments — seemed to have decelerated to a crawl. It was as if he had witnessed a play, performed for his benefit on a grand-scale set with a single performer. And yet there was a sense of time lost, for John found himself on the white marble concourse with no recollection of crossing the road or mounting the stairway.

The girl, of course, had vanished to her platform — but which one? He glanced up at the vast destination board. WINDSOR and ETON rattled off, giving way to ASCOT, TEDDINGTON and his own stop, RICHMOND. Further around by the snack bars and newsstands, backpackers awaited trains which would bear them to Poole and Portsmouth.

Perhaps she had entered his train. As he walked along the platform he told himself he was not staring into the carriages, searching for sight of the sequinned dress. Back at the barrier the guard blew his whistle. He boarded the train and pressed his wet head back into the seat, sweating in the sultry compartment as each swing of the carriage bore him further away from the city.

What was it about her that had seized him so fiercely? He was too young to experience those menopausal pangs of envy men suffered when they passed attractive girls. Mere lust, then? Or was it the odd incongruity of allure and energy that she embodied? Whatever the answer, he would never know. She had not seen him. He would never see her again. And yet the strangeness of the scene remained in his mind, replaying through facets of his memory like a half-forgotten piece of film.

That night he dreamed of the running girl, the glittering rain, the station steps stretching steep and endless into the night. Once more he saw her fly towards the train, once more he heard her heels tick-tock across wet stone with the clarity of a metronome. The sequinned dress spun out across her pale thighs again as she turned and raised her fingers slowly to her lips, a sensual Cinderella pausing on the palace steps. The slow-motion scene was just as he had experienced it, yet something had skewed now, contorting the moment from normality into an unhealthy fetishistic image.

When the vision at last released him he awoke unrefreshed, tangled in damp sheets, to find that Helen had already risen, showered and dressed.

He sat at the study desk in his dressing-gown and briefly recorded the dream in his notebook, as though the moment would somehow prove significant. That he had taken the diary from a locked drawer made him aware that he was hiding part of himself from Helen's eyes. When she breezily entered the room a few minutes later, he started as if caught with a guilty secret. She had dressed in a smart black suit which accentuated her copper hair. On Saturdays, she worked a half day at the department store where she was a book-keeper.

'What are you doing?' She peered over his shoulder, fitting an earring.

'Nothing.' He slipped the book into a drawer and turned the key, rising. 'Why didn't you wake me?'

'You were tossing and turning all night. You looked as if you needed the extra rest.'

'You look nice.'

'Senior management are coming in. We've been asked to make a special effort. If you're not doing anything this morning, could you get some shopping?'

John stuck his hands in his pockets and stared out of the window. 'Okay. I'll take Josh with me.'

'Surely you jest.' Helen swung her bag on to her shoulder. 'He left the house hours ago. Don't you remember what you were like at his age?'

Without thinking, he said, 'I've blocked everything that happened before I was nineteen.' He had meant it as a joke, but he saw the hurt in her eyes.

CHAPTER
3
Ixora

Scott Tyron was a twenty-seven-year-old Californian with bleached blond hair and a chocolate tan who reckoned he could pass for twenty-one on a good day. Today was not a good day. He was tired, hot and scared that he was going to fall. As he hung to the roof ledge thirty feet above the ground, he waited for the flames to reach the first of the chimney stacks before shouting for help. As the second chimney burst into flame he released one hand from the ledge and looked down to the huge canvas airbag below.

'Give it another five seconds, then drop,' called the voice from the studio floor.

'You're shittin' me, man. No fucking way.' Scott released his grip and dropped like a rock. On the ground it took three men to haul him out of the airbag. The director, a seasoned professional named Farley Dell whose fall from grace had coincided with the collapse of the British film industry, had spent the last two weeks attempting to coax a performance from a young man whose only claim to fame was an over-hyped rock album and a drug-related court case. His patience was at an end, his manner exaggerated and condescending, his voice filled with quiet fury.

'You dropped way too early, Scott. We warned you that we would miss the shot if you did that. We rehearsed this many times. You were perfectly safe up there.'

'Yeah, right. So was Vic Morrow.'

'Now we have to set the shot up again. But your PR people —' he indicated John and his assistant '— are planning to take you away in five minutes. The set will take over half an hour to redress ...'

'I don't do overtime, man, it's in my contract.'

'I am aware of that. I am just warning you that if we have to go into overage, it's not coming out of our insurance, it's coming out of your salary.' Behind them, a special effects assistant turned off the flaming gas jets which had engulfed the roof and its burning chimneys. The set lights had been doused, but the temperature in the hangar remained stifling.

'Hey, this isn't my schedule,' said Scott. 'My people requested an extra two weeks, if you remember.' He turned to the continuity girl, who regarded him impassively. 'Let's be honest, I wanted Paul Verhoeven to direct this, not some guy who's spent the last ten years making army training videos.'

The director rocked back in his chair and released a sour burst of laughter. 'Paul *Verhoeven*? Don't flatter yourself, sonny. On this budget you'd have been lucky to get Michael Winner.'

Tyron pulled the shoulderpads from his shirt and threw them on the floor. 'The money could have been there with a few script changes. You know, I had Ridley Scott begging for this project.'

'Fine, you're welcome to him,' said Dell. 'With all that backlighting we'd never have seen your face. Besides, if we'd taken money from the American majors they'd have made us write an upbeat ending.'

'I don't see what's so bad about that.'

'I'm glad you didn't set up script deals for Shakespeare. Ophelia pulled from the water, gasping but alive. Hamlet either forgives Gertrude and the King or goes after them with a magnum, depending on audience research.' Dell stretched out his hands. 'I can see it now. Scott Tyron in *Hamlet II: The Reckoning*. He's Back, and He's Madder Than Ever.' The continuity girl stifled a laugh.

This was only his second week, and already John was becoming familiar with the edgy humour of on-set arguments. Star tantrums were mostly manufactured by the publicity machine, Howard had explained. Genuine disputes were more likely to involve the set carpenters than the lead players. Film crews were usually united against a common enemy: wasted time. Hours, minutes, seconds of exposed film were all that counted. The set of *Playing With Fire* was not a happy one, but that scarcely mattered. An untroubled production was virtually regarded as the sign of a bad film.

Tyron's exit from the set was John's cue to take control. He stepped forward and lightly touched the actor's shoulder. 'We have a car waiting for you, Mr Tyron. This is my assistant, Paula.'

Paula gave their star a tight smile and led him from the hangar. The tiny blonde had been working in film PR for over ten years, and her confident charm allowed her to deal with the most temperamental actors. 'It'll take us around forty minutes to reach Shepherd's Bush, so we'll have to run you straight into makeup,' she explained, ushering him into the back of their hired Mercedes.

On his first visit to a film set, John had expected to enter a world of bizarre juxtapositions. But instead of finding himself among gladiators and chorus girls, walking between vast skyscapes of Mars and Atlantis, he merely discovered rows of wartime sheds, darkened hangars and deserted concrete fields.

On the first day of his new career, Howard had outlined his duties. The job would consist largely of ferrying artists to and from shoots and interviews, acting as little more than a well-paid servant. John had been warned that the hours were more 5 to 9 than 9 to 5. Senior staff members had earned the right to spend most of their time behind desks, arranging press conferences and writing releases. With performers such as Mr Tyron, whose reputation for bad behaviour was the only thing that kept him in the tabloids, John would be accompanied by an experienced assistant. Eventually the artists would learn to trust him, and he would be able to build his own list of clients.

Paula sat in the front of the car, leaning back in her seat to talk to John while their star stared angrily out of the window. 'I'll stay on at *Wogan* and take Scott back to the St James's Club afterwards,' she said. 'You go to the party.' Scott's ears pricked up. He turned from the window.

'Party? Man, how come *he's* goin' to a party? I'm the star, I'm the guy who goes to the parties.'

'No,' said John, 'you're the guy who plugs his movie on *Wogan*, then goes back to his hotel and learns his lines for tomorrow.' He gave a friendly smile. 'Believe me, this is one party you really wouldn't enjoy.'

'Believe you?' Tyron gave him an incredulous stare. 'Forget it, man, you're in PR.'

The party was held in the glass-fronted penthouse above Dickson-Clarke which Howard Dickson used as an office and part-time seduction centre when his wife was away visiting her health spa. By 7.30 the room was packed with a disconcertingly stereotypical group of media-types, aggressive chain-smoking agents, elegant models with distant eyes and expensive smiles, goggling financial backers who happily lost their production investments for the opportunity of telling friends that they were show-business angels, and an assortment of well-connected film distributors, advertisers and publishers. John's role in the proceedings was largely to ensure that no clients were left standing alone, and that those with spare investment cash were teamed with those who required it. Consequently, the hazy air was filled with the discussion of film, book and television projects, very few of which would ever see the light of day, at least in their intended form. This, everyone agreed, was partly because the British government regarded film subsidies as marginally less important than road gritting, and most projects were crap, anyway.

'So you've left Tyron sitting in his hotel room armed only with a buffet trolley and his script for company,' said Howard, steering John towards a pair of potential clients from the MI Group. 'He knows he's grounded but he'll still try to slip out for a little I and I later.' It stood for Intercourse and Intoxication. PR companies often used their own in-house slang to carry on conversations around their clients. 'I hope Paula remembered to warn the doorman.'

'We can't stop him leaving the hotel, Howard, They'll call us if he tries. Maybe I should have taken away his wallet.'

'What for? He can borrow cash on his face, and if he needs condoms he'll probably call by the studio, steal a couple of their mike socks.' The thought of Scott Tyron lifting the rubber sleeves from microphones forced a smile to John's face.

Howard was a fast-talking New Yorker with a sharp intellect which he kept hidden from his clients behind a barrage of risqué banter. At the age of forty he was also the titular head of the most powerful show business PR company in London. His partner, the Clarke of Dickson-Clarke, had suffered a massive pressure-related heart attack two years ago and was now enduring tension-free retirement in a Victorian seaside town.

'Listen, we have some hacks here from the Sunday sleaze papers. Dell refuses to let them anywhere near the set since they dug up the article on his conviction in the seventies. Go and see if you can interest them in something other than the buffet table.'

John pushed his way through the crowd and easily located the tabloid newsmen. They were wearing the cheapest suits in the room and were furtively shovelling handfuls of canapés into their mouths. The gossip press formed the other half of an uncomfortably symbiotic relationship with star PR. Although their careers were inextricably threaded together, the relationship rarely veered into anything approaching genuine friendship.

John was attempting to engage them in conversation when his eye was caught by a movement at the main entrance.

Park Manton, Dell's producer, was holding open the door. Thanking him as she stepped through it was the girl he had seen at the station. For a moment he wondered if the image in his dream had simply imprinted itself on someone else's features. But it was definitely her. Glossy black hair spread in a sable fan across her bare white shoulders. She wore a short black dress of simple design. The pale rope of flawless pearls lay across her throat.

His attraction to her was an obvious, undeniable fact. What puzzled him more was why he should feel this way. He had quickly come to see that his job would entail meetings with some of the most attractive women in the world, and yet, in eleven years of marriage he had effortlessly maintained his vows to Helen. While infidelity was a natural state for Howard, it was an area which John had barely considered exploring.

Between gulps of free champagne, the Sunday newsmen were complaining about their treatment by Scott Tyron's director. He half listened to their pleas, watching across the room as the girl excused herself from her escort with a polite smile. Slowly she made her way towards the buffet table, heads turning in her wake. At first he thought she was heading for him, but she moved on to the drinks table and poured herself a glass of champagne. Atar of roses hung faintly in the air where she had passed.

'Amazing, isn't she?' Howard appeared at his side as the newsmen sidled off.

'Do you know who she is?'

'I don't know her name. She's about to do some work on *Playing With Fire*. I can't remember which role she's landed. Check out your shooting schedule. Apparently it was big enough to get her signed up with the Diana Morrison agency.' Dickson-Clarke handled several of the agency's clients. 'Go and introduce yourself.'

'No,' said John quietly. 'I dare say we'll meet in due course.'

'For Christ's sake, John, it's your job, not a date. I know it's a hell of a lot different to what you were doing before, but you've got to get used to this business. With those looks she probably has enough attitude to split pack-ice, but she's a potential client. Talk to her. If you don't, I will.'

Howard's confidence was impossible to dent. He treated clients and friends alike with the cavalier attitude of a professional socialite, and people loved him for it. As he moved off into the crowd, John freshened his drink and looked around.

The girl stood alone, the radiant centre of the party. As he watched, she caught his eye and held it with a steady, purposeful gaze. He was tempted to turn around and check behind to see if she was looking at someone else. She must have remembered him from the station. Without realising it, he found that he had crossed the room to talk to her.

'We haven't met. My name is John Chapel.' He proffered his hand. 'I just started working for Howard Dickson.'

'Ixora De Corizo.'

Her hand was cold and small in his. Her voice lilted with a mellifluous, unplaceable accent.

'That's an unusual name.'

'My mother was French. From Provence.'

'Is that where you were raised?'

'No.'

She stared down into her glass as he searched for a way to extend the encounter. 'How's the film coming along?'

'The director's very sweet. We've only shot one of my scenes so far, so we haven't worked together much.'

'And Scott?'

'He doesn't seem very bright. He complains all the time that he's not being treated like a star, and the more he complains, the less it makes him a star.' There was a natural break in the conversation. She seemed in no hurry to leave his side.

'It's a funny thing,' began John, 'but I saw you a couple of weeks ago. It was a Friday evening, pouring with rain. You were dashing into Waterloo Station. You looked as if you were late for a train.'

'No.' Ixora waved the suggestion away with her hand. 'That's not possible.'

'It couldn't have been anyone else. You were wearing an evening dress covered in sequins. You looked — sensational.'

'Then I'm afraid it must have been someone who looks like me. I was away the whole week, visiting friends in Yorkshire. I didn't arrive back until it was time for the first of my scenes, three days ago.'

'That's strange. I could have sworn it was you.'

'I'm sorry to have disappointed you.'

'Oh, no, you haven't, it's just—'

She was watching him in a way that made him cease to attempt any explanation. 'Yes?' Her emerald eyes shone as she tilted her head. A heat sickness descended on him. He could feel the sweat blistering his palms, blossoming beneath his arms. For a moment it was as if he was high above the ground, looking down. He heard himself ask her about the role she was playing.

She laughed. 'I'm supposed to be Scott's jealous girl-friend, a true English rose. I was raised here, but I'm not English. Do you think I look English?'

'Far from it. You're far too exotic. South American. Perhaps your father's side—'

She cut him short. 'I never knew my father.'

John changed tack. 'How long have you been an actress?'

She smiled and raised her hand to her lips in uncon-scious reprise of her gesture on the steps. 'I'm not really an actress, I just do some occasional modelling. I don't need to work. My mother died seven years ago, when I was seventeen. She left me well provided for. She owned a very nice property behind Sloane Square. That's where I live now. So now you tell me.'

'Tell you what?'

'About yourself. You know, I speak, you speak. Party conversation.'

John glanced around the crowded room. 'How's it been so far?'

'Like the champagne.'

'Sparkling, or just flat?'

'Empty.' She turned her glass upside down with a smile.

'I'm sorry, I'll get you another.'

Returning with the glasses he was conscious of the others watching him. Ixora raised an eyebrow as he returned to her side. She was still waiting for him to tell her about himself. John thought for a moment. He suddenly felt the need to mention his marriage, as though it would act as a safety barrier between them.

'My turn.' He cleared his throat. 'I'm just entering my fourth decade on earth. I have a wife called Helen and a son called Josh, I live in Richmond and we have a cat called Mutley.'

'How formal you are!' She laughed again. 'Not at all the kind of person you usually find in public relations.'

'Why, what are they like?'

'Oh, you know. Arrogant and disinterested. A little too much surface charm. I guess urbanity is a hazard of the job.'

'To be honest,' John admitted, 'I don't think I really understood what was involved when I took this on. It was Howard who suggested the idea of a career change to me.' From the corner of his eye he saw his employer approaching.

'I see you've met Diana's latest recruit.' He sided with Ixora, facing John, an old trick of his. 'I came over to tell you that we're taking Diana Morrison to dinner. I've booked a table for six at the Lindsey House. Perhaps Miss De Corizo would care to join us.' He pronounced the 'z' as a Castilian 'th'. John knew Howard well enough to recognise that Ixora was not being invited for her client potential. She was the kind of girl he loved to be seen spoiling. Howard was a peacock, forever showing off before the female of the species, charming and shocking them in roughly equal measures. Most women saw through him immediately. They didn't realise that he expected them to.

'I'm not sure I can ...'

'Of course you can. Mr Chapel would love to escort you.'

'Really, Howard,' John protested, 'I can't.' Helen was already having trouble adjusting to his new working hours. Tonight he had promised to be home by nine.

'Excuse us for a moment.' Howard led him to one side, his smile fading fast. 'Listen, John, the least we can do is buy Diana dinner after the Sarah Monroe screw-up.' Last Saturday, someone had accidentally double-booked the temperamental jazz singer, resulting in a loss of revenue for Diana Morrison's favourite client. When the chanteuse had been informed of the mistake she had thrown an empty bottle of Jim Beam from her car window which had hit someone's dog. There was talk of a law suit.

'Why don't you call your wife and tell her you'll be late.'

John thought of Helen sitting angrily before the television and decided to stand his ground. Besides, there was something about Ixora that disturbed him. Her forthright manner failed to match her appearance. In his first two weeks he had already shepherded enough models to their interviews to know that they were defensive and suspicious in the extreme, a necessary counter-measure encouraged by the duplicitous intentions of the men they frequently attracted.

'I really can't, Howard. Thanks all the same.' He glanced at his watch. 'I have to go. It was a pleasure meeting you, Miss De Corizo.' As he made his farewells he was sure he could feel her eyes follow him across the room.

Helen barely looked up from the television when he entered. A single corner-light illuminated the lounge. She sat with her legs tucked beneath her, picking at the remains of some lasagne. A half-empty wineglass stood beside the plate. Despite the heat of the room she wore a cardigan. Helen was always cold. Whenever he and Josh played football in the park she would stand on the sidelines rubbing the flesh of her thin limbs until he guiltily called a halt to the game.

She pushed the plate to one side and stretched her arms along the back of the sofa. 'How was it?' she asked.

'Oh, you know.' It occurred to him that he should mention the exotic addition to his client list, but then he wondered if Helen might be jealous. Apart from the ex-girlfriend of Howard's who had trapped him in the kitchen at his Christmas party three years ago, he had never really given Helen any cause to be upset. 'Howard tried to get me to go to dinner with him.'

'If it was business you should have gone.'

'There were several other people going. I wasn't really needed.' He sat beside her. 'What are you watching?'

'It's about spiders.' The screen was filled with a close-up of sticky black mandibles manipulating a struggling fly into a gaping mouth. 'They always put this kind of thing on when you're eating. Did Howard find himself a date?'

'I suppose so. A model, new on the books, terribly glamorous.'

'Did you find her attractive?'

He gave an unconvincing shrug. 'I guess so, I mean, in a flashy way.'

'Isn't that the type Howard goes for, the tarty ones?'

'I didn't say she was tarty.'

'*Spiders in the group Theraphosidae are hairy,*' intoned the television announcer, '*and may develop a leg spread of up to eleven inches.*'

'No, you said she was flashy. Angela must be at the health farm again.'

'I believe she's gone to a conference in Edinburgh.'

Helen finished her wine and set the glass on her plate. 'She's as bad as him. I'm surprised you ever see them together. They're like sexual versions of those little weatherman barometers, you know, one always in when the other's out.'

Not like us, thought John. That's the subtext of this conversation. Infidelity is for other people. It was something the two of them half-heartedly discussed once in a while.

'*The male Diadem, or Common Garden Spider,*' the voice-over continued, '*must mate its partner very carefully to avoid being eaten by her immediately following intercourse.*'

'Do we have to have this on?'

'The cat's sitting on the remote and I don't like to disturb him. Have you eaten anything?'

John shoved the grey-backed Persian from the cushion where it lay snoring and thumbed off the television. 'Don't worry,' he said. 'I'll get something from the fridge. Howard wasn't pleased that I left early.'

'He'll get over it. He knows you'll soon be the hardest worker there. Why do you think he employed you? He remembers what you were like at Webber-Goldtrott. Don't have the cheese,' she called after him. 'It'll give you more bad dreams.'

John smiled as he took a block of Cheddar from the cooler. Ixora had made his night-fantasies flesh, and in doing so had exorcised them. Ahead lay only deep, untroubled sleep.

Or so he thought.

At 4.00 a.m., more troubled than ever, he slipped from Helen's side and headed for the silent lounge, to await the arrival of dawn, and the deliquescence of his night-time demons.

CHAPTER
4
Vincent Brady

The corpse lay in a circle of tripod-mounted spotlights, surrounded by coils of cable, as if forming the sacrificial centrepiece in some obscure video ritual. Two police officers, a detective sergeant and a photographer comprised the second wave of visitors to the scene. Earlier in the day a young constable had answered a complaint from the downstairs neighbour, and had broken down the door of the top-floor flat.

In the main lounge area he had discovered the body of a young black male, approximately six feet tall, over thirteen stone, hair neatly cropped in a fashionable flat top. He was aged around twenty-eight, and was lying in the centre of a blood-caked rug, his feet tied together with electrical wiring. His hands had been tied as well, but the flex had been pulled until it had stretched and broken, the plastic cover splitting so that the wire inside had bitten deeply into his wrists.

The flat was cleanly kept but cheaply furnished and anonymously decorated, probably rented rather than owned. It had been a home. It was now an abattoir.

Although its internal gasses had begun to bloat it, the body was muscular and healthy, stripped to the waist, clad in a pair of black Levi's 501s jeans. His feet were bare. Although there were a number of dried-out stab wounds on his face, neck and upper chest, the tissue damage was minimal, suggesting that the instrument used had been extremely sharp, possibly surgical. One deep wound stood apart from the others, protruding muscle tissue. Traces of blood could be seen all over the room; handprints on the walls, footprints smeared over the floorboards. There had been a hell of a fight, thought Sullivan, even though his legs had been tied. It was probably only terminated by the victim passing out from loss of blood.

'Well, it ain't a suicide, that's for sure.' Wyman, the photographer, had begun to pack away his equipment, anxious to leave. It was late, it was hot and the body was stinking.

'Of course not,' said Sullivan, taking his remark seriously. 'Knife suicides usually cut the inside of the wrist opposite to the cutting hand, then go for the throat from left to right, assuming they're right handed. Murder wounds are deeper, less tentative like these.'

An earlier search had turned up a dead Yorkshire terrier in the bedroom, which presumably explained why the corpse's eyes had been mutilated. A dying animal seeking moisture would cannibalise its dead owner. Identification of the victim had not been difficult. He had been discovered in his own flat. Vincent Brady, a local barman. Known and liked by his neighbour, who had described him as 'a decent type'. The bedroom and the lounge had been ransacked, but as yet it was impossible to tell if anything had been removed from the premises. So far, the only prints they had found in the flat belonged to the victim.

'Classic defence wounds. Look at this.' Sullivan tugged at his voluminous trousers and crouched beside the body, pointing to the slashmarks criss-crossing the dead man's palms and outer forearms. Reluctantly, the photographer joined him. 'There are also a couple on his lower back. He turned away from his attacker at some point, threw his arms over his face trying to protect himself. Odd.'

'Why?' asked Wyman, cupping his hand over his nose.

'The tied feet suggest premeditated murder, but the actual attack looks as if it took place in some kind of prolonged frenzy.' Sullivan's plastic-gloved hand moved Brady's right arm freely back and forth. 'He's been into rigor mortis and back out again. This must have happened quite a few days ago.' He pointed to one of the officers by the door. 'Oy, you're Mace, aren't you?'

'Yes, sir.'

'Well, Mace, where do you reckon the murderer was standing?'

Detective Constable Deborah Mace studied the corpse carefully, aware that Sullivan had a habit of throwing questions at his crew just for the pleasure of having to answer them himself. She thought for a moment, then shrugged. 'Don't know, sir.'

Pleased, the detective sergeant heaved himself to his feet and moved one of the cooling spotlights aside. 'Somewhere over here, I would say.'

The photographer gave an appreciative nod. 'How can you tell?'

'It looks to me like the victim lowered his arms for some reason. His attacker got a clear thrust in to his chest and pierced his heart and his left lung. He inhaled blood into his air passage, choked and fell.' Sullivan pointed to the floorboard beyond the rug. 'Attacker stood here and watched him die.'

'How can you be so sure he was standing there?' asked Wyman.

Sullivan glanced from the body to the rug and thought for a moment. 'Taking the pattern of the wounds we can assume that most of the heavy bloodshed occurred early on in the attack. The footprints on the floorboards are all close together, made by the victim, stumbling around with his feet tied. The rug is soaked with blood, so we know that the attacker hardly walked on it, otherwise we'd have found a set of more widely spaced prints around the room. Wait, I'm overlooking something.' Sullivan clearly enjoyed playing to an audience. 'We know where he fell right after he was struck. Stab wounds usually trail off in the direction of the assailant. Now, if we check the shape of the incisions.'

He beckoned to the other officers, then crouched to examine the victim's chest. Most of the cuts were deep and clean but there were a number of smaller, more irregular markings.

'Scrimmage wounds here. Cleavage lines there. He tried to pull away while the knife was in his flesh. The elastic fibres of the skin run in patterned directions. If a strike is made parallel to these lines, the wound closes easily. Across the lines, you have a gaping wound that bleeds badly. In removing the blade to strike again, the assailant tore across the victim's fibre-lines to produce wounds of increased severity. What about the weapon used?'

As no one came up with an answer, he continued. 'Plenty of elliptical cuts with neat pointed ends. That suggests a flat blade, very sharp indeed. At a guess I'd say a stiletto, shiv, professional attack knife.' Sullivan rose to his feet, knees clicking. Even with the windows wide open, the room reeked dizzyingly of excrement and decomposing flesh.

'Wyman, turn the rest of the lights off,' he called to the photographer, 'we're starting to cook.' He gestured at the corpse. 'So is he for that matter.' Red-faced and puffing, he followed Mace out of the room and down a short flight of stairs to the main door of the flat. 'We'll have to hang on here until forensics can run a drug check. Bloody late as usual.'

He and Mace had already given the flat a preliminary shakedown for illegal chemicals. 'Christ, I hate murders at this time of the year.' He pulled a somewhat grey handkerchief from his trouser pocket and wiped his sweating forehead. 'How do you stay so dry?'

Mace shrugged, but unclipped the top button of her shirt. 'I don't sweat,' she said simply.

'Then you'll go far.' Sullivan's gaze was drawn back up to the room they had just left. 'A find like that can turn the strongest stomachs. No amount of experience will ever take the feeling away.'

'I'm not worried,' said Mace. '"That which doesn't kill me makes me strong."' She gave him a thin-lipped smile.

Sullivan didn't need to follow Nietzschean philosophy to sense that he was being treated with condescension. It was a common problem with new recruits that usually disappeared in the shift from theory to practice.

'An iron constitution isn't the only thing you need,' he said. 'Simple trained observation comes in useful too.'

Mace gave her tutor a cool, appraising look. 'Are you saying I missed something?' she asked.

'Go and take another look at the body.' He followed her up the stairs and back into the baking lounge.

'Marks on the side of the neck,' Sullivan prompted after allowing Mace a minute of silent examination. 'Thin repeated pattern. A gold neckchain with a crucifix.'

'But he's not wearing ...'

'Because the attacker pulled it off.'

'Then how do you ...'

'Because it's in the kitchen.'

Together they stared at the glass of water which stood on the draining board. Dangling in it was a small golden cross.

'Why would anyone do that?' asked the young detective constable.

'I haven't a clue,' replied Sullivan, 'so might I suggest you label, date, name, case and number it as evidence until one of us does?'

CHAPTER
5
Watcher

On the following morning, the first day of September, John arrived early at his office. The Dickson-Clarke building had been remodelled during the eighties construction boom, and had suffered the worst excesses of Toytown post-modernism. It had tiny windows and Meccano-like extrusions ending in large nuts and bolts that most people mistook for scaffolding. Inside, the walls of the partitioned offices were dotted with neon triangles that gave everyone a ghostly blue pallor. Instead of being restful it was claustrophobic, like working in an aquarium.

John thumbed through the script of *Playing With Fire*. His old accounting expertise told him that at a mere four million dollars, the budget for the feature was alarmingly tight for its schedule. It would be essential for them to help Dell and his team to avoid any production delays.

The story was a noirish murder mystery, set in clubland London of the fifties. According to the call sheet, Ixora was playing one of the hostesses suspected of killing the owner of a nightclub. The style of the piece gently spoofed the films of the era, while hoping to provide an engrossing mystery of its own. The script was a cineaste's delight, filled with period in-jokes, but an unlikely candidate for box office success. Farley Dell, the director, hadn't had a hit since the early eighties. If he could carry the thing off, it was possible that the film might be destined for cult status, but 'cult' usually meant 'box office disaster'. John was wondering what else could be done to improve the film's public image when Howard arrived bearing coffees.

'What happened? You look like death.' He leaned across the desk and set down one of the cups.

'I didn't sleep well last night,' replied John. 'Weird dreams.' He attempted to arrange his body comfortably on his new steel chair. 'How was the rest of last night?'

'Okay. Diana's being as hard as fucking nails on this Sarah Monroe thing. We'll have to provide some financial recompense. There's no way she's going to let us off the hook.'

'I didn't think she would. How was Miss De Corizo?'

'She sat across the table with her elbows tucked in and her knees together and barely spoke a word except to mention you. She can certainly eat, though. Did you ever meet a model who wasn't on a diet? Well, this one's not. She's a human garbage disposal.'

'Wait, what did she say about me?'

Howard gave him a sly look. 'What do *you* care what she said? You're a happily married man, buddy.'

'I was just curious.'

'She thinks you're a gentleman, and you have nice curly black hair, like Superman. I swear to God that's what she said. And she's looking forward to working with you on a daily basis.'

'What do you mean?'

'Diana wants us — you — to take her on as a separate client. I told you you'd have your own accounts, I just didn't expect you to get one before you'd finished earning your first pay cheque. Diana needs to get Ixora's face shown around town. Most of her previous modelling experience has been overseas. She's left it a little late to start out afresh, but Morrison's prepared to bankroll some kind of launch for her. Dell says there's an extraordinary visual quality about her which comes over on film. What have you got on this morning?'

John raised the file in his hand. 'I've just started compiling ideas on promoting the movie.'

'Okay, take a look at this.' Howard laid the film can on his desk. 'Footage of Ixora at work. It's cutting room floor stuff mostly, out-takes from a couple of commercials, fashion shows, some unusable first footage from the Scott Tyron epic. Her role's already been reduced from the original script. She looks great, but apparently she has a long way to go before becoming an actress. Still, it should give you some idea of her potential.'

John sat alone in the darkened screening room as sections of ungraded film flared through the projector gate. The first few takes were two or three years old. Ixora twirled self-consciously in a floral print dress at the Trevi Fountain. Her hair was bobbed short, her skin as untanned as ever. Then she appeared on the green steel bridges crossing Les Halles in a variety of primary-coloured prêt-à-porter outfits, affecting an attitude of studied disinterest only while the camera held her in its sight. As the film slowed at the end of each take and allowed more light to flood on to the film stock, he watched her break into uncontrollable laughter as her figure faded in the rippling yellow glare.

The screen went blank. The next footage showed several takes from the Scott Tyron film. Ixora stood waiting for her cue at the foot of the nightclub staircase. She wore a glittering red ball gown and elbow-length red gloves. As the clapperboard marked the start of the take, she pulled free of the uniformed doorman who tried to grab her, then launched into diagonal flight up the stairway to the exit doors at the top.

He was watching the scene that had occurred at the station that Friday evening. The same damned scene. At the top of the steps she turned and slowly raised her hand to her mouth, calling out to someone offscreen. This is crazy, thought John. What I saw happened in real life, not on a piece of film. Every movement of Ixora's body was as he remembered it. Every step, every gesture was identical. And yet it felt as if there was something wrong, something missing from her performance which she had included in her original real-life version of events.

The take ended, to be followed immediately by an identical one. Again Ixora launched herself towards the shadowed steps, a glittering firebird in full flight. On the top stair she paused and turned, her hair swirling about her face. She raised a gloved hand to dark painted lips, called her mute line and ran on. As the takes continued, the simple set of movements was repeated over and over, as if taunting him with the imperfection of his memory.

When the film finally ended and the cinema lights returned, John pushed back into his seat and stared at the blank screen. How was it possible? What he had just seen had really happened, and yet Ixora had denied even being in London at the time. It could only be a bizarre coincidence, a fictional moment that somehow paralleled a real-life event. Now the memory would be even harder to erase.

If Ixora looked like a dream in the flesh, on film she photographed like a living fantasy. Why had no one picked up on her potential before? Presumably Dell had screen-tested her. Perhaps the problem was with her voice and its odd, unplaceable accent. There was a list of things he needed to find out; could she read lines? Did she have a good interview manner? He would have to examine her portfolio and pick out some decent transparencies. The thought of meeting and talking to her again was oddly daunting now that he had seen her on film. It was as if the camera caught a radiance within her which somehow changed the spectrum of light within the film stock, reinforcing the tones of her flesh. Whatever she wore, however she looked, it was plain that the camera loved her. In his previous job he had seen the early model cards of many present-day actors. It was amazing how terrible many of them looked until they had had their noses fixed, their teeth capped and their posture improved. But not Ixora. She was a natural beauty. There was a goodness about her, a basic warmth that showed within her obvious sexuality, and subtly added to it. It was a quality he had never seen before. There was something about Ixora that fascinated and aroused. He wondered if it would make working with her easier, or more uncomfortable. And how would Helen feel when she discovered that his first account involved spending extra-curricular time with a beautiful actress?

The woman on the sparkling stairway took a step forward into the light. Her flaring white dress was topped with a blood-red camellia. On either side the party guests applauded her arrival. Now they crowded forward as Violetta began to sing.

John lowered his glasses from the figure on the stage and studied Ixora from the corner of his eye. Her attention to the unfolding drama was total. He knew she would cry when Alfredo held the consumptive courtesan in his arms and begged her for forgiveness. As the familiar strains of the music flowed through the auditorium of the Coliseum, John recalled the meeting with Howard this afternoon.

'The truth of the matter is, John,' he had explained, a look of embarrassment crossing his face, 'I'd asked Suki to the opera tonight without realising that Angela was coming back to town this afternoon.' Suki was Howard's mistress, a compliant Filipino girl who seemed happy to appear and disappear at Howard's will, depending on the latest travel arrangements of his wife. Howard was not in love with Suki, nor was Suki in love with him; the situation was Victorian, one of mutual convenience. He was paying the rent on her flat. She was available to him at short notice.

'I want you and Ixora to use the tickets. The first night of *La Traviata*. The production's supposed to be excellent.'

'That's not the point, Howard. I can't cancel dinner with Helen at such short notice.'

'Are you two going out to eat?'

'No, but ...'

'This is business, John. There's something I should tell you. We need Diana Morrison. If we do well with Ixora, she's in the position of giving us David Glen.' Glen was a highly successful actor-turned-author who had just broken the million-dollar barrier on the sale of his new screenplay. Glen was a potential conduit to fame and fortune, because of his friendship with the Hollywood moguls and his ability to call on them when it came to casting a movie.

'Take her to the opera,' said Howard. 'I'll arrange for you to meet with some of the attending press in the intermission. The first thing we must establish in their eyes is that Ixora is a class act. We'll have her seen attending some of the better openings. I guarantee you that one of them will run a piece on her tomorrow. Helen will understand that it's business. Put her on to me if she acts up, okay?'

John hesitated, aware that Howard was testing his commitment to the job.

'Look, if you can't trust yourself not to fall in love with her, you're definitely entering the wrong industry.'

'Come on, Howard, it's not that.'

'Then what is it? You wanted your own accounts. Now you have to start earning them. Jesus, most men would jump at the chance to do what you are doing for a living! If you want to be a desk-jockey forever, tell me and I'll give the account to someone else.'

'It's okay,' he had replied, giving in. 'I get the message.'

And now they sat side by side at the front of the balcony, Ixora simply and stunningly attired in a glittering black dress and evening gloves. The production was sumptuous — overly so. Violetta's townhouse was an absurdly overdecorated palace of red and gold. The setting owed more to the decadent gaiety of *Die Fledermaus* than to nineteenth-century Paris. John fidgeted in his seat — another twenty minutes to go until the end of the second act. He looked about at the audience, frozen in their admiration for the new soprano. Most of them, anyway. Six rows back on the far side of the auditorium he caught the glint of someone's opera glasses. Whoever it was seemed to be staring at Ixora instead of the stage. As the scene progressed, he glanced back again and found that the attention of the man behind them had not wavered. The only way John could see was by turning around in his seat. After three or four attempts to study the watching figure, the elderly couple behind him began to stare angrily.

On stage, Alfredo discovered Flora's invitation and set

off in angry pursuit of Violetta as the curtain fell to tumultuous applause.

'There's someone watching you,' he told Ixora as they rose from their seats. They made their way to the small circular foyer at the rear of the balcony, and awaited the arrival of the press photographers. Ixora laughed as she noted the concern on his face.

'I wouldn't worry about it,' she said, lightly touching his shoulder. 'I once modelled for a perfume poster in Paris, Tendresse. I still receive mail about it to this day. Some of the things they send me — well, you don't want to know.' She flapped her hand away, brushing aside the memory.

'This man is watching you through his glasses. I could probably have him thrown out.'

'Don't be silly, John. You can't stop someone from staring.'

'I'll point him out to you.'

'No, really, I don't want to see. It's happened before.'

The journalists arrived. As they photographed Ixora in the doorway of the box, John wondered if the staring man was possibly among them. It seemed odd that they were standing here, manufacturing further images for people to stare at through the once-removed medium of their newspapers. For the first time he felt he had glimpsed a darker side of his new profession.

Twenty minutes later, they resumed their seats for the remaining two acts of the opera. As if to confound John's suspicions, the sixth-row seat behind them remained empty.

Tears rolled down Ixora's cheeks as Violetta cried, 'I have returned to life!' and fell dead upon the floor of her bedroom.

As they emerged into the sultry evening air of St Martin's Lane, John spotted Ixora's admirer once more. He stood a little way behind them at one of the foyer doors, his hands thrust deep in the pockets of his summer raincoat. He looked to be about fifty, but his thin black beard and moustache had probably added a few years to his appearance. The black curly hair which hung limply against his pale forehead was speckled with grey. His deeply sunken eyes remained on Ixora's back, never flinching or straying for a second. An expression of shock hung upon his features, as if he had just realised something terrible.

'I should go and ask him what the hell he's playing at,' said John, pointing out the shadowed figure to Ixora.

'Please don't.' She laid a cool hand against his chest. 'It's not important. He may not be well.'

'Do you know him? He looks as if he knows you.'

She gave her admirer a considered appraisal. It did not seem to bother her that she was being watched. 'No,' she said finally. 'I suppose it's possible that he's on the set during the day, but I can't remember ever having seen him before.'

As they rounded the corner heading for Trafalgar Square, John looked back to the steps of the Coliseum once more. Their observer was still leaning against the wall with his hands in his pockets, watching their departure with unconcealed displeasure.

'Ixora, are you all right?' John had ushered the young model ahead of him as they passed through the narrow alleyway connecting the Strand to Covent Garden. Now as the walls widened and he drew level with her he could see that the colour had drained from her face.

'I'm fine.' Her voice was little more than a whisper. 'If we could just get in from the cold.' He studied the raised goose-flesh of her arms in puzzlement. The evening was unbearably warm.

'We'll be there in a minute,' he promised. The

restaurant was a recommendation of Howard's. As he pushed open the door he was unsurprised to see low, soft lamplight reflecting on fussily dressed tables, a *fin-de-siècle* French nightspot where middle-aged executives could conduct liaisons without fear of discovery.

As soon as they had been shown to their seats, John slipped off his jacket, placing it between himself and Ixora. He caught his reflection in the coppery glass of the partition, the white shirt, red braces, grey tie, the polished black hair. And there beside him, the tall, curving elegance of her limbs, the spangled black dress, the glowing dark hair of a woman who had managed to turn every head in the room, and who, even more remarkably, had done so wholly unselfconscious of her ability.

He knew it was stupid and wrong, purely a male ego thing, but halfway through their starters he still felt like a schoolboy on his first date. Ixora delicately sliced the warm pigeon breast on her salad as she spoke.

'How does your wife feel about you having this kind of job?'

'She's still getting used to it. I was Howard's accountant for years. Big city firm, very straight-laced. I guess it drove me a little crazy. Anyway, I felt the need to get out, so I worked in merchandising for a while. Then I ran into Howard again and he offered me a job.' He slipped his fork into the steaming *coquille* on his plate. 'How about you? How did you start modelling?'

'I didn't begin until after my mother died. She would never have allowed such a thing. She was such a strict Catholic that she wouldn't even have approved of me wearing lipstick. She was from a small Spanish village. The other women wore black, went to church and cooked the whole time. We went there to visit her family every summer. It was very depressing, very small-minded, just gossip and food and religion.' Despite doing most of the talking, she had managed to finish her starter before he had barely touched his.

'I thought you said your mother was French?'

She pushed back her plate and thought for a moment. 'No, you must be thinking of someone else. She was Spanish, and my father was English. Why would I tell you she was French?'

'I'm sorry. Didn't you say something about Provence?'

'Did I? I forget. Well, we used to go to Provence too, you know.'

John watched as she momentarily lost her composure. He had always possessed a keen memory for the minutiae of casual conversation, and was convinced that he had heard correctly. Any further thoughts were shelved as their main courses arrived. Ixora had ordered some kind of heavy *paysanne* stew of braised hearts. He had opted for a simple dish of chicken.

'So, John, how do you spend your spare time? How do you live your life?' She was already on her first mouthful of the boiling stew. Anyone would have thought she hadn't eaten in a week.

'It's very boring, I'm afraid. I've been married for a long time. You grow to appreciate the comfort of routine. You know, meals at regular times. Friends over for dinner. You compare notes on child-rearing. Supermarket on Fridays, DIY on Sundays, trips to the seaside, that kind of stuff.'

'You sound as if you're apologising for the way you live.'

John shook his head. 'I'm not. I don't mean to sound smug, either. It's just how things are.' He refilled her glass. 'What do you do when you're not before the cameras?'

She seemed taken aback by the question. 'I don't know. The time just goes.'

'Well, do you have a boyfriend?'

A troubled look crossed her face. 'No — I had one, but

it didn't work out. The whole thing finished badly. I'm happy to be by myself, for a while anyway.'

'All right — what do you want from life?'

'What do I want?' She rolled her eyes to the ceiling. 'What I want! One part of me wants nothing more than to be at home and to live quietly. But the other side, oh, that's the dangerous part. I want to paint like a Pre-Raphaelite, sing like a diva and dance like Fred Astaire. I want to read minds, and learn to like oysters. I want to soar into the heavens like a rocket, to climb mountains in Nepal, to break the land speed record in a car of my own design, to fight a duel with one hand behind my back. I want to understand the past and see the future. I want to beat the Devil himself in a game of chance. Especially to beat the Devil.' Suddenly embarrassed, she resumed eating.

For a moment, John was unable to think of a reply. 'Well,' he said lamely, 'I hope your dreams come true.'

Now it was her turn to look surprised. 'I doubt they will somehow. I'm really very ordinary.' She was either impossibly naïve, or playing with him.

'Nobody can look like you do and say that.'

'You may not realise it, John, but every pretty girl has to make a decision. At an early age she is forced to choose. For a few brief moments in her life she can do anything, and go anywhere. She either uses that time or she lets it slip by. The first route is the most dangerous. It can easily destroy you, turn your head, hurl you into a kind of limbo where normal morality no longer exists and nothing is real, nothing has any importance beyond its market value. I don't mean the old cliché of the street prostitute, but something more sinister and subtle.' She lowered her fork and leaned forward, emerald eyes glittering darkly.

'I think that beyond the dire warning of the fallen woman is something far deadlier, the woman who survives at any cost, the one whose addiction to her physical appearance has robbed her of anything spiritual beneath it.' She took a sip of wine. 'I see them all the time, the other models, talking of marrying millionaires when they could be doing something for themselves. I have no desire to spend my life shoring up my looks, to survive on the men I can still attract when I'm old. I have no desire to pass my time in a series of increasingly desperate seductions, to fight and lie and fight....' Her voice had tightened, and suddenly she stopped.

'What I mean,' she concluded, a cool unfamiliar tone entering her voice, 'is that I don't want to be dependent on men all my life. I want to be able to stand alone. That's all. Excuse me.'

She pushed back her chair and left the table, dropping her napkin on to her seat.

It had not occurred to John that Ixora was under any stress, but it now seemed a possibility that the new emphasis on her rise to fame, her contract with the Morrison agency and her long hours on the film set were making their mark. He wished he knew the best way of handling the situation.

When Ixora returned from the cloakroom the waiters fussed around her, making sure that she was reseated comfortably. Her manner was calm and collected once more. Before John had a chance to speak she reached over and took his hand in hers.

'I'm sorry, that's not like me at all. It's just — you're so easy to talk to. You stay silent, you listen. Thank you.' She pulled him gently towards her and kissed him on the cheek. For a moment John was enveloped in the perfume of English roses, and something else beneath it — an exotic scent, wood and citrus, hard to define.

They parted at the head of the alleyway into the Strand, Ixora hailing a cab for Chelsea, John setting out for Waterloo Bridge to walk off his meal.

Soon he was above the ebbing river once more, surrounded by the comforting lights of the city. The strangest of feelings assailed him, as if he now realised what had really occurred in the restaurant. For the first time in his life, he felt that all that he held dear had been placed in danger. And the almost mystical intensity of that first innocent, grateful kiss was the vanguard of all future misery and destruction.

CHAPTER
6
Attack

John watched as the glistening red glider soared and dipped in the still air above the meadow. A few feet away, Josh manipulated the remote-stick to lift the plastic and balsa aircraft above the dusty, immobile plane trees of Richmond Park. Disturbed by the noise, a herd of deer took off for the sheltered shadows of a nearby copse. It was hard to believe that his son was only eleven years old. Already he almost reached his father's shoulder. His hair was cut in the fashion favoured by his style-saturated schoolmates. His clothes were covered in the correct colour-coded logos, symbols and slogans required for continued classroom survival. His dialogue was peppered with colloquialisms garnered from a variety of TV, video and music influences. In many ways he had become a miniature adult. Yet here he was, as happily engrossed with a model aeroplane as his father had been at exactly the same age.

'Everyone else does it,' he called as he dipped the glider low once more. 'Even teachers. So why is it bad?'

'I know it seems hard to understand,' John attempted to explain further. 'Swearing debases language. It's lazy, because it's easier to say *fuck* than to think of something original. I know it seems hip, because most of the people you like in movies and at school do it. But really, it makes you look stupid to other people. Not to your classmates. But you get used to swearing with them and it becomes a habit, and pretty soon you forget and do it in front of someone else, and *that's* when you look stupid. All I'm saying is, do it if you want, just remember that there are better ways of showing that you're a cool guy.'

'Like smoking dope. Just kidding.' Josh looked up from his remote panel long enough to regard his father with a wary eye. 'All this because I said *shit*. It's almost worth doing it to get one of the famous Chapel family lectures. You're so straight, Dad.'

'And you're a mouthy smartass. Let me have a go at that.'

'Swearing. You just damaged your character again.' Josh passed his father the control panel. 'Mother's upset with you, by the way.'

John concentrated on the aircraft buzzing noisily overhead. He was aware of Helen's coolness over the past two days. He just hadn't expected Josh to pick up on it. 'Why, what have I done?' he asked, trying to sound casual.

'Oh, the usual, working late. I think she thought you'd be home more with the new job.'

'I warned her that the hours would be longer. It's difficult for both of us, you know.'

'She misses you. I almost miss you. I think you should go and talk to her.'

'Hey, kid, it'll settle down in no time. And then you'll get to meet the stars, come and visit me on film sets, things like that. You can start collecting autographs. Did you know they sell for a lot of money?'

'Really?'

'Yup. And we'll get tickets for rock concerts, all the best seats. You'll be able to swank around to your friends about how you met Sting.'

Josh made a face. 'He's old enough to be my grand-father.'

'It's going to work out great. I'll have a talk with your mother. It'll be fine. Wait and see.' They watched as the droning vermilion glider circled endlessly against the sun like a poisonous, angry insect.

'Is she very beautiful, this woman you took to the opera?' Helen tugged at a blade of dry grass, affecting disinterest.

'I suppose so.'

'You always say that. You suppose.'

'That's because I'm torn between telling the truth, which is yes, she's very beautiful, and telling you a lie to spare your feelings. It was a press opportunity. They took some photographs, asked some questions. Then they printed her face in one of the tabloids, which was not what we wanted.'

'Why couldn't you have just gone to the photo call? Why did you have to sit through the whole thing with her? You've hardly ever done that with me.'

'That's because Josh was growing up, and anyway you don't like opera.'

'That's not the point.'

'And I could hardly leave her sitting by herself for the performance.' They sat beside each other on the sunlit side of the hill. In the distance, Josh's glider buzzed. John reached over and cupped Helen's face in his hands. 'I can't pretend to you that it's a chore attending these functions. I'd be lying if I did. But you must understand that it's what I do for a living now.'

Helen pulled herself free and smoothed her hair back into place. The August sun had freckled her unmade-up face. 'So, how would you like it if I got a job as a cocktail waitress?'

He sat back, exasperated. 'Now you're being stupid,' he complained. 'This is a career with some real horizons attached to it. Howard thinks I have a lot of potential.'

'Howard.' She spat the word. 'You're taking the advice of a man who has no respect for anyone or anything.'

'It'll work out, I promise. It's a new job, it involves a lot of socialising. There are bound to be long hours at first. Look at me.' He wobbled the excess flesh of his stomach. 'I'm a hollow reed.'

She smiled at last. 'You're right,' she admitted, 'I'm over-reacting. It's just that I love you very much. I like us doing things together. You're a good man. You're honest, and you're strong. I want you to share things with me, not with somebody else. That's only natural, isn't it? I just need reassurance every now and again.'

'Look at Josh.' He nodded in the direction of the boy, who was running toward the landed aircraft. 'He's growing up so fast. Soon he'll be studying for his exams and turning vegetarian and telling us off for having ruined the environment.'

'Expressing horror when he finds out we still have sex.'

'Quoting French anarchists.'

'Discovering Socialism.'

'And we'll be creeping out of the house just to get a little peace and quiet.'

She laughed again. 'That sounds fine by me. You promise that's how it'll be?'

He studied her hopeful brown eyes. 'Oh, without a doubt.'

'You've made an old married lady very happy.' Helen rose to her feet and watched the plumes of smoke unfurling from a distant bonfire.

This is how I always want to think of us, he thought. Helen standing on the hill against the flare of a dying summer sun, one hand raised to shield her eyes, the other holding down the hem of her skirt. Josh hurdling the stems of tall dry grass between us, running to collect the crimson aircraft. This is the life we have made for ourselves. This is who we are.

On Monday, John was forced to admit that his new career move was a strange one. All morning long he had racked his brains on the initial press releases for *Playing With Fire*, trying to imagine what would persuade a disparate group of magazine columnists to run articles on the film, when the only unique thing about the production so far was its uneventfulness.

The move, he reflected, had been the right one to make, even though he had been forced to accept a four thousand pound salary drop. Helen had been supportive of the change, and had happily offered to increase her own working hours. She had often expressed the hope that he would one day find a way to explore the creative side of his personality. But now, seated beneath the aqueous slats of light reflected from the venetian blinds, staring at a computer screen which refused to be filled, he began to understand how tough his task could be.

He was here to operate as a buffer between two self-serving barter systems. One involved the movie makers, the men and women who relied on the media to carry knowledge of their existence to the public. The other concerned the press and TV people, who had the power to turn a bad film into a national cult or reduce the public image of a performer to the status of a leper.

He watched Howard at work on the telephone, denying one publication an interview with the director, but sopping them with an exclusive on the leading lady, juggling one press launch against another. He had not realised that there was so much hustling involved.

'Your account, Ixora De Thing.' Howard's voice preceded him into the room. 'She won't do satellite. Why is it so hot in here?' He was striding about at the end of the desk, pulling at his shirt collar, interrupting John's flow of thought.

'The air conditioning isn't working. Why won't she do satellite?'

'It's not that she won't, it's us that won't let her. She's upmarket. Class. We don't want her beaming into council estates in the Midlands. The public should have to pay to see her.'

'If they watch her on satellite, they will pay,' John pointed out.

'Forget it. We've had this problem before. Diana West-lake, the woman who lived with the Amazon tribe; we negotiated with Sky, Superchannel, one of those, I forget which. She's concerned about the environment, I tell them, she's only doing the publicity to get her message across to a wider audience. Some station presenter with a seventy-dollar haircut and a suit made out of Tibetan rush-matting promises to stick to script.'

'What happened?'

'First question up, he asks her if she slept with any of the pygmies. So remember, you expand Ixora's profile, but not at the expense of her persona. Wendy'll give you her "A" list of stations and publications.'

Just before lunchtime John descended to the basement viewing theatre armed with another can of Ixora's rushes. In order to assemble an electronic press kit on the actress, he would have to dig up further usable footage. As the lights faded, the familiar interior nightclub set from *Playing With Fire* appeared on the screen. Ixora stood apart from the other players on the far right, but she might just as well have been standing spotlit at the centre.

Several mute out-takes had been spliced together. These were shots which, for one reason or another, had been rejected by the director as unacceptable. One revealed a microphone boom hanging below the standard level of screen cut-off. Another showed the camera crew standing patiently at the side of the screen — and there, kneeling beside one of the operators, was the man who had studied them so obsessively at the opera house. There was no mistaking the pale face, the thin black beard, the narrow dark eyes. It was definitely the same man and, just as before, his eyes never once flickered from the object of his agonised attention.

John returned to his office to discover an accumulation of Post-It notes on his word processor. Checking them out, he remembered that he had promised to meet a *Time Out* feature writer who was keen to do a piece on the Tyron movie. Perhaps he'd be able to secure a mention for Ixora.

'St Martin-In-The-Fields' read the yellow slip of paper. 'Derek Kommar, Crypt Restaurant, 6.00 p.m.' He reached the church a little after the hour, tacking between the peace protest taking place on the steps and the commuters heading for Charing Cross Station. The temperature rose steadily as he descended the stairs into the crypt. A pair of young Chinese women were setting up their music stands at the back of the room. The tombstones beneath his feet were covered by white iron tables and chairs. The crypt was mainly popular with students, who used it as an inexpensive winebar. Most of the tables were filled. Those who sat alone sipped red wine and pinned open the pages of paperbacks. It seemed an odd meeting place to have chosen.

Derek Kommar turned out to be an affable young man in a denim shirt and baseball cap who seemed to know more about the production of *Playing With Fire* than he did. In the course of a bottle of wine it was agreed that the magazine would run a cover article on Scott Tyron, and perhaps a sidebar on the history of the production. John presented the journalist with Ixora's newly printed port-folio, and suggested he keep an eye on her for the future. By 6.45 p.m. their business was concluded, and Kommar took his leave, heading into Soho for a movie screening. John was about to follow him through the exit door when he saw the subject of their conversation.

Ixora was seated in a dimly lit corner, leaning on the armrest of her chair with her chin cupped in the palm of her hand. She was alone. As he approached, she smiled awkwardly and rose to kiss him. She pushed a chair back from the table and pointed to it. Reluctantly, John seated himself, propping his briefcase against the leg of the chair.

'This is a welcome surprise,' she said, pouring him a glass of red wine and sliding it across. For a fraction of a second she looked ill at ease, as if he had caught her doing something private. 'I've never been here before. Isn't it strange? Nell Gwynne is buried no more than twenty yards from this table. Did you know that the monks of Westmin-ster Abbey used to come here to chapel before the twelfth century?'

'No, I didn't.' John shifted on his chair. The heat prickled at him. He wondered why she was here alone. 'It's very hot.'

'I know, it's wonderful, isn't it? It reminds me of home.' She brushed her hair back from her eyes and gazed around. She had just returned from the studio. Her face was scrubbed clean of makeup. It was the first time he had seen her looking truly relaxed. She wore a new white T-shirt and baggy, faded blue jeans with a heavy brown belt looped over at the waist. The effect was all the more alluring for being so deliberately casual. It was hard to imagine her behaving as an ordinary person, lounging in front of the TV, taking toast and tea back to bed. She seemed only to exist in this mode, designed more for other people than herself. It was, he supposed, one of the hazards of her profession.

'I suppose you grew up in the south,' said John, wondering which country she would pick for her child-hood memories tonight.

'That's right, the deepest south.' Her eyes held the distance for a moment, then refocused. 'I thought a friend of mine would be here this evening. I'm glad I decided to wait a while.'

John glanced at his watch. Helen had people coming to dinner at eight. 'I can't stop, I'm afraid. I'm late already.'

'I'll walk with you.' The force of her reply surprised him. Before he had a chance to say anything, she had pushed the glass aside and risen from her seat.

'Are you sure you don't want to wait for your friend?'

'I doubt he'll turn up now. You're going to Waterloo?' As they crossed the floor of the crypt she kept close at his heels, as if somehow seeking the protection of his shadow. As they reached the top of the stairs and turned into the sunlit street which led to Trafalgar Square, John had the distinct impression that someone was following behind them.

Searching the road ahead for a cab he stole a look back at the church, at the protesters and pedestrians thronging its steps like characters from an eighteenth-century litho-graph of London life.

They spoke little on their way to the bridge. It seemed

as if they were deliberately refusing to develop the conversational reference points between them, as if by doing so they would open up some taboo area, some point beyond which they would not be able to return. John wondered if she was as attracted to him as he was to her. He assumed not. That was, after all, the main requirement of a model, the ability to project her appeal. The difference was whether you chose to act on it and make a fool of yourself, or whether you were mature enough to look beyond the physical image and discover the person behind. In Ixora's case, the person behind seemed just as mysterious.

His attention was drawn back by a cab passing with its yellow hire light illuminated. As it continued over the crossroads, John turned to catch a glimpse of a figure rounding the far corner, and realised that it was a man who had been sitting near Ixora in the crypt.

Could it be that he was following them? Was it the same man, the one from the theatre, the one on the film set? Some psychotic who worshipped this beautiful woman, who had to be near her all the time, like the one who was obsessed with that actress, what was her name, Jodie Foster? In the angled amber sunlight he couldn't tell whether the figure had a trim black beard.

They crossed into the Strand at the corner of Villiers Street. If Ixora had noticed that they were being followed, she gave no indication of doing so. He was about to suggest that they should have more luck at the cab rank on the forecourt of Charing Cross Station when the figure launched itself at them. John spun at the sound of running footsteps, raised his eyes to where Ixora stood, startled, as their attacker — *her* attacker — descended upon her with his fists flying.

John had the impression of a tall, olive-skinned man with cropped black hair before he grabbed at the falling fist, trying to divert it from Ixora's terrified face. He forced himself in front of her assailant, trying to deflect the blows, but a long left arm struck out hard, balling its fist, passing over his shoulder and catching her hard on the cheek. As she fell to the ground, John swung wildly at his opponent, delivering a heavy blow to his midriff, knocking him heavily to the pavement.

As the figure rose John watched for his face, waiting to see the little black beard and moustache, the lank curly hair, but before he could confirm the identity of their attacker he had risen smartly to his feet, spinning around and launching himself away from them. Seconds later the scuffle was over and they were alone, as the fleeing figure sprinted into the traffic of the Strand and away into one of the sloping side streets that led to the river.

'Are you all right?'

He pulled her upright and checked her face. Blood was leaking from a split beside her right nostril. 'Here.' He pulled out a handkerchief and held it to her face. Several bystanders watched from a safe distance.

'Where's your bag?'

'I wasn't carrying one.' With the handkerchief clamped over her nose she pointed to her back pocket. Her wallet was still there.

'Show me.' He eased open her hands. Blood had congealed on her cheek. An area above her lip was turning blue.

'You're going to have some bruising. Nothing they can't cover up on set. Does it hurt?'

'Not really.' She dusted the knees of her jeans with her free hand. John slipped his arm through hers and forced a smile.

'Let's find a policeman. I didn't get a good look at him, but it must be the one who's been following you.'

'No.' Her fingers gripped his arm. 'Let's just — just sit

down somewhere for a few minutes. No police.'

'Ixora, some psycho just attacked you.'

'Please — I'll be okay, I just want to rest.'

'All right.' He searched for a suitable place, located a small café with outside tables and steered her inside to the bathrooms in the rear. When she reappeared, her face had been wiped free of blood but was robbed of any colour. There was a cut on her cheek, the dark shadow of a bruise. Her lip was slightly swollen. Luckily he had managed to deflect any real damage. He bought two coffees at the bar. They emerged into the dying sunlight and found themselves seats. She dropped into the chair and lowered her forehead on to the fingers of her right hand, studying the circular stains on the tabletop.

'I know the man,' she said simply.

'What?' He stared down at her, a cup in each hand.

'His name is Matteo. I used to go out with him.'

'Jesus, if you know him, we can have him arrested.'

'It wouldn't do any good.'

'Why not?' He raised her lowered face with the fingertips of his right hand.

'He's a photographer. I dated him for a while.'

'So what happened?'

'The usual, I suppose. He seemed something he wasn't. Faithful. Serious about me. There were other things. I finished it.'

'When was this?'

'Three, four months ago.'

'And he's still creeping around after you?'

'He was very possessive. When I stopped seeing him, he began to follow me all the time. If I met friends, he'd suddenly appear and interrupt us. I threatened to go to the police.'

'Why didn't you?'

'My career was just starting to break. He knows where I

live. I didn't want any trouble. I figured if I ignored him he'd eventually make someone else's life miserable instead.'

'I think we should talk to someone. They could at least put a watch outside your house.'

'Dear John, sometimes it's obvious you haven't been in this business very long. It's not the kind of publicity they want for the film.'

'This is more important, Ixora! This Matteo came to the set, didn't he? Why did you let him?'

'What do you mean?' Her face was a blank.

'He's in last week's batch of rushes, I saw him myself, the man from the opera house. You can't just walk on to a closed set. Someone must have agreed to let him attend the shoot.'

'Matteo? He wasn't on the set. He couldn't have been. I'd have recognised him.' She shook her head. 'We're not talking about the same person. Wait a second.' She dug her wallet from her back pocket and withdrew a crumpled photograph. 'This is Matteo.' Smoothing it on the table, she rotated it for him to examine. John found himself looking into the eyes of a man he had never seen before in his life, a foreigner in his mid-twenties, broad-nosed, handsome and arrogant.

'Wait, this man is much younger.' He was confused now. 'He's nothing like the one at the opera.'

'John!'

He twisted in his chair to locate the source of the call. An overweight businessman in a grey pinstriped suit was calling from the other side of the café. Lee Cavarett was sharing a table with two of his former colleagues. John had not seen any of them since the day of his failure to appear for his own farewell party. They nodded and smiled across to each other, unprepared to renegotiate their former acquaintance on new terms. The eyes of all three flicked across at Ixora, whose swollen face was turned away in embarrassment.

'Let's get out of here.' Ixora accepted his hand and they departed. Cavarett's wife was friendly with Helen. Perhaps news of his arrival with a beautiful, bruised woman would reach his wife's ears. Right now his only concern was to put Ixora in a taxi and get her home to safety. For all he knew, this lunatic could still be lurking around somewhere. He was aware of the manner in which they slunk away from Cavarett and the café. It was as if they'd been caught in the middle of some act of infidelity. Something about Ixora always suggested a clandestine nature to their meetings.

As the taxi bore her off she sat with her head against the seat rest, exhausted, not looking back. John returned to Waterloo, puzzled by these new events. As he studied the glistening river from the bridge, he thought of how long his life had sailed on a steady, unquestioned course. He could feel the tug of unfamiliar currents, strange winds rising to bear him into uncharted territory.

CHAPTER
7
Coroner's Report

The early part of September was a busy one for the residents of Bow Street police station. Covent Garden was still filled with tourists ripe for mugging, gangs of school sixth-formers threw their final criminal flings of the summer holidays, and the continuing hot weather turned normally placid motorists into homicidal maniacs.

Detective Sergeant Michael Sullivan was unable to find a quiet spot where he could read his coroner's report in peace. A hysterically crying woman was being comforted in his office, and the operations room was filled with Japanese students taking notes. He tried the door of a colleague's office further along the corridor, found it unlocked and settled behind her desk, only to be turfed out when she suddenly returned with several arguing officers in tow.

In exasperation Sullivan headed for the foyer of the pathology lab and made himself comfortable on one of the bench seats there. He preferred to read through the report than to spend an hour of explanation with the coroner Finch, who talked too enthusiastically of his work and smelled as if a gallon of aftershave had been poured over him, which it had, because of his aversion to the chemical smells which clung to his labcoat. Setting down his coffee, Sullivan spread the folder across his knees and began to read.

POST MORTEM REPORT ON VINCENT BRADY
Male
of 16 New Church Street, Vauxhall
Body identified by: L. Gardner.

Post mortem carried out at the Central Mortuary, Codrington Street, London WC3 at 10.00 a.m. on 2nd September 1991.
Observers present at the post mortem: Dr R. Land, Detective Chief Inspector I. Hargreave, Detective Sergeant M. Sullivan, Detective Constable D. Mace, PC L. Gardner, C. Wyman (Photographer HMCO), G. Samuels (Technician), Dr O. Finch (Her Majesty's Coroner).

HISTORY
The deceased, a barman, was attacked by an unknown assailant at his lodgings on or around 18th August. He was 28 years of age. On 26th August, police received a complaint from Mr M. Al-Kahffadji, downstairs neighbour to the deceased, concerning a bad smell emanating from the upstairs flat. The investigating constable, PC L. Gardner, gained forcible entrance to the property and discovered the body on the floor of the main lounge.

EXTERNAL EXAMINATION
The body was that of a well-nourished black male, 6'
2" in height and weighing 88 kg. There was no
clothing present on the upper half of the body. The
victim was wearing black jeans, no underwear, no
footwear. The right antecubital fossa showed a mark
due to damage in transport.

Sullivan released a derisive snort. Brady's plastic-encased
body had slipped out of their hands as they had lowered it
down the twisting stairs.

The following facial injuries were present: four areas
of abrasion on the front of the forehead, grouped
mainly to the left. These consisted: two 2 × 1 cm
sized areas, a 3 cm sized area above the nose, a triangular 2.7 cm sized area above the left eye. Bruising
was present inside the left eyelid, the upper and lower
lips. In addition there were five stab wounds. In each
case, the occipitale, parietale and frontal bones
prevented penetration of the blade to any signficant
depth. These wounds measured a uniform 1.2 cm.
Teeth were intact.

The report continued its detailed catalogue of scrapes,
cuts and bruises. Sullivan flipped the page and continued
reading. He had been correct in assuming that the murder
weapon was a narrow-bladed knife, probably surgical. The
range of injuries was impressive. Both pleural cavities and
one kidney punctured, a wound in the right sternomastoid
muscle to a depth of over seven centimetres. Subarachnoid haemorrhage covering the entire surface of the brain,
which, incidentally, weighed 1,500 g. Sullivan idly
wondered how much his own brain weighed.

Both wrists and ankles showed bruising of a width consistent with the cords binding the hands and the feet of the victim.

CARDIOVASCULAR SYSTEM
The heart weighed 410 g. The valves and aorta were normal. No significant coronary artery disease.

GASTROINTESTINAL SYSTEM
The tongue was cut and bruised, consistent with biting. The stomach contained remains of a recent meal, hamburger. The liver showed gross fatty change. The gall bladder, pancreas and peritoneum were normal.

He skipped on to Finch's notes at the bottom of the page. 'I was also informed that a blood alcohol test performed on the deceased revealed the level of 280 mg/100 ml and a urine alcohol of 295 mg/100 ml.'

CONCLUSIONS
1. This man died as a result of subarachnoid haemorrhage, due to the rupture of vertebral vessels, probably vertebral veins at the level in the cervical cord of C2.
2. These ruptured vessels were caused by a stab wound to the left side of the neck.
3. Although cause of death is described above, cessation of life could have occurred momentarily from any or all of the other wounds, notably the puncturing of the lungs and damage to the kidney.

A separate sheet clipped to the back of the report added Finch's notes concerning the time delay in finding the body, and the effect of stomach bacteria on determining the cause of death. He turned his attention to the red cardboard file lying on the seat beside his cup of scabbed coffee, the result of Mace's initial legwork.

'I can save you the trouble of reading that.' Deborah Mace had appeared in the doorway before him and pointed to the second file. She had thrown a baggy grey sweatshirt over her shoulders, about to go off duty.

'Be my guest.' Sullivan closed the folder and turned to face her.

'Vincent Brady was gay.'

'So?'

'So perhaps he brought someone back and the trade turned a little rougher than either of them intended.'

'I don't see that his sexual preference has any relevance.'

'What do you mean?' Mace looked irritated.

'You're talking about the tying of the body. Bondage is just as common in heterosexual relationships. And there's no medical evidence here to suggest he'd had sex.'

'Maybe he was just getting started. Nobody saw whether he came in alone on the night of the 18th. He was working the evening shift, 5.30 to 11.00, but he left just after 9.00. I talked to the rest of the pub staff. Brady never spoke to them much. Kept his own company. Besides, he'd only been there a couple of weeks.'

'They could have at least bothered to report him missing. Why did he leave so early?'

'He told the manager he wasn't feeling well, said he wanted to go home and go to bed. Obviously he had some kind of appointment arranged.'

'Why do you say that?'

'The guys he was on shift with said he changed into a new shirt before he left. He got all dressed up.'

'You know where he used to hang out?'

'I've got the name of a restaurant and a couple of bars, but I haven't been to any of them yet. Vice are going to send someone over for me.'

'Why can't you go?' asked Sullivan. 'Do you have a problem dealing with gays?'

Mace threw him a sour look and pulled the sweatshirt over her head. 'No more than I have a problem with anyone else around here,' she said finally. 'I've had my transfer accepted to Hackney as part of the staff decentralisation programme. This place is a lunatic asylum. Nobody knows what's going on. Nothing ever gets cleared up. I joined the force to solve crimes. Instead I spend my day filling out forms.'

'That's because you're a public servant, Mace. Your every move is accountable. I'm sorry we haven't got a nice simple investigation for you to handle, one with a beginning, a middle and an end. That's not how it works. I usually only get to see the middle bit myself.'

As he watched her stalk off into the noisy corridor beyond, the feeling he had first felt in Brady's apartment returned, a fear that this case would somehow spread beyond his control.

It was a problem with all of the murder cases that fell under the jurisdiction of Bow Street. Historically, Central London was not an area associated with an especially high murder rate. Therefore when a homicide investigation was opened, there were always plenty of officers keen to be assigned to the case.

He would request that Mace should not be replaced for the time being. There was something very odd about Brady's death, and the fewer people who became involved at this stage the better.

CHAPTER
8
Blood

'What's the matter?'

John pushed the loaded shopping cart to one side and focused his attention on Helen. She was in shirt-tails and jeans, what she called her 'shopping outfit', standing in the middle of the aisle, thoughtfully watching him. Behind her, Josh was attempting to eat a family-sized box of chocolate raisins before they reached the checkout.

'Nothing's the matter,' he replied. 'Why?'

'It's as if you were frozen to the spot. People can't get past.'

His mind had been far away. He looked up at the fluorescent panels chequering the barn-like steel roof of the supermarket. The easy-listening version of 'Message In A Bottle' was playing on the Muzak system. He hated this place, its vastness of choice, its impersonality, its cheery brightness. He pointed into the cart. 'Have you noticed they've even got ingredients listed on fresh pineapples?' he said with a sudden smile.

'Buy the tinned ones,' suggested Josh. 'More additives, but less chemicals.'

Helen slipped an arm around his waist. 'You're terrible at false *bonhomie*, John. Stop thinking about work so much and help me figure out what we're going to give Howard and Angela to eat tonight. It's bad enough that you have to go to this photo session this afternoon. I could have done with your help.'

And so they walked on from one aisle to the next, packing ravioli and trout and lemons and bottled capers, choosing from racks of Chablis and Chardonnay while somewhere far away the red dress swirled and lifted in the warm shadows of the dressing room, and blossomed like a rare sea anemone beneath the studio lights, and John became a prisoner of his unrecognised desire.

'Put that back, Josh, it's all sugar.' Helen removed a packet from the cart and thrust it back at her son.

'Your chance to win a brand new Toyota truck,' he said, temptingly waving the box back and forth before her.

'Tell him, John,' she pleaded. 'It's bad for you.'

'Christ, Helen, everything's bad for you.'

'Don't take the Lord's name in vain.' She slapped at him.

'Helen, John! I didn't know you shopped here. How are you both?'

They found themselves facing a smiling, pear-shaped woman in a shiny blue jogging suit. Sue Cavarett turned to John and appraised him. 'I'm surprised to see you helping Helen. I imagined the glamorous PR life would keep you away from such mortal chores.'

It was instantly obvious to John that she resented the success of her husband's former colleague. The expression on her face failed to conceal her jealousy. He suddenly remembered that Lee Cavarett had spotted him with Ixora at the café yesterday. A chill began to spread in the pit of his stomach.

'Isn't it typical?' Sue was saying. 'None of us see each other for ages, then it's twice in two days.' She waited for a quizzical look to appear on Helen's face. 'Because Lee bumped into John just yesterday afternoon, didn't he?'

'That's right, yes.' John shifted from one foot to the other. This was absurd. He had done nothing wrong, and yet his palms were starting to sweat.

'You never mentioned you saw Lee. Where were you, darling?' Helen smiled at him. He looked at her sharply, but it was an innocent question.

'Oh, at a café. I was with a client.'

'Really?' Sue Cavarett seemed surprised. 'Lee said you were by yourself. Sitting all alone with your coffee, poor thing. He thought perhaps you'd been stood up for a date.' She flashed a wide, bitchy smile at Helen. 'We really must have dinner soon. I'd better get on — if I forget the kiwi fruit my name will be mud.'

She fluttered her hand at them and drifted on with her trolley. John stared after her. Could Cavarett have actually failed to tell his wife about Ixora, and the strange intensity of their behaviour together? Perhaps he really hadn't noticed her. Perhaps she didn't exist in this mundane world, or could only be seen by certain people, those prepared to believe in something other than everyday reality. His thinking was becoming paranoid — and over what? He reminded himself that nothing had happened. And nothing was going to happen. He studied the woman beside him, guiding the cart around the end of the aisle, checking her list against the shelves, and knew that he could never do anything to hurt her.

*

The photographic studio was situated beside an abandoned cinema on a corner of the Edgware Road. As in the case of many such businesses, it occupied the most unlikely location imaginable to be involved in the manufacture of dreams.

One of the Dickie Feldman's assistants pulled the heavy black drape along its rail and turned off the rear wall lights of the studio. Feldman, the man who was about to step behind the camera, had requested that Ixora bring two outfits from the film in addition to the clothes that had been provided for her by the magazine. The group shots featuring the other stars of the film, minus Scott Tyron, who was filming inserts in the Derbyshire countryside, had taken place two hours ago against a curving blue-skied cyclorama. For a moment, the sawing of police car sirens brought the outside world into the studio, penetrating the thick blackout screens which covered the only window in the room. John was bored. Despite the presence of several large electric fans the air in the studio was stifling. The session had already overrun by an hour due to technical glitches, and Ixora had seemed on edge and uncomfortable, barely able to follow the photographer's instructions as he ordered her from one pose to the next.

Now, while John waited for Ixora to appear in her final outfit, the assistants pulled the dustcloths aside and lit the set to obliterate shadows. He was surprised by the ability of these professionals to create such potent illusions within such a minuscule space. The studio was cramped and cluttered. Its floor was covered in scraps of silver tape, arranged to mark out camera positions. Its hardboard-covered walls seemed in imminent danger of collapse. But then the lights were switched on to the set, and there stood a miniature masterpiece of illusion. A circular plastic jacuzzi was filled with water that had been dyed a brilliant shade of crimson. Behind this, paper ivy was stitched to a wall of fake stucco, emerald green clinging against shocking pink.

The cost of the session was being shared by *i-D* magazine, who had planned the fashion spread. Their designer was seated in a corner with the props boy discussing pastry casings. Feldman, the photographer, was impatiently pacing the edge of the set.

'You want to go and check on her?' he asked. He clearly saw John as little more than a paid minder. 'It can't take that long to put a fucking swimsuit on.'

John rose from the edge of the table and crossed to the small dressing room behind the cyclorama. The fans blew warm air against his damp shirt as he slipped behind the shifting wall. A linen curtain screened the dressing room. He felt for the edge of the cloth and tentatively lifted a corner.

'Ixora?'

The makeup girl was applying a final dusting to Ixora's shoulderblades. 'I'm just taking the shine off her skin,' she said. 'What do you think?' She took a step back and turned her charge to face him.

Ixora's brilliant emerald eyes shone darkly beneath heavy black mascara and a glitter-sprayed fringe. Her lips had been wetly frosted with crimson. The bikini cut deeply across her small breasts, pushing them into a cleavage, the bottom half scything between her legs in a tiny triangle. John's mouth fell open. She had been made up as some kind of Penthouse Pet, an image of whorish adolescence.

'John, I don't feel comfortable in this outfit ...' she began.

On the other side of the lights, Feldman was calling, 'Ixora, we're running late, honey. Just come out here and let me see you.'

'Wait, you should change.' John pushed her back and

turned to the stylist. 'You can't expect her to go out there looking like this.'

The stylist, a small Jewish woman with tinted red hair, looked bewildered. 'You don't like this look?' She raised the back of her hand beside Ixora's face. 'It's all the fashion now. So the man out there tells me.'

John slipped a dressing-gown over Ixora's shoulders. 'You understand that if any shots of you dressed like this got out, they'd wreck the image we're trying to create.' He turned to the stylist. 'Whose idea was it for her to look like this?'

The stylist pointed beyond the curtain. 'Speak to Mr Ponytail sitting in the corner.'

'John, if he says it's the fashion—' began Ixora.

'No, absolutely not. Stay here a minute, I'll sort it out.' Howard had warned him not to interfere in situations like this, but what else could he do? He climbed around the edge of the set and called to the designer. 'The outfit's all wrong. You'll have to go with what Mr Feldman has already taken.'

'Now, wait a minute,' said the designer, raising an accusing finger. 'This has nothing to do with you. You're here to drive your client home, nothing more. Deciding what she wears is a creative decision. You have no—'

Behind them, Ixora suddenly cried out. She had stepped forward through the curtain and was staring at the set, her eyes widening at the sight of the swirling crimson water. As her legs gave way she suddenly fell forward. John ran on to the set, just in time to break her fall with his outstretched arms. They laid her on the couch and moved a fan close to her face while the props boy ran to fetch a damp cloth.

'It's all right,' said Feldman, 'it's just the heat. It's happened before in here.'

John crouched at her side and bathed her forehead with

a wet flannel. Moments later, her eyes slowly opened and she started from the seat.

'Lie back,' advised John. 'You passed out. The heat . . .'

'No, I saw—' She closed her eyes.

'What did you see?'

'The pool. It's filled with blood.'

'No, it's just water, water with red dye added. They were going to ask you to stand in it.' He smoothed her fringe away from her eyes. She looked up at him.

'I can't stand the sight of blood. Never have been able to, not since I was a child.'

'Don't worry, there's no need to do any more shots. Just lie back and be still for a while.'

The stylist coughed behind him. He suddenly became aware that he was stroking her hair with the backs of his fingers. Embarrassed, he rose to his feet. 'The pool,' he said lamely. 'She thought it was full of blood.'

CHAPTER
9
Film

Dickie Feldman's popularity as a fashion photographer had survived three decades of sartorial folly, from Shrimpton, the mini and psychedelia through Westwood and the safety pin to yuppie flash, Nike rap and back to psychedelia. He captured them all with an eye for the era, albeit a jaundiced one, and he remained in business by never hitting a client and never missing an opportunity.

Tonight, as he sat back in his chair and watched the boy boxing up the last of the equipment, he was congratulating himself on the latter. Feldman prided himself on his unerring ability to spot a future media celebrity, and the De Corizo girl was the first model he'd seen in a long time who had The Look. There was something about her that flared into life beneath the lights, an odd translucent quality to her skin that made her appear as if she had been created in porcelain. The girl was tall, positively robust, and moulded with a sensuality that turned the simplest poses into classic photographic images. Once more he slid the magnifier across the first sheet of contacts and studied them frame by frame. It was almost impossible to decide which shots to go with. The magazine's young art director would probably use the stills that showed the designer clothes to their worst effect. That wouldn't be difficult, he thought, turning to the next sheet. Most of the outfits would only suit the most angular of models; hanging from the rounded shoulders of the general public their effect would be comical, uncomfortable and downright insulting.

The boy called out to say he was leaving. Feldman murmured a reply and waited for the outer door to close before rising from his seat and returning to the darkroom. Switching on the overhead bulb, he lowered his considerable bulk to the base of the plans chest and pulled out the bottom drawer.

The PR man had virtually bust a gasket when he'd seen his client in what the designer had euphemistically referred to as her 'clubbing outfit'. It was hard to see why he had objected so strongly, unless of course he was knocking her off. The clothes had been a little risqué, but nothing exactly shocking. Besides, Chapel had been right, she didn't suit the outfit. Her nature was too sophisticated for latex microgear. The only way to get the shots working would have been to make her angry or get her to cry.

Just then, of course, God had intervened and provided him with a perfect opportunity. Chapel had blown his stack, and the girl had freaked out at the sight of the water in the set. He was glad he'd been able to squeeze off a roll of film while everyone was still arguing.

Now he removed the envelope from its hiding place and shook the roll of film into the palm of his hand. He was well aware of what he hoped to find: frozen frames of anguish and anger, half on the set, half in the dressing room, the crying girl in her fetishistic garb, the PR guy and the art director arguing — all the elements of a classic series. He crossed to the other side of the bench and prepared the hypo basins. Naturally he would do nothing with the pictures that would jeopardise his standing with the magazine. No, for the time being these could stay in his portfolio. Then, if the girl became something of a success, perhaps it would be time to negotiate a deal.

He paused for a moment, listening at the curtain. The steel outer door to the studio had clicked, and for a moment he had heard the sound of the street traffic; the boy must have forgotten something. He picked up a black Pentel pen and carefully printed Ixora's name on the side of the film roll, replaced the cap and dropped the film into his shirt pocket, then pushed out through the curtain into the darkened studio.

'Tom, put some bloody lights on. You'll fall over something.' He spoke in the direction of the main door. No reply returned from the dark. There seemed to be chill air currents circulating in the room, but that was impossible. Goose-pimples had risen on his arms. Listening to the soft rhythmic breathing before him, it occurred to Feldman that he was facing an intruder.

'Tom?' he called, tentatively taking a step forward. Perhaps the door hadn't shut properly as he'd left. The kind of people he saw wandering the Edgware Road late at night didn't bear thinking about. 'I'm turning the lights on.' He tried to sound confident as he reached for the wall switch.

Suddenly a flashlight shone into his eyes and an arm slammed hard across his throat. He was shoved back to the floor, cracking his spine against the chair behind. He tried to sit up but his back hurt. It was impossible to discern anything of his attacker beyond a vague looming bulk. The torch remained unwavering before his eyes. A hand reached down and grabbed the front of his shirt, pulling him to his feet. Feldman lashed out with his right foot, but struck air. He was thrown back against the wall, stumbling over the tangle of extended tripods the boy had forgotten to clear away, jarring his shoulder against the brickwork.

The hand on his shirt found the roll of film and deftly removed it from his pocket, turning it over in the torch-beam. There was a strange sound, a grunted oath as the film was held motionless in the intruder's hand, then the metal shaft of the torch fell across his face, cracking bone and wrenching his head to one side.

A molten bar of pain glowed across the side of Feldman's head as he attempted to understand what was happening. The torch had been placed on a nearby work-bench, its beam still glaring in his face. The figure had gloved hands. It was a hot night. This was no tramp from the street seeking something to sell. A fresh streak of pain sent his hand to his face. He was losing blood. There was a buzzing in his head; a fracture? He wondered how long he could last before losing consciousness. The hands were attempting to expose the roll of film, but the gloves were preventing him from tearing the strip from its casing. The roll was bounced to the floor in anger, and a shoe fell on it with a sharp crack. The figure bent and rose, awkwardly pulling one of the gloves off. Before him a hand held a twisted peel of plastic between its fingers.

There was another pause. Feldman could not tell if he had momentarily lost consciousness, or if his attacker was motionless for some purpose. With the unravelled roll of film still in his ungloved hand, he seemed to be looking around for something. Feldman tried to push away from the wall but it felt as if his head was coming apart. He watched helplessly as the gloved hand reached down for one of the fallen tripods at his feet and unscrewed one of the lower leg sections. Rising once more to full height, the intruder raised the hand which held Ixora's exposed roll of film and shoved the container into the startled photographer's mouth.

Feldman felt the bitter metal on his tongue and gagged as leather-clad fingers forced it to the back of his throat. The film still trailed from it like a celluloid streamer as his assailant rammed it deep into his oesophagus with the aid of the tripod leg. Feldman's agonised cries were quickly stifled as his throat muscles flexed against the intrusion and he vomited copiously. Now the figure seemed to tower above him as he fell to his knees, his head forced ever backwards as the tripod shoved its way deeper and deeper into his windpipe.

Feldman was still attempting to scream as the hands pushed down with all their might, hammering on the end of the tripod stem. By the time the metal leg and the film roll wrapped around it had been buried to the hilt in his throat, Feldman knew that he had seconds to live. The bloody rictus of his mouth closed over the end of the steel tube and his body toppled sideways to the floor, where it lay in a cadence of convulsions. A single frame of film protruded from his shattered teeth, the unseen contours of Ixora's fetishistic celluloid postures lost like frozen shadows within his cooling flesh.

CHAPTER
10
Pursuit

'This trout is superb, Helen,' said Howard, removing a bone from his throat and taking a generous swig of wine. 'I wish Angela could find the time in her busy schedule to cook like you.'

'Howard thinks I spend too much time away from home,' said Angela by way of defence. She was small, dark-featured and delicate, and had confided to Helen in the kitchen earlier that she was having an affair with a twenty-two-year-old pizza chef called Wayne.

'If you spent a little less time at Champneys having your body shored up I'd be able to get a hot meal occasionally,' grumbled her husband, refilling his glass. 'I don't seem capable of operating the microwave without overloading its thermal capacity. Last week I made a chicken implode.'

Helen sent John an amused private look. Howard

Dickson was fast losing his youthfulness and much of his hair, if not all of his charm. It was common knowledge that his self-styled 'open' marriage was on the rocks. He alleviated his growing sense of insecurity by taking on mistresses in serial infidelity. Those who knew him well saw him as a perennial adolescent with failing self-esteem and an ego that prevented the problem from being aired. It surprised John that he still had any shred of respect left for his colleague.

'You'll have to eat with us when Angela's away,' offered Helen.

'That's a good idea. You could watch over him for me.' Angela eyed her husband suspiciously. 'Make sure he doesn't stray.'

'The way Helen looks tonight, I don't think she'd have to worry about me straying,' said Howard. They continued eating in an awkward silence.

'You two always seem so relaxed with each other,' said Angela finally, laying down her fork. 'Don't you ever argue?'

'Of course we do,' laughed Helen, glancing over at John. 'It's just that we've been together a long time. I guess we know each other too well.'

'That's right, you married young, didn't you?' said Howard. 'Surely that must have put a strain on things?'

'I had Jesus to turn to.' Helen cast her eyes to the table, embarrassed. 'Would anyone like dessert?'

Afterwards, thinking about their guests' behaviour over dinner, John could see just how badly Howard had fallen into a trap of his own making. He resolved to forget his own ridiculous infatuation with the troubled young model, and attempted to cast all thought of her from his mind. From now on he would spend more time thinking of his wife and son. Ixora could sort out her own bizarre problems without his help.

＊

But in the week that followed, he walked like a ghost in her wake. At the studio, at the daily rushes, at the press briefings and script conferences, he studied her face as the faintly outlined bruise paled to the tone of her cool white skin, he listened for the susurrant hiss of material caressing her body as she sat, he caught the scent of English roses in the air as she passed. The power and lightness of each movement touched his senses, the repeated postures of her limbs marking his vision, to imprison every gesture in his mind.

They spoke less often now, perhaps because each of them saw the danger in doing so. To all outward appearance, however, life was normal. At home Helen prepared meals, attended her church meetings, went about her book-keeping work at the department store. On John's free evenings they watched TV, laughing at silly jokes, airing petty grievances. John paid the bills, and rebuked Josh for damaging his school clothes. News of the photographer's death warranted a paragraph in the local paper. Until Thursday, no other irregularity disturbed the pulse-line of their domestic routine.

It began as a normal day, with a staff meeting in the first-floor boardroom. Howard held the chair. This morning he appeared in a haze of aftershave and sporting a new haircut that partially succeeded in hiding his baldness — an indication, other staff members suggested, that his wife was once more away from home.

'As you know, there have been developments on the Diana Morrison account,' he said, consulting his agenda. The others, five men and three women, checked their notepads. 'Sarah Monroe's UK tour completed successfully, no thanks to us, with a return date next February for the Island Jazz Festival. Diana has asked us to prepare some kind of promotional brochure for the event, and I'll be putting John in charge of that. Speaking of which, I've had a formal complaint from the art-director at *i-D* magazine that you attempted to pull rank on him during Ixora De Corizo's session last Saturday.'

He turned his attention to John, who shifted uncomfortably in his seat. 'You know where your responsibilities begin and end, John, at least you should do. You can only offer advice and hope that it will be taken. The guy's a little prick, we know that, we just find ways to work around it. Luckily it hasn't damaged our relationship with the magazine. Just be aware in the future, okay? And you're handling the radio show tonight.'

John checked his schedule. 'I have no record of this,' he said. 'What station?'

'BBC, Radio Five. The Simon Long show, 8.00 p.m.'

'Client?'

'Your favourite.' Howard smirked. 'Miss De Corizo. The subject is femininity and feminism. They've got a couple of other guests, some grumpy dyke from Camden Council,' he squinted at the schedule, 'and Barbara Cartland. I thought she was dead but apparently not. It'll be fairly grim but Ixora needs some radio practice while her audiences are still small, and you shouldn't be there for more than an hour.'

He turned his attention to the rest of the staff. 'The good news is that this brings us a lot closer to signing — you guessed it — David Glen, who in turn is about to sign his three picture deal with Paramount.'

The implication was lost on no one. If they had Glen and Glen had a deal with Paramount, they stood to handle the UK publicity for all three films. This was what Howard had always wanted, a break with the US majors for distribution PR. The key to Glen was keeping his agent happy, and that, by implication, meant keeping Ixora happy.

Helen was going to be upset. They were supposed to be

visiting friends for dinner tonight. As soon as the meeting had ended, he called her at the department store. The evenly modulated tone of her voice betrayed her annoyance with the change of plan.

Ixora had made it known that she would like to be collected for the radio interview from her house, so John turned his Volvo into the leafy crescent behind Sloane Square a little after 7.00 p.m.

The redbrick Victorian house sat back from the roadway beyond tall iron railings. The first touch of autumn showed on the tips of the hornbeams in the overgrown garden, the shedding leaves crackling beneath his shoes as he approached the house. The tiled porch was inset with pastoral scenes in stained glass. As he rang the bell he could hear her footsteps on the stairs. She was dressed in faded jeans and a crumpled T-shirt, and appeared to have been sleeping.

'What time is it?' She held the door wide and he ducked beneath her arm.

'Time to splash some water on your face and get dressed.'

'Good. Come up.'

There was no lights on in the hallway. Although the evening was warm and dry there was a feeling of dampness within the house. Following her to the floor above, he turned at the top of the stairs and examined the paintings which hung in cadenced rows, small brown studies of horses and hounds. In a corner of the landing stood an ancient aspidistra in a Chinese pot. Beyond this, a corridor took them to a broad gloomy lounge, hung throughout with suffocating velvet curtains.

Ixora ushered him in and excused herself, turning into another stairway that John assumed led to a less antiquated apartment. A formal table stood in the centre of the room, densely filigreed with flowers. The room's

decoration was overpoweringly Victorian, a formal chaos
of texture and pattern. Embroidered cushions filled a fat,
floral sofa. Every surface was covered with personal items,
small gilt-framed daguerreotypes, a rosewood tobacco-
box, ashtrays, crystal paperweights, china statues of dogs
and cherubs, a pair of brass Dürer hands, cut off at the
wrists and turned to heaven in prayer. If Ixora's mother
was indeed Spanish, nothing in the room gave an indication of her nationality. Quite the reverse; the accumulation of Minton and Doulton pottery, Staffordshire
figurines and Bohemian glassware pointed to a very
British background. There was enough of it to furnish a
small museum.

When Ixora returned she had changed into a black silk
blouse.

'Does someone else live here?' John pushed aside some
cushions and seated himself on the sofa.

'No, there's just me.'

'Isn't it a little large for one person?'

'It was Mother's house. Someone comes in to clean
twice a week.' She brushed her hair in the mottled gilt
mirror at the end of the room. 'I like living alone. You
should see some of the flats the other girls live in. Do you
have any idea how lucky I am?'

'But it must get lonely.'

'Not really. I have Lily.' John raised an eyebrow. 'She
should be around here somewhere.' She flicked back her
hair and crouched down, checking around the room. 'You
frightened her away. Lily, come out.' He followed her
gaze to a gloomy corner behind one of the dining chairs.
There, a black Persian cat hissed sourly at him, yellow eyes
glinting from the shadows.

The room felt suddenly cold. Something prickled at the
top of his spine. He rose to his feet. 'We're going to be late
if we don't get a move on.'

His anxiety eased as soon as they cleared the hall and stepped into the porch. The atmosphere of the house had made him uncomfortable. Ixora locked the front door and followed him to the car.

As they pulled away from the kerb, another vehicle appeared in the rear-view mirror. The face of the driver seemed familiar. His dark hair was curly, speckled with grey, and there was a thin black beard. He turned the car into the heavy traffic surrounding Sloane Square.

'Don't look round,' he said quietly. 'Remember the man from the opera?'

'Yes.'

'He's behind us.'

She immediately twisted around in her seat. 'God, you're right.'

'He must have been waiting outside your house. I noticed the car when I came in.'

'Do you think we should call the police?'

'Let's wait and see if he follows us all the way to the studio.'

From Victoria to Hyde Park, past Speakers' Corner and around into Oxford Street, passing the impressive façade of Selfridges to turn left into Great Portland Street, he watched as the Vauxhall Opel stayed no more than thirty feet behind. Ahead, Broadcasting House stood in the centre of the road like a marooned ocean liner. He parked diagonally opposite its main entrance and waited.

The Opel continued on for a block, then pulled sharply in to the left. John checked his watch.

'I'll see you into the foyer,' he said, holding the door for her. 'They won't let me go into the studio with you.' She was looking back over her shoulder, searching for the parked car.

'Are you sure you don't know who he is, Ixora?'

'Of course not,' she replied testily. 'He's just some crazy guy.'

They crossed the road and entered the building. After a few minutes, a harassed young woman with a clipboard collected Ixora and led her away into the labyrinthine tangle of tunnels that existed beneath the building. John thumbed through a day-old newspaper, glancing at the clock. Outside, the setting sun cast orange light against the glass doors of the building. As he watched the shadows shifting across the windows, he realised that one of them belonged to the figure of a man. Throwing the newspaper aside he leapt from the chair and ran to the entrance. As he did so, the bearded man moved hastily away along the pavement.

John set off in pursuit, and was about to grab at the coat-tail in front of him when the figure darted sideways through an ajar door into one of the building's basement exits. Seconds later, John found himself in a badly lit corridor that ran between the studios. Another passage bisected the path ahead. In which direction had he fled? John turned on his heel, listening. Staff moved quietly through these corridors because of the sound recordings taking place around them. Suddenly he heard it, a scuffle, shoes slipping on the dirty green carpet tiles. He ran ahead and saw the figure vanish into another of the seemingly endless passageways.

Halfway along this corridor a script-girl pushed open a door with her back, pen in mouth, coffee cups in her hands. John sent her sprawling as he dashed past, swinging hard at the end of the hall to catch sight of the figure as it disappeared down a short flight of steps, running further beneath the building like the white rabbit vanishing down a hole. He reached the stairway before the doors ahead of him had stopped swinging. His quarry stood pressed against the corridor wall, chest heaving. John could see now that he was not a young man. Could he run no further? Why else had he stopped? He was mouthing something through the glass. John reached forward and pulled open the door.

'— your life, stay away from her! Just stay away from her!'

John held up his hands for silence. 'I want you to stop bothering the lady, do you understand?' he said. 'You haven't any right to invade her privacy like this.'

'I have every right! Keep away from her.' And suddenly there was steel in his hand, the slim shaft glittering beneath the luminous ceiling panels. As he swung wide John jumped back, the edge of the blade slicing his jacket at the sleeve. His attacker shoved away from the wall and slammed hard against the firedoor opposite. The door jarred loose with a bang and he passed through into the alley beyond. As John ran forward a stinging sensation began in his arm. He clutched at his sleeve and realised that he had been cut. That moment of hesitation was all it had taken to injure him. The darkened alleyway was empty.

'Christ Almighty.' He lurched back into the corridor, striking out in the direction of the foyer. The burning had spread to his elbow, numbing his muscles. Blood was dripping from his sleeve on to his hand.

By the time Ixora emerged from her interview, a member of the St John's Ambulance Brigade had cleaned and bandaged John's arm. It was a superficial wound, but the knife had been sharp enough for the gash to require medical attention. Ixora was visibly upset, and remained silent on the journey home.

'I've got to go to the police,' he said as they turned into Sloane Crescent.

'Why?'

'The ambulance staff have to report all knife wounds. I'll try to keep your name out of it.'

Whether he wanted it or not, he had once more been

drawn into her world. With the problems they were having on the *Playing With Fire* set, this was exactly the kind of publicity nobody wanted.

At the gate, she turned and beckoned to the house. The wind had risen, and the tops of the hornbeams rustled somewhere in the darkness above their heads.

'Your arm must hurt,' she said. It was not sympathy he heard in her voice, but desire. The wind swept her hair across her face, and her pale hands rose to hold it back. The gesture was a familiar one, and recalled the scene on the steps of Waterloo Station. As he leaned back against the door of the car a lightness rose inside his stomach, heat spreading at his thighs.

'You can come in if you like,' she said softly.

'I can't, Ixora.' Around them the branches lifted and spread, exhaling like the sighs of children.

'You can, John.'

He began to feel giddy. Leaves scuttled over his feet. The road was deserted. The dark house robbed her figure of light. She withdrew a step, her features dissolving in the darkness.

John turned back to the car and threw himself behind the wheel, locking the door. As he twisted his key in the ignition and pulled jerkily out into the road he glanced up at the house, but Ixora had vanished in the undulating shadows as if her form had been absorbed into the restless night.

CHAPTER
11
Links

'Obviously he choked to death, blood and vomit. There was a fair amount of internal bleeding.' Finch sat back with his hands on the edge of the sink and dangled his thin legs above the floor. 'His bronchial tract's all torn up. Took a pretty strong arm, I should think.'

'What makes you think that?' asked Sullivan.

'There are signs that he fought back and failed. Discolouring on his arms. Crescent bruises on the inside left leg, probably a shoe heel. He was pinned against the wall. The angle of the marks suggest that the attacker was taller than him.' Finch rose to his feet, his knees cracking. 'Something was used to stuff the film down his throat, a stick of some kind.'

'We found a section of camera tripod smeared with blood and fragments of skin tissue. No fingerprints. Is there anything else you can tell me?'

'You know, this reminds me of another case we had in here, a man with a peacock feather stuck—'

'We caught him, Oswald, remember?' Michael Sullivan did not wish to be reminded of past disasters. He had travelled to the coroner's lab in order to obtain some kind of sneak preview of Finch's autopsy report. Due to the extreme violence of the crime and the lack of an immediate motive, there would be an unusually detailed and well-attended post mortem. Although pressure would be on Finch and his men to deliver their findings quickly, Sullivan knew from past experience that this could still take days. And that was more time than he had to spare. As the body had not been discovered until the studio had been opened on Tuesday morning, and Oswald had estimated that death had occurred approximately sixty hours earlier, they were already faced with a cold trail.

'We'll talk some more, Oswald, thanks.' He rose to leave, eager to be free of the cloying chemical stench emanating from the surrounding slabs. He checked his watch as he stepped into the lift, noting that he was running late for his next appointment. Despite his reluctance to do so he had been encouraged to appoint a new assistant, but Bow Street Station remained understaffed, and most of the remaining detectives were double shifting.

It didn't help that most of the foot force was occupied with tracking a highly organised gang of muggers operating in the area. Working in groups of twenty to thirty members they were steaming through the local stores, denuding upper-income shoppers like a plague of locusts. Irate storeowners were daily storming the duty desk demanding action because so many overseas visitors had been physically assaulted in the raids.

Sullivan had inherited the Feldman murder thanks to the wonder of electronic technology. Although the case would not normally have fallen under his jurisdiction, the newly computerised workload rota, ACID, or Advanced Criminal Identification Database, switched cases via the section's local area network system, so that above a certain workload level cases were passed to the station best equipped to handle them. Deciding factors included the number of detectives available, staffing levels and availability of technical equipment. If Bow Street, in its present chaotic state, was still being handed work from other areas, thought Sullivan, things were worse out there than he had realised.

Raymond Land was a smartly dressed doctor in his early forties whose meticulous, some would say obsessive, attention to detail made him one of the finest forensic experts in London. He and Sullivan were as opposite as two men could be. Twenty-eight years old but looking much older, Sullivan had the appearance of a man who lived alone and did not possess an iron. The doctor looked as if he'd been born in a suit. Land was a member of the General and Administration Division, although he had graduated from the biology section. There he had worked in criminalistics, specifically the comparison of contact traces, in body fluid grouping and in computerised blood indexing. Sullivan had worked his way up through the force from the rank of constable. Their tolerance of each other was born of respect rather than anything more amiable.

Right now, Land was annoyed at being kept waiting for twenty minutes. He sat behind his cramped desk squaring piles of papers by their corners as Sullivan knocked on the door.

'As you know, Michael, the material submitted to us by your reporting officers was a complete mess. Much of the proforma documentation was inaccurate and minimalistic. Where do they train these people?'

Sullivan took a seat before the doctor. It was best to

ignore these complaints. With limited report time available to them his men were rarely able to live up to Land's exacting standards. 'Do you think I'm right?' he said.

'Well, yes I do,' Land grudgingly admitted. 'I've jotted down some notes. They may be of use to you.' Sullivan was unable to suppress a warm glow of satisfaction as he accepted the notepad. The doctor was aware of his limitations as an analyst. To extend the old proverb, he could identify a tree from its bark samples without comprehending the layout of the forest. Wisely, he left that part to others.

The next section of the investigation was already underway. Every client featuring in Feldman's appointment book for the last month had to be traced and interviewed. Tracking them down was proving difficult, because the photographer's diary was an indecipherable mess which presumably he alone had understood, and his employees were freelance, which meant that they were constantly moving around the capital.

As Sullivan walked back along the Strand towards Bow Street Station, he turned up into the piazza and cut through the tourist-infested cafés of Covent Garden. Taking a seat and ordering himself a coffee, he opened the pad and began to examine Land's neatly printed notes. It was all there, hardcopy corroboration that Vincent Brady and Dickie Feldman had been murdered by the same person.

Sullivan thought back to Brady's stuffy South London flat and Feldman's windowless Edgware studio. Both crime scenes had been airtight; both rooms had contained the same lingering aroma. Sullivan hadn't registered the fact at the time. Smell was one of man's most powerful and undervalued senses. It was possible to locate the exact time and place of a distant memory from certain scents. It was only as they had been closing up the studio that he remembered where he had experienced the odour before, a sweet smell beneath the stench of decomposition. It was then that the threads between the cases had begun to draw together.

He unfolded the sheet he had torn from his police jotter and checked it against Land's notes. The problem was that no matter how many common elements there were between the two crimes, lack of similarity in their surrounding circumstances meant that they might never have been compared. Now, however, it became blindingly obvious that the crimes were related. From the two sets of notes he carefully wrote out one combined list:

1. *Aftershave*
Its pungency had suggested nothing else. As the smell had long since dissipated, how possible would it be to track down the brand from memory?

2. *Ferocity of Assault*
In both cases, the extreme violence of the killing suggested an impulse attack. Unpremeditated murder, spontaneous and unnecessarily cruel. Perhaps the killer had been formerly institutionalised. Run a check on recent escapes and releases from mental clinics.

3. *Lack of Motive*
Neither victim had enemies, drug or criminal connections. No robbery had taken place in either case.

4. *Entry*
Neither of the premises showed evidence of forced entry. Either the attacker knew his victim or had access to both buildings.

5. *Skin Tissue Matches*
Microscopic epidermal slivers beneath the nails of

both victims bore matching structure. Not enough skin was missing to show scars on the attacker, however.

6. *Nail Marks*
Two crescent cuts on Brady's arm, one on Feldman's neck. Smooth, rounded nails — the commonest kind, but still a match.

7. *Thread Matches*
This connection, Land had been forced to conclude, was tentative at best. A number of identical fibres were found at both crime scenes. All that linked them was the absence of any identifying origin at the respective sites.

8. *Unidentified Substances*
Also common to both crime scenes were several minute chips of metallic paint, red in colour, possibly from a weapon brandished at the victim on both occasions. Samples sent to Chemicals dept for analysis.

9. ???

And here was something else, the strangest link of all. On the draining board in Vincent Brady's kitchen he had found the half-filled tumbler containing a crucifix on a chain. According to his workmates, Brady was religious, and usually wore the cross around his neck. He was seen wearing it on 18th August. And in the bathroom of Feldman's studio, a gold *hai*, the Jewish symbol for life, removed from the chain around its owner's throat and dropped into the toilet.

Had Brady and Feldman removed the symbols themselves? If not, it meant that the murderer had removed them after their deaths — the clasps of both chains were unbroken. To Sullivan it was the first real indication that he was dealing with more than a mere criminal — it signalled the disordered workings of a deranged mind. And there was no way of knowing how soon someone with such a mentality might commit another atrocity.

CHAPTER
12
Matteo

John's new career remained a mystery to his wife. At dinner the previous Saturday, Howard had explained to her the need for a company that could handle press interviews, personality profiling, agent deals and contracts, but John could tell that she saw it all as rather pointless and expendable. Helen could not see that PR had much tangibility as a career. Her parents had been farmers, working in a world where there was little time for frivolities, and she had retained much of her mother's puritanism. It was a trait she had tried in vain to check. She had once confided that she longed to be passionate instead of practical, but that violent emotions had never come naturally to her.

John, on the other hand, had always held his feelings at bay, subconsciously realising that he had traded any youthful grand plans for the quieter pleasures of family life. This was an area of guilt that neither of them discussed, and they both knew why. On summer evenings Helen caught him standing in the garden with his hands in his pockets, staring into the distance, lost in thought. At these moments he was unfathomable and unapproachable, and she simply waited for him to return to her once more, a faraway smile fading on his face. Her patience with him had always been a source of wonder.

As they cleared the table together he listened to her plans for the week, watched her flick a strand of unruly red hair from her eyes as she stacked the dinner plates.

'We have the Hutchinsons coming over after Josh's school play,' she reminded him. 'I know you're not crazy about them, but at least they arrive with a decent bottle of wine and never stay beyond ten thirty.'

'What date is that?' He started to rise from the table.

'I've told you twice. You're not listening.' She pushed him back into his seat. 'Stay there, I don't want you making a mess of my kitchen.'

'Where is Josh, anyway?' he called as she left the room.

'Out with Cesar, where else?' she replied. 'I've a feeling the pair of them are up to something. I found a box of matches in Josh's blazer this morning. I think they may be smoking. You'd better give him the old "if you could see inside a lung you'd be sick" lecture.'

The telephone rang. Helen's hands were wet. She searched for a towel in vain. 'Can you get that, darling?' she called. 'If it's Josh, tell him he can have an hour and no more.' Their son usually rang at this time with an elaborate, implausible excuse for his late return.

'John? Is that you?'

He recognised her voice instantly, and glanced uneasily towards the kitchen extension. 'Ixora, what's the matter?'

'I feel guilty about calling you at home, but I didn't

know what else to do.' She sounded as if she'd been crying.

'John? Who is it?' Helen came in wiping her hands on her jeans, her interest piqued. 'Is everything all right?'

He covered the mouthpiece with his hand and turned to her. 'Just work.'

'John, are you still there?'

'What's happened?' He tried to make the inquiry sound casual.

'He forced his way in here …'

'Who?'

'The man who followed me when we left St Martin's. Matteo. Oh God, this is so hard on the phone. He tore my dress …'

'Wait there. I'll come over, just — wait.' He replaced the receiver slowly, trying to restore his composure. Helen was seated behind him, a look of consternation on her face.

'Who was that?'

'Someone from work. I have to go in for a while.'

'Oh John, not again, not tonight! It's the first evening we've had alone together for ages.'

'I'm sorry, there's nothing else I can do.' It would be best for both of them if he left quickly without further explanation. He kissed her lightly on the lips and pulled his jacket from the back of the chair.

By the time he pulled up outside the house, night had fallen. The wind had begun to rise, tearing the first few dying leaves from the trees in the dark garden.

She opened the door on the second ring and stumbled into his arms, bursting into tears. As he stepped back from her he could see that the top of her dress was torn apart. He quickly pulled her inside and closed the door. As usual, the house was in semi-darkness. He groped about for the hall lights and switched them on.

'Christ, what did he do to you?' The top of her chest was stained with a pair of livid blue bruises. Scratches covered the upper part of her left arm. Her lower lip was cut.

'He rang the bell — I couldn't see through the glass and opened the door. He pushed his way in, shouting at me.'

'What was he saying?'

'I don't know, I think it was something about you.'

'This is nuts. He isn't even the one who attacked me at the BBC. Why would he mention me?'

'I told you, he's jealous. I tried to reason with him, tried to make him leave but he wouldn't go. Then he grabbed me and hit me. I began to scream and he ran out.'

'You have to go to the police, Ixora, this has gone far enough.'

'No, I can't do that.'

'Why not, for Christ's sake?'

'Don't you have to report to them as well? What will they say if we tell them about two separate assaults by two different people? They'll want to know more, and then the press will get hold of it, I know they will.'

'Maybe you have a point.' He threw up his hands in despair. The whole thing was becoming crazy. 'Look, I'll go and see this Matteo. Where does he live?'

'No, John, I don't want you involved in this. I'll deal with it in my own way.'

'What are you going to do, buy a pit bull? Come on, Ixora, you're my only client. If anything happens to you I'll get the blame. Where does he live?'

'I won't tell you.'

'Fine. I'll find out for myself.'

She followed behind as he headed for the kitchen, and the bag which lay open on the scrubbed pine table. She grabbed his arm as he ran through the pages of the leather

address book. 'He's dangerous, John, he could hurt you.'
'Yeah, and I could hurt him. I'll be back soon.'

He had read enough of the address to know that it was in the most run-down part of King's Cross, sandwiched somewhere between the bookies, the porn shops and the cut-rate hotels. He located the block of flats in the triangular section of land bordered by canals, gas-holders and a weed-covered network of shunting yards. The building was due for demolition soon, and had been allowed to fall apart in order to escape listing as a place of historic interest. Parking his car in the forecourt, he slipped a small tyre-iron from the tool-kit on the front seat into his jacket pocket. If there was trouble, he would be ready. As he searched the laundry-laden balconies, he wondered how Ixora had come to meet someone living in a place like this.

The man he sought lived on the seventh floor and, incredibly, both lifts were out of order. On the stairs he passed a wheezing old woman laden with shopping bags, but she refused his help when he offered to carry them for her. The graffiti-smothered corridors stank of urine and boiled cabbage. More than half of the flats were boarded up.

On the seventh floor, none of the lights were working on the balcony. Heavy metal music pounded behind closed doors. The flat he sought had a steel panel bolted across the entrance lock. Finding no bell, he rapped his knuckles against it and waited for the sound of bolts being drawn back, bracing himself for trouble. He saw at once that the man who opened the door was the same one he had encountered with Ixora. His Mediterranean features were heavy and handsome, his hair slicked back in a fashionably square cut. Deep brown eyes glowered beneath a ridged forehead. He was dressed in a white vest and jogging slacks; hard-packed muscles bunched in his broad neck and tattooed chest. Although no more than five feet seven inches, he looked powerful and dangerous.

'Okay, Matteo. Do you know who I am?' asked John.

As he recognised his visitor, Matteo's expression sharply transformed. John had been ready for some kind of aggressive reaction, but now he suddenly saw that this was the last thing on his mind. Instead of anger, he saw fear. Matteo held the door wide.

'Yeah, I know who you are. You better come in.'

The flat was filled with huge, cheap items of furniture, as if Matteo had moved from a larger flat and had tried to cram its contents into half the space. Stacks of boxed video, stereo and home computer units suggested that he was either an electronics retailer or a fence.

He led the way to an equally cluttered kitchen, opened a battered refrigerator and yanked out two cans of beer. Throwing one across to John, he gestured to a chair.

'I don't know what to tell you, man, 'cause whatever I say you won't believe me.' Matteo's accent placed him as Spanish-American.

'Try me,' said John. 'I'm pretty gullible. Let's start with why you go around punching defenceless women in the face.'

'You don't know, man, you just don't know what's been goin' on here.' He shook his head sadly. If he's attempting to elicit sympathy, thought John, he's picked the wrong man.

'You're involved with Ixora, right?' He pointed a finger.

John took a slug of beer. 'What do you mean, *involved*?'

'You work with her.'

'Yes, I do. She could have had you thrown in jail for assault, but she let it go. Why should she do that? Why the hell are you following her?'

'I'm not following her, man. I've got better things to do

with my time than chase around after that bitch, believe me.'

'That position's already been filled,' said John. 'Do you know that she's being watched all the time?' He wondered if the man who had attacked him in the corridors beneath Broadcasting House was related to Matteo, or even in his employ. 'Christ, you went to her house tonight and you hit her.' He was trying to stay calm, keeping his voice in a low, soft register, but the thought of this sweat-stained lowlife threatening Ixora barely allowed him to keep his anger in check.

'Fuckin' right I hit her, man. You would have, too.' John watched the self-satisfied smile spreading across his opponent's face and the tyre-iron began to weigh heavily in his pocket, the metal warming to his body temperature, as if somehow becoming an extension of his flesh.

'She told me your name — John? Well, listen, John, my business is with her. She's been driving me fuckin' nuts. You should really stay away from her, as far away as possible. She's a special kind of jinx. A bad omen. Like, if you saw her at sea, your ship would straightaway hit a fuckin' rock, you know what I mean? Bitches like that shouldn't be allowed to walk around.'

Matteo had just raised the beercan to his lips when John leapt from his seat, the tyre-iron suddenly in his hands. Slamming Matteo's head back against the refrigerator door, he pinned the steel bar across his throat, crushing his windpipe. 'Now listen to me. I want some answers out of you and fast, otherwise I'm going to choke the air out of you until you're dead. Nod your head.'

The head moved rapidly up and down. Unable to catch a breath, Matteo's face was beginning to blacken. John relaxed his grip slightly. He had surprised himself, but although his pulse was racing he felt calm and in control of the situation.

'Okay, now start at the beginning. Where did you two meet?'

'Far 'way from here. You never hearda the place, it's so far away. I took some pictures of her.'

'What kind of pictures?'

'Not the kind you're thinkin' of, believe me.'

'And you followed her here to London?' Perhaps Ixora had made a bad career move, taken a lucrative modelling job and posed for a few nude snapshots. It wouldn't be the first time such a thing had happened. He thought of Crawford, Monroe, Madonna. 'Were you blackmailing her?'

'Maybe, but not 'cause I wanted to.'

John tightened his grip on the tyre-iron once more. Matteo's face began to suffuse with trapped blood. 'Then what, you made her have sex with you?'

'No, man, you got it all wrong. *She* came on to *me*. Thought she could buy me off. I'm tellin' the truth, she tried to kill me. Look at this.' He slid his free hand beneath the bar and turned his neck to John. Two small, deep gashes had been cut several inches apart, narrowly missing his jugular vein. The wounds were freshly scabbed. Fear flickered in Matteo's eyes. Whether or not he was telling the truth, he seemed desperate to be believed.

'I don't understand,' said John. 'Why on earth would she try to kill you?'

'Because I know about her past, man. I'm probably the only one, and now she's gettin' this big career she doesn't want it fucked up by someone like me. She gets me into bed with her, takes me to the fuckin' moon and back, then waits till I fall asleep and tries to cut my head off with a fuckin' carving knife.'

John took his knee from Matteo's chest and eased up on the bar. He fell forward in his chair, gasping for breath.

'Why did you attack her in the street? Because she'd come at you with a knife?'

Matteo stopped massaging his throat. He looked puzzled. 'Wait a minute, you're gettin' your wires crossed. I hit her 'cause she did *this* to me.' He gestured around the room. 'She ruined me, man. You think I was always like this? I was a professional photographer, I was bringin' in the big money. I'm livin' in this sleazebag shit because of her. When I found out what she'd done I came after her to get back my share. I found her swanning around with you and I guess I just saw red.'

John felt that he was somehow misunderstanding their conversation. Each explanation made less sense than the last. Down the hall a child had started screaming. He dropped the tyre-iron to his side and tried again. 'Okay, you say she seduced you, then tried to stab you. Let's forget about her reasons. When did this happen?'

'Two nights ago.'

So he was lying after all. Ixora had told him that they hadn't seen each other for two months. Besides, two nights ago she'd been getting the smoked-salmon-and-baby-rack-of-lamb treatment at Le Gavroche with the head of the agency and some guy from the *Daily Mirror* Entertainments page.

'I'm going to choke you again if you don't stop lying to me, Matteo. This happened two months ago.'

'Two *nights* ago, man.' He threw John a wounded look, as if surprised that he wasn't being taken seriously. 'Take a look at the wounds — do they look a coupla months old to you?'

John's sense of reality was starting to shift. What had he got himself into by coming here? He raised the tyre-iron to Matteo's throat once more and pushed hard.

'She lies to you, man,' Matteo was crying in rasping breaths. 'She's a disease with no known cure. Hurting me won't make no difference. You're being taken for a fuckin' ride, you're a career move, a stepping stone. She lies to you just like she lies to everyone.'

As John walked through the stinking corridors of the block of flats, the photographer's rasping chuckle echoed on in his head.

On the way back to Chelsea he almost broadsided a truck by failing to notice the traffic signals at Hyde Park Corner. The more he discovered about Ixora, the less he understood. Even if it transpired that she had never lied to him, he wondered if he would ever really be able to trust her.

Nothing about Ixora seemed clear or straightforward. Her behaviour, her very presence seemed to elicit abnormal responses from the men who came into contact with her. Being so attractive, so desirable, she was forced into a position of constant demurral, and this was bound to make enemies for her. But Matteo seemed an unlikely candidate for any kind of romantic dalliance. Living in squalor, nursing grudges against the world, he may have grown obsessive about the glamorous young model everyone admired. Perhaps he felt Ixora represented everything that was wrong with his life.

John pulled to a halt outside the house a little after 10.30. Ixora was waiting in the hall as he pushed the front door open. She was wearing a cream silk blouse fastened high at the neck, and a plain black skirt. At odds with the elegant severity of her clothing, her face reflected pain and confusion. He walked past her into the lounge and switched on one of the table lights. As he did so, the Persian cat fixed him with a malevolent eye.

'I don't know why you always have to make it so dark in here,' he muttered irritably. 'Let's throw out some of the shadows, shall we?' He crossed to an oval rosewood table by the heavily draped windows and switched on a second light. The room was unbearably hot, the boiler pumping scalding water through creaking pipes, even though the evening was mild. Ixora followed obediently behind him, sitting in the armchair he indicated for her.

'I've just had a meeting with your friend,' he said quietly. 'Matteo says you were with him on Tuesday night.' Ixora shifted forward in her chair and started to speak, but was silenced with a raised hand.

'Let me finish. He says you seduced him, and then you tried to kill him. He insists that you *ruined* him, whatever the hell that means, which is why he attacked you in the street. Now, either he's completely crazy, or you know something you're not telling me.'

'John, I don't see how you can think for a single second that I would hide anything from you.' Her voice was filled with indignation. 'He's a habitual liar. Everything he says is untrue. Why do you think I stopped seeing him?'

John was not fully convinced. 'Where did you meet?'

'In Barcelona, a long time ago. He was a photographer, a very good one. He came here and looked me up. But things didn't go well for him. He lost several big assignments.'

'Why?'

'Drinking. Fantasising. Acting wild, I don't know. He treated me as if I had been placed on earth to save him. John, this is crazy, either you learn to trust me or you don't, I have to know. Please don't turn out like the rest.'

'What do you mean?'

She waved her hands in a gesture of dismissal. 'You're not like the others. You didn't go after Matteo just because it was the right thing to do. Can't you see what's happening between us?'

He shifted uneasily. 'You tell me.'

'You have to learn to trust your basic instincts, John. Why do you think you're trying so hard to help me?' She reached her arm up around his neck and kissed him lightly. Her lips were surprisingly cool. John felt as if he had touched a live wire. In the few brief seconds he had seen her on the steps of the station, he had never dreamt that this moment might actually come.

He took a step away from her and turned to the hall, where a grandfather clock had begun to chime. Ixora crossed her legs in a slither of nylon, watching him, waiting for his next move. She was, without doubt, the most beautiful woman he had ever seen in his entire life. The chimes ceased after the eleventh. Helen would have grown bored waiting for him. She would probably be in bed by now, reading.

'I have to go, Ixora,' he said finally. 'You understand that. I'm a married man.'

'I know.'

'I love my wife. There's too much at stake.'

'I know.'

'You'll be all right now.'

Before she could protest, he left the house and walked back to the car. Seated with his arms across the wheel he found himself unable to drive away. Ixora represented everything he had dreamed of and would never have. She was like a member of an alien species, so far beyond his reach, and yet she wanted him. All the drama, sensuality and adventure he had ever craved was here, just a few steps away from where he sat. This was the moment. Now or never.

CHAPTER
13
Passion

Leaving the door of the Volvo unlocked he took a single pace forward, then another.

As he reached the porch of the house he saw the front door swing slowly inward, felt the carpet beneath his feet, watched as the paintings on the walls paraded past. He remembered the floral patterns of the curtains, dense and English, lilac and iris, bowls of old flowers with petals as dry as paper and sodden, rotting stems, steeped in the ullage of a thousand blooms, bitter blues and deadening yellows, reds as cold as long-dried blood.

Then he was in the flower-filled bedroom, and her advancing face gleamed dully in the lamplight that spilled in from the windows. The bed was covered in a quilt of gleaming patchwork gold, with the figure of a woman woven Klimt-like through the shining fabric.

Ixora's silken blouse parted beneath his fingers, dissolving like strands of spiderweb, revealing the translucent flesh of her neck, her small solid breasts. As the cloth slid from her skin she arched her back, flexing her long spine until the gleaming black fringe fell back from her eyes to touch the golden bed beyond. His arms linked behind her waist as he lowered her on to the auroral quilt, bathing her body in shades of saffron and sulphur. They removed each other's clothes and he knelt between her cool white thighs, his chest hair brushing her face in an arc that seemed to send sparks of static leaping in the dark. Her body was cool and moist to the touch, her tongue like iced velvet as it flickered in his mouth. As they joined together and his body became a part of hers, it seemed that the room itself changed shape, intensifying and deepening, and the flowers surrounding the bed dropped their sticky perfumed liquor from each pale taunting stamen; sickly blossoms crowded his pulsing vision, their urgent growth whispering in his ears as he drove himself into the dark vault of her body, his senses blurred by the pounding of his blood.

The scent of her flesh clung to his nostrils as he fell to the golden threads below, salt tears dripping into his eyes. He could scarcely catch his breath. She lay with an arm thrown across her face and her torso twisted to one side, a Pre-Raphaelite maiden, Ophelia at rest upon a riverbed of gold. He tried to find his voice, but she placed a cold hand across his lips. Even in the near darkness he could tell that she was crying.

She lay silent and unmoving as he dressed. There was nothing he could say that would add to their knowledge of each other, no word that could not damage the unspoken bond between them.

Fully clothed, he returned to the edge of the bed and reached for her, but her hand eluded his. He took his leave, unable to judge her changing mood, and glanced back on the stairs at the scented bedroom with its damaged marble virgin.

On the landing below he briefly had the impression of someone standing stock-still in the darkened hallway, breath held back. Needles prickled up his spine as he quickened his pace to the foot of the stairs and the safety of the porch beyond. Outside in the rustling garden he looked back up at the bedroom window and realised that there was nothing in the hall but some wayward manifestation of his guilty conscience. Once more he saw her body on the quilt, the alabaster thigh, the outstretched hand, and his pulse quickened.

By the time the Volvo nosed its way through the twisting Richmond backroads it was far past midnight. As he entered the bedroom Helen laid her book on the counterpane and removed her reading glasses.

'You were gone a long time,' she said lightly. 'Everything all right?'

'Uh, there was a problem at the office.'

'Well, tell me about it.'

He thought for a moment, unused to the practice of lying. 'There's a photo-call for the *Playing With Fire* stars tomorrow and the press have got wind of trouble on the set.' The story was a half-truth, passable as a first attempt. Several tabloid journos had been questioning staff on the studio lot, trying to unearth a scandal. He tried to sound casual but his words seemed forced and false. This kind of deception was a new, unpleasant experience.

'I hope it isn't always going to be like this, John.' Helen retied the top of her nightgown tightly. 'It's not fair on Josh. You were supposed to go over his homework tonight.'

She'd believed his story. Amazed, he breathed a sigh of

relief and began to unbutton his shirt. 'Maybe I should take a look at his books. Where are they?'

'He'll have already packed them in his bag. On the chair by his bed. Don't wake him.'

John made his way silently across the landing to Josh's bedroom. The boy lay nestled in the pillows, breathing lightly, the pale glow from the hallway touching his face. As he stood watching the slumbering child a guilty alarm assailed him once more, as though it took such a moment as this to remind him of how much he stood to lose.

When he finally returned to his own bedroom, the passion he had felt for Ixora that night had been swamped by a far more overwhelming feeling of fear.

CHAPTER
14
Hargreave

Detective Sergeant Sullivan thoughtfully sucked a boiled sweet and watched as a funnel of seagulls swirled behind the chugging riverboat. At the stern rail a young couple were tossing handfuls of bread at the swooping birds. Sullivan often chose this method of travelling to work, joining the motorlaunch at Greenwich pier to alight in Westminster less than half an hour later. This morning he was surprised to be hailed by a senior colleague.

'Hello, fancy finding you here.' A heavy-set, pepper-haired man was tacking towards him with an overflowing coffee cup in one hand and a leaking Danish pastry in the other. 'I didn't know you were a south of the river man. Sorry about this — I missed breakfast this morning.'

Sullivan hauled himself to attention, instinctively wondering if his tie was straight. Detective Chief

Inspector Ian Hargreave's joviality always made him feel nervous, as if his relaxed mood was liable to evaporate at any second, to be replaced by something more exacting and far less convivial. He was regarded as something of a living legend by the majority of the London Met staff, an awkwardly unorthodox man whose circuitous approach to his cases proved a constant source of bafflement to those students attempting to emulate his methodology. He was known to have his favourites, and shamelessly shunted personnel whenever it suited his requirements.

Sullivan was surprised and flattered that Hargreave remembered him; the two men had exchanged few words recently, and those mostly by telephone, as Hargreave was now based in the newly converted Serious Crimes Division which had been opened above the old tube station at Mornington Crescent.

'This is a civilised way to enter the city, isn't it?' said the senior officer. 'One of the few genuine pleasures afforded to the working man. Another being a visit to the barber.'

Sullivan laughed. 'It has to be a real one, smelling of Brylcreem,' he pointed out.

'Oh, absolutely.' Hargreave leaned on the railing beside him. 'Ever been to Andy's in Chalk Farm? The snick of the scissors. Cut-throat razors. Something for the weekend. Marvellous. Your name.' He clicked his fingers. 'Michael Sullivan, isn't it? I understand you made sergeant.'

'Yes, sir.'

'Drop the sir business, would you? You're not on duty yet. I read your report on the Vauxhall case, Mr Sullivan. Very interesting. Sullivan ...' He turned the name over thoughtfully, dipping the Danish into his cup and splashing coffee on to the deck. 'No relation to the music man, by any chance?'

'Not that I know of,' replied Sullivan.

'Pity. One of the senior detectives is a big G and S fan.

Oh well, never mind. You've drawn yourself a link between Vincent Brady and this Edgware Road case, is that right?'

Sullivan explained his reasons for assuming the same attacker in both cases. Hargreave seemed genuinely interested. 'Tell me,' he asked through a final mouthful of Danish, 'what was on the film?'

'The film?'

'The roll in Feldman's throat. Didn't Raymond Land have it printed up for you?'

'I — don't know. Surely there would be no point . . .'

'Why not? I skimmed the crime officer's report. The studio door hadn't been left open and there were blackouts on the windows, so there was no reason to assume that the roll had become exposed. And, of course, the majority of it was jammed in his throat.'

'But wouldn't the acids in his emetic ejection—'

'You can call it vomit,' interrupted Hargreave, flicking flakes of pastry from his moustache, 'I've finished eating.'

'— wouldn't the acid have affected the chemical balance of the emulsion?'

'No idea, old chap.' Hargreave gave the sergeant a playful punch on the shoulder and almost knocked him over the side. 'The thing about Dr Land is he's a stickler for procedure. Unless you specifically request him to send you all the exhibit information he'll only provide you with the elements he personally considers to be relevant. I suggest you have a talk with him. The other thing that interested me in your report was the crucifix in the glass of water. What do you make of that?'

'I'm not sure, but we also found Feldman's neckchain down the toilet.'

'Probably a *hai*.'

'That's right.'

'The Jewish symbol for life. What an odd thing to do.

Sounds as if your killer is into some kind of Eastern occultism.'

'Why do you say that?' asked the sergeant.

'Bloody hell, man, I'm not doing all your work for you,' snapped Hargreave suddenly. 'Officially I'm not allowed to comment on your findings even though I attended the Brady post mortem. Until such time that you request my surveillance of the case.'

Sullivan knew that if he did so, his chances of receiving any personal recognition in the investigation would be negligible. Perhaps Hargreave was issuing him with a challenge.

'I have a few theories that I'm following up,' he lied. The penetrating gaze returned by the inspector was thankfully severed by the bump of the docking boat.

They parted by the Playhouse on the embankment, Sullivan cutting up towards Covent Garden and the chief inspector heading for the Northern Line. Hargreave had made the sergeant aware that he had missed something out in his report. It was up to him to discover what it was before the case was lifted from his jurisdiction.

'Of course we attempted to develop the film,' said Raymond Land, impatiently gesturing Sullivan into his office. 'I sent it to a toxicology expert.'

'What did he test for?' Sullivan dropped cigarette ash on to the spotless tiles, then shifted aside a neat stack of notebooks to perch on a corner of the doctor's desk. Land's eyes perceptibly narrowed.

'First of all, I wanted contact traces.'

'You were more interested in fingerprints than what was on the film?'

'Certainly,' replied the doctor with indignation. 'There was never any suggestion that the film contained anything pertinent to the case.'

'But it was shot film, it had been exposed, presumably by Feldman himself.'

'Yes, but if the murderer was attempting to dispose of incriminating evidence he would surely have taken the roll with him. Finding no fingerprints, we then tried to develop the exposed footage.' He donned his bifocals and consulted his file. 'Of the thirty-odd exposed frames, twenty-two frames were too damaged to develop. Nine were test lighting shots of the set he'd had built in the corner of the studio ...'

'The lagoon thing?'

'Right. The remaining four were of one of his models. Again, these were blurry test lighting shots, very poor quality, not posed setups. I doubt very much if you'd be able to identify the model from the condition of the prints.'

'Why didn't you let me have these?' asked Sullivan, holding up the grainy black and white reproductions. He knew that computer enhancement could produce a much clearer image, given time. They were in the process of interviewing every model Feldman had recently photo-graphed, but surprisingly few were even in the country at the moment.

'I imagined you would have spoken to everyone he filmed by now, Sergeant,' replied Land. 'The most basic procedural sense would have dictated that.'

Sullivan felt his face burning as he left Land's office. As he turned the corner he glanced back to see the doctor realigning the items on his desk, obliterating the traces of Sullivan's presence.

CHAPTER
15
Suspicion

'Because he's checked out of the fucking hotel, that's why!' shouted Howard, sending a secretary scuttling back into the corridor. 'I want him found within the next half hour. Call the airport, check the railway station, try anything you can think of.'

'What destination shall I ask them to check?' called the secretary.

'Jesus Christ, how the hell do I know? Call his agent.'

'I tried that. He's not answering his phone.'

'I'm surrounded by assassins. Good morning, John, where the hell have you been?' John stood in the doorway with his jacket over his arm. Howard towed him into the room.

'I didn't get any sleep last night.'

'Try and sleep on your own time. Tyron checked out of

his hotel this morning, taking all his luggage. No one's seen him or heard from him. The press conference at the Piccadilly Meridien is due to begin in three quarters of an hour. He's supposed to be here right now taking coaching from me. You got any bright ideas?' John thought for a moment. This morning Tyron was supposed to stand before the press with his arm around the director, acting supportive and disproving the rumour that the temperamental star wanted him replaced in mid-production.

'That wardrobe girl, what's her name, Lucia something. It looked as if he was starting to get something together with her. Has anyone called her?'

'John, you're a genius. Paula, get back in here. Find out what that girl's name is and call her. You'll have to fax the director at the hotel and warn him.' Paula slid back into the room, listened to her new instructions and slid out again. She moved silently and efficiently, as if she was on castors. Howard suddenly swung an accusing cigar in John's direction. 'Tyron and some UCLA buddies of his hit the hotspots last night after they finished filming. One of the script girls was with them for a while and reckons they consumed their own body weight in coke before deciding to move on, cutting lines on the top of a jazz bar piano, for Christ's sake. She left when Scott started grinding his teeth and picking fights. If we can't find him, the director and the producer are going up on that press stand and lying themselves blind, which means you'll be right behind them with your notes. You have notes?'

'No, but I can make some.'

'Do it on your way to the hotel.'

Upon his arrival at the Meridien, Paula called to warn him that the wardrobe girl was missing too. 'They'll eat you alive if you go up on that platform without some positive news,' she warned. 'Some of these people are like viruses, they seek out your weaknesses and attack them.

Don't let 'em make you defensive, 'cause then you're dead.'

'Thanks for the encouragement,' he said and hung up. He knew the way people like Tyron behaved. The star would not give Farley Dell or the producer, Park Manton, the chance of upstaging him at such a powerful press gathering. It was just a question of stalling for time until he showed.

At the appointed hour John stepped into a smoky, low-ceilinged hotel suite filled with impatient journalists and photographers. As he walked past the confused producer to the centre of the baize-covered panel table, all eyes turned to him. His throat felt as if it was filled with dry sand. He coughed into his fist and tapped the microphone.

'Ladies and gentlemen, if you'll just bear with me for a few moments.' He waited for silence. 'Before we get to the main purpose of this press conference, it has come to my attention that some newspapers have been referring to our leading artist, Scott Tyron, as "the new Tom Cruise". I know Mr Tyron does not think that this is an appropriate press title for him at this stage in his career, so I would like to discourage its further use. Now . . .'

Behind them, the doors opened and Scott Tyron sauntered in. He was dressed in a gold-embroidered cowboy shirt and faded Levi's. He was what they'd come to see. As he passed on his way to the microphone he hissed in John's ear, 'Hey, this is *my* show, man, so just butt out, okay?' Then the famous profile faced front, the smile widened, the eyes twinkled, the journos breathed a collective sigh and the room strobed with camera flashes. Dumbfounded, John dropped back into his seat.

'Apparently he couldn't sleep at the St James's Club so he decided to check out of there and into the Atheneum,'

John explained to Howard over lunch. 'He says he just forgot to tell anyone.'

'And the wardrobe girl, where did they find her?'

'In his bed at the St James's. It seems he forgot to tell her he was going as well, which was a shame because they were wearing each other's clothes.'

'Then how come he looked so good at the press conference?'

'He bought a whole new wardrobe and charged it to us.'

'When this picture is finished I'm going to kill him. I understand that you've got the press referring to Tyron as the "new Tom Cruise". You should have checked with us before you did that.' He smiled. 'Still, if it sticks, I'll give you a rise. How's Ixora?'

The change of subject threw John for a moment. What did Howard mean? Could someone in the agency have found out about them?

'Fine,' he said carefully. 'She has a few interviews coming up, nothing spectacular, but there's still a while before the film wraps.'

Howard was watching him intently. 'Uh-huh,' he murmured finally. 'Dell says she'll never make an actress. What do you think?'

John cut into his steak, considering the question. 'I know what he means. There's something about her delivery that's awkward, as if she's always too conscious of the role she's playing. I've seen some of her out-takes. She seems to have trouble handling a character whose nature is radically different to her own.'

'And I've been busy telling Diana Morrison that we can turn her protégée into a media celebrity. If we don't come through on this, she'll crush any chance we have of getting David Glen to the table. The woman is a barracuda in a blouse. First the Sarah Monroe fuck-up, then the Tyron movie turning into a damage limitation exercise — if we can't deliver here, I need to know now so I can cover my ass.'

'What do you want me to tell you, Howard?'

'That you can come up with an angle like you did on Scott. Something that guarantees us prime-time coverage in the week preceding the UK premiere. We need to build some kind of mystique around her, an air of mystery.'

'She already has that. Unfortunately we can't use it.'

'Why not?'

John gave a wry smile. 'I don't think anyone would believe it,' he replied.

That afternoon they were to resume location shooting in North London. John and Ixora met for lunch in St James's Park, passing beside lake fountains which sprayed a fine mist, seeding the dusty late summer air with soft crystalline light and the promise of autumnal calm. Ixora's pale hands linked loosely across her white cotton blouse, fingers idly rolling the pearls at her neck. He loved the way she walked, with long, slow steps, like a bird stepping over water, the way she turned her head to listen to music playing in distant traffic. Everything about her made him feel proud to be at her side. She seemed interested in everything around her, making small sounds of pleasure as she watched the swans lifting from the lake, old ladies basking in sun-dappled deckchairs. She found delight in the smallest things, and through her eyes John felt that he was rediscovering the city around him.

'I've been thinking,' he said, 'after the film has opened you should take a vacation, somewhere hot. Do you still have family in Spain?'

A blank look crossed Ixora's face, as if she had not considered the whereabouts of her family in ages. 'I — yes.'

'Well then. You could visit them.'

'But would you come with me? Last night wasn't just something that happened, some kind of aberration ...'

'I know, Ixora.'

'I'm frightened of losing this feeling.'

'So am I.'

She suddenly looked very young and unsure of herself. 'Suppose it just keeps growing. Suppose it hurts your wife.'

'It's already hurt Helen without her knowledge, because I love her and I have betrayed her.'

'Then we must agree to become no more involved than we are right now. Men have affairs all the time, and they hardly ever leave their wives. A simple affair — an agreement.'

'Agreements can be renegotiated. You should know that.'

Ixora checked her watch. A pair of construction workers passed, turning back to ogle at her. 'I'm due back at the location in twenty minutes. It's Scott's big scene. Are you coming to watch?'

'I want to kiss you but someone might see.'

'There's no one around.' She turned herself to his chest and slipped her arms around his waist. Through the mist of the fountains they might have been mistaken for love-struck teenagers.

Scott Tyron stood at his mark, impatiently waiting for one of the grips to fix the door of the telephone kiosk.

'He's shorter than I imagined,' said Michael Sullivan, gesturing in the direction of the leading player. One of the sound men cupped a hand over his headphones, glanced around and scowled. 'Why is his face orange?' Sullivan whispered.

'To counteract the natural light,' replied John, leading him away from the sound crew. Before them, the grips were pasting gaffer-tape Xs on the pavement for the extras to reach their marks. 'In this scene,' John explained, 'Scott has just found out that his girlfriend is alone in her flat with the killer, so he's calling her from the public booth. It's not a real telephone box.'

'Why not use a real one?'

'The director wanted it to be in the same shot as the girl's flat window.'

'That's the flat, up there?' The sergeant pointed to a lighted room above a shop. They stood in an awkward cluster, the sergeant, the director, the camera crew, the sound engineers and the lighting cameramen, the continuity, makeup and props personnel, all roped off from a curious public on the south side of Muswell Hill Broadway.

'That's only being used for the exterior of the flat. The interiors are being filmed at a flat in Highgate.'

'Let's have some quiet, we're losing light.' The director held up his hand for silence. John half expected the traffic noise to die away at his imperious command.

'Turnover.'

The cameraman checked the gate. 'Rolling.'

'And — action.'

The grip held a white plastic film slate before the lens. 'This is *Playing With Fire*, scene fifty-three, take one.'

The extras began passing by on the pavement. Scott Tyron bounded unnaturally to the door of the telephone box and wrenched it open.

'Cut.' Tyron walked away from the box. The extras stopped walking. Everyone else went about their business.

'Is that it?' asked Sullivan, disappointed.

'I'm afraid so,' said John. 'The actual phone call is going to be looped over another scene which they've already shot.'

'How long did all this take to set up?'

'Six hours.'

'Good lord, I could do a day's work in that time.'

'That's exactly what these people have done. They started at five o'clock this morning.' John led the chubby young sergeant away to a mobile canteen at the side of the road. 'What is it you wanted?'

'I have a photograph of you.' He withdrew a crumpled monochrome square from the ziploc bag in his filecase.

John looked puzzled. 'I suppose it could be me,' he said. 'Where did you find it?'

'Inside a dead man's body.' He explained about Feldman's murder. John had already heard. For a day or so it had been the talk of the office.

'Don't worry,' said Sullivan cheerfully, 'you're not a suspect. We've yet to find any motive for the killing. Nothing seems to have been stolen. He was wearing a gold Rolex, had a wallet full of banknotes – untouched. Who is the woman in the picture with you?'

John studied the photograph carefully. Ixora's face and right shoulder, half in shadow, eyes closed. He wanted to lie but realised that it would be easier just to omit detail.

'One of the models we were shooting that day,' he said simply.

'Perhaps you remember her name.'

'Ixora De Corizo. She's here on the set.'

'Just double-checking her ID,' said the sergeant. 'I actually spoke to her a few minutes ago. A very attractive lady.' He took back the photograph. 'I was hoping there would be a reason for the killer choosing this particular piece of film to ram down Mr Feldman's throat. Can you think of one?'

For the briefest of moments a cool cloud of fear touched the back of John's mind. Something best forgotten ... he exhaled, shook his head. The feeling had passed. 'I'm afraid not,' he said at last. 'If I do think of anything, I'll ring you.'

The sergeant handed him a card. 'My private line,' he said. 'Call whenever you like.' He made as if to leave, then paused and turned at the edge of the pavement. 'Perhaps I've been watching too much of this,' he said, gesturing at the film crew, 'but I keep wondering if he might have got the wrong victim.'

'Why do you say that?'

'When I spoke to Miss De Corizo she told me she was angry with Feldman for taking pictures of her that he wasn't supposed to ...' Why would she have told him that? John wondered.

'That's right,' he said aloud. 'He wanted to photograph her in a particular outfit. It was too sexy.'

'This is the thing,' said Sullivan softly. 'I got the feeling that she wasn't telling me the complete truth. Do you suppose she could have returned to the studio to retrieve the film he took? The careers of these girls are very carefully orchestrated, aren't they?'

'Certainly.'

The sergeant hopped off the kerb and back on. He seemed to be thinking aloud. 'That's what occurred to me when I first looked at the pictures, so I did some checking in the area. The video dealer two doors along from the studio was locking up for the night when he saw a woman returning — walking fast, he said.'

'How does he know it was Ixora?'

'He identified her from the photograph, Mr Chapel.'

'What are you saying, she came back and murdered her photographer because he didn't capture her best profile?'

'You misunderstand. Perhaps I've seen too many movies, but imagine this. She comes back to ask him not to develop the film. The lights are off, and perhaps Feldman doesn't hear her knock. She goes away — but someone has followed her, someone who thinks she's gone inside. It's dark in the studio ...'

'Feldman was murdered by mistake? Ixora was the intended victim?'

The sergeant shrugged. 'Too many movies,' he said with a smile.

CHAPTER
16
Acquiescence

It should have ended there.

His first visit to the shadowed bedroom of the house in Sloane Crescent should have been his last. But now that their bodies had touched and the looks and smiles which had passed between them had finally coalesced into something real, there was no thought of stopping, only the search for a way forward.

At the start of the third week in September John found himself travelling through Cheapside in a cab on his way to a meeting, lost in thought, and suddenly the weight of his decision seemed in danger of overpowering him. The unusual Indian summer had continued unabated and unbearable. As the taxi approached St Paul's Cathedral he looked up to see the sun hovering high and hazy in a lemon-tinted sky. Tourists still alighted from the coaches ringing the roadway, but the cathedral was large enough to coolly swallow them within its nave. On a sudden impulse he asked the cab driver to pull over.

Slumping into a pew at the back of the cathedral, consumed in the calming gloom of the ancient building, he tried to make sense of the new path his life was taking. This was one of his favourite places to sit and think. In the crypt below, Nelson and Wellington slept for all eternity. Behind him, Japanese tourists shuffled past whispering to each other. If God was trying to make a point about life carrying on, he got the message.

At home, the new school term had begun, and Josh was no longer hanging around the house complaining of boredom. Helen's book-keeping job kept her busier than ever at the department store, now that her supervisor was absent on extended sick leave. She seemed to enjoy the extra work. He and Helen had been married so long that they no longer consciously checked on each other's welfare.

Helen was practical and strong, never emotional about their relationship, yet capable of bursting into tears while watching a Disney movie. Although his perception of their marriage had changed dramatically in the last few days, John doubted that his wife had noticed anything different, not because she was unreceptive to change but because outwardly nothing had altered.

The morning after he and Ixora had made love for the first time, the young model had entered the Dickson-Clarke offices to drop off her updated composite shots, and had walked by his office. The look which had passed between them was enough to signal their shared sense of guilt. John's face flushed hot when he thought of the moment.

The worst part was his awareness of his actions, his shame at the betrayal of his marriage. But beyond this, compensating for so many conflicting emotions, were his stolen evenings with Ixora, the two of them laying side by side on the cool golden eiderdown, speaking softly in the light of the dying sun. At first they tried to set what was happening between them in some logical context, but already they had learned to leave the subject alone. Adultery had no excuse, and a woman like Ixora defied rational explanation.

What did he really know about her? Where had she come from? Who were her friends? Why had her ex-boyfriend accused her of ruining him? He no longer cared. The more he saw her, the more nothing else mattered except being with her. He knew that he had fallen in love. Ixora reawakened the child in him, restoring his sense of wonder at the world. It made him sick to realise it, but John was actually beginning to resent the time he spent at home in the company of his wife.

He had met Helen when they were both still at school. At the age of seventeen John had been bookish, awkward and uncomfortable in the company of the opposite sex.

Helen had been invited to his best friend's birthday party, but he honestly thought that she would not appear because she seemed to spend all of her spare time studying, and she carried an air of aloofness about her. To his amazement she had attended, looking strangely out of place in her pale blue dress when the other girls all wore Levis and sweatshirts. She even agreed to dance with him. For once, John's shyness remained at bay while he plucked up the courage to ask her out. They had dated for a while, kissing and cuddling in parks and cinemas, and she admitted that she had only come to the party because she knew he would be there.

Making love had been a frightening, thrilling experience, the first time for both of them, and Helen had bled badly. Although the act of sex became a natural part of their life together, Helen's strong religious background ensured that a feeling of guilt always assailed her.

It had been decided that John would read mathematics at Bristol University when he left school that summer. Helen was set for business studies at North London Polytechnic. Although they spent every weekend with each other, there was no consideration of a wedding. Neither of them carried the maturity of their age, and marriage was something that happened to adults.

Then Helen became pregnant, and everything changed overnight. Her parents' faith was staunchly Catholic, his own were vaguely Protestant, and their respective fathers actually came to blows at a family gathering. When John walked from the gates of his school he also left behind dreams of university. He addressed the financial problems of his impending marriage by finding employment as a shop assistant, and studying a night course in accountancy.

By successfully swaddling their son's birth within a marriage contract, John gained respect from Helen's parents and respectability in the neighbourhood. But eleven years of suburban existence had left him feeling culturally desiccated and prematurely middle-aged. His life had not followed the path he had intended. Helen had found peace in Christ. He had discovered no such solace.

He asked himself whether it was the banality of his existence that caused his attention to stray to Ixora, or whether he was simply attempting to justify his actions by presenting a balanced case for infidelity. He thought he had reconciled himself to life with Helen long ago, but Ixora had revived the familiar ache of dissatisfaction.

In his mind he returned with her to the house which stayed dark and cool on the brightest of days, to make love amidst the shadows and the threads of gold, surrounded by settling motes of dust, to feel her legs grip his in the tautness of orgasm. And then he was in the cathedral once more, every nerve end tingling with fear and desire and energy, and suddenly he knew that with her anything was possible, that there were no boundaries.

He rose from the pew and walked briskly from the church, scattering a party of bewildered Americans, his next appointment forgotten.

As the cab drew up at the house he saw her at the first floor window, as if she had known he might come for her. Pushing the unlatched door wide he threw aside his case and ran to the stairs. He found her at the entrance to the bedroom, her dark eyes frozen on his face. In undoing his shirt she tore away most of the buttons, loosening his erect member from his trousers before they had taken a step inside the room. The ferocity of her attack was matched by his own. As he collapsed onto his knees and then his back, she mounted him easily, hauling her sweat-shirt above her head and freeing her breasts, forcing her pelvis down into his, sealing his mouth with hers, her hair closing like a curtain over his eyes, obscuring his vision until darkness absorbed their writhing bodies.

They lay together on the floor of the room, their sweat quickly drying as they pulled apart. Ixora's hair was plastered to her forehead, her eyes downcast. She was as beautiful as ever. Neither of them spoke as they dressed. The scent of Ixora's flesh lingered on his body. At the head of the stairs he turned to face her. 'Can I see you tonight?'

'No, but we still have a while. Come with me.' She pulled on her sweatshirt and straightened it out, then pushed past him and ran down the stairs, laughing. 'Let's get out of here!'

'Wait!' he called back, 'where are we going?'

'Why do you always need to know, John? Where's your sense of adventure? Hurry, or we'll miss the sunset.'

She ran around to the passenger side of the car and

waited impatiently while he fumbled with the keys. 'I'll direct the way. All you have to do is drive.'

The Volvo threaded through the afternoon traffic to the embankment and followed the river, crossing at Vauxhall Bridge and turning into a no-man's land of wasteground and warehouses. 'This is the place, turn here.' She slapped her palm excitedly on the dashboard.

Ahead of them, standing alone, was a bizarre Victorian building covered in red, white and blue stripes, with flowers in polished copper pots and watering cans sprouting from every ledge and windowsill. Ixora jumped from the car and ran inside, emerging a few minutes later with a bottle of champagne and two glasses. They helped each other on to the embankment wall. Ahead lay the river, sluggish and sparkling. The wine was none too cold, and sprayed over her hands as she attempted to fill the flutes.

'A toast before Old Father Thames,' she said, standing up on the wall and raising her glass high in the air. 'To us, and the future of love.

> "Now folds the lily all her sweetness up,
> And slips into the bosom of the lake:
> So fold thyself, my dearest, thou, and slip
> Into my bosom and be lost in me."'

'What's that?'

'Call yourself an educated man? Tennyson. Now it's your turn.' She tilted her glass, light refracting in his eyes. 'Come on.'

'I don't know any poetry.'

'Don't be silly, everyone knows a bit of poetry, even just a line.' She pointed ahead. 'Look out there, beautiful sunset, reddening sky, reflections in the river, me by your side; surely it must bring something to mind.'

John thought hard. 'Wait, I remember something.' He counted the metre with his forefinger.

> '"If ever flattering lies of yours can please
> And soothe my soul to self-sufficiency,
> And make me one of pleasure's devotees,
> Then take my soul, for I desire to die."

'I don't know what it is.' He frowned at the crystallising water. 'I don't even know how I come to know it.'

'It's not very cheerful. I'll buy you a decent book of verse. Every Victorian knew his poetry inside out. It wasn't considered at all unmanly, you know, just cultured.'

'Why can't I see you tonight?'

'I have to meet some friends. I wasn't expecting you.'

'Neither was I. I guess I was having trouble making it through the day.'

'I prefer you stronger than that, John.'

'I'm stronger when I see you.'

Her eyes followed a police launch crossing the river. 'You have a wife and a son.'

'I know.'

'Don't you think about hurting her?'

'Of course.'

'And you still want this?'

'What do you think?'

'No,' she said, raising her eyes to his. 'You have to say it.'

'Yes,' he said hoarsely, and then, clearing his throat, 'yes, I do.'

'Thank God.' She pulled him close and released a shiver as the sun slid behind the darkening cityscape, and the first autumnal breeze pimpled the black waters below their feet.

CHAPTER
17
Pall Mall

'Not again, John. It's been every night this week.'

'I'm sorry, but what can I do? The releases have to be sent out by tomorrow.' For once he was telling Helen the truth. Everyone was staying late to help dispatch electronic press kits and photographic material to the networks. In the offices behind John, secretaries were phoning ahead to the stations forewarning them of incoming deliveries. He swivelled his chair back to the desk, freeing the telephone cord. 'Howard's done all the groundwork. I can't just let him down.'

'What about letting Josh and me down? I know the job's important, but I spend all my time waiting for you to come home.'

'Helen, I warned you about the hours when I took the job. We still get weekends together.'

'I'm trying not to be shrewish about this, John, but Josh

has barely seen you in weeks. He badmouths you all the time. This is classic Oedipal stuff. Next he'll want to kill you and marry me. He'll probably turn out gay. You think that's a good thing?'

'You never know. It might improve his dress sense.' Click and buzz. The receiver was dead in his hand. His internal-directory telephone rang.

'John.' Ixora's voice, velvet on the line. 'I'm in your reception. I can't stop long. Do you have a minute?'

She was wearing a short black skirt and a high-necked silk blouse. The outfit looked too simple not to be expensive. He moved to kiss her, but she warned him away. Howard was talking to his secretary in the corridor behind them.

'Where are you going?'

'Coming back. Diana had people she wanted me to meet. A Japanese magazine — they want to do a photo-spread, costumes from the film. The pay is stupendous. I got your message. Why did the police want to talk to you again?'

'It was just a phone call. It seems that we were the last people to see your photographer alive. The shopkeeper definitely confirmed that it was you he saw. They asked me if I knew why you went back there that night.'

'To the studio?'

He studied her face. 'Did you?'

The answer read instantly in her eyes. 'Oh John, I did. I should have told you, I know. You offered me a lift and I said I'd take a cab, remember? I waited for ages but just couldn't find one. I didn't like standing around on the corner, so I went back to the studio to order a taxi from there. I knocked on the door but there was no reply, so I left. I assumed that Feldman had locked the place up for the night. It seemed odd at the time, because he couldn't have cleared up in the studio so quickly. Luckily there was a cab right outside. I explained what happened to the fat little sergeant when he came to the shoot. Do you think I did the right thing?'

'How was Diana?' asked a bass American voice. Howard had walked up behind them. He slipped an arm around Ixora's waist. A brief flinch showed in her eyes.

'She was fine. Very complimentary about you, Howard.'

'That's a first.'

'I have to go. John, I'll see you soon.' She gave a formal wave and headed for the door.

'There goes one hell of a woman,' Howard murmured appreciatively.

They finished addressing the packages a little after ten. Releasing the rest of his staff, Howard put his head around John's office door. 'Why don't you get off home, John? Someone has to wait for the courier to collect everything.'

'My next train isn't for a while,' replied John. 'I don't mind doing it.'

'Suit yourself. I'll let Paula go. See you in the morning. If Helen gives you any grief about working late, put her on to me.' If I do that, thought John, she might find out just how rarely I work late. He turned out the overhead strip-lighting and began to read beneath his small desk lamp.

He realised that he must have been dozing, for the front doorbell caused him to react with a start. He expected to find a crash-helmeted motorcycle messenger waiting in the foyer. Instead he found Matteo. He was leaning against the night bell with his eyes half closed, dressed in a black sweatshirt and dirty grey chinos. Sweat glistened in his hair and eyebrows.

'I figured you'd be here.' His speech was rushed and clipped, as if he'd been dosed with amphetamines. 'She said she was coming to see you.'

'If you're referring to Ixora, you missed her. She left a while ago. I'd appreciate it if you would leave me out of your fantasies.'

'Fantasies, that's fuckin' great.' He slid against the wall. 'Are you gonna let me in or what?'

'Forget it. Go home.' He started to close the door.

'Wait, wait, I can tell you some things.' He hopped back at the door, desperate. 'She's killing me, man, literally killing me. I can prove what I'm saying if you wanna hear me out.'

'Why should I believe you? You lied before.'

'No, I didn't, wait. She makes love like it's the end of the world, right? Am I right?'

John's momentary waver gave him away. Matteo seized the moment, pushing the door wider and stepped inside, reaching out to John's jacket. 'That's 'cause for her it *is* the end of the world, do you see? If you wanna know the truth, ask her about her parents.'

'They're dead. Her mother passed on seven years ago and her—'

Matteo brushed his hand back and forth. 'No, no, no, the *truth*, man, they died together. Ask her how it happened. Or I could tell you right now.'

'And you want money for the information, don't you?'

'What can I do? She wrecks my life, then she won't give me a fuckin' penny!' he shouted in John's startled face. 'I need money. I'm willing to help you. Check up on her past and you might not be so anxious to see her again. I don't want the bitch back. I want her dead. I want to see her cut into tiny fuckin' pieces. Somebody should hear the truth.'

'That's it, you're out of here.' He propelled Matteo to the door and shoved him beyond it. The sudden thought that he might be dealing with Feldman's murderer made him push all the harder. Matteo continued to hammer at the door as he returned to his office. He noticed with some surprise that his pulse was pounding.

And yet, he couldn't shake the feeling that Matteo was really harmless, a petty blackmailer who seemed scared more than anything else. It made no sense. Christ, if he really was a murderer, he'd have to be pretty stupid to threaten Ixora's life in front of a witness. John sat back in his chair to await the arrival of the courier.

Pall Mall owes its name to the Italian ball and mallet game that Charles the Second had enjoyed playing so much with his mistresses beneath the elms of St James's Park. Unfortunately, carriages passing between the Palace and Charing Cross had thrown up fine clouds of summer dust, blinding the players and making them choke, so in 1661 a new road was built and named for the Queen, Catherine of Braganza.

Although it is still officially Catherine Street, it is known by the name of the pastime upon whose alley it stands: Pall Mall. Tonight, as always, the road was open to public traffic but its broad pavements were deserted, save for one angry, frightened man.

Matteo had not formulated a plan beyond visiting John Chapel at his office, and he'd done exactly what he'd promised himself he would not do, wrecking his one chance of credibility by losing his temper. He crossed between the taxis waiting outside the Royal Automobile Club and tried to figure out what to do next. Perhaps he should go to Sloane Crescent and confront Ixora with what he knew. Could that help either of them now?

He had reached the corner of Waterloo Place before he became aware that someone, or something, was following him. A shifting blackness revealed itself at the edge of his vision. As he descended the bank of pale stone steps leading to the Mall itself, he listened for the sound of shoes slapping on gravel, moving away, somewhere off to his right. To one side stood the exhaust-blackened facia of Admiralty Arch, leading to Trafalgar Square. Before him was the broad pink tarmac of the Mall. In the distance, sparkling beyond hazy lamplight, the low bulk of Buckingham Palace.

On the other side of the road, the lofty planes and elms of St James's Park rustled in darkness, as they had for so many centuries. He leaned against the statue at the foot of the stairs and lit a cigarette with a shaking hand.

He heard the sound again, closer now. There was someone behind him, of that he was sure. His skin cooled fast in the warm night air, dripping chill droplets of sweat between his shoulderblades. From the first night he had spoken to Chapel it had occurred to him that he might be in danger. He was strong, muscular, capable of taking care of himself. Chapel had merely been lucky enough to catch him by surprise in his flat. He would not let such a thing happen again.

The roadway ahead seemed desolate and devoid of vehicles. In the blazing amber lamplight a visitor could imagine it restored to former glory as a fashionable ladies' promenade. Matteo was more intent on crossing it without being attacked.

He finished the cigarette, dropping it to the white concrete promontory and twisting his shoe over the stub, then raised his head. There was a bad feeling in the air, something sour and godless about the night. It would be best to walk up the middle of the Mall as quickly as possible, heading for the roundabout at its far end, then to branch away in the direction of Chelsea. That's what he would do. How surprised the bitch would be to see him!

Setting off down the steps he noticed from the prickling of his skin that the wind had suddenly picked up, and was sending handfuls of leaves scuttling past him like rats. He rounded the edge of the statue as the steel arc cut a glittering rainbow through the night air. A swish, then a silence. Matteo staggered lightly, hands reaching up to his surprised face. What had happened? The tips of his fingers probed his wet chin and reached the edges of his mouth as pain began to blossom like a poisoned flower. Now his fingers were within his stinging cheeks, the razor-blade having parted the meat of his face so cleanly that at first his mouth seemed merely to have widened into an absurd smile. He could not scream, for the action involved dilating the very flesh which had been cut.

Aghast, he ran into the light, then into the roadway, the lower half of his face a broad river of crimson from smile to sweaterneck. Without voluntary command his legs kicked to life, pumping hard, carrying him forward towards the Palace and its fountain.

As he fled, he looked over his shoulder to see a windswirled figure shimmering in his shadowed wake, closing the gap with each powerful footspring. And as he watched, the diamond light of the blade soared again across his face, scoring his forehead, slicing the tip of his nose, narrowly missing the blood-gorged veins of his neck. He found voice now to scream, and the pain of doing so only made him scream louder.

And on he ran, shoes beating out a rhythmic tattoo on the pink tarred gravel, as the blade once more appeared from nowhere to rise and fall across his neck and down his back, opening his sweatshirt and tracing a crimson microline on the flesh of his left arm. The deserted roundabout lay just ahead and, imprisoned behind black lacquered railings, the distanced serenity of Buckingham Palace itself. Weren't there always guards there, police?

Now his attacker was one full pace behind. As if participating in a lethal game of touch, Matteo knew that he had to reach the railings first or he would die.

His mistake was in passing the fountain on the left. The distance he had to travel was further than a path to the right. As he ran for the clear stretch from the fountain to the railing he slipped on the spray-slick steps and stumbled, just as his attacker appeared from the other side.

This time the razor fell to his chest, three times, four times, tattering the sweatshirt, slicing its way to his heart and severing a valve. Blood flecked the bronze fountainhead and spattered the steps. As his body was lifted high, it trailed in the roadway, speckled the pavement and dripped on the railings of the Palace itself. Matteo's limbs thrashed in the final grimace of death. At any moment police could come running; but for the taker of the young man's troubled life there was still a little work to do.

Sullivan had been dancing at a nightclub in the Charing Cross Road when his pager sounded. If he had not taken the rare decision to enjoy himself on his night off, he might not have been found within the required radius of the call-out. As he turned into the western end of the Mall he noted the constables, the squad car and the ambulance pulled over on the verge at the northerly side of the fountain, and mentally figured the discovery of death to be around fifteen minutes earlier. He had pulled a jacket over his T-shirt, vaguely embarrassed by his casual state of dress.

There was something odd going on. The constables and the ambulancemen were standing around, as if waiting to be told what to do. 'Who was first here?' he called. One of the Palace duty officers ran forward.

'I saw it first, sir.'

Sullivan looked around at the clear sweep of the drive. 'Where is it, then?'

The officer raised a nervous finger to the spiked top of the Palace railings. Sullivan's mouth fell open. Wedged a full ten feet above the ground was the corpse, grotesquely doubled over like a bizarre colonial monkey-statue. It had poured a large dark patch on to the Palace gravel.

'Christ Almighty, what if the Queen looks out?' cried Sullivan, raising a hand to his forehead.

'She'll probably ask him if he had to come far,' suggested the constable. Sullivan shot him a silencing look.

'Well, don't just stand there, get the bloody thing down,' he said.

'There's a call for you, sir.' One of the mobile unit drivers was holding a receiver above his car door. Sullivan accepted the handset.

'Clear out the body, rope off the area and get out quickly,' said Hargreave, his voice crackling with static. 'Andy and Fergie are on their way back to the Palace. They should reach Admiralty Arch in about six minutes.'

'Well, I'm sorry to offend their sensibilities, Mr Hargreave, but we've got an extremely brutal murder here.' Sullivan released the reply button.

'Personally speaking, Sergeant Sullivan, I don't give a ferret's fart for the crowned heads of our fading empire, but these orders don't come from my department. Now get a bloody move on.'

They dragged the body unceremoniously from the railings, and were about to zip it into a plastic bodysack when Sullivan stopped them. 'Wait, leave it here for a minute.' He pushed the ambulancemen away.

'You heard the chief,' said one of them. 'We've got six minutes.' Sullivan ignored him and turned the body over, feeling in the back pockets of its blood-soaked jeans. He pulled out a wallet and flipped it open. The travelcard within identified the victim. He checked it against the corpse. Something glittered within the slashed sweatshirt, a glint of steel and ivory over the heart. Gingerly, Sullivan lifted away the strands of wet cloth to reveal an old-fashioned cut-throat razor. It had been closed and rammed so far inside the victim's heart that his skin had all but closed over it.

He checked the wallet again. Another snapshot, a polaroid. He was laughing this time, his arm around a drinking buddy. He held it against the travelcard. In both pictures their victim was wearing a heavy gold chain around his neck. A large crucifix dangled from it. He allowed the body to fall back and rose to his feet, searching the ground.

'Sir, we've got less than three minutes,' pleaded the constable, 'before *they* arrive — Andy and — you know.' He made the shape of a beachball in the air.

As they bundled the bodybag into the back of the ambulance, Sullivan ran to the fountain and peered into the shallow ring of water. He spotted the crucifix almost immediately, rolled up his sleeve and fished it out.

'They're at the gate.'

Sullivan looked around. With the exception of the police tape marking off a section of the railings, everything was packed away. 'Let's get out of here,' he said.

Sullivan instructed one of the constables to return in his own car, and rode in the back of the ambulance with the cadaver. As it reached the gate with its lights off the ambulance passed by the royal car, heading in the opposite direction. The driver craned his head in a vain attempt to catch a glimpse of the royal couple, while Sullivan hunched over the corpse.

The moment he had seen the severity of the attack on the victim, a sinking feeling had settled in his stomach. A blue-black graze showed at the back of the victim's neck where the offending chain had been torn away and immersed in water. The crucifix had been there in the fountain trough, but not the chain. Why? Because the chain had clearly posed no threat. No, it was the symbol of Christ that the murderer was interested in. This was more than a religious quirk. It was a signature. This attack had proven the most ferocious yet, and the gaps between the murders were getting tighter. But he could sense something more about the murderer, a spoor of malevolence. Tonight he had arrived in the wake of evil.

Sullivan had left behind a foot detail who would quietly comb the bushes and trees surrounding the Palace. Although he knew that they would find nothing, he was thankful to be travelling in the opposite direction, back towards the sheltering lights of the city.

CHAPTER
18
Wrap Party

'Why is it still so warm? So late in the year. It's like the sun doesn't want to leave.' The lacework shadowed her naked body with brocade tattoos, like filigreed wounds.

'Come away from the window.' John rolled over in the bed to where she had lain. The thick Irish linen beneath his torso was cool to the touch, as if it had not been able to draw warmth from Ixora's body. The waning sunlight was suffused by the dust which covered the tall bedroom windows, transforming them into opaque saffron panels. Ixora stretched her arm to touch the glass, as if the moment held a distant memory. Then she let the heavy jade curtain fall back in place, shielding them again from the light.

'We could always stay in bed.' She glanced along his body. 'I don't suppose we have to go.'

'We spend all our time in bed. It'll be good for you to mix with other people. Besides, it's a big career mistake to miss your own wrap party.'

'Oh, come on, John. After all the trouble on the set, everyone saying nice things to each other when they're really praying they'll never have to work together again?' She dropped to the edge of the bed, idly trailing her hand across his stirring genitals.

'I'm still your advisor, Ixora.'

'But you're in my bed. It's not so easy to take you seriously.' She released a throaty laugh.

'Why not?' John tugged the golden quilt over his stomach.

'You're just a man in bed. Not so dignified. Freckles on your shoulders. Fat little tummy.' She reached her hand beneath the quilt and shook his flesh. 'This is woman's territory. The bedroom.'

'I don't think many feminists would agree with you.'

'Then they're fools. This is the easiest way to control your sex. There is nothing more pliable than a man in a state of constant expectation.'

This time their lovemaking was slow and deliberate, their caresses relaxed and light. Their bodies moved in as stately and calm a fashion as a skiff skimming the surface of a lake. By the time they had risen, washed and dressed, the sun had long set, and they were late.

'Tell me something,' asked John, knotting his tie in the mottled wardrobe mirror. 'After your father died, why did you and your mother move here?'

'Alexandra — my mother — had lived in this house as a child. It belonged to her family. We had no other relatives in Spain, and the house had long been vacant, so we took possession. We were happy here.'

'I thought you said that you hated having to visit your Spanish relatives every year.'

'Tell me what you think of this outfit. I borrowed it from a friend of mine in Wardrobe.'

John studied her reflection as she stepped into a black silk dress. She never spoke of her father. John realised that he didn't even know his name. Then he remembered what Matteo had said. 'How did your father die, Ixora?'

One foot raised, she momentarily lost her balance. 'An accident. He'd been drinking. His car left the road.'

'How old did you say you were?'

'Did I say?' She thought for a moment, or pretended to think. 'Seven, I suppose. Perhaps eight.'

'But I thought—'

'It won't be worth going if we don't get there soon,' she cried out suddenly. 'Zip me up?'

His fingers brushed her shoulder above the dress, leaving bloodless marks behind. Her skin was icy to the touch. He supposed that she would explain her reluctance to discuss her family at a later date. After all, what could be so bad about her past?

'Let me give you some romantic advice, honey. There are those who love — there are those who wait — and there are those who wait on tables, and that's what you do, so could you take the fucking ashtrays away and empty them?' Scott Tyron turned back to the group that clustered before him. 'Fucking career-waitresses. Where was I? Oh yeah, that was after I did the time travel movie, the bratpack thing. This was at a time when they thought that if you had Michael J. Fox, a flying saucer and a theme tune by ZZ Top you had a sure-fire hit and a bunch of roman numeral sequels. Six fucking months of my life, and if the movie had turned out to be any more of a dog it would have shed on the audience. Amateurs, man.'

John turned his attention back to Ixora. 'How did you ever manage to kiss that guy in your big scene?' he asked.

'I thought of chewing garlic but I just kept my teeth closed. You want some punch?' They made their way over to the side of the studio, where a bar had been set up on trestle tables.

'Aren't you all supposed to exchange little gifts with each other when you leave?'

'We already did that yesterday. The set designer does needlepoint. Mine's staying in a drawer. Besides, the ritual seemed a little too cute considering most of the crew have been exchanging body fluids for the last six weeks.'

Studio C looked as inhospitable at night as it did in the day, a timeless place, devoid of outside intrusions, a blank space ready to adopt any character it was given. John felt it was like being inside a vast packing crate, waiting to be filled and turned to use.

By the time they had arrived, the wrap party had already divided into cliques. The director, producer, lighting cameraman and focus puller stood with most of the speaking-part cast on one side while sparks, chippies, extras and ancillary services were on the other. Ambitious trainees hovered between the two sides, accepted by neither. The editor and the composer were in attendance, although their work was just beginning. The film had finished two weeks over schedule and nearly a million dollars over budget. Compared to the director's last film, this was thrift.

Park Manton, the producer, passed them with half a dozen punch-filled cups between his fingers. 'Our right-on film school graduate,' he said, nodding at an earnest young woman who was speaking angrily to one of the crew, 'has now discovered that Eisenstein theory isn't always uppermost in the crew's minds. She's just been offered a moustache ride by the lighting cameraman. Farley tells me that he's very pleased with your big romantic scene. He says you have a great deal of potential.'

'Thanks, but he told me he doesn't think I'll ever be much of an actress,' said Ixora.

'Women like you have a special ability,' said Manton. 'You know what that is? The eerie power to cloud men's minds.'

'I suppose I should take that as a compliment. Scott thinks I should have paid him for the privilege of kissing the man worshipped by millions of women.'

'You should wait until you get as old as me before you start paying them, darling.' Manton moved off. 'I'll catch you later.' On the far side of the studio someone switched on the sound system, and a jazz tape began to play loudly.

'I know your profession is all about timing,' said a voice behind them in what sounded suspiciously like the start of a prepared speech, 'so I feel I must apologise for my own.' Sullivan coughed into his hand, embarrassed. 'Er, timing, that is.' Ixora threw John a 'help me' look.

'Ixora, this is Detective Sergeant Sullivan, remember? We all met on location the other day.'

'I'm sorry.' A look of recognition crossed her face. 'Of course I remember. It's been a crazy week. Sergeant, how are you?' She held out her hand, and for some reason Sullivan kissed it. Perhaps he thought that was what you did with actresses.

'I wouldn't disturb you on such a festive occasion were it not for the murder. Another one, that is. Another murder.' He shuffled awkwardly.

Ixora turned, the smile fading from her face. 'John, what is he talking about?'

'I don't know any more than you. Who's been murdered?'

'Mr Dominguez. You do know a Mr Matteo Dominguez?' He was watching Ixora's reaction.

'Matteo is dead?'

'I'm afraid so. He was stabbed to death late last night. It

was kept out of the papers for reasons of security. Perhaps you could answer a few questions?'

Outside, the night had cooled, and dense stars packed the sky. Free of the No Smoking signs, Sullivan hastily lit a cigarette. The backlot was still and silent. The sound of the party's tape deck could not penetrate the studio doors.

'Your name was in his telephone book, and there were some photographs.' He removed an envelope and passed it to Ixora.

'I thought he had returned them all,' she said, surprised.

'They were sealed in a small safe we found in his flat. This is an informal talk, so you don't have to answer, but what was your relationship to him?'

'We went out a few times. I hadn't seen him for quite a while.'

'Can you remember the exact date when you last saw him?'

'It would have been a couple of months ago. I suppose I could look it up in my diary.'

She was absently shuffling Matteo's photographs in her hands. John leaned over and examined them. A few dated black-and-white glossies, Ixora with her arms around friends, nothing more.

'To be honest,' said Sullivan, 'I came to you first because of your connection with the death of Mr Feldman.' He withdrew an absurdly tiny notebook and folded back the cover, then hunted for a pencil.

Ixora was shaking her head, speaking quickly. 'Nothing like this has ever happened to me before, and now there are two dead people. Do you think it could be something to do with me?'

'Please try not to be alarmed,' said Sullivan hastily, raising his hand, 'but you are a definite link. I think we're going to find that both men died by the same hand. I didn't tell you this, but there's also an earlier murder which we believe to be connected. Mr Dominguez somehow impaled himself on a railing ten feet high. Also, whoever did this would seem to possess considerable strength, because the murder weapon was found —'

'Were there fingerprints on it?'

'— inside his body,' finished the sergeant. 'This is a very dangerous person, most likely suffering from severe mental trauma. At this stage I simply need to discover if either of you know of any such person. And for the record, I need to know where you both were last night.'

John paled. Matteo had come to his office and accused Ixora of being some kind of lunatic, for God's sake. He would have to lie, just as she had omitted to mention her last encounter with him. He cleared his throat. 'Uh, I worked late.'

'Did anyone see you leave?'

'The night security officer hadn't been at his desk all evening.'

'Don't worry. I can check on that.'

'I took a meeting at my agency ...' said Ixora.

'This would be a model agency?' Sullivan licked the end of his pencil.

'Theatrical. I called by Mr Chapel's office to pick up a cheque. I saw him, his boss was there too, I think. After that I went home.'

Sullivan seemed stumped. He reluctantly closed the notebook and slipped it back into his jacket pocket. 'I have other questions,' he said unconvincingly. 'I'll want to ask you things later.'

'Fine.' Ixora glanced across at John. 'I don't think either of us are leaving the country.'

Sullivan sucked his bottom lip. 'Well,' he said at last. 'I'll be going, then.'

'What a strange little man,' said Ixora, as they watched him walk away. 'Why ever did he go into the police force, do you think? He hasn't got much sense of authority.'

'You and I need to talk,' said John, grabbing her arm.

Ixora shook herself free. 'What about?' she asked.

'He came to me last night.'

'Who? Matteo? Why would he do that?'

'To warn me away from you.'

'John, this is ridiculous! If you could hear yourself ... you don't seriously think I had anything to do with his death, do you?'

'Not directly, no. But you must know more than you've told me.'

'If I do, then it's because I'm trying to protect you!' she cried out. Suddenly her face crumpled as her composure broke. 'I could never allow you to be hurt. Don't you see, if I wasn't in love — so infatuated with—' She pressed her hand against her chest, fighting for breath. 'There never has been anyone — and none of this—'

'Ixora, calm down.' He took her in his arms and rested her face against his lapel. 'I'll take you home. Forget about this now.' He had seen proof that she wasn't a good enough actress to lie to him convincingly. But if she wasn't lying, she was certainly omitting to tell him the whole truth. Why, to protect him? From what? Perhaps for now it was better not to ask. Sooner or later he would find a way to make her open her heart to him.

CHAPTER
19
Saunders

'Heard you was with the film stars last night,' called the duty officer as Sullivan passed through into the station. 'Suppose you'll be after a starring role next.'

'Let me take over here for a while,' said Sullivan, sending his temporary assistant away from the computer. He settled his ample rear onto the swivel stool and punched up the forensic reports on Brady, Feldman and Dominguez.

One of the WPCs tapped his shoulder as she passed. 'They're saying you took a famous film star out to dinner last night,' she said. 'Who was she?'

'I visited the studios on a business call,' he said irritably. 'For God's sake go and make some tea.'

Earlier in the day he had correlated the common circumstantial factors between the three cases. Now he

was looking for something more positive, something that
would point the way forward to outside suspects. Most of
the routine interviews had already been logged into the
computer's main data store. The system, set up under the
supervision of Ian Hargreave four years earlier, automatically matched victims of serious crimes throughout the
network to see if any correlating factors suggested links
between cases. Hargreave had realised that a number of
investigations remained open simply because information
had not been exchanged between areas. His system also
compared recorded suspect-interviews with the victim's
background information, searching for common elements.
As the accumulated data scrolled down the screen, his eye
ran over the factor match-list:

VICTIM NAMES: BRADY, V./ FELDMAN, R./
DOMINGUEZ, M.
PHYSICAL DESCRIPTION/
AGE/**PLACE OF BIRTH**/NATIONALITY/
HABITS/ASSOCIATES/LEISURE PURSUITS/
EMPLOYMENT HISTORY/ EDUCATIONAL
LEVEL/
RECORD OF DETENTIONS/COURT CONVIC-
TIONS/
NATURE OF OFFENCE/
INFO/RECORDS IN OTHER POLICE DEPTS/
ADDITION INFO/

The two common elements caught his eye. First he
summoned up the birthplace details. All three men had
been born overseas. The computer listed their entry dates
into Britain, but not their cities of origin. He made a note
to call Carl Phelps in Immigration. The other area of similarity lay in their previous occupations. The computer
showed that all three had experience of working within

the media industry. Brady was a former model, and had occasionally written columns for *Amateur Photographer* magazine. Feldman's background presented him as a fully fledged showbiz character, shooting flattering portraits of famous and infamous alike. His greatest successes had stemmed from recording the fashion excesses of the seventies. Matteo Dominguez had spent time briefly as a freelance photographer. He and Feldman had shared a number of photographic subjects and knew many of the same people, although in such a small London-based industry this was hardly surprising.

Sullivan added his notes to the file and saved it, running off a back-up disk of his own. He drained his tea mug and rose from the chair. Time for an informal chat with Oswald Finch, his man in the morgue.

'Hello there,' called Finch cheerily. Sullivan was surprised to find the lanky coroner tying a tag on to the toe of a corpse.

'I thought they only did that in the movies' he said, pointing to the body.

'Standard procedure, old boy,' said Finch with a smile. 'Of course, you know all about the movies now.' His grin broadened. 'Aren't you supposed to be having some torrid affair with a famous actress?'

'No, I am not,' complained Sullivan. 'Have you got anything interesting for me on Dominguez?'

'He's on the bench right now. Let's have a look at him.' He beckoned the sergeant, obviously waiting for a chance to show off his handiwork. The corpse came as something of a shock to Sullivan. Innumerable plastic clips pinned back flaps of dried flesh, as if the body had been specifically arranged for display.

'The attack on him was incredibly ferocious,' said Finch, jabbing the edge of the gaping chest wound with his ballpoint pen. 'The razor was shoved clean into his heart — the toughest muscle in the body — the blade was extremely sharp, of course, and it was driven by a very strong hand. Now, if you look at the *Quadriceps Femoris*, here.' He indicated a wide slash on the young man's thigh through which extruded a fibrous red tongue of meat. 'It's a very leathery, broad muscle, used for powering the legs into ambulatory motion. It's not very easily cut, and yet, as you can see, the right hand portion has been virtually severed. As you can imagine, this was the last wound to be inflicted. He'd have fallen down at this point. The surprising thing is that his muscles weren't tensed when he expired.'

'I don't understand,' said Sullivan.

'Well, if he'd been climbing the railings to escape his attacker, he'd have braced his feet like so,' Finch adopted a semi-crouching position. 'Like a mountaineer. Then ...' he raised his arms, 'one final haul over the top — he slips — falls back on to the spikes ...' Finch pointed a bony finger at his own calves, 'and the legs are still tensed, you see? But this musculature here is completely flaccid.'

'What do you think that proves?' asked Sullivan, bewildered.

'Dominguez didn't climb the railings,' replied the coroner, thoughtfully sucking the end of his biro. 'He was hurled.'

Sullivan's next stop was at the office of Raymond Land. The forensic report on Dominguez was compiled under the aegis of the supervising doctor, and rather than wait for his findings to filter through the system, it made sense to obtain the information as early as possible. Land's legendary reluctance to reveal any findings prior to the completion of the report only encouraged Sullivan to goad him.

Land had also made it known that he was dismayed at having to work with a junior like Sullivan. With the linking of a possible third death, a murder as serious as this required the full attention of senior investigating officers from Serious Crimes, and although Hargreave was now officially in charge he was still allowing his promising young sergeant to continue with the groundwork. Land, on the other hand, had no patience with those he considered less knowledgeable or experienced than himself.

'Just tell me if you have an origin for the murder weapon,' asked Sullivan, following the doctor around his desk. 'Come on, Raymond, please don't make me wait another two days.'

'I'm surprised you're interested in the case,' sniffed Land, 'I thought you spent all your spare time dating film stars.'

'Has this information been posted somewhere?' asked the sergeant.

'Give me one good reason for not keeping you waiting.' Sullivan breathed heavily through his nose. He would have to play his trump card. 'I think we've got an honest-to-God serial killer on our hands. Three bodies in three weeks, with Dominguez's death following the M.O. you suggested for Brady and Feldman.'

'I think that's unlikely in the extreme,' said Land irritably. 'Serial murders are very uncommon in the British Isles. Given the ferocity of the attack, this Buckingham Palace thing is more likely to be a case of aggravated assault. Dominguez was acknowledged to have a violent temper. Admittedly, the frenzy in which he was killed —'

'I wouldn't suggest this if I didn't believe it.' The sergeant knew he was risking his nascent reputation by laying claim to the discovery of a serial killer. Contrary to public consensus, such entities were still an extreme rarity outside of the USA, and many an officer senior to Sullivan had made a fool of himself claiming to have uncovered one.

'Unless you can produce some solid evidence to support the claim, I'm not considering that option in my report.'

'Surely the crucifix in the fountain is a strong enough link,' said Sullivan heatedly.

Land consulted his notes. 'There were blood splashes all around the fountain, adding to evidence of an extremely physical attack. I know it's tempting to fit the case to the theory, but there are other factors to take into account. I assume you know about the drug connection?' He raised a quizzical eyebrow.

'No,' Sullivan admitted.

'It's clearly documented in the witness updates. According to friends of his, Matteo Dominguez had recently taken to selling cocaine. He was falling in debt to the wrong kind of people. A month ago I understand that he actually reported a death threat to this very station.'

Sullivan swore beneath his breath. How could he not have been aware of that?

'I'm afraid you'll have to gather your material a little more carefully if you're planning on maintaining credibility around here,' said Land, removing his spectacles and closing the file. Furious at his loss of face, Sullivan rose to leave. In his eagerness to fit the facts he had cut procedural corners. Land placed a cool hand on his arm. 'Don't feel too bad,' he said, concern showing surprisingly in his voice. 'We've all rushed into things. It's part of the learning process.'

The evening traffic was a motionless ribbon of light and steel from the Spaniard's Inn to Highgate Village.

'Let's park here,' suggested Ixora. 'We'll never get any closer.' Against John's advice, she tucked her black handbag under the passenger seat.

'I'm not sure we should have come,' he said as they joined the walk toward Kenwood House. 'It's too risky. A lot of Helen's friends from church will be here.' The final concert of the season had already begun, its audience entirely covering the emerald hill which sloped down to the lake and the orchestra beyond. The air beneath the trees was humid and heavy. Dense clouds of midges swarmed in the lower branches.

'I'm your client, John, and this is a legitimate business exercise. Besides, you could do with the fresh air. It might stop you worrying so much.' They picked their way between the picnic hampers and found a space to sit. The orchestra had begun with the sprightly overture from Offenbach's *La Vie Parisienne*.

John searched the surrounding area uneasily. Normally, Ixora's presence blunted his conscience to the point of rendering it inoperable. Tonight, fear of discovery returned feelings of shame. As she lay back against his chest, lost to the music, his anxiety increased by the minute. She had no idea of the strain being placed on his marriage, and why should she? Hadn't he been the one encouraging the affair from the start? Adulterers usually returned to their wives. He wondered if Helen had already begun to grow suspicious.

Behind them, a group of picnickers laughed softly in the dark. He jerked his head around and stared after them, trying to recognise the faces.

'God, you're tense,' said Ixora. 'Try to enjoy the music. This is one of my favourite places. Why don't you open the wine?' He emptied the contents of the carrier bag they had brought.

'There's no corkscrew.'

'Damn, I'm sorry — it's in the glove-box.'

'I'll go back for it.' He raised her head from his chest.

'Ask someone here for one,' said Ixora. 'You can't go all the way back. You'll never find me again.'

'I'll only be a minute, I promise.' He rose to his feet and climbed awkwardly back through the tangle of arms and legs. The walk back through the park failed to reduce the feeling that something was wrong.

As he approached the car, he was shocked to find it in the process of being broken into.

'Hey, what are you doing?' He broke into a run as the figure rose from the door and started off along the pavement. As the running man passed beneath a street light he caught a glimpse of the now familiar goatee beard. He remembered the knife slashing his arm in the corridors of the BBC and warily slowed to a walk. To his surprise the figure slowed too, catching his breath against a low garden wall.

'I just want to talk to you,' called John. On the occasion of their previous meeting, he sensed that the man had struck at him in panic rather than anger. He took a step forward, unsure which of them should be the more frightened. The figure remained immobile, breathing hard. Behind them, the distant sound of the orchestra filtered through the trees.

'Just tell me who you are. Why can't you leave us alone?'

'I wish I could, but it's not as simple as that.'

'What do you mean?'

The figure pushed away from the wall and turned to face him. John could see now that he was much older than he had at first thought. 'I'm Ixora's husband.'

'You're crazy. She isn't married.'

'I'm sorry to disillusion you. Her name isn't De Corizo any more, it's Saunders. If you don't believe me, look inside the bag she always carries with her. I think you'll find the marriage certificate in one of the zipped pockets.'

'Is that what you were doing at the car? Trying to take something from her bag? What the hell do you think gives you the right?'

'I have every right! Take a look at the certificate. It's the only way you'll ever believe me. There's no point in asking her about it, she'll deny everything. Read what it says on the licence, then call me. I'm in the book.'

'Why should I?'

'Because if you don't, Mr Chapel, you could well be the next one to die.'

John glanced over his shoulder at the Volvo. By the time he turned back, the figure had vanished into the gathering autumn mist.

He ran to the car, fumbled the key into the lock, and pulled Ixora's black leather bag from beneath the passenger seat. He found the usual contents — lipstick, compact, tissues — and there in the zipped side pocket, a square brown envelope. Opening the glove compartment and turning on its small map-light, he pulled the hammered vellum sheet from its sleeve. The certificate documented the union between Anthony James Saunders and Ixora Seraphine Baptiste De Corizo. It had been issued in the city of Bristol three years ago. He pulled a pencil stub from the glove-box and scrawled Saunders' home address on the inside of his cigarette packet. The corners of the certificate caught and folded as he shoved it back into the envelope. It was pointless to confront her immediately; she would only lie to him, just as she had in the past.

He would take her home after the concert, then arrange to visit Saunders. If he really was who he said he was, why would he behave so erratically, first attacking John, then trying to warn him? It seemed that everyone who touched Ixora's life started acting crazy. As he walked back beneath the sheltering trees, John grew determined to confront his suspicions and understand what kind of woman Ixora De Corizo really was.

CHAPTER
20
Discovery

The medieval city of Bristol lay at the confluence of two rivers, the Lower Avon and the Frome. Long ago its docks had prospered on the trade of tobacco, molasses and cocoa; its Royalists had defended their stronghold in England's civil war. Now, after the massive destruction wreaked by the bombing in the Second World War, there was precious little left to reflect its origin. Tired of watching the endless grey concrete walls sweeping by the train window, John returned his attention to the address in his hand. He had spoken to Saunders this morning, had agreed to meet him on neutral public ground, a small area of parkland near the Clifton Gorge suspension bridge.

Saunders had refused to divulge much further information on the telephone beyond the fact that he kept a flat in London, and that he had been following Ixora for some time. He had also insisted that John would have to come to Bristol before any further explanation would be offered. Luckily, *Playing With Fire* had now entered its post-production phase, and he was able to get away.

Saunders arrived late. He came running across the dry grass as if he was frightened that John had decided not to wait for him. He was wrapped in a filthy grey raincoat, its belt knotted untidily at the waist. Beads of sweat glistened on his face, as if he was sickening. Wary of their purpose in meeting at all, the two men remained several yards apart from one another.

'Stay where you are,' called Saunders. 'Just answer my questions, yes or no. I want to know what Ixora has told you. Do you understand?'

'Yes.'

'When you met her, did she tell you that she was single?'

'Yes.'

'*Lie.* Did she say she was a virgin?'

John took a step forward. 'She didn't say anything about that, and I don't think—'

'Shut up.' Something gleamed in Saunders' hand. John became aware that he was holding a gun, training the thing at his face. He had never seen a real firearm before. The effect was more disturbing than he had imagined.

'She told you her background was, what — French?'

'Spanish.'

'*Lie.* She said that her father was killed in a car crash?'

'Yes.'

'*Lie.* She told you she's twenty-four?'

'Yes.'

'*Lie.* She loves you, wants your respect, but above all, wants you to trust her?'

'Yes.'

'*Lie, lie, lie!* You've really fallen for it, haven't you? You're married, of course.'

'Yes.'

'Why is it that after a certain time, a married man will believe anything he is told by a beautiful girl?'

'This is different, I was working with her, I had no intention of getting involved …'

'Be quiet. There's nothing more revolting than hearing other people's excuses for their lack of moral fibre.' He slowly paced around John, the gun held between his hands. 'I'm not so sure now that you're even worth saving. Smarmy expense-account media wideboys like you are two a penny. Who would miss you?'

'My wife and child.'

'You should have thought about them earlier. Now, of course, you're in it up to your neck.' And over my head, thought John. So many crazy people were suddenly populating his life that it was starting to feel normal.

'You'd better listen to me carefully,' said Saunders, walking closer. 'Whatever happens, Ixora must never marry again. I am a doctor. I have a private practice here in Bristol, and I spend three days a week in my London consulting rooms. Three years ago I took a vacation in Florida. I met Ixora there. We quickly fell in love, and after an idyllic two weeks together, we returned to England to be married in a registry office. If that surprises you, consider that I was then forty-four years old, lonely after a disastrous divorce, and Ixora was like a dream come true.' He stopped pacing and rested with his back against a tree. 'She was the personification of all my desires, charming and beautiful, full of life. But most of all she loved me, or so I thought. It took me a while to realise the truth.'

'Which is?' asked John wearily. He was getting sick of being a captive audience for everyone's crackpot opinions about Ixora.

'She is — unwell. Unbalanced. Mentally ill, if you like, suffering from paranoid delusions. She believes all men to be her enemies, that they will all eventually try to harm her. She thinks she's being persecuted by someone, a representation of all her inner fears.' Saunders' choice of words made John wonder if he was a psychiatrist. 'She is liable to hurt herself, and those around her — especially those who are closest to her. You've seen what happens when men succumb to her charms. The boyfriend, the photographer before him. She should really be put away in some place where she can't harm anyone.'

'Wait a minute,' shouted John, his anger growing steadily. 'It seems to me that it's the men around her who cause all the damage. Christ, you're the one who tried to stab me!'

'I didn't want to hurt you. The knife was for protection. I was just trying to warn you away.'

'Are the two of you still legally married?'

'No. Ixora and I were a divorced over a year ago.'

'Then why the hell are you still hanging around her?'

'I try to watch over her. Don't you see, I'm compelled to ensure that she causes no harm to herself, or to others.'

'Are you telling me that she's a murderess?'

'I didn't say that. She — causes bad things to happen.'

Suddenly the source of the problem became obvious. 'You're still in love with her, aren't you?' said John, removing his hands from his pockets and taking a step forward.

'No! That's not true.'

'Yes you are, she left you, and you couldn't handle it. You still can't accept that she's gone. So you hang around, spying on her, trying to screw up her chance of a life with anyone else. That's it, isn't it?'

'No — I just want people to stay away. God, I realise how that must sound—'

'Do you honestly think she'll take you back? No wonder she hasn't said anything to me. I can imagine how embarrassed she must be about the whole thing.'

'No!'

'I'm going now, Saunders.' John took a step back. 'If I see you hanging around again, I'll have you thrown in gaol.'

'No!'

He saw the recoil from the pistol before he heard the retort. A chunk of bark exploded from the tree trunk beside his head. He darted around the oak and ran as hard as he could down the grassy slope towards the bridge. A second shot echoed across the gorge, then a third, the air parting sharply above his head. He refused to stop, and did not look back until he had reached the busy roadway far below. When he finally turned around, Saunders was nowhere to be seen.

John was not a superstitious man, but he was forced to concede that some people attracted bad luck. Ixora seemed to be a magnet for madmen and murderers; as if she gave off some kind of electric signal that only reached those with irregular brain patterns, drawing them to her.

Perhaps he should include himself in that lineup. After all, he was doing things he had never done before in his life. He'd undergone a transformation from suburban man to lead player in a *noir* thriller. And if he was honest with himself, there was even an attraction to it. At home Helen waited, faithful and constant, a determined homemaker in a world of kids and casseroles, a world he no longer felt a part of. Out here, Ixora beckoned to a realm of dark, deceitful luxury, where risks were taken for high rewards. Didn't the most tender fruit always hang from the highest branches?

Now more than ever, he felt that Ixora was worth each new risk. When he thought of her, the image of Helen receded in his mind. It was not until he reached the station that his pulse returned to normal, and he could not be sure if its pace was due to the woman or the gun.

There was still the question of Ixora's 'marriage'. Although he understood her reasons for concealing it, the subject had to be faced. How could they continue with these lovesick men lurking around every corner? The good doctor was dangerous, to himself as well as others. He began to wonder how many more he had yet to meet.

John checked his watch as the train arrived at Paddington. Howard would be pissed off with him, disappearing without any warning. Perhaps it was best not to go in at all today. He rang Ixora from the station concourse and waited for the answering machine to kick in, then remembered that she was dubbing her lines today at the De Lane Lea sound studios in Soho.

He caught her just as she was leaving on her lunchbreak. She looked relaxed and refreshed, with a casual eloquence of style that reaffirmed her beauty with every movement. She told her friends she would see them in an hour and, slipping her arm in his, walked with him into Old Compton Street. They succeeded in usurping one of the small wicker tables at the front of the Soho Brasserie and ordered a freezing bottle of Chardonnay.

'Well,' asked Ixora, pleasantly surprised, 'to what do I owe this unexpected pleasure?'

'I've just been shot at by your ex-husband.'

Her face fell. 'What are you talking about?'

'Does the name Saunders ring a bell? The bearded man who's been following us everywhere? Sorry, just to clarify things, this is not the one who turned up skewered on the Buckingham Palace railings, this is the other one, the one you swore you'd never seen before in your life. The one who stabbed me in the arm, remember?'

'I was frightened that something like this would happen. John, he's not my ex-husband. He's not anything. He's — I don't know what, crazy or something—'

'Give me a break, Ixora. I've seen the marriage certif-icate. It's in your handbag.'

Her eyes studied his for a moment. 'Then you'll also have seen the envelope it came in.' She pulled the bag to her lap and fumbled angrily inside it. 'If you take a look at the postmark you'll see it was sent to me just two weeks ago.' She pulled the envelope from its pocket and slapped it onto the table. The frank-mark was issued with a recent date. 'It's his idea of a bizarre joke. Oh, you should have seen the letter that came with it! He's sending me the certificate to show how our love can be legitimised in the eyes of God. He's worshipped me from afar but could never reveal his love. He's my protector, he's been put on the Lord's good earth to ensure that I come to no harm, I'm the living personification of all his dreams, pages and pages of bullshit.'

'Do you still have it?'

'No, I threw it away. I kept the certificate because it was too crazy to part with. I was planning to show it to you when I had this all sorted out.'

'What do you mean?'

'I've been to the police about it, John.'

'Christ, why didn't you tell me?'

'Because I wanted to do something about it myself. I don't want you running around screening my callers, acting the PR agent in our private life as well! You have enough of your own problems. I wanted to do it myself. I didn't think it would backfire like this. I take it he missed?'

John smiled. 'He missed.'

'He was probably using airgun pellets. That's what these people usually do.'

'I don't think so. His first shot killed a tree.'

'Then the police will pick him up, won't they?'

'If I tell them.'

'Why wouldn't you?'

'I've seen enough of PC Plod already. Anyway, I'm not too sure what to believe right now. I know you're still not being completely honest with me. Saunders knew too much about you, Ixora.'

'I guess he's done some research. He hangs around outside my house, remember?'

'He also says you lie to me all the time.'

'For God's sake.' She rested her knuckles on her hips, exasperated. 'Let's get this over with. What sort of lies do I tell you?'

'About your background. He says you met in Florida three years ago ...'

'That's ridiculous. Three years ago I was living in Barcelona. John, this has gone far enough, all right?'

'I'm just trying to get things clear in my own mind. If he's made all this up, if he's living out some kind of fantasy ...'

'Look around you, people do it all the time.'

'... then how did he know that I'd find the licence in your handbag?'

'I can't remember when I put it there, but I suppose he saw me do it.'

'I want to believe you, Ixora.'

She rose from the table and slipped her jacket back over her shoulders. 'No, John, I'm not so sure you do. I think perhaps you're ready to go back to your family for a while. Subconsciously you want to return to your wife and your son, and you're looking for an easy way out. You want to stop believing in me so you can leave behind a clean slate.' She tilted her head back and lowered her sunglasses. 'If that's true, then you'd better tell me now, John, because I'm in this deep even if you aren't.'

'You're wrong, I'm with you all the way. I just have to be sure.'

'You can't say that, that's the woman's line. Besides,

nobody's ever sure about anyone in this situation. The wives occupy the moral high ground, the mistresses wait and cry, the men stall both parties because they want the best of everything. Triangles consist of one indecisive man and two decisive women. It's all guilt and recrimination, and nobody mentions love.' As they left the restaurant she darted a Kleenex beneath her shades. 'Well, I'm mentioning it. I love you, John. I love you. If you want me to wait, that's what I'll do, I'll wait. But there finally comes a time when you have to commit yourself fully. Saying that you love someone isn't enough. There has to be total trust on both sides. It's like teaching someone to swim, the moment when you take your hands away. You say you love me, but you've got to trust me with all your heart before you get it all back. Remember that.' She turned and smiled. 'All your heart.'

'All my heart, huh?' He took her hand and led her across the sunlit road. 'You're going to be late for your dubbing session.'

'No I'm not.' She checked her watch. 'I still have plenty of time.'

'Not if I have anything to do with it.'

They made love in the top floor suite of Hazlitt's Hotel in Frith Street, with the windows wide open and the soft pale yellow curtains billowing to admit the clattering of restaurant kitchens, the honking of the traffic, snatches of music and the conversation of friends meeting outside pubs and winebars, an unending torrent of street noise. And all around them the dazzling sunlight fell, casting a golden radiance across Ixora's pale body and filling the air with shimmering atoms of dust. It felt so good to be touching her away from the deadening, mildewed gloom of the house in Sloane Crescent. He lay down with his head against Ixora's breast and listened. Below, the air was acrid with shouts and traffic fumes, the sheer weight of humanity making itself heard, and he felt a thrill to be at the centre of so much life, to be able to share it with such an extraordinary woman. He prayed that the moment would never end.

But it did, and they dressed in comfortable silence, and left the hotel like illicit lovers, which Ixora pointed out was exactly what they were.

She returned to the dubbing studio an hour and a half late. He decided to delay Howard's wrath until the next day, and headed home to Waterloo.

Today the bridge seemed broader and even more sunwashed than ever before, but as he boarded the train his euphoric mood began to dissipate, so that by the time he reached Richmond he felt wretched. He wanted to be there with Ixora when she undressed for bed and when she sleepily awoke in the morning. He wanted to know what clothes she chose from the wardrobe, what she prepared for breakfast. He was frightened that Helen would ask him something so trivial and ordinary that for a moment he would forget himself and reply with some damning blunder.

More than that, he almost wished he would.

Helen was in the garden when he arrived, bringing in the last of the washing. She proffered a cheek as he passed, passively received the peck and moved on to the ironing board. She was wearing baggy jeans and an old check shirt of his with the tail hanging out. An Australian soap opera shrilled from the portable TV on the kitchen counter.

'How come you're home so early?' she called into the corridor.

'My meeting with Howard was cancelled. Is the water hot?'

'Should be hot enough for a shower, if that's what you want.'

'You read my mind.' John kicked his shoes beneath the bed and unbuttoned his shirt.

'Give me your trousers.' She appeared at the door with a red plastic washbasket in her arms.

'They're fine.'

'They're creased. Put them on top.' She laid them across the top of the basket and followed him to the bathroom.

'Where's Josh?'

'Over at Cesar's. He's staying there the night.'

'Is that a good idea? You know how nuts they are together.' He turned on the shower taps and adjusted the water.

'I said he could.'

He had showered at the hotel, but showered again for safety, lathering his chest so that he smelled of a familiar brand of soap. Afterwards he towelled himself dry, gelled his hair and pulled on his old grey sweatshirt and jeans, walking barefoot into the lounge. Helen was sitting in the centre of the sofa, patiently unwinding a tangle of wool.

'Dinner won't be ready for hours,' she said. 'If you had called, I could have put it on earlier.'

'Don't worry. I'm not hungry yet. I've got plenty of work to do, anyway.' He seated himself at the dining table and placed his briefcase before him. He was surprised to find it unlocked. He must have forgotten to lock it at the hotel.

'Tell me something I'm interested to know,' said Helen.

'Sure, what?'

'Did you have a good time today?'

'In what way?'

'At the hotel.'

His stomach dropped. He ran a hand through his hair, trying to think, trying to sound casual. 'I'm — not with you.'

'I'm aware that it's me you're not with. Who is she, John?'

'Who is who?'

'For God's sake, John, the woman you're having an affair with! Is she a client of yours?'

'I don't know what—'

'Don't lie to me, John. I may be many things, but I'm not a complete fool. I've known for long enough. Each day brings new outrages. Just don't insult my intelligence by denying it.' His stomach was churning. It was hard to think above the pounding in his chest.

'Today, for example. Howard called for you this morning. He wanted to know where you were. I told him I had no idea. This afternoon you left the hotel Visa slip in your back trouser pocket. I even listened on the extension when you took a call from her the other day.' She concentrated on unwinding the wool in her lap. 'What offends me most is that you're not even trying to hide it. Either that, or you're hopeless at having an affair.'

'I haven't been able to make any sense of what's happening to me,' he replied, turning slowly to face her. 'If I had known how I felt, I think I would have tried to talk to you.'

'Well, we're talking now.'

'How did you —'

'— find out in the first place? I don't really want to give you the satisfaction of knowing. And I'm not going to ask why you did it. It's obvious. Christ, it's all the women's magazines ever talk about. You gave up the chance to be someone because I got pregnant before you'd left school. Then I made it worse by admitting that I'd done it deliberately, because I wanted you and I wanted us to have a baby.' She threw aside the wool and rose from the sofa. 'A decade or so down the line I've turned into some kind of sitcom housewife and you've hit menopause ahead of schedule. We're a case history, you and I. What would the magazines say about that? They'd say I'm to blame, and they may even be right. But you know, John, it didn't have to be like this. It's this because you chose it.' She wiped her cheek with the back of her hand, trying hard not to cry. 'I've already told Josh. He's staying at Cesar's because he wants to be away from you. I think for both our sakes you'd better make other accommodation arrangements until we get this sorted out, don't you?'

'Why are you being so damned sensible?'

She turned at the door, her eyes filled with cold fury. 'Because somebody has to be, John, and it's certainly not going to be you. Not while this damned woman has you bewitched.' She shook her head, as if trying to awaken from a dream. 'I must say, your sense of timing is really terrible. And once again, so is mine.'

'Why?' he asked.

'Because, my love,' she replied, resting her hand on the front of her shirt, 'I'm ten weeks pregnant.'

That night, as the landscape darkened beneath banks of rolling cloud, the continental breezes which had held them in a pocket of late summer warmth suddenly died away, and the first frosted winds of autumn swept in across the city.

AUTUMN

CHAPTER
21
Departure

The first serious storm of the season broke in the scudding sky above them just as John was unloading the last of the boxes from his car. Balancing the bulging cardboard carton on one knee he tried to kick the gate open with his boot, but the heavy rusty springs set behind the stile made it impossible. He wondered where Ixora could have gone. She had been under his feet just a minute ago. A brilliant flash of lightning illuminated the house, transforming it into a shuttered stage set.

'Ixora,' he called, 'come and give me a hand!' He could see the open front door and the empty darkened hallway beyond, but there was no sign of her. Reluctantly returning the carton to the car seat he ran back into the house. Why did she never put the lights on? He walked to the foot of the stairs and called up. 'Ixora, everything's getting soaked. Darling, where are you?' Thunder broke with a bang, rattling the windows. The lights were off in the kitchen. He tried the switch. There was something wrong with the house's electrical system. None of the lights seemed to work with any regularity.

'Ixora, where on earth are you?' With the next flash of lightning came a feline cry. He turned on his heel to find her curled against the wall, hands clawed over her terrified eyes. He knelt down beside her, his touch bringing a fresh whimper of fear. 'Hey, come on, it's only a storm, high up in the sky. It can't hurt you.'

'God is angry at losing his angel.' She looked at him with uncomprehending eyes. 'Papa?'

'It's me, Ixora.' He folded his arms across her shoulders. 'Don't be frightened. I'll look after you.'

'Papa. Don't let it happen. Please don't let it happen.' Her hands clutched at her face.

'Nothing can harm you. Come with me, I'll take you—'

'No!' She grabbed at his hand as he rose. 'Stay with me!'

And so they remained, huddled beneath the stairs in the darkened house, while the rain filtered through the trees, drenching the seats through the open car door, pooling into the hallway and soaking the unpacked boxes which stood on the flooded tiles. Later, as they lay in bed listening to the rain, John wondered how their new life together would ever work.

It was impossible to see truly inside Ixora's mind. There were parts she simply closed off to the outside world, so many things for which she had no explanation. The map of her heart contained shaded areas of misinformation, territory forbidden to all who would pass. At night she fell asleep as quickly as a cat. By day she was shepherded between studios, dubbing dialogue for the last film, attending auditions for the next.

Two weeks after Helen had asked him to move out of

their home, Ixora suggested that he share the Chelsea house with her. It was too big for her to look after alone, and it would save him the expense of renting a flat. For two miserable weeks while he decided what to do he had stayed on at the house in Richmond, sleeping in a child's bed in the spare room, watching as Helen stepped silently aside to let him pass on the stairs.

Josh refused to meet, speak or have anything to do with him, and spent all of his spare time at the homes of his schoolfriends. It was tempting to think that Helen had turned him against his father, but John doubted this was the case. In one of the few curt notes he had received at the office, Helen had informed him that Josh's school grades were suffering because of his home situation. In a custody battle she would naturally be awarded the boy. He missed Josh terribly, but knew there was no way of winning back his affections at the moment. He was strong-willed and independent, with a cynical attitude that prevented him from relying much on either parent. In John's one brief conversation with his son, it seemed that the boy was trying to come to terms with the separation in his own way, and would eventually be prepared to discuss his feelings.

Helen had barely been present at the house while he had been deciding where to go, preferring to pay extended visits to her neighbour until he was gone. Finally, he had decided to move in with Ixora.

On the advice of friends, Helen had hired the services of a tough young lawyer with feminist leanings. The proceedings would not be pleasant. As Ixora's budding career could not allow her to be named as co-respondent, an excuse would have to be manufactured. Helen was proving as efficient at handling the paperwork as she had been at organising the house, or her book-keeping department at the store. She had set about it with a cool intensity that she applied to every job she undertook. He had to admire her lack of emotional hysteria. It was as if she had been waiting for something like this to happen.

When he had first informed Ixora of his wife's discovery, she had offered to disappear from his life, allowing him one last chance to return home. They had both known the answer to that one before she had finished her little speech. Still, they were careful to tell no one of their relationship, for fear of how it would affect the meticulous creation of Ixora's public image.

And good times followed, as they gradually dismantled their doubts about each other.

A freezing weekend in Devon was spent trudging across frost-flecked moors.

Ixora arranged a dinner party during which it was revealed that a) she could create a mean Shrimp Creole, and b) she had friends of her own, although they were people she had mostly met on modelling assignments.

Farley Dell successfully negotiated a development contract for another movie and threw a party to celebrate, during the course of which he drunkenly promised Ixora the leading role. It later transpired that he had done this with everyone.

The seed John had planted in journalists' minds bore fruit: Scott Tyron appeared on magazine covers billed as the new Tom Cruise. And Ixora taught him to read poetry, something he began doing for her sake and actually ended up enjoying.

There were no further sightings of Ixora's 'guardian', and John began to assume that he had frightened the doctor away for good. Only a handful of nagging doubts remained, locked at the back of his mind — and these soon seemed hazy and foolish.

At night he lay by her side beneath the golden quilt and watched the rainwashed moon dance on the ceiling, and anything seemed possible. His bridges were burned. His marriage was over. His life was moving from its solid, grey bedrock on to shimmering, shifting ground. It was an exciting, terrifying prospect.

CHAPTER
22
Sullivan

Sergeant Sullivan looked at the wristwatch his girlfriend had given him and checked it against the clock on the wall. The damned thing was slow again. He slipped it from his wrist and wound the minute hand forward. He knew that he would have to run against established procedure in order to continue now. He also knew that if he waited any longer for the appropriate clearances, he would run the risk of allowing his suspect to strike again. It was a classic procedural problem. The main elements of his theory were now in place. He felt that he was ready to apprehend the murderer of Brady, Feldman and Dominguez. He was sure that he knew the identity of the killer, and the name of his next victim. He had compiled a file of largely circumstantial evidence, but needed a clincher, something cast iron that would carry a conviction. And he knew that

Hargreave would never have agreed with his working methods.

Serious crimes investigations were a matter of team-work, in order to reduce the possibility of personal error. Sullivan was aware that he had already omitted information from his report that could lead others to the same conclusions he had reached. But what else could he do? Time was slipping by, and with each passing day the trail cooled a little more.

He folded together the last of the computer printouts and slipped them into a ziploc file bag. He had reached a decision. After the arrest had been made he would be able to justify his actions. The evidence he had provided in his report had been deemed too conjectural for the issuing of a search warrant. He would act alone, but he would take care to provide himself with an escape clause. Locking up his desk, he headed across the hall to Sergeant Long-bright's office.

Janice Longbright was a woman to be feared and worshipped in equal portions. Her tenacity and commit-ment to the force were exemplary, and her strange beauty had long ago captivated most members of staff. With her waved auburn hair and red lipstick, she looked like some half-remembered postwar British starlet. As well as being ambitious and independent she was having an affair with Ian Hargreave, which made her a dangerous confidante. She and Sullivan were virtually the same age, and had trained together. He knew he could rely on her.

'Michael, come in. I never see you any more.' She waved him to a seat and indicated the untidy stack of reports on her desk. 'I've been bogged down with casework. We've got muggers snatching briefcases by drawing a knife across the inside of the victim's wrist. Three people in intensive care so far. Apart from that, everyone else is tied up with this extraordinary business at the Savoy. Bodies turning up all over the place, and a bunch of amateur witches helping with the investigation. The press is having a field day. How are you?'

'I was wondering if you'd do me a favour. I was supposed to be meeting one of the pathology doctors here, but he's had to go out. If anyone calls for him, could you tell them where he'll be?' He had decided that it was not safe to tell her the rest of his plan.

'Certainly,' said Longbright. Sullivan handed her a page of instructions.

'It's important,' he explained. 'Just read the caller what's on the paper. I'd rather trust you with it.'

'No problem. But don't be such a stranger in future.' As she watched him leave, a look of mild puzzlement clouded her face.

Saunders' London flat was located in one of the post-modern Docklands developments below the East End's Commercial Road. Its buildings were earmarked by the kind of architectural appendages that seemed solely designed for attractive brochure photography. Saunders' block was flanked with attenuated brick turrets, each peaked with a red wooden globe atop a large blue triangle. It was a look which, in the two years since its creation, had already begun to date horribly.

Sullivan climbed the steps and buzzed the video entry-phone. He knew there would be no reply. Saunders was attending a meeting at the London Clinic, and would be there until lunchtime. It was a simple matter for the sergeant to arrange entry to the block of flats with the security officer, who resided on the ground floor in an office the size of a large broom cupboard. He knew that it would take much more persuasion for the young man to turn off the alarm system and provide him with a pass key. After flashing the appropriate credentials he explained that the doctor was helping the police in a confidential matter concerning missing drugs.

'I'll have to call Dr Saunders before I let you in,' said the guard, reaching for his telephone book.

'You won't find him at the clinic today,' said Sullivan casually. 'He'll be at the station helping us, or may already have left to come here. Try this number.' He passed over a slip of paper with Janice Longbright's extension printed on it. The guard dutifully rang, explained and listened. At length he was satisfied and replaced the receiver. 'She says he just left and is on his way back, and that he left instructions to admit you.'

'Quite right,' said Sullivan. 'When you're helping with police work, every minute may count.' Convinced, the guard relented and produced his keys.

Together they rode to the fourth floor of the building and walked through the pastel hues of a heavily carpeted corridor to the doctor's flat.

'I should come in with you,' said the guard, eager to watch.

'I'm afraid that's not possible,' said Sullivan. 'Reasons of security. I'm sure you, of all people, understand that.' He gave a conspiratorial wink. 'You can wait for me at the lift if you like.'

Three rooms — kitchen, lounge, bedroom — adjoined each other, unimaginatively decorated in corporate shades. The south-facing windows had a view of the sluggish grey river. The lounge had been turned into a consulting room, with a Victorian writing desk and seating units fitted against the far walls. Saunders had a degree in psychiatry, but he was breaking the law by using residential property for the transaction of business.

He found the first corroboration of his suspicions in the small white-tiled bathroom beyond the bedroom. The pervading citrus smell of aftershave, the same smell that had saturated Brady's apartment and Feldman's studio. Unfortunately, there was no solid proof of this beyond his own memory of the previous crime scenes. But now, more than ever, he was convinced that his theory was correct.

Raymond Land had provided him with links between the first and the second murder. Sullivan himself had discovered a number of factors joining the second and third. Again, there was the ferocity of the attack. Again, the appearance of nail-marks on the arms. The unident-ified metallic slivers that had been discovered by the bodies of both Brady and Feldman were also present on Dominguez's clothes.

But then had come the break. The photographer's clients had reappeared as acquaintances of Dominguez. The model, De Corizo, had briefly dated him. The model's PR man, Chapel, had been visited by him — and a new character appeared behind the scenes. Dr Anthony Saunders.

The De Corizo woman had reported him as some kind of sex pest who had taken to following her at night. Further investigation had revealed what the model had naïvely neglected to tell him: that Saunders was in fact her former husband. A file search had turned up the registra-tion of the marriage in Bristol three years ago. Divorce had been filed and granted two years later.

That explained other anomalies. One, no forcible entry to property; the doctor could have gained admittance by identifying himself as De Corizo's ex-husband. Two, the ferocity of the attacks; a routine check on Saunders had revealed that he himself had been previously institution-alised for mental disturbance. Sullivan had been surprised to find that this was not at all uncommon in the world of professional psychiatrists. The doctor had suffered a temporary mental collapse and subsequent bouts of violent behaviour. He had confided to friends that this state had been caused by the stress of his 'divorce'.

Sullivan opened the bathroom cabinets and checked beneath the sink, smiling at the neatness of his theory. The model is unwittingly photographed in racy poses by the photographer. The photographer dies. The model is pestered and injured by an old flame. The old flame dies. Finally, he possessed what he had been missing all along — a motive. Insane jealousy.

Obsessed with Ixora, furious because he cannot have her for himself, Saunders attacks and kills all those who would try for her hand. At least, it was a motive for two of the murders. The only evidence of the doctor's involvement in Vincent Brady's death was a dubious testimony drawn from a tobacconist opposite Brady's flat, who had seen someone who approximated Saunders in appearance leaving the crime scene around the estimated time of the young barman's murder.

Circumstantially the evidence was strong. But as yet, it was still not enough. Sullivan returned to the lounge and sat at the desk, trying each of the drawers in turn. He uncovered medical reports, pharmaceutical mailers, invoices, business letters. There had to be something more here, something that would condemn the man.

Then he saw them — the same tiny scraps of red paint, clustered around the handle of the bottom desk drawer. Withdrawing a small polythene bag, he carefully flicked them away from the handle with the blade of his penknife. Bingo — a forensic connection. Returning the bag to his pocket, he continued the search with renewed vigour. In the tie-drawer of Saunders' bedroom wardrobe he discovered a large crucifix, and a leather-bound Bible, marked off at several pages. A link with the religious artefacts removed from the victims, albeit a tenuous one.

At the base of the wardrobe, buried beneath pairs of shoes, he discovered a large cardboard carton. He pulled it towards him and removed the lid. Press clippings and photographs of his ex-wife, dozens of them, certainly enough to prove a case of obsessive love. This was getting better all the time. Sullivan smiled to himself. He was on a roll.

What else? Doctors always kept appointment books. He returned to the consulting room and searched the desk top. Odd that there was a jar filled with pens, but no notepad or diary. He walked to the window and checked the book-filled ledge beneath the curtains. Nothing much there. Four floors below, walking briskly across the main concourse, Saunders was returning to his flat.

'Shit!' Sullivan registered the figure and darted behind the curtains. He looked back into the room, wondering how much time he had left. In the centre of the desk, above the leg space, was a thin drawer he had overlooked. He rattled it a few times, but it was locked tight. Kneeling beside it and inserting a length of straightened clockspring into the hasp, he used the flexiblade on his pen knife to push the latch back long enough to spring open the drawer. There they were — notepad and business diary. Outside, the lift began to whine as someone summoned it. Sullivan threw open the appointment book and checked the date. Three patients were listed for the afternoon, nothing after 4.00 p.m., then — red felt-tip lettering, scrawled across the evening portion. A single word. TONIGHT.

Sullivan drew a breath. He felt as if he'd hit the jackpot. No time or place mentioned. How would he find out Saunders' plans? Outside, the sound of the lift had changed in pitch, prior to arriving at the floor. Sullivan threw the diary back in the drawer and glanced at the notepad. The top page was covered in scrawls and doodles. He tore it free, stuffed it in his pocket and returned the pad, slamming the drawer and locking it.

The lift doors had opened.

Saunders must have stopped to speak with the security man. Sullivan looked for another way out. If he was found now, everything would be ruined. Where could he go? He ran to the bedroom and yanked open the window just as Saunders and the guard entered the flat.

The ledge outside was wide enough to stand on, but only just. He pulled the window shut behind him and it closed with a click, the lock falling firmly back in place. Great. He was determined not to look down, but it was the first thing he did. He had to move beyond sight of the windows. The further set were separated by a large blue granite sphere. He would have to straddle it to reach the next flat. If only he had kept his promise to lose some weight this year.

Far below, leaves blew across the concourse, piling against the railings which ran beside an inhospitable river Thames. There was nothing for it but to raise his leg and reach across the ball to the far side of the ledge. He had never hated post-modern architecture as much as he did right now. Having achieved a purchase with his right hand and foot, he shifted his body weight across. For a moment it seemed that he would sway back out into the sky and plunge to the river below. Then his left arm and leg followed across and he was safely around the sphere.

He found himself peering into a neat, empty kitchen. The pivoting ventilator window above the counter was fixed with a ratchet lock and held partly open. With a single twist of his hand, he was able to snap the flimsy butterfly screw holding it in place. The frame wasn't large enough to climb through, but it allowed him to reach down and unlock the main window. In less than a minute he was standing on the counter of the kitchen, noting the half-empty bowl of muesli and coffee cup, spoor of the single city executive.

He listened at the adjoining wall. Saunders sounded royally pissed off. He was shouting at the security officer for losing his man. While he waited for an all-clear, he unscrewed the notepaper from his pocket and examined it.

The sheet was covered with drawings of Ixora, clothed and naked. Saunders really had it bad. Sullivan was about to fold the paper up again when he noted the tilted writing in the corner. Today's date, then a hastily scrawled rendezvous. *Midnight — Hungerford Bridge*. As soon as he was out of here, he would return to Forensics and try to get a match on the red shavings in his pocket. Then he would head for Hungerford Bridge, to lay in wait for Saunders and his intended victim.

CHAPTER
23
Intruder

'There's a letter for you.'

'I don't see how. Nobody knows I'm here.' He took the envelope from Ixora and examined the handwriting. 'It's from Helen. No stamp. She must have delivered it by hand. I wonder how she found out where I was?'

'Perhaps she rang your office and asked.'

'*Nobody* knows I'm here. I wish you'd leave some lights on.'

It was a little after 10.00 p.m. Ixora was standing in the gloomy hallway in her dressing-gown, preparing for bed. 'You know how much I like the dark. What does it say?'

'I rang home and asked for Josh. She wouldn't let me speak to him. She's telling me to stay away from him until we can agree on a divorce settlement.'

'That's not fair. She knows how much you love him.'

'She wants to hurt me back. I can't say I blame her. But she has no right to stop me from seeing my son unless that's what he wants as well.' John folded the letter back into its envelope. 'Don't ever hurt people, Ixora. It's a terrible, cruel pastime.'

'We all damage each other without meaning to.'

'And sometimes we do it deliberately. Let's go to bed.'

Ixora made hot chocolate and they drank it at the kitchen table, listening to the wind and rain batting against the leadlight windows. Finally, they doused the few lights and climbed the hall staircase. John slipped his arm around Ixora's narrow waist, guiding her ahead of him.

With the heavily brocaded drapes that she had relined and hung around the gilded four-poster bed, their bedroom had taken on the overwrought aspect of a Burne-Jones painting. At least it kept out the chill draughts that geysered through the rattling window-frames at night. The sprawling house needed at least thirty thousand pounds worth of work to be spent across its four floors. Ixora had a small allowance, left to her in perpetuity by her mother, and the rest she made from modelling. The building itself was worth a fortune, but he could well imagine that nothing in the world would ever persuade her to sell it, or indeed to change a single piece of furniture.

As they lay in bed he fulfilled his nightly ritual of watching her face in repose, and wondered what would become of them. Suddenly he felt deathly tired, as if the weight of the world was upon him. This idyllic feeling of romance seemed too much like a temporary state, a schoolboy rite of passage. Although he knew everything about the way she spent her days, he knew nothing of how she really felt, or what she really wanted. For years now, Helen had been an open book. There were no secrets she could keep, no feelings she could not help but show. They had grown too alike across the years. It had stripped away their ability to hide emotions from each other. Ixora was a different case entirely. Almost everything she did seemed to possess a hidden motive. He liked that — for now. But he could sense a time approaching when he would need to understand her better if their relationship was to continue its growth.

'John?' She sleepily pulled the covers from her pale throat.

'Mmmm?'

'You'll never leave me, will you?'

'No. Of course not.'

'And you will learn to trust me?'

'You know I want to.'

She opened her eyes. 'Wanting to isn't enough.'

'I will. In time. You have to tell me more.'

'If I tell you something now, something totally honest, something I've never told anyone, will that help?'

'It depends. Will it help me to understand you?'

'I think so, yes.'

'Then try.'

Ixora pushed herself up in the bed and turned to him. 'I admit that I've lied to you in the past.'

'What about?'

'My father, for a start. I didn't love him. I was terrified of him.' She lay back and studied the ceiling. 'When I was ten years old, we lived for a while in a small village on the coast of Spain, near Barcelona. I loved it there, but, oh, how quickly I came to hate it. On Saturdays, my parents would take me to the sea and we would swim together. Then, one morning, my mother couldn't join us, so my father and I went alone. Once we were in the water, my father — a great, dark man — carried me out, where he would hold me on my stomach with outstretched arms, helping me to stay afloat while I practised my swimming strokes. This particular day, the horizon was dark with an approaching storm, but we went swimming anyway, and he lifted me up to practise my strokes, but his hands — his hands slid over my chest, and his fingertips inside me, and he began to whisper in my ear, terrible things, dreadful evil things.

'I was so shocked that I slipped away into the water and nearly drowned, and as he tried to haul me up I hit him and hit him and screamed at the top of my voice, so he held his hand across my mouth. I couldn't breathe, and might have choked if the lifeguard hadn't seen us and become suspicious. My father dragged me back to shore and we never spoke of the incident again. But from that day on I never let him touch me, not even for a goodnight kiss. I just wanted him to die.

'I think that even now when I'm with a man, it's very hard for me to rid myself of that dreadful, stifling memory. Do you understand?'

'God, Ixora, that's terrible.' John moved closer and slipped his arm behind her head, holding her to him. 'It's not surprising you've had trouble coping with lovers in the past.'

'You know, sometimes I still believe that out there, somewhere, concealed in the dark, there is a man like my father, someone who waits to cause me the worst harm in the world. He waits and waits for the day I make a mistake, then he will take me away into eternal darkness. That is what I fear.'

'You've an overactive imagination, Ixora.' He cradled her head against his chest. 'Go to sleep.'

'Out there in the dark,' she murmured sleepily. 'Lost inside the storm. Waiting for me. Always waiting.'

Moments later she was asleep, the dim light from the streetlamp beyond the windows casting aureoles of light across her eyelids.

*

He woke with a start.

There was someone in the house. A muffled thump from below, somewhere at the foot of the stairs. Ixora's head was still on his chest. Gently, he eased it off on to the pillow and checked his watch. 11.15 p.m. He slid from the sheets, pulled on shorts and a vest, then groped beneath the bed. His hand closed on the torch he kept there as a safeguard against the house's arbitrary lighting system.

The landing was in darkness. He tried the switch beside the bedroom door, but nothing happened. This was a great time for the electrics to play up. He peered ahead, but could see nothing. His head felt heavy and sore, as if he had been drugged. He could hardly hold his eyes open. Perhaps he was still asleep, and dreaming. Reaching out for the banister rail, he switched on the torch and slowly descended the stairs. As he moved the beam, the shadow of the grandfather clock in the hall twisted and grew across the ceiling.

From the corner of his eye he sensed a movement in the dark beneath the stairs. Reaching the bottom step, he turned the beam into the corner, reflecting the sheen of deep mahogany wall panels. He walked further into the hall, shifting the cone of yellow light.

To his left, the hem of the heavy embroidered curtain covering the side door of the house drifted lazily back and forth. He knew that it was there to block the draughts, but as he reached to pull it aside a bout of nervous nausea assailed him. Caught in the torch beam were a pair of eyes, glittering ebony pupils widening in shock. John shouted in surprise and backed up. Behind him a small table fell noisily on to its side as the heavy black shape divorced itself from the doorway and darted past, heading for the stairs.

John spun on his heel and ran back to the banister, his

fist closing on empty air behind the moving figure. Suddenly he thought of Ixora, sleeping above. It was as if the dark man of her dreams had suddenly sprung to life, and was now heading to claim her.

They took the stairs two at a time, John slipping on a carpet-rod and falling heavily, dropping the torch, its beam spinning crazily as it bounced back to the hall. His head spun as he rose to his feet, his mind clouding, tipping the stairs into a vertiginous spiral. He grabbed out at the handrail and hauled himself upright. The form at the head of the stairs had suddenly stopped in its tracks, waiting, its back turned to John.

The climb seemed to take forever. As he looked up, the figure appeared at the end of the tunnel, receding still further. In the next moment he was upon him, and the figure was lashing a long arm at his face, pushing him back. The blow connected. He felt a burst of pain in his eye and cheek. For a moment he was weightless, balancing on the edge of the stair. Then, his arms outstretched, right hand fighting for purchase on the smooth wall, he fell headfirst backwards to the foot of the stairs. His last conscious thought was for Ixora's safety — and his own survival.

CHAPTER
24
Handcuffed

A looping necklace of white lights twisted back and forth between the lampposts of the South Embankment. In the past hour the wind had steadily risen, drawing chill air across the river and spinning the wind-operated neon sculpture which stood atop the Hayward Gallery in ever faster patterns. Sullivan tightened his jacket across his chest as he headed for the bridge. On his left were the illuminated picture windows of the National Film Theatre, to his right, the whipping ripples of the Thames. Hungerford had originally been built as a footbridge across the river in the early 1840s. Now, sandwiched between Waterloo and Westminster, it served the trains leaving Charing Cross Station. On its east side a narrow bridge still operated beside the tracks. Two thirds of the way across from the station a curved observation bay thrust out over the water.

Sullivan could see the figure of a man there, leaning against the railing with his back to the river. He assumed that Saunders was early until he remembered that his own watch was running slow. He quickened his pace as he reached the double flight of steps which led to the walkway. The doctor was alone. His victim had yet to put in an appearance.

Sullivan felt sure that this final act would provide a logical conclusion to the investigation. His reconstruction of the crimes had suffered from one fatal flaw. If Saunders was driven to murder through overwhelming jealousy, why had he not killed his most hated rival for Ixora's affections? Perhaps he had been toying with John Chapel, waiting for the perfect moment to strike. Perhaps Chapel had proven harder to catch unawares. Perhaps the order of the destruction of Ixora's men was random; logic was not the doctor's strong suit. Whatever the reason, Sullivan was convinced that he would now witness the final confrontation between the two men.

He had decided against making contact with John Chapel himself. He knew that he was compromising Chapel's safety by not informing him of his findings, but there was nothing to be gained by warning him that the police would be interrupting their encounter. On the contrary, Chapel might not show up if he thought that the whole affair was about to go public.

As Sullivan left the shadow of the staircase, moving into the illumination of the bridge, he could see Saunders' face clearly set in profile against the riveted steel girders. His fists were clenched at his side, his eyes shut tight. He seemed to be muttering to himself.

Sullivan had not had time to consider how he would approach his man, beyond the procedural duty of making an arrest. Saunders would obviously be armed, and Chapel was probably aware that this encounter could prove dangerous, given his own knowledge of the ongoing murder investigation. Any dialogue that took place between the two of them would be wary, to say the least. The trick would be to get some kind of admission from Saunders prior to his victim's arrival.

Climbing to the top of the stairs, Sullivan knew that he was acting against all orders. He should have arranged for a back-up foot patrol on the bridge, but the request for one would have opened the way for all manner of questions he hadn't the time to answer. His best approach was to be forthright and fast. He wanted to handle this alone. Christ, it was the chance for him to establish his career with one masterstroke. Any disciplinary action taken for failing to follow procedure would be eclipsed by the success of his capture. With this in mind, he strode towards the doctor and laid a firm hand on his shoulder.

'Waiting for someone?'

The figure spun around to face him, his eyes wide in surprise. 'What?'

'I asked if you were waiting for someone.'

Saunders regarded him distractedly then moved away a few feet, staring back at the pathway across the footbridge. There was no one else in sight. A little further along, one of the safety meshes between the railway track and the walkway was missing, and had been temporarily covered with strips of orange plastic that rattled in the wind. Sullivan moved closer. Out of uniform he could have been anyone.

'Listen to me carefully, Saunders. I know what you've been through. You can't stand seeing anyone else touch her. I'm going to give you one last chance to reconsider your actions tonight. Unburden yourself. You can do it.'

Saunders turned back to him, angry now. One hand jumped into his coat pocket. 'Who the fuck are you?'

'Police.'

Suddenly Saunders' hand was out of his pocket and holding a gun. Catching sight of the gleam from the short barrel, Sullivan had time to register the virtual harmlessness of the bore before bringing his knee into Saunders' stomach, doubling him over. He twisted the pistol from his hand and threw it over the railing. Tightening his grip on Saunders' arm, he brought it higher behind his back and hissed into his ear, 'I'm arresting you for attempted murder, and in a moment I'm going to explain your rights. Do you understand?'

'You're crazy!' cried Saunders, trying to squirm free. 'Trust the bloody police to get it all wrong.'

'I know you're waiting here for your ex-wife's lover.'

Saunders thrashed about. 'Let me go, or we'll both end up in trouble.'

Sullivan twisted his arm harder. Something was wrong. He wasn't getting the right response at all. There was a rattling sound on the tracks, as if a train was coming. He looked up but could see nothing.

'Let me go, you bloody fool!' Saunders squirmed in his grip. The rattling grew louder, but there was no train. A flock of startled pigeons exploded from their nest in the girders.

'I want to hear you say it, Saunders.' Sullivan was starting to panic. He had no idea what to do next. 'Tell me what you're doing here! You're waiting for John Chapel, aren't you?'

Behind them, a dark figure appeared on the side of the tracks, outlined against the girders. Saunders sounded genuinely surprised. 'Chapel? You really *are* crazy. I'm not waiting for Chapel. Now for Christ's sake, let me go. You'll die too if you don't!'

Sullivan loosened his grip. 'Are you threatening me?'

'This is a matter for the church, not the police,' said Saunders derisively. 'You're way out of your depth.'

Sullivan removed one hand and felt inside his jacket, closing fingers around steel. 'I'm taking you in. You'll have plenty of time to explain yourself.' He quickly slipped the handcuff over Saunders' left wrist and snapped it shut, dropping the remaining cuff onto his own arm.

'What the hell are you doing?' screamed Saunders, trying to pull himself free. 'We have to leave the bridge!'

Sullivan braced his legs and kept his ground. 'Why? You have a meeting here arranged for midnight.'

Realisation dawned on Saunders' face. 'You're the idiot who broke into my flat.'

'Your security guard admitted me. I know everything, Saunders. It's all over.'

'Then you know that I came here to surrender.'

'Surrender? What do you mean?'

'Look over there!' Saunders pointed up at the figure on the tracks. There was a muffled explosion, and the air beside the sergeant seemed to split apart. Sullivan turned to find a short steel shaft jutting from Saunders' face. It had entered his open mouth, a clear six inches protruding from the back of his neck. Blood sprayed over the sergeant's chest as his captive became a dead weight and fell to his knees, the cuffs yanking painfully on his wrist. The figure on the tracks was moving forward, stepping across the thrumming railway lines. Pigeons whirled around it like windtossed rags.

The handcuffs bit deep into his wrist as Sullivan pulled at the fallen body beside him. It would barely budge. There was a click and a hiss of compressed air as their pursuer reloaded. Saunders' body was twitching violently as his blood leaked out in dying jets, slicking the walkway. Sullivan painfully hauled the corpse towards him. He had to get off the bridge. He knew he would never be able to get Saunders' body down the steps, but perhaps someone would spot them.

He succeeded in pulling the body to its feet just as the figure fired again. This time the steel shaft clattered uselessly against the iron balustrade of the walkway. It seemed to have come from a crossbow, or a speargun. Saunders' body was lying against him as he tried to manoeuvre it against the protective barrier. He had to hold the body still so that he could reach his keychain. As he released his free hand the corpse rolled down, bursting through the plastic warning straps which covered the missing barrier and falling on to the darkened track, pulling Sullivan back with it.

He looked desperately around but could see no sign of his attacker. They were in a terrible mess. Saunders' corpse was grotesquely splayed across the track, Sullivan's arm trapped beneath it, part of his coat around his shoulders and part wedged under the corpse, the keys to the cuffs in one of the pockets. As he tried to roll the body aside, one of the Charing Cross trains hooted, preparing to leave its platform.

Panic seized him as he tried to haul the body up into a sitting position. The rails pinged as the train began moving toward them. The keys, thought Sullivan, everything depends on getting the keys. Around him, sleepers creaked and girders groaned as they took the weight of the approaching train. His breathing turned into ragged sobs, his hands slickening with blood as he pulled at the loose dead weight of Saunders' body. With little more than a few yards to go, he and the corpse succeeded in righting themselves before the train bore down on them.

Sullivan was clutching the rolling body with both hands, his back and arm muscles screaming in pain as he turned his grisly burden from the railway line and the carriage slammed past in a rush of displaced air.

He would have to let go of Saunders with one hand in order to reach the keys. For all he knew, the keeper of their rendezvous could still be waiting to pick him off. He shoved against the dead weight with his shoulder, pushing it back through the barrier that separated the railway from the footpath.

'Help me!' called Sullivan, but there was no one to hear him. Saunders' body had collapsed to the floor of the walk once more, pulling him over. Stretching his free hand into his coat pocket, he found it empty. The keys had to be in his jacket breast pocket. His hand had just closed around them when he felt the weight beside him suddenly lighten. Turning in alarm, he watched helplessly as Saunders' body was raised and cradled in his murderer's arms. As the head tilted back into a triangle of overhead light, the sergeant was able to see who he had come to meet. His mouth slackened in surprise.

'You have got to be fucking kidding me,' he said finally.

'Sorry, no joke,' came the reply. 'This is deadly serious.' Saunders was released over the side of the bridge.

Sullivan's arm was almost wrenched from its socket as he was dragged halfway over the railing by the falling body. He felt the skin around his left wrist tear open as the corpse dangled from it. The pain was unbelievable, but there was something to frighten him more. His thrashing legs were being lifted to the height of the rail. Seconds later he was upside down and slipping over the balustrade, his cries torn away in the sour wind which howled beneath the bridge. Another train trundled overhead, leaving the illuminated city for the darkness of the urban necropolis, as Sullivan plunged into the icy river water.

The corpse sank faster, as if leading their rapid descent with a will, and Michael Sullivan found himself following his wretched destiny into the filthy blackness of the river below.

CHAPTER
25
Howard

'Wake up, John.'

The shadows of leaves came into focus. He was staring at the ceiling. Morning sun filtered through swaying branches at the bedroom window. He tried to lift his head, but the pounding forced it back to the pillow.

'You banged your head last night,' said Ixora, pressing a cool flannel to his brow. 'You must have slipped on the stairs.'

'No, there was somebody waiting there—'

'I heard you fall. I came down moments later.' She smoothed the gilt counterpane around his body. 'There was no one else.'

'Then he must have managed to get out.'

'The front door was still locked on the inside, John.

Only you and I were in the house. Just lie back and rest. I've called the office to say you'll be in late this morning.'

'Did you speak to Howard?'

'Yes.'

'How was he?'

'You'll find out soon enough,' replied Ixora.

'I was relying on you, John.' Howard swept around the office like a caged animal mapping the limits of its confinement. 'How could you let me down like this? We had Morrison *this* close to signing the whole show over to us, and now this. How could you lose your sense of discretion over something as delicate as this?'

'What's happened?'

'David Glen has been calling to speak to you. Does the name ring a bell? David Glen and the million-dollar screenplay, the same David Glen who's represented by the Morrison Agency? It turns out that he and Scott Tyron — who Glen wants for the lead in his movie — meet up in LA yesterday, and are lunching in Spago or one of those other restaurants where the diners are more interested in power-fucking each other than tasting the food, and Glen mentions that Diana Morrison wants us to handle his deal, to which Tyron says, "Forget it, David, you can't trust those bastards at Dickson-Clarke." And Glen asks, "Why not, Scott?" and Scott replies — and listen carefully, John, 'cause this is the punchline — "They're unprofessional. They fucked up my publicity on *Playing With Fire* by turning me into a Tom Cruise clone, but worse than that, one of them ended up fucking my co-star."' Howard thrust his hand menacingly. 'You want to tell me about this?' Before John had a chance to answer, his intercom buzzed.

'Hold all calls, Jane.'

'It's not a call. It's your son. He's here in reception.'

John's finger jumped on to the talkback switch. 'Don't let him leave. I'll be right there.'

Howard turned in anger. 'Where do you think you're going?' he shouted. 'There's no time left to sort this out.'

'Nor this,' said John, grabbing his jacket from the back of the chair and leaving the room. He supposed it was inevitable that Howard would eventually find out about their affair. He had been warned of the consequences of becoming involved with his clients; Howard had made it plain that such actions constituted grounds for dismissal. But for now, he forced himself to put the problem out of his mind and concentrate on his son.

Josh was standing awkwardly in the steel-and-plexiglass reception area, his hands folded together before him. He looked more adult than John had ever seen him. He'd gained a little weight, and his shoulders seemed squarer, his expression cool and serious. He kept his eyes downcast as they greeted each other. John wanted to hug him, but decided that it would be best to keep his distance until he could gauge the boy's feelings.

'Come on, let's get out of here.' He opened the main door and ushered the boy through, tousling his hair. As his son had initiated the meeting, he forced himself to remain silent, allowing Josh to open the conversation. For the next ten minutes they walked to the Embankment in silence. It had just stopped raining, and the street air was still pleasantly fresh.

'How are you, Dad?' asked the boy finally as they waited to cross the road.

'All right. How is your mother?'

'Driving me crazy.'

'Well, I hope you're looking after her.'

'I try to, but she keeps telling me not to grow up like you. And to stay away from you. She thinks I'm at school today.'

'It was very brave of you to come and see me.'

'I wanted to.' Josh turned to him, his brow furrowed. 'Mum says you're living with her.'

'That's true.'

'So you're not coming back.'

'I don't think your mother would want me back,' he said, sidestepping the question. They wiped off one of the benches overlooking the river and sat, the sun appearing as a pale halo above the clouds.

'She's very angry with you. It's all she ever talks about. She spends most of her time at the stupid neighbour's. And her cooking's got really lousy. Do you want to come back?'

'To be honest, Josh, I don't know. I've been with your mother a long time, from before I was really a man. In a way, I never had to grow up. I never learned what life was really like. I hid away from everything. Now things are different. It's changing all the time. I like that.'

To their right, a train trundled across Hungerford Bridge. A knot of figures were huddled together on the walkway. They were pulling on a set of ropes which hung from the railing.

'Mum says that you're only thinking of yourself.'

'Well, to an extent that's true, because I want to understand more about my life. But I have to think of you and your mother as well. I have to do what's right for all of us. What's happened to our family is my fault, but the problem between your mother and me isn't a new thing. It's been there for a long time now, only neither of us did anything about it. What I did brought it to the surface.'

'Are you going to give her a divorce?'

'I suppose so, if that's what she really wants.' But now, of course, there was a pregnancy to consider. He decided not to mention it to Josh until he and Helen could decide on a course of action.

There was a shout on the bridge, and the knot of figures craned over the railing. Somebody fired a flashgun.

'Do you love this woman enough to leave me and Mum?'

Christ, thought John, what a question. Only a child could ask something like that. At Josh's age, emotions were still quantifiable, as if one could be weighed off against the other.

'I do love her, yes, but I don't want to lose you.'

'It's very complicated, isn't it?'

'It's part of being an adult.'

'Bummer.' Josh consulted his sneakers.

'You can do something to help, you know.'

'What?'

'Let me see you more often, to talk like this.'

'I would have before, but, you know ...'

'I know.'

'Hey, look. They're taking something out of the river.' Up on the bridge, they were hoisting a pair of dripping brown bundles over the railing. 'Neat,' said Josh excitedly. 'Maybe it's dead bodies, like a suicide pact or something. Can we go and watch?'

'No. Let's get something to eat,' said John, hauling his son to his feet. 'You've got a very morbid imagination.'

'So would you, hanging around the house right now,' replied Josh, clambering on to the seat for a better view and wrinkling his nose with pleasure.

They walked up into Henrietta Street, heading for Joe Allen's. John knew that the restaurant would be warm and busy, conducive to easy conversation.

'If you want, I could probably get Mum to meet you,' said Josh, drizzling ketchup over his grilled chicken. 'If you want.' They were sitting in a far corner of the restaurant, surrounded by too many plates of french fries.

'Then if you get back together, I take a hefty commission.'

John narrowed his eyes as he watched the boy. 'You're a smart kid,' he lisped in his movie-star voice. 'And you know what happens to smart kids.'

'They get dropped in the river at night,' they said in unison, repeating the line from a horror video they had once rented when Helen was out.

'What do you say you and I go fishing one weekend?'

'Fishing is for dweebs. Bowling's cooler.'

'Fine by me.'

'So, do you want me to or not?'

'Do I want you to or not what?'

'You know.' He winked. 'Fix up a meeting. Be nice for you to get back with Mum in time for Christmas.'

'You're really pushing this, aren't you? We'll see. Keep eating.' He shovelled the rest of the chips on to Josh's plate.

Slowly, they found a way to talk of the things Josh had always preferred to discuss with his father. John could see that they had tentatively arrived at a new level of under-standing. For the first time ever, he felt that he had held an adult conversation with his son. Finally he pushed back his chair and patted his stomach. 'I'm stuffed. You want some more fries?'

'Are you kidding? And leave no room for dessert?' He reached across and wiped a spot of ketchup from John's chin. 'Mum said that if I saw you, you'd try to buy me off with stuff to win back my affections, so I'm going for the biggest ice cream on the menu. I could have a brandy poured on it.'

'You could try and die in the attempt. She said that, did she?'

'Yeah, but it's okay, you don't have to buy me off. I still love you.' He concentrated on wiping his plate clean, to avoid the embarrassment of catching John's eye.

'And I love you, Josh. I'm very proud of you, you know.'

'That's great, Dad.' He scrunched up his eyes and grinned. 'You want to take me shopping?'

'Where the fuck have you been?' shouted Howard. He was standing in the centre of the corridor with sheaves of documents sprouting from his fists. Everyone else was in hiding.

'I was with my son,' said John quietly. 'We had some things to sort out.'

'Great! We're in the process of losing the most important account we've ever had, and you're off spending quality time with your goddamned family. I thought you understood what this job entailed. Now that you're back, perhaps we can pick up where we left off. Get in my office!' He slammed the door behind John and strode to the window, clenching and unclenching his hands. 'Let me get this right. You're having an affair with Ixora De Corizo.'

'It's more than that, Howard. I've left my wife for her. We're living together.'

Howard fell back heavily into his chair, the colour draining from his jowls. 'You're kidding me, right?'

'Would it be better if I was?'

'What did I tell you when you joined? Huh? Don't shit where you eat. What's the first thing you go and do?'

John watched Howard, disturbed by his reaction. His anger seemed to far exceed the crime. Surely any ill feeling could be patched up with a phone call to Glen.

'Why did you do it? And why with her?'

'What do you mean?' asked John, puzzled.

Howard was shaking his head in mock amazement. 'Well, how do you think she got the job?' he asked, leaning across the desk. 'A model with no previous acting experience?'

'She was chosen by the director,' said John. 'Wasn't she?'

'Well, that's one way of putting it. Let's just say she gave the greatest performance of her career before she reached the cameras.'

'You're telling me she slept with Farley Dell to get the part?'

'I don't know whether they got any sleep in. Wake up, John, for God's sake.'

John rose to his feet, blood suffusing in his face. 'How do you know this is true?'

For a moment Howard seemed about to speak, then he waved the thought away. 'Look, let's just forget this conversation happened. You should still have stayed away from her.'

There was no doubt in his mind that Howard was lying — but why? John could feel a chill sweat starting to trickle down his back. He searched the air for some rational lead to the conversation. 'Wait, you're telling me to stay away from the clients and yet you're the one—'

'Hey, I'm the boss.' Howard stabbed a finger at his chest. 'Everyone knows about me. It's different. And I'm a fucking sight more discreet than you've just been.'

'I didn't tell Tyron.'

'Then maybe she did.'

'No.' He moved towards the door. 'Ixora wouldn't have any reason for doing so.'

'Wouldn't she? Maybe she knows something you don't. Listen, John, when you came here I warned you that you'd be dealing with a different race of people. The men and women who populate this industry aren't like normal folk. They kiss you and then they kill you. There are guys out there who will pay to have you cut if you cross them. There are women with angels' faces who behave like Typhoid Mary. You have to treat them carefully and handle them from a distance, as if they were viruses. Everyone's out for themselves. Don't trust anyone, especially not the one you're sleeping with. You remember me saying that?'

'No,' said John. 'I really don't.'

He clipped three sets of red lights on his way to Chelsea before reason brought his anger under control. By the time John parked in Sloane Crescent the sun had vanished behind lowering cloud, and it was starting to rain.

He found her in her usual position, seated in the embroidered bedroom, watching his arrival from the window. There was not a single light on in the house. He switched on the dressing-table lamp as she rose to greet him. After their embrace, he placed his hands on her shoulders and seated her on the edge of the bed.

'I understand less about you each day, Ixora,' he said quietly, recounting his conversation with Howard. She did not try to interrupt him, but waited until he had finished before she spoke.

'John, do you remember the first time we had dinner together, and I pointed out how different you were from most of the people I'd met in this industry? You're doing it again.'

'Doing what?'

'Being naïve. Think it through. You know there's no love lost between Scott Tyron and me. Why did he ask me to re-dub my lines three times?'

'I suppose he wasn't happy with your performance.'

'My performance is the director's problem, not his. Right from the start he wanted me out of the film, because he felt I was deflecting attention away from him. The press coverage I received during the production was phenomenal, thanks entirely to you. Scott complained to Dell, who ignored him and kept me in the film. The only way

Scott could get his own back was by replacing my voice during the post-production. And who does he want to use as a vocal replacement?'

'I saw the audition tape go through. I can't remember her name.'

'She's a woman called Lindsey Hall. She's David Glen's girlfriend, John. Don't you get it? Scott's going to be playing the lead in Glen's movie. Howard wants the new film and its writer signed up through the Morrison Agency — my agency. Diana Morrison is naturally anxious to put me up for a role. Scott doesn't want me getting any more publicity on *Playing With Fire*. In his opinion I've had too much already, because of my connection with you. He doesn't even want me to audition for the new picture. He'd rather see Glen's girlfriend signed. So the only way the account will go to Howard is if I'm not in the deal.'

'How do you know all this?'

'Because I heard today that Howard asked Diana Morrison to drop my audition so that he would get the account. Diana apparently said no, because you're doing such a fine job with my publicity, and she sees my career building. My guess is that Howard had already found out about us, and it didn't fit in with his plans. His only option is to break the bond between you and me.'

'You think he made up that story so that I would finish with you, and he could get the account?'

She sat back against the bedpost, tired. 'You tell me, John. That's what it looks like.'

John was shocked. He knew that business always came first with Howard, but never expected him to lie to his own staff, his own friends ...

'How close did you come to believing him?'

'After all that's happened lately, very close indeed,' he admitted. 'I can't work with someone who'll say anything to get what he wants. How can I ever trust him?'

'People like Howard will betray anyone for money. He has betrayed you, John. You must do something about it. In my country ...'

'Which country is that?'

'... a situation like this would have to be confronted. I'm so very tired. I have to sleep.' She lowered her head to the counterpane and closed her eyes. With his hand resting on her cool bare shoulder, John numbly watched the final glimmer of light refract through the rusted trees of their garden wilderness.

CHAPTER
26
Glimpses

In the four long years that she had been secretly engaged to Chief Inspector Ian Hargreave, Janice Longbright had rarely seen him display any public emotion apart from anger. Today, however, Raymond Land had called to request his attendance at Sullivan's autopsy, and he had refused, citing personal involvement with the deceased. After replacing the receiver Hargreave stood in the corner of the operations room, silently looking down into the street until Janice lightly touched him on the shoulder.

'It's not your fault, you know.'

'You can't say that.' Hargreave remained facing the window, his hands thrust deep in his trouser pockets. 'It was my recommendation that got him promoted. I should have realised that he'd go behind my back, try to handle the whole thing by himself. It was a fault of his. I should have kept a closer eye on him,' he said. 'If I hadn't been so intent on wrapping up this bloody Savoy business, I would have seen that he was advancing the investigation on his own. I should have hauled him over the coals for not surrendering all of his files to me.'

'How did you know he was holding information back?'

'Thinking about it now, it was obvious. He couldn't have reached his conclusions from the report he'd submitted to me.'

'Do you have the full document in your possession?'

'No. I've managed to assemble most of his notes, but not all. It's over there, on the desk.' He indicated the scruffy, file-filled office behind them. Janice saw the redness in his eyes. She wanted to touch him, but continued to observe the rules that kept them apart during office hours. Hargreave was considerably older than her, and in a position of advanced responsibility. Knowledge of their relationship would undermine their authority, or so they thought. In reality, everyone in the station knew of their protracted affair and enjoyed the convoluted rituals they had evolved to preserve its secrecy.

'Have you read through them yet?'

'Yes. Sullivan's evidence points clearly to his suspect. He constructed a faultless argument for Saunders' capture and arrest. He should never have gone there alone.'

'Well, it's over now.'

'Not at all,' said Hargreave. 'The case hasn't closed with Saunders' death.' The tone of his voice alerted Janice at once. As he walked away from the window, she followed closely behind.

'You don't think he had the wrong man?'

'I'm sure of it. Come inside. Close the door.' Hargreave had decided to work out of Sullivan's office. In some indefinable way he felt it would bring him closer to understanding his colleague. 'I warned him about the perils of impatience. You end up cutting the evidence to fit your theories, and making false assumptions. He wouldn't involve anyone else because he wanted to take all the credit. He paid for that decision with his life.'

He pulled open the top drawer of the desk and removed a stack of red plastic files. 'I really can't blame him for arresting Saunders. The bloke was living a bit of a fantasy life. He'd spent six weeks as a voluntary patient at a private mental clinic. His personality profile suggests that he's a creative thinker, but not a very rational one. He got married to the model, Chapel's girlfriend, after knowing her for two weeks.'

'Chapel is seeing the girl?' asked Janice, surprised.

'That's right. He's left his wife for her. It rather increases the likelihood of their involvement, don't you think?' He pulled out another of the files. 'Sullivan got corroborating evidence of Saunders' emotional instability from several of the people he spoke to. Most of his friends agreed that he was subject to violent outbursts of temper. Sullivan had found a motive, obsessive jealousy, and a bloody good one in my opinion. What he didn't have — and what he allowed himself to overlook — was a pattern of logic. He writes here that Saunders was intent on removing anyone who stood between himself and his ex-wife. Then why start with the small fry? Feldman merely photographed her. According to Chapel the Latino, Dominguez, may have been blackmailing her, but with what? No supporting evidence has ever been found. Vincent Brady's death had a matching M.O. but there's no link whatsoever with De Corizo or Saunders. Why go after them? Why didn't Saunders start with Chapel, the man she was currently living with?' Hargreave's mood began to lighten as he opened the folders one by one and examined them.

'You said Saunders was irrational and obsessive.' Janice crossed to the coffee machine and filled two plastic cups.

'He obviously wasn't thinking very clearly.'

'If anything, obsessives think too clearly. They get bogged down in factual minutiae, plans and timetables. But Sullivan didn't see that. He'd uncovered the identity of his murderer. To make his theory work he needed a victim. Impatience again. Chapel was the obvious choice. Anyway, the subsequent meeting on the bridge alters our perception of events.'

'Talk me through it.'

'Join me for lunch.'

'It's a deal.'

They ate huge bowls of steaming spaghetti carbonara beneath dusty Chianti bottles in an unfashionable Sicilian restaurant behind the Royal Opera House. In summer, when the windows were opened and the clatter of the kitchens momentarily ceased, you could hear the tenors and sopranos practising tricky *obligatos* in the rehearsal rooms.

'Imagine the scene,' said Hargreave, wrapping the sticky spaghetti around his fork. 'Sullivan discovers that Saunders has a gun registered in his own name, and he knows he's arranged to meet someone, he assumes Chapel, on the bridge at midnight.' Hargreave was waving his fork at her, flicking sauce on the tablecloth. There was spaghetti hanging from his moustache. She still loved him.

'I understand he had previously taken statements from Chapel, and the model.'

'That's right. I doubt there were any surprises from her. A roll of the eyes and a plea of ignorance. One interesting thing. She called the station a while back to report that Saunders had been pestering her, claiming to be in love with her. She'd asked for someone to look into it. Naturally, we did nothing. Chapel's statement makes more interesting reading because it's coloured by our sergeant's perception of him. His response to questions is bland enough, but Sullivan reckoned he was reacting guiltily, not telling the whole truth. Perhaps Saunders had already contacted him. Chapel's not saying.' Hargreave's fork screeched on the plate, raising hackles on Janice's neck.

'So, this morning I put a casual call through to his office, just to ascertain his whereabouts the night before last. First he claims that there was no meeting arranged for midnight, reiterating that Saunders hadn't contacted him. Then he says that they had an intruder at the house — this just two hours before Saunders' established time of death, mark you — and that he was knocked on the head, or so he thinks.' Hargreave removed the sheet from the file and held it close to his face, smearing sauce on it.

'He remembers coming to, bruised, some time later. His girlfriend had been woken by the noise, and had found him lying at the bottom of the stairs. She thought he'd simply slipped in the dark, and had taken him up to bed. Apparently there's something wrong with the electrics, and the lights are always going out.' He peered hard at the paper. 'I should have brought my reading glasses, they use such small print for these things. Chapel can't remember the exact sequence of events, but he reckons that the prowler might well have been Saunders. But why should it be Saunders if, as Chapel claims, they hadn't been in contact with each other? Is he lying, I wonder? Whether he is or not the question remains, who was Saunders meeting on the bridge that night?'

Janice dabbed daintily at the corner of her mouth, hoping to balance Hargreave's gastronomic pyrotechnics with her own good manners. 'What do you think really happened?' she asked.

'I think Sullivan reached the rendezvous at the same time as Saunders, but before the person Saunders had arranged to meet. He accused Saunders, who went off the deep end, and Sullivan was forced to handcuff him. Then

what did Saunders do? Shoots himself, not with the loaded
and undischarged handgun we found in his coat pocket,
but with a diver's harpoon? If he's killed people before,
surely he'd just shoot the arresting officer, unlock the cuffs
and escape.'

Hargreave loaded another forkful and prepared to lift it.
Janice moved back, out of the way. 'All right, somehow
Saunders got shot. What, he doesn't fall to his knees, but
climbs over the railing in order to take Sullivan with him?
That's a pretty determined suicide. No, Chapel — or
whoever it was — kept his appointment, hiding on the
other side of the girders, against the railway tracks. He
shoots at Saunders, not realising that he's been hand-
cuffed. When he discovers what's happened, he's forced to
kill the cop as well. Something prevents him from
reloading the harpoon — maybe it's jammed. So he jumps
down onto the walkway and upends the body, tossing it
over the side. What can Sullivan do but follow it down
into the river?' Hargreave wiped his plate clean with a
piece of garlic bread. 'What a terrible bloody way to die.
Let's get back. Our young friend was fond of storing additional information in his desktop IBM. With any luck we'll
find the code name he stored it under.'

As they paid and left the restaurant, the sergeant turned
to Hargreave. 'Suppose it wasn't the same person who did
this, Ian? We could be looking for more than one
murderer.'

'I don't think so,' replied Hargreave, holding the door
for her. 'The M.O. fits perfectly. And just so that it doesn't
break the pattern, when our boys hauled the bodies from
the river, they found that Sullivan was wearing a gold
neckchain with a crucifix attached to it. Immersed in
water. Just like the others in the file.'

'There was a photographer on the bridge, by the way, a
freelancer for the *Daily Mirror* who happened to be

passing. He got some shots of the bodies being lifted from the water, but I understand they're a little too gruesome to be used. We slapped a restraining order on the publication of the shots, but someone is bound to come sniffing around.'

'If we don't get this sorted out damned quickly, the press gag is going to come off in a few days anyway. The only way I've been able to hold it on is by citing the Buckingham Palace connection and branding it an act of terrorism.'

'There's something about the investigation that bothers me,' said Janice. 'There's no logic to it. It just seems bad, poisonous, as if anything at all could happen. I know how unprofessional that sounds.'

'No. I know what you mean. There's an element underneath all this that I can't get to grips with.' Hargreave withdrew the stub of a cigar and stuck it in his mouth. 'It's as if I keep glimpsing something from the corner of my eye, but when I look directly, it's gone. I don't know who's safe, and who to warn.' He lit the cigar, flicking the match to the gutter. 'Because I don't know who's next.'

CHAPTER
27
Out

John had been deeply disturbed by the phone call he had received from Bow Street police station. Saunders was dead, and so was the young sergeant who had questioned them. Perhaps he and Ixora were also in danger. The chief inspector who had called seemed unwilling to divulge the circumstances of their deaths, and John had been unable to find any mention of the tragedy in any of the day's newspapers. Was it possible that the police suspected his involvement with Saunders and were trying to trick him into an admission of guilt?

Although John had been scarcely able to provide a substantial account of his movements two nights ago, Hargreave did not attempt to accuse him of direct involvement in the case. News of the call had also worried Ixora, who was frightened that some hint of scandal would reach her agency or worse still, the press.

According to this man Hargreave, Saunders and Sullivan had died together in the course of the investigation. Perhaps they had been in a car accident.

As much as news of the deaths had shocked him, nothing could top the revelation that Howard was manipulating him to gain future business contracts. His colleague had been out of town on business for the past couple of days. Now John wondered how to handle the problem. He was aware of the risk that a showdown could place on his new career, but there was a moral issue to be resolved. John permitted himself a tight smile as he darted through the Strand's morning traffic. A moral issue; that was something he hadn't considered for a while.

He found Howard in the reception area of a recording studio situated behind the pungent vegetable market in Berwick Street. He was waiting for Park Manton, who had just been viewing the newly dubbed *Playing With Fire* footage. John figured that it would probably be better to wait until Howard returned to the office, but anger and impatience took control.

'Why did you lie to me?' he asked quietly, pacing before Howard, who was lounging uncomfortably across the seating units.

'John, for Christ's sake sit down, you're making me jumpy.'

'I know you lied, I just want to know why. You know you won't be given Glen's film unless you have Scott Tyron's cast approval, and you won't get that unless Ixora is out of the way.'

'John, this broad is fucking up your head. Who told you that?'

'Just tell me if it's true.' John stood over him, clenching and releasing his hands.

'Tyron is doing Glen's movie, yes, and he doesn't want Ixora in it. That's the way it goes.'

'So you tell me she's screwing around, just to protect your contract?'

'You got it all wrong. The first part, that's just business. Tyron doesn't want your lady outshining him, but it may interest you to know that he doesn't want Dell to direct either, even though the old man was promised it, and he doesn't want the first assistant who answered back once too often, or the wardrobe mistress who made the mistake of telling him he was a thirty-four waist. You know what it's like. Films die and careers get killed for all the wrong reasons. There's nothing malicious in it, it's just showbiz.'

'Then maybe I picked the wrong career after all.'

'Christ, John, will you lighten up? Thanks to good PR agents, Marion Morrison's name was changed to John Wayne. Girls screamed over Rock Hudson and Jimmy Dean while they were out cruising Boystown. Carmen Miranda got away with cocaine in her platform shoes. Nothing is what it seems. It never has been.'

Howard returned his attention to the new issue of *Screen International* as John's temper began to flare. It was important for him to hear an admission of a lie from Howard. It would prove to him that men chose to slander Ixora because they couldn't have her. It would remove the last traces of mistrust he still harboured about her.

'I want to hear you say that Dell didn't sleep with her, Howard. You said it to help keep a contract, not because it was true. Tell me he didn't.'

Howard's broad face rose above the newspaper. He wrinkled his nose. 'Just fuck off, John, will you? If you're that concerned you can go and ask Dell yourself, but it won't do you any good because he'll just tell you how he passed her on to me.'

'You're lying.'

'I warned you, you're not playing in the little league any more. This isn't like your old job. I wanted Ixora on our books. I used whatever I could to get her to stay. These are big deals, big money, and you either grab them when they're offered to you, or they roll on by and someone else gets them.'

John was breathing hard through his nose. He knew that Howard was lying. Otherwise, he'd never have expressed surprise at the news that he and Ixora were living together. Listening to his justification of his morally bankrupt lifestyle was making him sick.

'That's the deal, is it? You just take what you want, lie through your teeth and screw who you like.'

'You must be the last straight man, John, 'cause I swear I've never met anybody as naïve as you. Besides, you're in no position to lecture me about marriage.'

'I've left my wife for Ixora because I'm in love with her. That's a lot different to what you're doing.'

'And what am I doing?' Howard's eyes grew wide and innocent.

'Approaching everything in life as if you can either screw it or buy it.'

'Well fuck me and let's do lunch.' Howard threw up his hands, laughing. 'You know what happens to movie people when they go to hell? They hand out business cards. Welcome to the real world, pal.'

John lunged forward and grabbed him by the throat, hoisting him to his feet. Although Howard was physically larger, he was out of shape. When John threw him against the foam sofa unit, it tipped over backward and he cracked his head against the window behind, splitting the glass. The receptionist screamed as Howard struggled to right himself. John's heart was pounding out of his chest. If Howard jumped, he was ready. But the man floundering before him, jammed between the units, was not about to fight back. As he rose, John saw that he was bleeding from a cut on the back of his head. Howard reached up and gingerly touched his wound. 'Jesus Christ,' he said, 'I'm cut.'

'Look, Howard—'

'You've got about an hour to get your stuff out of the office before I have the locks changed,' he shouted, shoving past on his way to the toilet, his hand across his face. 'If you come anywhere near the building after that, I'll call the police, you got that?' He turned to the bewildered receptionist. 'Get this guy off the premises, he's a fucking health hazard.'

John spoke to no one as he cleared his belongings from the Dickson-Clarke offices. Most of the staff were at lunch, but one or two of the secretaries threw him strange looks as he walked down the corridor with a taped-up card-board box beneath his arm. A sense of reason had returned to him now. He could see the events of the past more clearly.

Howard's male vanity had refused to allow him to admit that he had been unsuccessful in seducing Ixora. He couldn't handle the fact that his sexual dynamism was starting to lose its velocity. And firing John was an easy way to prove his willingness to work for Diana Morrison.

Now that Ixora had finished the film there was no immediate work for her in sight. Money would be a problem for the two of them, particularly with the possibility of divorce proceedings approaching. He wondered how he could break the bad news to her. He knew that he would never return to his old career in finance. As he walked through Covent Garden with the cardboard box under his arm, he was aware that he had taken a gamble, shedding the normal lifestyle of his suburban neighbours for something closer to the edge of life.

If he had not lost his temper, he would have realised that Howard was trying to give him some real advice. He was adrift in a moral grey area, sandwiched between his past and an uncertain future. Unless he was prepared to make a stand he would never discover his true capabilities, or even secure another job.

Even though he had not believed Howard, John could no longer be sure about Ixora. The mistrust remained with him like a pebble in a shoe. He found new meanings in her guileless poses, her injured eyes, her innocent explanations. He took to questioning her, casually, lightly, less from genuine interest than to see if he could catch her out. And still he sought signs of her past, interrogating the few of her modelling friends who had known her longer than a couple of months until they gave him odd looks and changed the subject. Ixora's former life remained sealed off, and she volunteered no further tales from it, knowing that he would no longer merely accept her word.

Their affair had stalled in an area of caution and distrust. Although their love for each other was growing steadily, the emotion was tempered with suspicion.

On the Thursday afternoon of the following week, John's first full week of unemployment in years, Ixora entered the house in tears. She had just returned from a studio in Wandsworth, where she had been shooting test shots for a French television commercial, and threw her arms around his shoulders.

'Come on, what's the matter?' asked John.

'You're going to be so angry with me,' she cried, dampening the neck of his sweatshirt. 'I've smashed up the car. I came out of a side turning on to the Embankment just by the Albert Bridge and hit a parked lorry.'

'Stop crying, it's all right. Here.' He pulled a handkerchief from his pocket and wiped her nose. 'The main thing is that you're not injured. Anyway, it's a Volvo. You can't have done that much damage if the other vehicle was parked.'

'That's just it. The truck's load shifted and fell on the car, scaffolding equipment, it went everywhere and made such a noise.'

'My God, you could have been killed!' He held her tightly against his chest. 'You're not hurt in any way?'

'No, I was clear by this time. I know you said we'd have to be careful with our money from now on ...'

'Don't worry, the insurance will take care of it. I guess we'll have to rely on public transport for a while.'

She sniffed and thoughtfully fingered the pearls at her throat. 'I could sell my pearl necklace. It's supposed to be very valuable.'

'Don't be ridiculous, your mother gave you that. I know how much it means to you. Don't even think of such a thing.' He was about to kiss her when the telephone rang.

'I'll get it.' He reached across to the kitchen table and raised the receiver. 'Hello?'

'John?'

It was the first time that Helen had contacted him directly since they had separated. Startled, he raised his eyes to Ixora's face. She seemed to sense who was calling, and released herself from his embrace. 'It's Helen,' he whispered.

'I wondered if we could meet somewhere.' The softness of her tone surprised him.

'Uh, sure. Was this our son's suggestion?'

'I think it's about time we talked to each other, that's all.'

He thought fast. 'Fine. Where?'

'I don't — is Ruby's still open in Camden High Street?'

'To my knowledge.'

'There, then.'

'Okay. Can you manage Saturday lunchtime? We'll behave like civilised people.'

'Civilised people,' she agreed. 'Name your hour.'

'One o'clock.'

The line went dead, leaving him staring at the receiver. 'What did she want?'

He looked at Ixora, barely seeing her. 'To talk,' he said simply.

Camden's cramped markets were segregated by the canal's lock-gate system, and operated beneath and beside a narrow humpbacked bridge covered in posters for political rallies and fringe theatre productions. The streets were always crowded here, largely with people who expressed their ideologies through their appearance. John made his way over the bridge towards the restaurant past old hippies and young punks, skinheads and rastafarians, students and yuppies, locals and tourists. After all the recent ambiguity and confusion in his life, he suddenly realised how much he was looking forward to seeing Helen again.

He spotted her through the steam-smeared glass, sitting at the bar lost in thought.

Far from gaining weight in her pregnancy, she had lost it, entirely to her advantage. As she greeted him she moved with a lightness he had not seen in her for years. She slipped the jacket from her shoulders and revealed a slender figure encased in a black woollen suit. Her stomach barely showed at all.

'What do you think?' she asked with a nervous smile. 'I finally gave up carbohydrates.'

'You look great,' he said, unsure whether he was supposed to kiss her, and deciding against it. 'You always said you wanted to do it.'

'Too bad it took a major upheaval in my life.' She spoke without rebuke, almost affectionately. 'I think the baby's going to be on the small side, though.'

'When is it due?'

'The end of April. There've been no problems so far.'

Summoned by the waiter, they made their way to the table. Helen ordered carefully, denting the waiter's hauteur by interrogating him relentlessly about ingredients.

'So,' he said when they were alone once more, 'how have you been?'

'Okay, I suppose. I've been spending a lot of time at the church. We've opened a non-denominational advisory centre for teenagers. It keeps me busy. I never realised there were so many disturbed people around. Josh is fine, doing better at school. Life goes on. What about you?'

'Howard fired me last week. We had a terrible argument. I'm afraid I hit him.'

'That's not like you, John.' Was it his imagination, or was there a hint of amusement in her voice? 'What did you fight about?'

Things were going so well that John was reluctant to bring Ixora's name into the conversation. 'It was an ethical thing.' he explained in honesty. 'I told him I didn't think it was right for him to emotionally manipulate his friends in order to make deals.'

'That was very noble of you, if somewhat naïve.' The subject was dropped with the arrival of their starters. Instead they discussed Josh, who already wanted to enter art college when he left school, and the house, which badly needed a new roof. Mention of his perilous financial state was avoided, although he knew it would have to be broached when the subject of maintenance arose. With any luck he'd find a solution to the problem before she needed to find out. Helen already had enough to worry about. Brisk banter masked their real emotions from each other. John was surprised and disturbed by the effect of seeing her again. She openly admitted that she was missing him.

'Listen, John, I won't launch into some speech about how Josh needs a father and how much I want you back,' she said, setting aside her fork. 'Since we split up I've learned a lot about looking after myself. I couldn't simply return to our old life. Perhaps it was too structured. But most families draw comfort from order. I can understand what happened between us a little better now. I suppose time is giving me a vantage point.'

'Helen—'

She raised her palm to him. 'Let me finish. It's taken a lot of courage for me to come here and say this. I don't know that I could ever trust you again, not fully, not just because you lied but because you found it easy to do so. The truth is that I do still love you very much. I always wonder where you are, what you're doing, if you're all right. That's loving someone, isn't it? A large part of my life has been spent taking you into consideration. Maybe it's too much to give up entirely. Particularly as I'm carrying our child.'

He studied her eyes, surprised and touched. The last thing he had expected from her was any suggestion of a reunion, and now he found himself seriously considering the possibility.

To say anything more at the moment would be wrong. She was working the idea through in her own way. It would be best for him to suggest something positive for the future. His life with Ixora was fast and strange, always on the edge of something dangerous. His marriage to Helen had become prematurely middle-aged. Surely with her help they could create something between the two extremes? He had to admit that the thought interested him.

'We could meet up again in a few days,' he suggested, helping her into her coat. 'What do you think?'

'That would be nice. I was thinking that it might be an idea to put the divorce proceedings on hold for a while.' She turned and gave him a peck on the cheek as they left the restaurant. 'At least, until we've had a further chance to talk.'

Walking back across the bridge alone, a warm glow filled his heart. Clearly Helen was serious about the possibility of their reunion. Their final decision would have to be a mutual one. She could not be let down again.

CHAPTER
28
Tunnel Vision

'This place is supposed to be exclusive,' said Howard, tapping his cigar butt over his empty coffee cup. 'Look at this lot. What a fucking shower. The advertising people will be moving in next, and then we'll have to find somewhere else to go. It'll be like the Groucho Club all over again.' The muffled thud of the downstairs disco vibrated the soles of his shoes through the carpet. He watched a young man in an off-the-peg dinner suit massaging his nostrils with a distinct lack of subtlety as he exited from the toilet, then turned back to his dinner companion. It was nearly midnight, and the club was filling up fast. Long-legged women in tiny black skirts lounged against the gilt walls as they searched for men they could pointedly shun.

'So this is all sorted out, then?' he asked, anxious for a

physical manifestation of their truce. Diana Morrison leaned forward and smiled, which was a mistake as she was peering over a low shaded table-lamp, and the lighting made her look like the mirror demon in *Snow White*.

'I suppose so, although you must realise that Ixora is my baby as it were,' she said, 'and I did so want to put her up for David's project.'

Diana had her Shirley Temple voice on. It made him ill to hear middle-aged women adopt the vocal characterisations of little girls. 'But there'll be other parts she can audition for, Diana. She's hot right now, and she's bound to get more work when the film premieres. I don't like trade-offs any more than you do, but it ties us all in with Paramount, and that's good for everyone no matter how many of the projects go into turnaround.' He waved a waiter over with a single finger, which he then twisted to point to Diana.

'We'd like some more coffee in fresh cups I think, and — Calvados, darling?' For a brief moment the waiter, who had been studying Diana's intricately braided coiffure in order to get tips for his night course in hairdressing, assumed he was being offered a liqueur. 'Make that the twelve year old. Actually, you can leave the bottle.' Howard waved him rudely away and switched his attention back to his accomplice.

'You know,' said Diana, fishing about in her handbag for a cigarillo, 'we could actually make a fair amount on this deal if we tie in a director ourselves.'

'Who did you have in mind?'

'It's more a process of elimination. I don't suppose McTiernan's available for at least two years. To get Spielberg interested we'd have to stick some kids in the script and take the razor attack out, and for David Lynch I guess we need an S and M scene with dwarves, although it is an upmarket slasher so he might be interested.' Diana flicked ash from her false eyelash. 'I haven't got your attention, darling.'

'I'm sorry,' said Howard awkwardly, 'I think I just saw someone I know. The oddest thing — will you excuse me for a moment?' He walked from the table as Diana was still replying and followed the curving staircase downwards. On the landing above the disco a fire door swung slowly to a close. He caught it just before it clicked back in place.

The cement corridor beyond was lit only by the emergency exit sign. Beneath it, a dark figure was walking quickly away. Clubbers often came out here if they wanted to smoke a joint. The air was acrid with marijuana. Howard stood with his hands by his side, unsure of himself. His head felt foggy, as if he had been inhaling the fumes for too long. The figure was retreating around a corner.

'Wait for me,' he called, running off along the corridor. Motes of dust flicked red in the light of the exit sign, blurring the hastening shape ahead. The walls seemed to be narrowing as he ran. Before him, the figure turned and waited for a moment, then set off at a renewed pace, like Alice's White Rabbit.

'Need to talk to you, for God's sake,' said Howard, losing his breath. As he stopped running, the figure stopped too. The corridor curved down and appeared to twist, as if heading back into the ground. Redness from the emergency sign saturated the walls, making them look as if they were bleeding. Suddenly it began to grow cold, the temperature dropping fast. He could see his breath forming.

'Christ, this is ridiculous. Come over here. I have no quarrel with you.' The figure, blurred by dust and smoke, remained silent and motionless, yet somehow it seemed larger than before.

'Well, you can't say I didn't try.' Howard turned to go,

but the path back had stretched into an endless tunnel.

'What the hell is going on?'

The floor was steeper than he had realised. The icy air was growing harder to breathe. He ran a few steps forward, his sense of direction growing confused. It didn't seem possible, but the ground below tilted still more sharply and the corridor walls ahead narrowed to a pinpoint. He was hallucinating, that was it. The dope in the air had penetrated his lungs.

He turned back just in time to see something large and black roaring at him like a banshee.

With a scream of fear he set off along the tunnel, sweat dropping into his disbelieving eyes as the walls continued to close in. The creature behind was almost upon him, the echoing footfalls landing on top of his own. On either side, the walls were brushing his body.

The crimson exit door to the club appeared before him.

He had almost reached it when he felt a searing pain across the back of his neck, and realised that he had been slashed with something sharp.

He raised his hands to the wound and turned, his eyes widening when he saw the blade of the sword. 'Christ, are you out of your fucking mind?' he cried, staggering slightly, the pain in his neck worsening. Suddenly he was being pushed back towards the wall. He slammed hard against it as the cutlass curved deeply and slowly across his shirt, splitting it wide and cascading blood on to his stomach. Now the razor swept faster and faster back and forth, cleanly severing cloth and skin, fibre and artery, popping open fleshy wounds as his trousers turned black with blood. By the time the blade had reached its final descent, Howard's body had slipped in its own juices to the flooded floor, his face a chaotic blur of blood and bone.

Hands reached down and wrenched the tiny gold cross

from Howard's gaping throat, dropped it into a half-full Volvic bottle and screwed the cap back on. The last thought in the publicity agent's dying brain was that somehow he had wandered into the pages of Diana's gory screenplay.

CHAPTER
29
Apprehension

There was a shift of weight in the bed. A movement of air beside him. He rolled over and opened his eyes, to be greeted by darkness. The curtains surrounding the four-poster bed were pulled shut.

'Ixora?'

'Go back to sleep.'

'What time is it?' He pulled himself up against the bolster, attempting to massage the soreness from his throbbing temples.

'Late. Four, maybe.' The voice came from the far side of the room. The effort of pulling back the curtain brought a renewed stab of pain. The hours of darkness spent at Sloane Crescent were taking on a hallucinatory quality. He had not slept this heavily since the night he was attacked on the stairs by one of Ixora's 'obsessives' — that was how he thought of them now. Last night he had drunk the best part of a bottle of Scotch waiting for her to return home.

'Why are you so late?' He coughed and shoved back the thick counterpane. Ixora was wriggling from a slim black tube of silk which drifted to the floor in a pall of warm perfume.

'I went for a walk afterwards. I needed some fresh air. They were very nice, but we all drank a little too much schnapps.' A few days earlier Diana had arranged a dinner for her with some German film makers who had expressed an interest in starring her in an upcoming television serial. Now that he had been fired from Dickson-Clarke, John could no longer act as her chaperone, and as Howard had yet to reassign her account, Ixora had been forced to attend the function alone.

'What time did you leave them?' he asked, rubbing the sleep from his eyes. 'You must have been walking for a long time.'

'Why do you sound so suspicious?'

'I'm sorry. It's just that I thought you'd want to be with me.' He knew he was being pathetic. He was a grown man, he didn't need comforting. 'Listen, I realise how that sounds. The most beautiful girl in London comes home to me at night. I'm not complaining.'

She sat on the side of the bed and slipped her arm around him. 'You know I would rather have been with you, but this was business. I have to keep my contacts up, especially now that you're out of work.' She rose and turned from him, dipping to remove her tights.

'What's that?' He pointed to the crimson stain on her right calf. Caught in the thin shaft of light which bisected the room from the street, it had the lividity of a wound.

'Where?' She examined her leg carefully. 'Dietmar dropped a bottle of wine on the floor and it splashed everywhere. Good thing I was wearing black.'

When she had left the house, his first thought had been to run from floor to floor switching on every single bulb, washing away the shadows with an incandescent display of light, but this was an action he had been forced to dismiss at the risk of an electrical overload. The old house was wired up in an alarmingly makeshift manner, and he could not afford to renovate it. Instead he had sat in the dark as she did each night, listening to the ancient gramophone and waiting for her return. Even the cat hid from him, fleeing from room to room as he passed through the house. The normality of their life together, minimal at the best of times, seemed to be vanishing completely. He walked to the window with the golden counterpane pulled around him, watching as the rain fell into the trees and the empty street.

'Come to bed.'

He obeyed, and she slid her body on to his and bit his neck, raising a lurid weal. 'I hope you're not still tired,' she whispered, smiling in the dark. 'You've had enough sleep for one night.' As she raked her nails lightly across his stomach, a familiar fire grew within, and he turned to receive her pyretic embrace.

'My God, look what you did to me.'

He twisted to catch sight of his back in the bathroom mirror. Scarlet striations slanted from his spine to his shoulderblades. 'This has been a hell of a week for sex. Ixora?' He leaned out into the upstairs hall, heard voices at the front door. Moments later, she appeared on the landing. Despite the early hour, she had already bathed and dressed in jeans and a sweater. She did not return his smile. Her pale-knuckled hands were knotted over her stomach.

'The police are here, John.'

'What do they want?'

'They've come to arrest you.' She glanced over her shoulder at the front hall. 'Howard Dickson was murdered last night. They received an anonymous phone call saying you did it.'

The ground fell away so fast that he almost lost his balance. Even before he could begin to think of a response, damning thoughts came crowding in. They had fought in public. He had physically attacked Howard. The receptionist had seen them. He had been locked out of his office. Murdered last night — last night he had spent the evening alone. No alibi. No witnesses. Nothing to protect him.

Nothing at all.

Over the next few hours, faces and figures passed like the tableaux of a funhouse tunnel. Everyone was very reasonable. Two young officers waited while he shaved and dressed before leading him to an unmarked squad car. Neighbours had watched discreetly through parted net curtains. At Bow Street Station a woman sergeant had offered him coffee, and allowed him to call his lawyer. As soon as he arrived, the formal procedure began.

Detective Chief Inspector Ian Hargreave, who on the telephone had seemed like a benign if unpredictable uncle, now showed a darker side to his personality as he listened to John's stammered denials with a fading smile.

'I'm sure you appreciate what the gravity of the situation demands from us,' said Hargreave. 'In an English court of law you are tried for a single criminal offence, and in this case the offence is the murder of your employer. From a legal point of view, your appearance before me is coincidental to our earlier conversation.' Hargreave dug out the stub of a cigar from his top pocket and examined it with distaste before jamming it in his mouth. 'Off the record I have to say it suggests that even if you aren't guilty of murder you're heavily implicated in the surrounding circumstances. Even Mr Phelps here must be aware of that.' He gestured at John's lawyer, an absurdly young man who sat beside his client riffling through a pile of untidy notes as if expecting to find a legal instruction manual.

'Mr Phelps?'

The young man raised his head, his eyes swimming hugely behind thick spectacle lenses. 'Yes? Oh, yes. Yes indeed. Well, let's put it this way, Mr Chapel, if you were a racehorse I wouldn't bet on you.' He released a yelp of a laugh and returned to his search.

'What happens now?' asked John. 'I've never been arrested for murder before.'

'It's quite simple,' said Hargreave clearly, as if explaining to a child. 'Sergeant Longbright is going to take a detailed statement from you, in the presence of Mr Phelps here. After that, if I deem it necessary, Mrs De Corizo will be asked to sign a search warrant of her property, because to continue the enquiry I have to look for physical evidence of the crime, that is, something that will match forensically with data taken from the victim. At this point I may require you to visit the scene of the occurrence accompanied by my liaison officers. If you have any further questions, I'm sure that Mr Phelps will be happy to answer them.'

Hargreave excused himself from the interview room and returned to his office three floors above. Howard Dickson's body had been discovered by a doorman in a nightclub fire exit at a little after 2.00 a.m. that morning. Although his wallet had provided proof of his identity and profession, it was not until Hargreave had arrived on the scene at 7.30 a.m. that the connection to John Chapel was established. The corpse had been slashed to ribbons by a large, heavy blade, not found on the premises. Dickson's dinner companion, a woman named Morrison, was being treated by her GP for hysterics. Hargreave put in a series of calls, first to Raymond Land over in Forensics.

'We have nothing as yet,' admitted the doctor, checking his screen. 'If this death really is linked to the others, I need some non-attributable prints to compare. The interior handle of the exit door appeared to have been wiped clean and the corridor walls are too porous to hold anything.'

'What about the Volvic bottle?'

'There are some interesting fragments. I've got a call in to the SCU, see if I can run it through their AIL equipment, but I'll need a report from you to get clearance.'

'You should have it by tonight, Raymond.' The Serious Crimes Unit possessed an expensive argon-ion-laser device that could reveal normally indetectable fingerprint traces on crime exhibits by exposing surfaces to 38,000 watts of electrically charged argon. Alternatively, the bottle could reveal hidden prints by being dropped into liquid nitrogen at a temperature of minus 196 degrees centigrade — but that would make the exhibit brittle and prone to damage.

'There's a scratch of red paint on the wall of the bottle I'm quite interested in,' said Land. 'It's the same colour as those flakes your boys collected from Feldman's studio. No murder weapon this time, but it seems obvious that the wounds were made with a very large knife, possibly a sword or scimitar of some kind. It's a favoured gangland weapon, I believe. I've spoken to Finch and he agrees. I want your permission to remove the fire door at the club.'

'What for?'

'The lower half of the door is smothered in scuff marks. Some of them look quite fresh. Sometimes when we're handling a hit-and-run, we enclose the vehicle inside a plastic tent, heat up a superglue compound and pump the fumes into the tent. A polymer forms over the marks and shows them up in a kind of 3-D relief. I'd like to do that with the door.'

'How long will it take?'

'Couple of days at least. How's your man?'

'Chapel?' Hargreave pulled pensively at his cigar and tipped back his chair. 'He had a motive, and the opportunity. He has just about everything we need for a conviction ...'

Land could sense the hesitation in his voice. 'Except?'

'He doesn't have the right personality profile. I want you to go over your conversations with Sergeant Sullivan again in detail. The boy may have sounded bull-headed and arrogant to you, but he knew something more. His views shouldn't have been dismissed so easily by any of us.'

Land took the point. Hargreave knew the doctor well enough to see that he would have given the sergeant a particularly rough ride. 'I'll go through my notes and see what I can come up with,' said Land, signing off. 'Good luck with Chapel. I'm glad I have to deal with an exact science.'

Two hours later, Janice Longbright entered the office with a file containing the copied affidavits. She seated herself opposite Hargreave and crossed her legs in a slither of seamed nylon. Her auburn hair had been lifted from her shoulders and tied with a tortoiseshell slide. More than ever she seemed like a forgotten fifties filmstar. She was thirteen years younger than him, but age never seemed a problem between them. It was all the more unfortunate that their time together was always spent discussing work. Hargreave forced his attention back to the details of the case as the sergeant handed him a photocopy of Chapel's statement.

'As you can see,' she said, 'he's consistent and accurate

with his times. We have the entire interview on tape if you wish to hear it. One vague area emerges in his conversation, and that's concerning the reasons for his dismissal. He gave me some gobbledygook about a disagreement over contracts, but I had the feeling that there was a more personal reason behind it. He's anxious to keep Miss De Corizo's name out of the papers because of her career, so he may be hiding some connection there.'

'How did he react to the ring?'

'I tipped it out of its plastic bag on to the desk in front of him and the colour drained from his face. He obviously recognised it at once.'

'But it's not his.'

'No, it's a lady's eternity ring, red gold, Victorian, although I suppose it could be worn by a man, on his little finger. There's a blood splash on the inside, so it must have been on the floor when the murder was committed. No telling how long it was there.'

'And yet Chapel reacted violently to the sight of it? Curious. I'm not sure that we can keep him in on the evidence we have at the moment. It's a good job his lawyer's incompetent. Anyone else would be screaming blue murder by now.'

Janice slowly shook her head. 'I have to admit, I really don't think it could be him.'

'It's a bloody shame, but I have to agree with you,' said Hargreave. 'Still, we should get a statement from the studio receptionist who saw Chapel physically attack his boss.' He tapped Janice's document with his forefinger. 'He says right here that he has no way of proving his whereabouts at the time of the attack. If we were dealing with an isolated crime, I'd reckon Chapel was our man. But the only way any of the other deaths make sense is if they're links in a chain. And there's no way that Chapel could have participated in all of the earlier killings. I managed to unlock Sullivan's case data on the computer — password Michael, there's imagination for you, he might have bothered to put Gilbert or something — and ran through it with the thought that he was intending to build a case against Chapel, but it's impossible to construct. He's always in the wrong place at the wrong time. No, I'll sign his release, but we're going to have to keep him under close surveillance until all the forensic evidence is in.'

There was a knock at the door and a confused-looking Phelps entered. He approached Hargreave's desk nervously. 'I wondered how much longer you're likely to be,' he began. 'My client hasn't had anything to eat since ...'

Hargreave rose and slapped a hand on his back with a hollow clap. 'Relax, Mr Phelps, we're not going to detain either of you for much longer. This is your first experience of a Serious Crimes arrest, I take it?' He eyed the lawyer eagerly, as if searching for cracks. 'Possibly even your first time in an interrogation?' He guided him towards the door. 'Well, now that you've visited us you mustn't be a stranger. If you'd like to see any of us at short notice, get caught shoplifting.

'Fire your law firm as soon as you get out of here,' whispered Hargreave, pointing at the young lawyer as he released a distraught John from his confinement in the holding bay. 'You were arrested for murder and they sent you a junior. Unbelievable.' He had expected to see some sign of grateful relief in Chapel's face, but the man seemed emotionally paralysed, either with fear or anger, his skin as slick and pallid as a corpse. He walked to the door as if he was being operated by remote control.

'Before he gets to the bottom of the steps outside I want someone on his tail,' hissed Hargreave to Janice. 'I don't care who you send, but make sure they have some smart clothes and enough dosh on them. Chapel's the type of bloke who eats out all the time.' Two weeks ago a certain PC Bimsley, one of the foot-surveillance operatives working on Bow Street's anti-mugging operation, had failed to make an arrest because his suspect had contacted a fence while dining in an expensive Mayfair restaurant, and Bimsley had come out without his credit cards.

'Have your man call in every three hours. If Chapel decides to part his hair differently, I want to know about it.' He paused in the doorway, thinking for a moment. 'Of course,' he said, 'the same thing goes if someone tries to murder him.'

CHAPTER
30
Past Times

With bad weather bringing the West End traffic to a stand-still, the cab was forced to detour through the rain-sodden backstreets of King's Cross, past the towering black iron gas cylinders and the dripping trees which lined the canal. John stared from the window and saw nothing. All he could think of was the ring they had found near Howard's body, the Victorian gold ring that Ixora's mother had bequeathed to her, and now he was willing to concede the unthinkable; he saw that she had led him to the brink of darkness.

She was the murderess who had provided herself with a perfect alibi, he was the adoring accomplice who was all too willing to sacrifice himself at the altar of her beauty. With him at her side there was no lie she could not tell, no crime she could not commit. The night Saunders had died he had been attacked in her house and left unconscious.

What had happened in those missing moments? Last night, she had returned at some unearthly hour with some cock-and-bull story about dinner with the Germans. The crimson stain on her leg was, according to her, a splash from a bottle of wine that had been spilled. But what if it had really been a splash of blood? It was so obvious now when he looked back at it, and yet the police had not wished to interrogate her. Could they really be as blind as he had been? Surely the doorman at Howard's club would have remembered seeing her? And where was Ixora now that he needed her? Upon leaving Bow Street he had called the house, but there was no reply.

The cab slid over to the far side of the road as it turned into Royal College Street, narrowly missing a traffic sign. His mind was a blur of unrealised images and unanswered questions. As the deserted roads gave way to traffic and pedestrians once more, his thoughts spiralled into alternative theories. Could Ixora really be capable of committing murder? Even supposing that she could physically perform such feats, what on earth could she ever hope to gain by it? Saunders had harassed her, but what of the others? Was she simply shielding someone, the 'dark man' of her dreams? Could she even be tracking the real murderer, and incorporating herself in some bizarre guilt-absolving scenario? The more he considered the possibilities, the less likely it seemed that she could be guilty of such monstrous acts.

But if she wasn't implicated in the murder, what the hell was the ring doing there?

When he finally arrived at Sloane Crescent, there was no sign of Ixora. The house was cold and empty. He rang the Morrison Agency, to be told by the receptionist that Ixora had not called in today. He took the hall stairs two at a time, running to the bathroom and upending the wicker laundry basket, searching for the tights she had removed so hastily in the middle of the night. Kicking around among the clothes on the floor, he found no trace of the incriminating article. Where else to look? One by one he emptied the bedroom drawers on to the floor, checking each item of clothing.

Next, he headed for the cupboards in the study. This was where she kept her photo-albums, the ones she had so coyly refused to show him when he had first moved in. Hauling back the burnished mahogany doors, he pulled down the gilt-edged volumes bound in red leather and threw each open in turn. Here and there were sterile model shots and stills of Ixora being pinned into dresses, glimpses into the fakery of fashion advertising, but on every page there were missing panels. Two of the volumes were completely empty, their photographs removed in haste, mounts and torn corners clustered in the bindings.

The bottom drawer of her desk proved to be locked, with no sign of a key. After a few minutes he managed to crack open the lock with a kitchen knife. The contents proved uninteresting, except for the diary in which she wrote some evenings before retiring. Here a handful of pages had been removed with scissors or a sharp knife. It made no sense. Now more than ever her past was a blank, as if it had been deliberately and systematically erased. As she had not been born on British soil, he supposed that there was no point in trying to trace her family background through St Catherine's House.

He was about to throw the diary back into the drawer when a fold of paper slipped from the back of it. A typewritten list of male names and telephone numbers, twenty-five in all, including those of Matteo and Saunders. Why should this have been hidden away? He was stuffing it into his shirt pocket when he heard the front door open.

'John? Are you home?' Her heels clicked on the hall tiles. He slammed the damaged drawer shut and looked back across the ransacked room. 'John, where are you?' She appeared in the doorway, blue winter coat buttoned tight to her neck, black and white checked scarf thrown loosely over it, a living fashion plate. Her eyes widened as she surveyed the mess, pulling off her gloves. 'Whatever happened here? When did they let you go?'

'Where have you been, Ixora? I was arrested for murder, and you went missing.'

'Where do you think I've been? With your lawyers, where else? What on earth have you been doing?'

'If you've really been to the lawyers, you'll know that they had to let me go.'

She paused halfway through unbuttoning her coat, nervously watching him. 'You sound strange. I know it must have been an awful experience for you. There was no point in me waiting at the police station. I thought it would be more useful to take legal advice. Mr Phelps arrived just as I was leaving — he said you'd been freed. I called the house but there was no reply.'

'Ixora, why do you have no past?'

She continued unbuttoning the coat, speaking with casual deliberation. 'What do you mean? Of course I have a past, everyone does. I just don't go on about it. You know about my parents, they—'

'You have no pictures of them.' He pointed to the albums which lay scattered over the carpet. 'You've removed them all.'

'Oh, *that*. Yes, I removed them ages ago. They were all mixed up with my model shots. I wanted to keep them in a separate book.'

'Which is where?'

'God, John, you're so suspicious. I think it's in the attic, I can't remember. If you want to see them, I'll find them for you. But not right now. It's been a terrible day and we could both do with a drink.'

'Wait there. I'm not finished yet. Your diary—'

'You've been in my desk? I have the key, how could you—'

'I broke open the lock.'

'John, you had no right!' She came forward and examined the shattered drawer, horrified. 'That's my grandmother's escritoire, it's been in the family for years!'

'Half the entries in your diary have been torn out. Where are they?'

She threw her hands wide, flummoxed as much by his attitude as the question. 'If you must know, those pages were so full of bad times that it depressed me to read them back. I wasn't thinking very rationally at the time. You're not the only one who's been going through a lot. Your lawyers told me that we've been lucky the press haven't hounded us out of the house yet. They've managed to get hold of the story now, did you know that? There's a photograph of the nightclub in tonight's *Standard*, something about "murder in high society". It won't be long before the tabloids are at the front door, and I don't need to tell you how the publicity will affect all the work you've done. Just remember that you're not the only one involved in this.' She poured tonic into two gins and passed him one. 'So, have you got any more questions for me?'

'Yes.' John held up the list of names. 'What's this?'

'It's a list of all the men I'm sleeping with, what did you think it was?'

'Seriously.'

'It's called networking. I typed it out for Diana Morrison. Influential contacts, mostly media folk. And before you say it, yes, I know Saunders is down there, but I can explain that very easily. You see …'

'The ring!' he shouted suddenly, unable to contain himself any longer. 'Why was your mother's ring found at the club? Explain to me what it was doing there.'

She paled suddenly, one hand instinctively closing over the fingers of the other. 'My God, I have no idea,' she said hoarsely. 'Are you sure it was mine?'

'Positive. When was the last time you wore it?'

'I don't know. Several weeks ago. Do you remember, one day you asked me why I wasn't wearing it, and I told you I'd taken it off to have a bath? I thought I'd lost it that day. I searched all over the house, and it turned up in the bedroom.'

'Where did you wear it after that?'

'Wait, I think I had it on for that awful photo-shoot, the one with Feldman. I don't recall seeing it any later. But if I lost it at the studio, how on earth could it have travelled all the way to the nightclub?'

'I don't know. Maybe someone wants to implicate you in this.' He rose and took her in his arms. 'You know, it's as if I have to reinvent you in my mind each day. As if you only exist from hour to hour, with no past and no future. I want to trust you, Ixora.'

'Until you do, there's nothing holding us together but the present moment.'

He lifted a lock of hair from her eyes and studied her face. 'Then that's what we have to work on. And the only way we can do that is by understanding the past.'

'That would mean finding out who's doing this, and why. I won't have you putting your life in danger.'

'It's already in danger,' replied John. 'Someone is trying to frame both of us for murder.' He released her and walked to the window. 'Maybe this whole thing is being staged for our benefit. It's as if there's someone out there plotting our destruction, watching our every move. But why? What the hell are they waiting for?'

'Stop it, John,' said Ixora, 'you're frightening me.'

'I'm frightening myself,' said John.

*

On two further occasions in the next week he was summoned to Bow Street police station to expand on his previous statement, but in every other aspect the Met's case against him seemed to have reached a reluctant hiatus. Nor did any further explanation come to light over Ixora's missing ring. The subject was quietly dropped, and became something to be sidestepped whenever their conversation moved in its direction.

In the last week of October John signed on with a media headhunter, who studied his CV with a jaundiced eye and announced that there was, of course, no possibility whatsoever of finding work this side of Christmas.

With no money being deposited into his bank account, John's overdraft began to reflect mounting debts. Despite his recent encouraging lunch with Helen, demands for legal fees arrived from her lawyers to cover their costs and — somewhat optimistically, thought John — from Mr Phelps for his passive role in the police proceedings against him. In addition, Josh's school expenses required prompt payment, and a heavy monthly mortgage had still to be met on the house in Richmond, as had a variety of joint hire purchase agreements.

With his credit card statements no longer cushioned by company expenses, John found himself sinking fast in financial quicksand. Although Helen had communicated through her solicitor that she would continue to meet some of their household costs, he saw that something would have to be done quickly, and that someone would have to be tapped for a loan.

Ixora kept him hopeful for the future, studying the employment sections of the papers with him, and asking her friends about the availability of jobs. Her own career had begun anew, with a lucrative Japanese modelling contract lined up and the promise of a rewarding television role in the new year. The release of *Playing With Fire* was set to receive its world premiere in London, the exact date and place to be arranged as soon as conflicting release patterns could be untangled by the distributors.

In the last few days of the month, John was sent for two interviews with public relations companies, one involved in sport sponsorship and the other in television, but although both seemed to go well he was not contacted again for either position.

Now that it grew dark so early, the house seemed even gloomier. On the days when he was not swallowing his pride by visiting old friends and awkwardly sounding them out about employment, he found himself sitting at the bedroom window as Ixora had done, watching for her return.

One day he tore up the floorboards on the landing and attempted to rewire the electrics, but the antiquated system of hidden, frayed wires eventually defeated him. He lived for the moments when she bustled into the house, swathed in chill air, laughing and chattering about how terrible the day had been, and how glad she was to see him. At night he stacked the bedroom fire with logs and they made love beneath the cover of the golden quilt, exploring each other with a slower, more tender passion than the angry energy they had fought to expel in the last sweltering weeks of the summer.

In these quiet, comforting moments the promises they made meant something, and gave him hope for the future. But as he watched the faces dancing in the flames of the burnished bronze fireplace, he found himself thinking of his wife and son, and a series of images played through his mind. The hospital waiting room on the night Josh had been born. The three of them playing Scrabble on the floor of the lounge. The smoothness of Helen's arched neck. The look of concentration she wore when she was reading. He wondered how their next meeting would go. She had called to arrange another lunch in a week's time.

The hour was approaching when he would have to define the course of his life for once and for all.

CHAPTER
31
Assassin

Between the towering Ionic columns of Selfridge's department store stands an eleven-foot-high statue of a woman holding a large double-faced clock. She is known as 'The Queen of Time', and she guards the entrance with a majestic grandeur that few modern department stores ever achieve. On Friday the second of November, at precisely four minutes to noon, as the hands of her timepiece prepared to overlap, a scruffily dressed man marched with determination beneath her feet on his way to the store's toy department on the third floor.

Here, below the distorted bleat of canned carols, a financially strapped character actor reduced to making appearances as Santa Claus waited in the spectral gloom of his illuminated styrofoam grotto, ready to disorient and terrify small children into being good.

In true commercial Christmas spirit, the children's floor was a world of primary-coloured fluffy collectables and batteries-not-included interactive videotoys, many of them starting at £99.95.

At the entrance to Santa's Grotto, harassed mothers and nannies lined up their wailing charges, readying them for their first major confrontation with an ethical problem in the real world. The children shuffled forward through the eerie mechanical tableaux of spasmodically slaving elves and diseased-looking goblins which were meant to enhance the magic of the season, and braced themselves for weighty problems concerning the value of duplicity (about having been good all year) and the reward of same.

Pushing his way through to the front of the line, the dishevelled man set about climbing the snow-clad polystyrene hill that sheltered Santa's little rest area and changing cubicle. On the far side, he lay flat against the hill and watched as jolly old St Nicholas attempted to calm a ululating infant by seesawing a vermilion plastic pony before its horrified eyes. Finally, checking his watch and seeing that the appointed time had been reached, he dug into his jacket and removed a small handgun, which he carefully trained on the back of Santa's deeply unconvincing wig.

He looked up to the roof of the cavern, where a hundred twinkling bulbs glittered in a man-made midnight sky, and for a moment it seemed as if he was standing on a real hill, staring into the infinity of the universe.

'This is for you, my love!' he cried, realigning the gun and squeezing off a single shot which reverberated through the fairy labyrinth. As the screaming began, he looked down to see that the top of Father Christmas's head had exploded over the surprised infant. The child was thrown clear as the rotund body toppled slowly to one side and fell to the floor, pumping blood across the artificial snow and spattering a set of cheeky lightbulb-nosed reindeer with spots of crimson.

His mission fulfilled, the assassin slumped back against the styrofoam skislope and awaited the blessed arrival of the authorities.

'Does this mean that I'm officially cleared?' asked John. He found his visits to the police station oppressive and disturbing. The corridors were always filled with anxious people. Tension crackled in the air. How the staff managed to survive in such surroundings without becoming traumatised was a mystery.

'In due course you'll be notified in writing that you are no longer regarded as germane to the case,' said Hargreave, 'but yes, Mr Chapel, it does mean that you are cleared.'

John took down his raincoat and rose to leave. 'Tell me something,' he asked, 'did you ever really think it was me?'

'I'd have to say no to that,' replied Hargreave. 'Although I thought you were somehow involved. I still do. I'm just not sure how.'

'Can you tell me about the man you've caught? I mean, why did he do it? How do you know it was ...'

'I think you'd better leave before I change my mind, Mr Chapel,' said Hargreave wearily. 'There's still a lot of work to be done before we close the lid on this.'

After ushering his former suspect out of the door, Hargreave returned to his desk and sat with the case's physical evidence files spread before him. If anything, the investigation made less sense now than it did before. Donald Peter Wingate, forty-five years old, an unemployed builder, had confessed to everything. More to the point, he had confessed to anything. He had immediately surrendered himself after the shooting of the Santa Claus, anxious to be taken into custody.

His shabby King's Cross flat was wallpapered with photographs of all the current top models, mostly clipped from magazines and newspapers. Ixora's picture was among them. In preliminary conversations with the arresting officers, Wingate often referred to 'his girls', about whom he obviously nursed an obsession. He admitted frequently tracking attractive young women to their homes and watching them from a distance, and disclosed that he had been following this daily ritual for two to three months.

He explained that he worshipped the models' great beauty, and hated it when other men pestered or tried to touch them. He attempted to explain his involvement in each of the killings currently under investigation, but his conversation repeatedly deteriorated into rambling thought association. Mr Wingate was full of explanations, and precious few of them made sense.

The tabloid press had a field-day with a variety of SANTA'S PSYCHO SLAY headlines. Hargreave had a tough time making sure that the cause of the attack and the names of the models were kept secret from the journalists.

Subsequent investigation showed that Wingate had been interned in various mental institutions for the past seven years of his life. When arrested, he was found to be in possession of a small-calibre handgun and several rounds of live ammunition. When asked to explain his attack on an innocent store employee, he simply said that his girls would be pleased when they knew what had happened, although he denied ever having actually met or spoken to any of them.

Hargreave was far from happy. Donald Wingate seemed like an exaggerated version of Sullivan's original suspect, Anthony Saunders. Their backgrounds held uncomfortably close similarities. The main difference was that Saunders had gone on to become a victim.

Each fresh admission of Wingate's guilt brought with it a reverse effect. The inspector checked off his notes, running through the pages point by point.

Wingate was able to recite the correct locations of each of the crimes, although his fingerprints were not found anywhere. Yet he insisted that he had never worn gloves. He knew the names of all the victims and how they had died, and yet he could not remember where he had met them. Wingate had explained the motive for each of his attacks as that of jealousy. But Hargreave had conducted hundreds of criminal interrogations, and it was usual for such a person to show signs of emotional betrayal, or at least of nervous tension.

As their suspect was of doubtful mental stability, a police psychiatrist had attended each of the interview sessions. She was in agreement with Hargreave. Wingate seemed to know just so much about the crimes and no more, as if he had read up on each case and learned the circumstances by rote. He was unreliable, inconsistent, a self-confessed former white witch. But then, each time they were ready to dismiss the possibility of his guilt, he would reveal some point that had been withheld from the newspapers, something that only the police and the killer could possibly know.

'This final murder makes no sense at all,' he said to Janice as she came on duty. 'He says he did it because one of the girls wanted him to, but insists that he's never met any of them or even spoken to them on the phone. And he can't remember which one gave him his "orders". And why a Santa Claus, for Heaven's sake? Why not just some passerby in the street?'

'Killing an ordinary person certainly wouldn't have drawn so much attention,' said Janice. 'Perhaps it had to be someone outlandish. Did you ask him about the immersed crucifixes?' The sergeant seated herself on the far side of Hargreave's desk, stole a swig of his coffee and turned his notes around.

'He says he can't remember why he does that either. As he's been living the life of a vagrant, we can't prove his whereabouts on any of the nights in question. Although I'm damned sure that the doorman of the club wouldn't have let him in looking the way he does. There are a dozen other inconsistencies in his stories, and the details vary every time. And yet ...'

'What?' Janice surveyed the files which swamped the desk.

'He knows about Dominguez being found on the railings. He knows that the razor was inside his body. He knows that Howard Dickson was killed with a sword. We've told nobody about that. What do you reckon?'

'Simple,' said Janice. 'He's a nut. I'm not being facetious. He has an impaired, distorted memory. Who can tell what his priorities are? If he didn't do it, how could he have obtained inside police information, short of breaking in here at night? I'd say that until you uncover irrefutable proof of his innocence, you've got your man. What does his hospital file say about his past behaviour?'

Hargreave tamped the end of a thick cigar against its case and lit it. 'I don't know,' he answered. 'It was forwarded to the Wandsworth Clinic two years ago. They were the last people to treat him. I spoke to them this morning, but nobody seems to recall what happened to the file. The doctor who handled his case has since left. They also had a small fire which damaged part of the records office, so there's more delay and confusion. We're still looking, but God knows how long it's going to take.' He removed the cigar from his mouth and studied the glowing tip. 'I think there's an element we've overlooked throughout this.'

'What element is that?'

'The occult.'

'What, because of the witchcraft thing? A lot of mental patients have a strong belief in the occult listed on their personality profiles. It's very common.'

'It's not just that. A number of the victims were religious. Several wore crosses, which were removed after death.'

'What about Santa Claus?'

'Saint Nicholas. Blasphemy, perhaps, a false god. Let's find out.'

'How?'

Hargreave rose and reached for his overcoat. 'We ask a priest,' he said.

CHAPTER
32
Father Connor

'We meet again,' said Helen, raising her glass. 'More neutral ground.' She checked around the restaurant approvingly. 'One good thing about the separation. We're eating out more often than we used to.'

This time it was a cluttered fake-French bistro in Chiswick, a point roughly halfway between their two houses. Helen's swollen stomach was finally becoming noticeable, but she still seemed slim and full of energy. John, on the other hand, looked and felt terrible. True, the police had cleared him of a murder charge, but the strain of too many nightmare-plagued nights had begun to take its toll.

'You look rather tired,' she said, reading his thoughts. 'You're not still having bad dreams?'

'I don't think you'd believe me if I told you.'

She squared her shoulders to him, beckoning. 'Tell me.'

'I've been involved in Howard's murder investigation,' he said, clearing his throat. 'I knew these people that — died. I didn't know them very well, I just — knew them. I was released,' he added hastily. 'They caught the man. But the police thought I was connected to the case somehow.'

Helen frowned at the darkness beneath his eyes. More than anything else, she hated not understanding his new life. 'This is so unlike you, John. Things always used to happen to other people, never to you.'

'Well, I suppose all that changed.' He was granted a reprieve from further explanation as the waiter appeared to take their lunch order.

'You know I went to Howard's funeral?' she said when they were once more alone.

'No, I had no idea. How was Angela?'

'She bore up very well. Some reporters tried to interview her at the graveside. I was rather taken aback to see your name in the paper, something about you being the last person to see the victim alive. It was a non-story of course, they were only dragging it out because minor royalty sometimes visits that club.'

'I felt terrible when I heard what had happened to him, responsible somehow.'

'Have you found a new job yet?'

'Nobody is prepared to employ me until after Christmas.'

'Things must be difficult for you.' She smoothed her napkin across her lap. 'I thought we ought to meet today because time is pushing on. After our last lunch together, I consulted the lawyers about freezing the proceedings, but they advised me not to do so. In case it didn't work out between us.'

'You mean if we don't reach a decision soon, we'll wind up getting a divorce whether we want it or not.' John brushed a lock of hair from his eyes and tried to look as if he was savouring his wine in a relaxed manner.

'That's right. I'm told that the case could be dealt with very quickly.'

'How quickly?'

'The end of January. It's the condition of adultery that paces it up. Plus the fact that both parties consent to the divorce.'

'Ah, but do they?'

'You tell me, John.'

'I still love you.'

'Enough to come back to me?' Helen leaned forward and crossed her hands, waiting for a reply. An awkward silence fell between them. He hadn't expected her to demand a decision over lunch.

'I need more time to sort things out,' he explained. 'It's complicated. How's Josh?' The shift of subject was badly handled.

Helen instantly took offence. 'Your son is fine. It's you I'm worried about.' She removed the napkin from her lap and rose. 'He wants you back, and so do I. We both think you need to be saved from yourself.'

'Helen—'

'Listen, John, you can't have it both ways. There's no point in us meeting again until you've reached a decision.' She forced a smile, but he could see disappointment in her face. 'Just don't make me wait too long.'

He watched her slowly leave the restaurant. As she reached the door she dipped her head, as if she had something caught in her eye.

Father Matthew Connor was not a modern priest. He did not raise money by holding bingo sessions in some newly built church extension. He refused to abbreviate hymns, and did not illustrate his sermons by having the parishioners' children prance about with teatowels on their heads. He preached heavenly redemption, eternal damnation and very little in between. His craggy face, deep-set eyes and bushy brows seemed designed to encourage this endeavour.

'Naturally, I'm very involved with Satan,' he said, walking between the pews collecting hymnbooks after Monday's evening service. 'And I suppose he is with me.' He gestured to the stack of hymnbooks. 'The boy used to do this, now he's forever going missing in the evenings. Football season. A good lad but as they say, a walk through the ocean of his soul would scarcely get your feet wet. I trust you'll take a drop of something with me?' As they entered the gloomy vestibule, Father Connor reached into his cupboard and poured two very decent measures of whisky into a pair of tumblers.

'Oh yes,' he said cheerfully, 'I take a great personal interest in Hell. I can explain this business of putting the crucifixes in water, if that's what your main concern is.' He sat back in his tattered armchair and savoured his drink for a moment. 'It's a Middle European thing. Did you ever see those vampire films now, the Dracula chap? Awfully afraid of the crucifix, and of all its manifestations.'

'Yes, I'm familiar with the films.'

'We get Dracula from Vlad the Impaler, of course. Romanian, I think he was, and a very real person. If you remember, Dracula didn't just have problems with the crucifix, there were a number of other things that gave him grief. Cloves of garlic, hawthorns — representing Christ's crown, running water. There are many items which have developed religious significance. But some of these things cancel each other out, water and the crucifix in particular.'

'You mean the murderer dropped the crosses in water to nullify their effect?'

'Yes, but rather to nullify their *after*-effect, their lingering holiness, as it were. You've got a very religious person here, preparing to commit a heinous sin beneath God's gaze, and here's a religious symbol strengthening His power about the victim's neck. You don't want to kill someone just to have them gain redemption in Heaven. Best way to de-activate it is drop it in water. Must be fresh though.' He made it sound a simple mechanical process, like stripping a car engine.

'What do you mean by fresh?'

'Water that's been run from a spring or river, a source that isn't still.' Hargreave thought of the Mall fountain, the bottled water — even in Brady's kitchen there had been a bottle of Perrier in the fridge. The water in the glass had simply lost its carbonation by the time the body was discovered.

'Of course,' Connor continued, refilling his companion's glass, 'you have your odd man out with Father Christmas.'

'What do you make of that?'

'Well now, Saint Nicholas is mentioned in Greek texts as early as the sixth century. He saved the little children you see, but it was the Germans and the French who produced the modern day myth. His feast day was dropped from the ecclesiastical calendar, and I imagine that there are purists for whom the celebration of such a saint in certain circumstances would constitute religious blasphemy.'

'I don't understand. What circumstances?'

'I'm given to understand from what I read in the awful tabloids that your Santa was a man of the Jewish faith,' explained Connor. 'And that would rather mean that your murderer was having a joke with you, wouldn't it?'

Hargreave's cheerful demeanour faded as he rose from his seat. 'Thank you, Father,' he said, offering his hand. 'It looks like I may need to call on you again.'

WINTER

CHAPTER
33
Dark

'You spend too much time moping around the house,' said Ixora. 'It's not healthy.'

John was standing at the window with his back to her, watching as a fresh squall of rain spackled the swaying leaves beyond the glass. From somewhere above came the steady drip of water leaking through a ceiling. 'I have to think of a way to make some money,' John replied. 'It's the wrong time to be looking for a job, and I can't start up on my own without capital.'

Ixora raised her eyes to the ceiling. 'The roof will have to be repaired if this rain keeps up.'

'At least that will be covered by your insurance.'

'It would if I had any.'

'You're not insured?'

'I never got around to it.'

He looked back at her. 'Where are you going?'

'Audition for a commercial.' She was dressed in an expensive black woollen jacket and skirt, part of the wardrobe she referred to as her 'combat outfit'.

'It's Christmas Eve,' he said absently, turning back to the window. Ixora laid an arm across his shoulder with a tired sigh.

'Stop thinking about the past so much, John. What's done is done.'

'I just want to understand it,' he said. 'Why do you think that guy killed Howard?'

'Who knows? I'm trying not to think about it.'

'Well, I can't help it.' Nothing about the recent past felt satisfactory or resolved. Any attempt at analysis merely reminded him of his doubts about Ixora.

'I don't suppose they'll ever find out. These things are never clear cut.' She moved her hands around his waist. 'Who are you blaming?'

'For what?'

Ixora shrugged. 'Losing your job, Howard's death, everything. You wander about the house like a soul in torment. And you don't trust me.' The room had suddenly grown dark around them, casting her eyes in pools of shadow.

'You don't know that.'

'Yes, I do. If you completely trusted me, you'd have shown it.'

'How?'

'I think you'd have asked me to marry you.'

'Christ, Ixora, it's hardly the right time. I'm not even divorced yet.' And I'm not completely sure that I want to be, he added mentally.

He had called Helen half a dozen times in the past two weeks and had yet to catch her at home. Christmas gifts hand delivered to her and Josh had been returned unopened. Last night he had waited until Ixora was asleep before ringing the house at 2.15 a.m. but there was still no reply. Could she have met someone? Perhaps she had changed her mind about wanting him back. If she failed to contact him, the divorce would continue to proceed.

'Let's do it,' Ixora cried suddenly, clutching at his arms, 'The time is never going to be right, don't you see? Let's not wait any longer. It may be the only way you'll learn to have faith in someone again. Making a decision will make you strong.' She forced him back from her. 'Propose to me, right now.'

'Don't be silly, Ixora …'

'You know, properly. On one knee.'

He suddenly saw that she meant it. There was a feverish light in her eyes as she slowly pushed him down before her. And at that moment he realised that she was right, that this was the only thing that would keep them together.

'Say the words. Four words.' She ruffled his hair. 'We don't have to name a date.'

Suppose he did it. They'd face the bad times together, side by side as man and wife. She would be his forever.

'Ixora—' He tried to clear the dryness in his throat. 'Will you — marry me?'

She clasped his hands together before them, arranging the pose like a photographer at a wedding. 'Yes, John, I'll marry you.' She lowered her face to his. 'From now on,' she whispered, lightly biting his neck, 'nothing will ever be able to harm us. Nothing at all.'

The tree had already begun to drop its needles. Helen crouched beneath the brittle branches with a dustpan and brush, cursing her decision to buy the damned thing in the first place. It had all been part of her attempt to keep up appearances, to make it seem as if everything was normal in the house. At the time it had seemed so necessary to prove that John's departure had not upset their daily routine. Now that pretence was over.

Josh was hardly ever at the house, so Helen spent more time with her church group. She had been reluctant to mention the separation to her few friends at the advisory centre, for fear of the questions they would ask. But the truth had quickly been discovered, and her fellow parishioners had rallied on her side against John and husbands in general.

Outside, the sleet rattled across the windows like handfuls of hurled gravel. She emptied the dustpan and searched for something else to do, straightening the Christmas cards on the mantelpiece as she passed. Josh had just returned from Cesar's house. She could hear him thumping around in the bathroom, washing before dinner.

This would be their first Christmas Eve alone. Her parents had moved to a retirement complex in Spain, and the thought of sitting with John's family while they avoided mentioning their son was too grim to contemplate. That left an ailing grandmother in a home in Chichester, two weird cousins and an uncle no one in her family could stand. Some Christmas.

She wondered why she had not heard from John. Either he was delaying his decision until after the festivities, or he couldn't bring himself to admit the truth; that he was happy where he was. Even so, it was odd that he hadn't sent his son a gift. If it wasn't for Josh's efforts they would never have met for lunch.

Tonight, instead of wrapping presents and opening wine as they had in previous years, she would attend her church service alone, and, if necessary, pray for her husband's soul. She plucked a silver ball from beneath the tree, where it had fallen from the dying branches. If John walked through the door this minute, she wondered if she would be able to resist taking him back. She despised his weakness, his falling for the oldest trick in the book. It was humiliating to have her desirability as a mate called into question. After lunching with John that first time in Camden Town, she had suddenly felt a desire to understand the enemy.

That afternoon she had watched Ixora from the garden of the house in Sloane Crescent. At first she could see only a shape drifting before the windows on the first floor. Then quite unexpectedly the front door had opened, and Helen had shifted into the darkness beneath the dripping hornbeams, scarcely daring to breathe as she waited for a first glimpse of the woman who had stolen her husband's heart.

The figure that had emerged was tall and sinuous, moving as lightly as a feather, carried along by the winter gale.

Helen was shocked by the appearance of her rival. Keeping her distance, she had stepped into the road and watched in dismay until Ixora had turned the corner. The thought of John succumbing to someone so youthful and glamorous was shattering.

Yet there was something shameless and unhealthy about the woman. Lately, Helen had felt herself growing more susceptible to feelings of Godlessness in others, and she had sensed a kind of suffocating, harmful presence in Ixora. She knew that nothing good could come of their union, even if it was legitimised in church.

Bitterly, she recalled her own cheerless ceremony in a freezing registry office so many years ago, how she had listened to the truncated text with her head bowed, as if the simplicity of the service would reduce the sin and shame of her pregnancy.

Her mother, who could cite a dire warning for every

occasion, had cautioned John that an elaborate wedding was the sign of a doomed marriage. Thank God, he had told her, that they'd decided against an ice sculpture for the reception buffet. She smiled at the memory.

'I thought you said we were eating at eight.'

The silver tree ornament in her hand cracked, leaving a red hairline across her palm. She looked up to see Josh standing in the hallway drying his hair. His resemblance to his father was more in evidence each day.

'There's no need to creep around like that,' she said, irritably brushing the shards from her hand into an ashtray. 'They've forecast terrible weather. I didn't think you'd make it back in time. You can lay the table. And try calling the cat again, will you? I can't believe she's outside in the rain.'

While she drained off the vegetables at the sink, Josh called to her from the dining room. 'I was reading about this kind of thing. Male menopause. He's proving his manhood, like when apes bang on their chests. That's why he hasn't called.'

'And I'm supposed to take him back so that he can pull me around by my hair.' She stood a colander under a saucepan and poured sprouts into it. 'It's not as if she kidnapped him, for Heaven's sake. He's an adult, capable of making his own decisions. He's supposed to be sensible.'

'I don't think common sense has much to do with it,' Josh called back. 'It's just chemistry, glands and hormones, like sap rising in—'

'I get the picture, thank you,' she snapped, lifting the filled plates and carrying them into the hallway.

The sudden plunge into darkness made her miss her footing and stumble across the threshold of the room, dropping both meals in the process.

'Mum?'

Helen tried to rise from her knees, but the fiery pain in

her ankle forced her down. Broken china surrounded her hands.

'Josh, where are you?'

'Over here, by the door. Are you all right?'

Slowly her eyes adjusted to the gloom. 'I think so,' she said, testing her ankle. 'There are some candles in the drawer by the sink. Is the whole street out?'

Josh's silhouette appeared at the window. She rose to her feet, keeping the weight from her sore ankle.

'Next door's dark. Perhaps it's an electrical overload. Don't move.' He headed for the kitchen. Moments later she heard the drawer being opened. The silence of the dining room was broken by the sound of the storm gathering overhead. A faint yellow haze bled through the curtains from the street lamps beyond. Slowly she made her way to the window, leaning against the chairbacks as she went.

The street was rainswept and deserted. Above the house, the rising wind moaned through dark cables, shifting them from side to side. She could no longer hear Josh moving about in the kitchen. The house had suddenly become as silent as the dark, as if all sensation was being muffled, swallowed up. Helen peered out, cooling her forehead against the cold glass. Sleet was catching on the immaculate lawn of the house next door. The lurid array of coloured Christmas lights which framed their porch was now a string of rattling dead bulbs.

Suddenly the sight was replaced with a face, inches from the glass, crimson mouth formed wide in a shocked shrieking circle, whites displayed around surprised black pupils. Helen screamed and fell back from the window just as it exploded over her, showering heavy glass shards across the dining room table.

She crawled across the floor to the front wall of the room, heedless of the glass beneath her knees.

'Josh! My God, where are you?'

Her hand touched something hot and fleshy lying on the floor. With a cry she recoiled. The cuprous smell of blood was on her fingers. She raised them in front of her eyes. There was blood everywhere. It was pumping from something right beside her, pooling around her legs. Confused and terrified, she began to cry.

A second pair of windows burst inwards, shattered in unison, glass fragments chiming and clattering to the carpet.

Josh had run back into the room. Suddenly his thin arms were around her, dragging her aside to an armchair. He dashed into the hall and threw the front door wide, halting before the felled pole which had brought the power line down into the side of the house. The cable fizzed and crackled against the wet earth, glittering with tiny blue sparks.

In the desecrated darkness, his mother cried out as she saw the shredded body of the creature that had been hurled into the room. The cat lay twisted on the floor, its back broken, its innards protruding. As the animal's blood dripped from her hands, Helen began to shake, and her conviction that demonic forces were gathering about them began to develop an unbreakable grip.

She knelt before the flickering figure of Christ, her hands clasped in fervent prayer. The Christmas service had ended, and the church was now deserted. The verger was waiting beside the opened far doors. He could damned well wait, she thought. Her communion with God was more important. Although her wrenched ankle made walking difficult, she had insisted on attending church alone. Some prayers could not be shared.

The neighbours had wanted to call her a doctor, but she had refused the idea of medical attention. They were concerned for the welfare of her unborn child, they said, and the traumatic after-effects of shock. It was funny how they never spoke to her the rest of the year, except to complain about smoke from the barbeque drifting near their washing.

She had left Josh and the neighbours to nail chipboard across the broken windows. A team from the power company had appeared within the hour to shift the cables away from the house. They had been unable to promise restored electricity for Christmas Day. Everyone had been so quick to offer rational explanations. The storm had brought the pole down against the windows. The cat had been standing on one of the ledges. She had shivered and listened, unconvinced.

Now, as she knelt on cut knees before the garishly painted statue of the Lord, she prayed for forgivenness, not for herself, but for John. A bright, hard pain was beginning to burn within her swollen belly, a signifier that the gathering diabolic forces had tonight achieved their aim.

With a bitter wind moaning at her back, and the candles flickering smokily about her, she prayed for her husband's divine deliverance. From Ixora. From evil.

CHAPTER
34
Flight

Hargreave sat in the darkened observation room waiting for the officers to lead Donald Wingate from the chamber next door. He was unable to light his cigar until the room had been vacated, because the lit end would show through the two-way glass that stood between them.

For the past two hours they had listened to Wingate answering questions in a flat exhausted monotone. It was Boxing Day afternoon, and the third psychiatric session that week which had been attended by Hargreave. He swung the chair around to face Raymond Land, who was not looking at all pleased.

'Well, what do you think?'

'Ian, I'm a forensic doctor, not a psychiatrist. This isn't my area. You should talk to the chaps who've been conducting the interviews with him.'

'True,' agreed Hargreave, searching his jacket for

matches, 'but you were directly advising the original officer in charge of this case, and as he was killed in the course of duty I think you've inherited an extra share of the involvement. Besides, if I question the interviewing doctors they'll just give me psychiatric gobbledygook until their reports are ready, and you know that won't be until the New Year.' He lit the cigar and sat back, loosening the knot of his garish tie. Land looked at him doubtfully. Nevertheless, Hargreave noticed that he had made notes while observing the interview.

'You saw his charge sheet, arrested for shooting Father Christmas, and his claims to the murders of half a dozen people. He'd have been kicked out of here if it wasn't obvious that he'd actually used live ammunition. Now I need to know if this man has a classifiable mental disorder.'

'That won't be so easy to define,' said Land. 'There's not much of a line between neurosis and mere unhappiness. He's self-centred, manipulative, insensitive; classic signs of a personality problem. How was he when they picked him up?'

Hargreave checked his file. 'Sweating, pale, fast pulse-rate. The arresting officer thought he was having a heart attack.'

'That would merely be an advanced anxiety state, consistent with the action of firing a gun, tells you nothing. Psychopaths rarely understand the consequences of their actions. They don't learn by experience, don't really care what happens to them. They have no conscience. They tend to be defiant toward society, and successfully resist therapy. Shooting at Santa Claus suggests paranoia to me. He's in the right age bracket, forty-five, and from his responses today he would seem to be sexually maladjusted. Paranoics often set off on what they see to be their mission in life by basing all their logical thinking on a single accepted false premise.'

'In other words, Wingate could think he's been placed on earth to remove a particular type of person who might harm him ...'

'Exactly. There are many types of psychosis, brought on by everything from alcohol to rogue hereditary genes, but you'll have to consult an expert for those.'

Hargreave looked around the tiny anteroom. 'There's supposed to be at least one observing psychiatrist in here acting as a control, but there's no one available. They're all away for Christmas, probably skiing.'

'I always prefer to work through,' said Land. 'The West End's nice and quiet. I assume the tie you're wearing was a Christmas present.'

'From my ex-wife,' said Hargreave. 'That's how much she hates me. What did you get?'

'The hits of Andrew Lloyd-Webber, sung in Welsh.'

'Stone me. Someone's got it in for you too.'

They both turned back to the window, and the empty room beyond.

'You know, listening to the inconsistencies in Wingate's answers, it sounds to me as if someone's spun his compass so hard he has no idea which way he's facing. Mentally, that is.' Hargreave lit his cigar with relish. Janice had bought him a box of them for Christmas, the one decent gift he'd received.

'Why do you say that?'

'He's scrambled up over everything in his life — except the murders. He's got times, places, details that half the investigating officers aren't even aware of. It's the testimony of an eye witness, plain and simple. I'd swear he was there.'

'Then perhaps you'll have to accept that he did it,' said Land, irritably wafting the smoke aside. It was common knowledge that the only factor still delaying the case was Hargreave's reluctance to accept Wingate's guilt.

'Believe me, Raymond, I want to accept it.' Hargreave knew that he had to be more circumspect in his findings than anyone realised. The Home Office had taken an unhealthy interest in proving Wingate's guilt, partly because one of the murders had occurred within the vicinity of the royal household, but also because Wingate seemed to have obliterated his personal background so thoroughly that some form of organised terrorism was suggested.

Checking through the interview transcripts he had noted Wingate's deep-seated belief in Satan, and his conviction that the Devil could perform his work through human channels. But he still didn't buy it. Watching as the broad, shuffling man had been led from the room with his head bowed, hands knotted together with rubberised straps, he had been assailed with the feeling that far from seeing the Devil at work, he was merely being palmed off with one of his disciples. Before each session, he had watched their suspect sizing up his interrogators, readying his replies in measured tones. Something about the performance just didn't ring true.

'I'm going to draw up a new list of questions for Mr Wingate,' he decided. 'I don't know how I'll do it, but I'm going to catch him out.'

It was John's first Christmas without visits from argumentative relatives, without lounging in front of the television after too much turkey, complacent in the knowledge that his next meal was already being prepared. He and Ixora hid themselves away on the first floor of the house in Sloane Crescent, planning and speculating, looking to the future and carefully avoiding any mention of the past. They attempted to cook, with Ixora exhibiting total ignorance of typical British Christmas cuisine, and were finally forced to rely on takeouts.

John carried out some minor repairs to the roof, but the bad weather prevented him from tackling any major work. It had been mutually decided that they should not buy presents for each other. Instead they added to the nest egg, that small amount of money they had pooled in their joint account from a handful of John's surrendered insurance policies and the sale of Ixora's few stocks left to her by her mother.

'There are a couple of paintings on the landing that might be valuable,' Ixora suggested, tearing off a section of pizza and folding it into her mouth. 'And there's the furniture.'

'We're not that desperate yet,' John replied, knowing that they soon would be. Outside, the snow that had settled on Christmas Eve had ripened to sienna-coloured slush. As it was too expensive to heat all of the rooms, they confined themselves to the bedroom and the kitchen. With so few hours of daylight, they rose late in the day, reluctant to forsake the warmth beneath the golden quilt.

On the day after Boxing Day, Ixora was called back for a second audition and John found himself seated before the telephone, wondering whether to call Helen. He couldn't believe that they hadn't spoken to each other over Christmas. Finally he lifted the receiver and dialled. To his surprise, the call was answered.

'Mum's just come back from her prayer meeting,' said Josh. 'Why didn't you call us?'

'I tried your number lots of times, Josh. I thought you must have gone away to Nan's.'

'Maybe there was something wrong with the phone. I tried to get Mum to call you but she wouldn't.'

'Why not?'

'There was an accident here on Christmas Eve. A power line came down and some windows broke. It killed the cat and Mum's knee got cut.'

'That's terrible. I can't believe she didn't call. Are you okay? Is everything all right now?'

'Yeah. I spent Boxing Day over at Cesar's house because our lounge windows were boarded up. His stepfather bought him a load of Nintendo stuff for his PC. We played Super Mario a lot. Mum's been out with the church most of the time. Dad . . .' Josh allowed a silence to fall between them.

'Yes?'

Josh lowered his voice. 'Mum's in the next room. She's acting really strange. Praying all the time. It's not much like home any more.'

A sickening wave of guilt swept over him. At least they'd still be a family if he hadn't torn them apart.

'Josh, let me speak to her.'

'I don't think she wants to. She's changed.'

'Is she there now?'

'Yes.'

'Ask her to come to the phone.'

There was the sound of the receiver being set down. A minute later, Josh returned.

'She won't speak to you, Dad.'

It made no sense. Things had been improving, hadn't they? He spoke to Josh for a while longer, but too much remained unsaid beneath their conversation. He promised to ring the boy again in a few days.

Depressed by the call, John decided to go out and buy Ixora a present. Their Christmas had been too frugal, he decided. It was time to put a little *joie de vivre* back in their lives. He had seen a slim silver bracelet in the window of a jeweller's in the Fulham Road. It would be his engagement gift to her.

At Barclays Bank in Sloane Square, the cashier looked at him blankly. 'There's not enough money in your account to cover this withdrawal,' she said simply, sliding the cheque back beneath the glass.

'That's impossible,' he said angrily, drawing out his chequebook and checking the stubs. 'There's over two thousand pounds in there.'

'The computer says not.'

'There must be a mistake. Can't you double check?'

'Wait a minute.' She pushed away from her desk and consulted the central computer. A woman in the queue behind him released a theatrical sigh. Finally the cashier returned with a slip of paper in her hand.

'That's your balance,' she said, passing him the slip.

He glanced down at the amount. Five pounds. The bare minimum required to keep the account open. How could that be?

'Can you tell me when the last withdrawal was made?' he asked. The cashier consulted with her colleague at the next window, while the woman behind him blasted out a hiss of annoyance that was the product of a lifetime spent on the stage.

'This morning,' said the colleague. 'A lady in a red dress. The co-signee on your account. Said she was going away. Can't blame her in this weather.'

All of his old fears came flooding back. It was as if they had never been away. He ran out into the street, his soaked shoes splashing water over his trousers, muddying his coat. By the time he reached the house he was badly out of breath. The house was in darkness. She was taking his money and running out. And to think he had finally begun to believe in her!

He sat in the kitchen, his wet clothes steaming, trying to tamp the flames of his anger, trying to remain rational. The attempt failed. He ran to the bedroom, climbing on a chair to check the suitcases on top of the wardrobe. Where was the large one with the handle, the Samsonite? He couldn't tell from looking at the endless clothes hangers whether she had packed anything or not. Where was the black outfit she said she couldn't travel without? He pulled out drawer after drawer, his frenzy building with each new revelation of supposedly missing clothes.

She'd gone from the house, then, never to return, vanishing into the cool dark drizzle just as she had arrived, with no trace of her origin or her destination. Perhaps he could still catch her. She'd never get a taxi in this weather. How would she get to the airport?

Without realising what he was doing, he found himself outside, heading down the path, running the length of the Crescent, turning past the Royal Court Theatre. On the far side of the street he spun around, starring into the distance to watch for cabs. Nothing was stopping in the rain. No amber hire lights shone from taxi roofs. As he turned back he almost collided with her.

Ixora's eyes were wide with surprise. He was obviously the last person she expected to see. Unable to think, unable to see through the rain and his own tears, he seized her arms and began to shake her back and forth.

'Where the hell have you been?' he shouted. 'Where do you think you're going?'

She looked guiltlessly up at him. The rain had plastered her hair to her forehead. Instead of a suitcase, she carried a plastic Sainsbury's shopping bag.

'What do you mean? I've been to the audition. I'm coming home.' She tried to pull free, twisting from one side to the other. 'You're hurting me!'

'Tell me where you're going, damn it!' He shook her harder. 'Why did you steal the money?'

'Let go before I scream!' Her eyes widened and she pulled an arm from his grip, pushing him in the chest until he released her and stood panting in the rain.

'I didn't steal the money,' she shouted at him, 'I took it out — to pay for our wedding! It was supposed to be a surprise but you've ruined it!'

John was confused. 'What do you mean?'

She furiously threw the shopping bag to one side. 'I mean I've done it, I've arranged everything, and because some of the bills have to be paid in advance I withdrew the money to cover them. I was going to replace it before you found out ...'

John held up his hand. He'd had enough of this. 'You don't have any money to replace it with, how could you ...' Then he saw the paleness of her bare neck. The necklace was gone, the heirloom of perfect pearls that her mother had bequeathed to her.

'Are you happy now?' she screamed at him, tears sheening her eyes as she thrust her hand deep into a pocket and withdrew a fistful of paper slips. 'I pawned the necklace to cover the loan. I didn't know how much I'd get so I took the cash out first to meet the bills. Do you want to see the receipts?'

John took a step back, aghast. 'Oh, Ixora, I'm so sorry,' he murmured.

'No,' she cried, bursting into tears. 'I'm sorry, because you've ruined everything. All the hard work, all the planning, all ruined.' With her hand over her eyes she shoved past him and ran off along the road. The shopping bag lay on the pavement, bright oranges rolling to rest in the gutter.

By the time he reached the house she had gone, and this time there were real signs that she had left — clothes tipped out, suitcases missing. The china money jar on the kitchen mantelpiece that contained their emergency funds lay shattered and empty on the floor.

The front door stood open, water pooling in the hallway. He searched the street in both directions, calling her name, slipping in the puddles, his soaked shirt stuck to his chest. There was no one on the street, not even a shadowed figure in the distance. Ixora had vanished into the darkening afternoon, and this time he knew he would not discover her so easily.

Perhaps his arid years in suburbia had blunted his ability to love and be loved. He had been given a second chance to live, and he had managed to screw it up. All that had been asked of him was to trust and love unquestioningly, to prove his faith in one woman.

He knew that if he was ever to see her again, he would never let her leave his sight, for fear of losing her completely. Reaching the gate of the house he bent double and vomited, filled with the horror of his loss, a stomach-dropping hurt that deepened with each passing moment.

Ixora had gone. She had gone, forever.

CHAPTER
35
Vanished

Settled in what had become his usual position, Hargreave watched and waited in the observation chamber as Wingate was led in and shackled to the heavy steel chair in the centre of the room. Over the past week the prisoner had become increasingly violent, lashing out at the detention officers and managing on one occasion to loosen the front teeth of an interviewing doctor. Now it had become necessary to keep him under various forms of restraint around the clock.

For the past two weeks Wingate had been detained at a high security holding bay in a building behind Tottenham Court Road. The centre had been converted from part of the old Middlesex Hospital, but as it was only suitable for short-stay patients, Wingate would have to be shifted on before the commencement of a state trial.

To date, Hargreave's biggest stumbling block lay in the establishment of Wingate's innocence according to his ability to distinguish between right and wrong. In the absence of any earlier knowledge of his whereabouts, his mental and medical history had to be re-created in full from scraps of scattered information.

Did Wingate understand the nature and gravity of his actions? His lucidity was variable at the best of times, yet he seemed quite capable of making basic moral judgements. When questioned about the deaths, his face blanked. The murders presented a paradox. After all, if they were premeditated, why were they carried out with such extreme violence? His motives were shadowy; he had killed the men who exploited 'his girls'. Was this enough reason to encourage such frenzied attacks? Had he known the victims, or were they merely designs in a broader pattern only he understood?

Janice Longbright entered the chamber, quietly sealing the door behind her. For the past week she had been sifting through resident information from hostels, hotels, hospitals and day-care centres, trying to find someone who had seen or heard of Donald Wingate, so far without any luck. On the forensic front, however, the news was more encouraging.

'More positive matches for you,' she said, tapping Hargreave lightly on the shoulder. She handed him the latest lab update.

'I can't read it in here,' whispered Hargreave, never taking his eyes from the window. 'Tell me what it says.'

'They've got a second confirmed pairing.' Earlier in the week, fibres from Dominguez's jacket were found to be identical to those removed from Wingate's trousers. 'Remember the minute slivers of skin they found beneath the fingers of his left hand? Raymond Land reckons that the SEM's particle analysis reveals skin structure consistent with scar tissue.' The Scanning Electronic Microscope was a powerful and versatile weapon in the forensic armoury. 'Apparently Dominguez had a tattoo removed from his left arm some years ago. Land's got a positive match with it.'

'Looks as if that about wraps it up,' said Hargreave. 'There's not much else we can do.'

'What about De Corizo's ring?' asked Janice. 'Any idea what it was doing beside Dickson's body?'

'It had been in his jacket pocket. Must have popped out when he fell.'

'How did you find that out?'

'He chewed gum, and he was neat.'

'I'm not sure I follow you.'

'He'd removed a piece from his mouth earlier and put it in the foil wrapper until he could find a place to throw it. The wrapper was in his pocket, and had picked up an impression of the ring. Still doesn't explain why he had it in his possession, though. Any results on the red metallic particles?'

'Land's assistant says they were sent out for emission spectograph tests and that part of the sample batch was destroyed when it was heated. The rest is apparently still in transit.

Hargreave pulled out a stool and indicated that the sergeant should sit. 'Now that you're here, stay and watch this,' he said, pointing to the window. 'It's something I asked them to do. I wanted to see how Wingate would react.'

In the room beyond, the doctor had removed something from his pocket and was holding it before his patient in a closed fist. A glass of water stood on a small table between them. The doctor uncurled his fingers to reveal a small gold crucifix. For nearly thirty seconds Wingate remained motionless, his eyes fixed on the glittering cross.

Then he slowly opened his mouth and released an eardrum-piercing scream, his arms struggling against the restraining straps, hands grasping at the air. As the doctor reached forward and dropped the cross into the tumbler, Wingate's head fell forward and he slumped in his chair, held in place by his bonds.

Hargreave rose from his seat and paced before the window. 'I don't understand it,' he said finally. 'That was my ace in the hole. I was convinced he wouldn't react.'

'What made you think he was innocent?'

'Because there's something I've forgotten,' said Hargreave, 'something I either overlooked in Sullivan's notes or missed in the crime reports.'

'The murders ended with his arrest.'

'Don't you think I know that? Someone's being clever and I don't like it.'

'More than that,' said Janice, holding open the door. 'You can't prove it.'

It was two weeks now since Ixora had vanished.

The first two nights had passed in sheer misery, as he sat up waiting, praying for her return. Even at that stage he had become convinced that he would never see her again. Ixora never said anything she didn't mean. She was not a woman to make idle threats. Shattered by this thought he had emptied the cocktail cabinet, only to spend the next day nursing a monumental hangover.

Three days after their argument, Ixora had failed to appear at Shepperton Studios for a day's work on a new building society commercial. Diana Morrison had been quick to call her at home. 'Well, do you know where she might have gone?' she had asked John irritably. 'It's inconsiderate and unprofessional of her, and it harms our good relations with the agency. Did she say how long she was going away for?'

'I have no idea. I'm not in the business any more.'

'Of course not, I forgot. Poor Howard. Well, I must dash. You will let me know if you hear from her?'

'I was going to ask you the same thing.'

'You don't think we should call the police?' she added as an afterthought. 'I mean, after all that's happened …'

'I've already called them.'

'Well, I don't know what gave you the right to do that. I hope you didn't mention the agency. We've had enough bad publicity as it is.'

'Don't worry, I didn't mention you.' He could not be bothered to argue with the woman.

'I should hope not. It's the least you can do, after all the trouble you've caused.'

'What do you mean?'

'Forgive me, but didn't you beat Howard up in public?' Her voice grew heated. 'None of this started until you arrived. I must say you always struck me as rather suspicious. Not quite PR material.'

He suddenly realised that it was Diana who had denounced him in the anonymous phone call. 'You called the police the morning after Howard died,' he said numbly.

'I never trusted you from the start,' she snapped. 'I still don't. For all I know you may have murdered Ixora as well as Howard.'

'I would have thought even you would understand that I love her,' he said, throwing down the receiver. As he lay back on the quilt, a sense of desperation closed over him. The house was even gloomier without her. The light seemed to stay away, driven off by darkness. Bloated by the encroaching damp, the paper on the ceiling had started to peel and lift.

He had to find her, but how? She had no close friends to speak of. He had spoken to a couple of the other models, ~~~ had no idea of her whereabouts. Where was her family? He had found nothing of importance among the papers in her desk, but she had to have documents, policies, certificates — everyone did. Perhaps they were stored with a relative, somewhere on the continent. He returned to the desk, opening the forced drawer and turning it out onto the quilt. The only item he had failed to examine in his previous searches was a dog-eared paperback book, which he now picked up.

TEACH YOURSELF SPANISH.

Why should she want to do that? Surely Spanish had been her native tongue. It was one of the subjects he had not been allowed to discuss with her. Once more he examined the diary with its jagged core of missing pages, wondering whether she had destroyed them to protect some shameful secret, or hidden them safely to vouchsafe their value.

That night John escaped from the oppressive gloom of Sloane Crescent and embarked on an evening-long drinking spree. It was something he hadn't intended to do, and had not done for years, but by ten o'clock his mind was pleasantly anaesthetised with vodka, and he was talking to a bar-propped woman with backcombed red hair in a hotel in St John's Wood.

'That's the trouble,' he concluded, watching his companion arrange a line of olives beside her empty glass. 'My mistrust drove her away. She was the woman of my dreams.'

'There's no love without trust,' agreed his companion. 'My name's Geraldine. Would you like to buy me a drink?'

John tried to focus on her but she kept moving around. 'Why, are you thirsty?'

'No, I'm a lush.'

'Fair enough.' He ordered another round. 'You want to be careful. I think you've had one too many.'

'How can you tell?' she asked with a smile.

'You're getting blurred.'

The bartender brought the drinks over. Geraldine removed the olive from her martini and lined it with the others. 'Self pity is a lousy way to attract women,' she said. 'Going on about the girl of your dreams. It's not very attractive.'

'I'm not trying to attract you. I'm trying to get drunk.' He flicked a peanut at her.

'You're doing a pretty good job,' said the bartender.

'Forget this girl,' said Geraldine. 'Go out with me instead.'

'No thank you,' said John. 'I'd never be sober.'

He left the bar and caught a taxi to Soho. Then it seemed that events occurred in brittle flashes, tableaux of lurid colour and sound. He remembered a spirited argument in a pub in Old Compton Street, loud music, a crowded club — or was it a casino? — some pushing and shoving. After that, everything faded to black.

He slowly regained consciousness to find himself on the floor of Ixora's bedroom, fully dressed. As he tried to lift his head, a fierce pain shot between his eyes, lodging in his brain, jarring it with every movement. He tried to discover the time, but the face of his watch was smashed. His right trouser leg was torn. Dried blood caked his hands.

'Oh God . . .' He slowly hauled himself to his feet. The bedroom alarm clock read 3.15 p.m. His mouth felt mink-lined. When it came to hard drinking, he had always been an amateur. When he staggered into the bathroom, the mirror revealed a swollen, livid patch below his right eye and a deep gash across his forehead.

What the hell had happened last night? He checked his — Thank God he still had his wallet. He had left the house with forty pounds, all the money he had left in the world. He opened the billfold now. Empty. It was hardly surprising. He checked his other pocket and found it stuffed with crumpled sheets of paper. Digging deep, he pulled out the contents and laid them on the counter beside the sink.

There was nearly two thousand pounds, mostly in fifty pound notes.

'Jesus Christ, what have I done?' He sat down hard on the edge of the bath, trying to think.

An hour later he had thrown up twice, shaved, showered and drunk four cups of strong, hot, black coffee. Tablets had faded his headache to a dull throb. As he disinfected and dressed the cut on his forehead, the events of the previous night began to piece themselves together.

The two men he had met in the pub, he had told them about Ixora and they had insisted that he needed cheering up. They had taken him to the casino. He winced as he remembered telling them he had never played cards in his life. Now he recalled that they had arranged for him to borrow some money. But how much? And what on earth had he given them in return? He double-checked the pockets of his suit and turned up a folded business card belonging to one Murray Mancuso, Offshore Investors Ltd. There was a telephone and fax number, but no address.

He returned to the bedroom but the smell of alcohol still permeated the air, so he made the phone call from the kitchen. At the other end of the line a distant telephone rang, but there was no reply. He replaced the receiver and resolved to try again later.

How had he ever managed to get home? He smoothed out the fifty pound notes and placed them carefully in a drawer, vaguely recalling the minicab driver who had helped him to the front door. One thousand nine hundred and seventeen pounds. Unable to think further, he opened the bedroom windows and crawled back beneath the quilt, ashamed of his behaviour, appalled by his naïvety.

His dreams were filled with threatening shadows and half-explained acts of violence. In the midst of it all, he saw Ixora wading from a pool of blood, a bridal veil obscuring her eyes. Someone was shouting at him, someone else laughing. Ixora was in tears, begging him to stay, or perhaps to leave.

He awoke in hazy sunshine, his head clear, the room freezing in the light of a fresh morning. Rising and dressing, he headed for the kitchen, his drunken binge blurring into a distant bad dream. There was a letter on the front doormat bearing his name, manually typed. He tore it open.

The thin sheet of paper inside was a receipt. From Offshore Investors Ltd., for the amount of three thousand five hundred pounds.

How could he have been so stupid? Where had the rest of the money gone? He had spent £1,583 on an evening out, getting ripped off with cheap champagne in some illegal gambling den, then being thrown out after he had sobered up enough to complain. He'd been conned, as if he was an eighteen-year-old kid up from the suburbs with his first pay packet. At least he was still in one piece … Then he read the rest of the receipt, and a dropping sensation filled his stomach.

The amount to be repaid within two weeks, at 22 per cent interest, doubling to 44 per cent within one month.

He was dead. He was history. He had nothing; no savings, no job, a mortgaged home, occupied by his pregnant almost-ex-wife, school fees to find for his son. He felt as if he had been led through the seven deadly sins one by one, with lust leading the way. Hadn't sex shoved him into this mess in the first place? No, Ixora had fulfilled a need within him, right from the start. If only he could have accepted her love unconditionally. Without Ixora he was rudderless, a man with no purpose.

He knew that there was only one way out. Wherever she had gone, wherever she was hiding, he would have to play detective and find her.

CHAPTER
36
Hunting

Ian Hargreave turned into Sloane Crescent and checked off the house numbers in pairs until he reached John Chapel's residence. It took him several shoves to free the rain-swollen wooden gate. The detached Victorian villa would soon need repairs if it was to maintain its value. The window frames and the green-painted eaves were peeling badly. The roots of the nearest hornbeam were obviously damaging the brickwork, much of which was crumbling into fine red powder.

He thought of his own flat in Muswell Hill and knew that he would never be able to afford such a house as this. But at least he was high above the city, where chill winds swept the air clean and freshened the skin. Chelsea was claustrophobic, he thought to himself, too many cars jammed into the streets, too many people trying to stay smart. He rang the doorbell and stepped back, looking up at the rain-smeared windows.

The sight which greeted him was far from smart. Chapel looked as if he'd fallen into a threshing machine. An encrusted gash scarred his forehead, and one side of his face was swollen with dying yellow bruises. His shirt was unironed, the knees of his trousers covered with dust. He seemed surprised and not at all pleased to see him.

'I'm sure you remember me, Mr Chapel,' he said, offering his hand. 'Can I come in for a moment?'

Chapel stayed silent, but held the door wide. The hallway beyond was hidden in gloom. As if suddenly realising that he was not alone, he clicked on a battery of brass light switches. 'I'm sorry,' he said vaguely, 'I'm used to being in the dark.'

'You weren't sleeping?' Hargreave looked about the hall. Sour cold air filled his nostrils. There was rising damp here.

Chapel snorted. 'Sleeping? God, no. Come on through. I'll see if there's any coffee.'

The kitchen appeared to be the only room that was currently occupied. A week's washing-up stood in the sink. In the corner, several floorboards had been cut and raised. Hargreave cleared a pile of newspapers from a chair and seated himself at the table. 'Doing a bit of DIY?' he asked.

'There's something wrong with the lights. I've been trying to patch it up. I suppose you're here about the case.' John filled a kettle and plugged it in.

'I have a bit of a problem, Mr Chapel.'

'You accused me of murder, you might as well call me John,' he said, extracting a pair of mugs from the sink and rinsing them. 'I thought it had all been cleared up.'

'Quite a lot of people think that. We have a man in custody, an ex-psychiatric patient with a history of violence-related mental problems. He's given us a full confession.'

'Why did he do it?'

'That's one thing we haven't had much luck finding out. Anyway, I haven't accepted the confession yet.'

'Why not?'

'Because whatever his level of involvement in the murders, it still doesn't seem to be as central as yours.'

'Wait a minute, you cleared me.'

'That's correct. Don't misunderstand, this is purely a social call.' Hargreave stared glumly into the steaming mug set before him. The milk had bits in it. 'Your girlfriend, gone away for a while, has she?'

Chapel did not reply. He didn't need to. His face had drained to the colour of greaseproof paper.

'I assume she's left you.'

Still no reply. Hargreave hoped he wouldn't attempt to lie. He obviously wasn't very good at it. He appeared to be under a great deal of emotional stress.

'Well, I'm sorry to hear it. She was very charming, very beautiful.'

'Look, I don't know where she's gone. If you want to talk to her, you'll have to find her yourself.'

'Fine, fine.' He took a sip of bitter, burnt coffee. 'When did she leave? Did you argue? Do you have any sugar?'

'Actually, I stabbed her and stuck her under the floorboards.'

For one terrible moment Hargreave wondered if he was serious.

'This is important, John,' he said sharply. 'She's at the heart of this whole business and you know it. Now, suppose something's happened to her? Don't you care?'

'I care too damn much, that's the trouble. I was so jealous, checking her out for lies, hating every moment she was out of my sight. I was filled with this rampant paranoia that she might be up to something behind my back. I couldn't imagine what she saw in me, so I didn't believe she really loved me. I guess that's what happens when someone ordinary falls for someone extraordinary.'

'What happened the last time you saw her?' Hargreave asked.

'I mistrusted her once too often. It was over some money she'd borrowed. She said she would never see me again, and walked out. She kept her word.'

'Have you tried tracking her down?'

'None of the people she works with has heard from her. She failed to turn up for a modelling job. I'm beginning to think she's not even in the country.'

'That's right, she's French, isn't she?'

'Spanish.'

'There's no address in Spain, no relatives?'

'There are, but she was very secretive about her past. She never let me know where her family lived.'

'I could run an Interpol check for you, if you like.' For the first time since he had entered the house, he saw Chapel show an interest. 'It shouldn't be difficult. Do you have a photograph of her?'

John dug in his shirt pocket and produced a small picture, taken on the set of *Playing With Fire*. Hargreave carefully examined it.

'Seven murders,' he said. 'Seven odd, ritualistic deaths, and now a disappearance. I need you to think, John. There's something about this that doesn't make any sense. Something that begins with you meeting Ixora. Try to tell me exactly what happened on the night you met.'

John thought back. 'It was at a party. She was with her agent, I think. I was with my boss. I knew we were going to be working together. We introduced ourselves ...'

'Who first?'

'I did. I asked her where she was from. She said something about France. Provence.'

'I thought you said she was Spanish?'

'I can't remember. She was — French living in Spain, I guess. As I said, she hardly ever referred to her past. Actually, I'd seen her before that night.'

'Really? Where?'

'At Waterloo Station. I think she was running for a train. I asked her about it when we met, but the funny thing was she denied ever having been there.'

'What else did she say?'

'What do you want me to do,' he asked, 'remember the entire conversation?'

'If necessary, yes. You and Ixora are the only two who managed to emerge unscathed from all of this. There has to be a reason why.'

'What if there isn't? What if this man of yours just went nuts for no reason at all? People do that, don't they?'

'Yes,' conceded Hargreave, 'sometimes they do. But when that happens the violence usually occurs between family members, and it's over in a few moments. Such murderers don't plan meetings with their victims in advance. They don't arrange to be admitted into buildings. They don't wait until their victims are alone. And they don't cover their tracks by wearing gloves.'

For the next hour and a half, they recalled every detail of the early meetings between John and Ixora, with dates and descriptions of everyone present.

'If there's anything else, I can't think of it,' said Chapel finally, wearied by the endless painful reminders of their time together.

'I have a man whose future freedom may depend on your memory, John,' said Hargreave. 'Remember that. I want you to stay in touch. More than that, I want your help.'

He had another reason for encouraging Chapel to help

him clear the case. In London, the Metropolitan Police Force was directly answerable to the Home Secretary. In the last ten days, Hargreave had been telephoned twice for progress reports. If something didn't happen soon, he had no doubt that someone very senior would want to arrange an enquiry into bungled police procedure.

One more week. The department had been given seven days to advance the Crown's case against Donald Wingate, or find another culprit. And the chances of doing that were looking ever slimmer.

It reminded her of a thirties doll's house, prim and perfect, with a sloping red tiled roof, whitewashed bricks and matching bay windows. It was situated in a wide, tree-lined avenue in what she took to be the smarter part of Richmond. As she parked the car, Janice noticed the lack of life signs in the street. Suburbia, she thought. House-wives at ironing boards, kids at school, husbands at work and only a distant barking dog to bring the picture to life. No wonder she chose to live in Kentish Town. The tube station escalators never worked and the streets were filthy, but at least it was populated by the living.

'You must forgive me,' said Helen. 'I only have herbal tea. Would you like milk?'

'Yes please.' Janice balanced a dainty cup on her broad thigh while Helen tipped the jug. The lounge was spotless, and reflected the middle-income middle-class lifestyle of its occupants. Restored fireplace, thirties mirrors, couple of paintings — bland but original — a pleasant room, but too tidy. One unusual feature, though; a larged wooden crucifix nailed to the wall.

Helen had nothing in common with the woman her husband had left her for. She was small and freckled, pleasant faced, with coppery hair pinned up neatly and very little makeup.

'You were saying,' prompted Janice as she carefully shifted the tiny cup.

'My husband is not a religious man. I don't think he particularly approved of the time I spent with my worship group. I don't know why people are so frightened of religion. Now that he's gone, I've become quite involved with a number of projects. At the moment I've joined a work party renovating St Anne's in Soho. It keeps my mind away from thoughts of John.'

Janice consulted her notes. 'You said you and he had considered a reconciliation.'

'I had lunch with John a couple of times and we discussed the prospect, yes.'

'But your divorce is nearly through now?'

'That's right.' She paused, then seemed to reach a decision. 'You see, after John left, I discovered I was pregnant. There's dramatic irony for you. Our marriage began and ended with an unplanned pregnancy. John had stayed with me for the sake of our child once before, and I knew in my heart of hearts that he would do it again. But at Christmas I lost the baby. There was an accident, the storm brought a power line down. It could have killed us. The following day, I had a miscarriage. The doctor said it was brought on by the shock.' She shook her head sadly. 'I knew then that John wasn't coming back. That this was the way she could take him from me forever.'

'Who are you referring to?'

'Ixora, of course.'

'You think she had something to do with the accident?'

'I'm sure of it.'

'But how is that possible?'

Helen touched her finger to her lips, thinking. 'Do you believe that there are evil people in the world?'

'Yes, I do.'

'Then,' said Helen, 'believe in Ixora.'

CHAPTER
37
Storm Front

With a loud crack, the last piece of the floorboard came free. John knelt down and shone his torch into the cavity, following the path of the wiring with his free hand. Much of the rubberised coating on the wires had flaked and cracked open, exposing gleaming copper strands. No wonder the top floor lights flickered and died whenever two or more were turned on. Trying to repair the wiring was keeping his mind from dwelling on Ixora's whereabouts. Surely she would return to the house sooner or later? How could she have loved him if she found it so easy to stay away?

Something scuttled out of the torch beam, hopping across the ceiling lathes into the shadows. Ahead was an ancient junction point, an unruly knot of spliced wires sealed within white ceramic holders. The cabling slipped from his fingers and vanished into the darkness. Cursing, he repositioned himself by the hole and lowered his arm in until his shoulder was resting on the floorboards. But instead of reaching the junction, his fingers closed around a slim square box.

He slowly pulled the object toward him, careful not to let it slip from his fingers. As he removed it from the hole, he was surprised to find himself holding a child's diary. The mottled lock on the front still held, but its dusty cardboard strap had fractured with age. Rocking back on his heels, he opened the cover and examined the flyleaf:

The Property of I.D.C. May 1979

The handwriting was that of a girl in her early teens, firm round letters painstakingly printed with a fountain pen.

As he was studying it, something slid out from the pages and fluttered to the floor. He picked up the flower and held it to the light, a cluster of faded crimson petals with attenuated stalks. Finding the page from which it had fallen, he noted the printed appellation: Frangipani.

Several other blooms lay bright and brittle between the back pages of the diary, each one neatly labelled. Cordyline. Allamanda. Ginger Lily. Feathery fern-like leaves from a Flamboyant tree. Carissa, a five-pronged white flower with a dried plum-like fruit attached. Finally, a perfectly preserved plant stem with an array of small red flowers at its tip. Ixora. They were West Indian plants.

All thoughts of repairing the lights forgotten, John turned the book over and began at the front. Three pages in, he found an address.

'Family of De Corizo. 77 Grass Street, Castries, St Lucia.'

There followed what seemed to be a chronicle of everyday events, but it was inscribed in an indecipherable French patois, presumably in the fashion of teenagers the world over, to protect it from Ixora's parents. The diary ended halfway through the book, in what appeared to be mid-sentence. On the opposing page there were two addresses in someone else's handwriting. A local doctor and a parish church, St Marks, both situated in the town of Castries. These were followed by another date.

If Ixora was West Indian by birth, why had she lied? Was this where she had gone, returning to her natural home? He rose, walked to the telephone and dialled International Directory Enquiries. He had no luck finding a number for the family residence, but eventually the operator was able to trace St Mark's parish church, St Lucia. John thanked him, checked the time difference, then redialled.

The line was terrible, and rang for ages before being answered. The pastor of St Mark's was unavailable, but would he like to speak to the church administrator?

The woman who came on the line had a powerful Caribbean accent. He pressed his ear against the receiver and listened hard. After understanding that she would help him in any way that she could, he read out Ixora's family name, carefully spelling it.

'If you wait I'll look it up in the parish register,' she replied. 'May 1979?'

'That's right.'

'This may take some time.' The line went dead.

Twelve minutes later, the receiver was raised. 'Yes, we had a De Corizo family on the island, the only one. The address you have is correct.'

'I can't find a number for them.'

'No, you wouldn't. The Corizos died in the August of that year.'

For a moment, he thought he had misheard. 'Who died exactly?'

'I have the details here. Jack De Corizo, aged forty-nine years, Clarissa De Corizo, aged thirty-eight years, Ixora

De Corizo, aged seventeen years. Mother, father and daughter.'

'But that's impossible.' It couldn't be right. For a start, Ixora's age didn't tally correctly.

'That's what's listed in the records.'

'Someone must have made a mistake.'

'They're in the records because they're buried here,' explained the administrator. 'At least, the parents are.'

'Does it say how they died?'

'We don't have that kind of information. You could ask the pastor. He'll be back tomorrow.'

'Thank you.' John lowered the receiver and sat back.

Ixora was dead, or so somebody thought. And if she really was dead, who the hell had he fallen in love with?

He looked around the room. Everything had taken on an unfamiliar air. He pulled up a copy of the Yellow Pages and thumbed through it, writing down the numbers of the nearest travel agencies in the area.

His third call paid off. She had booked a flight to St Lucia on 27th December, using her own name. A one-way trip.

The British West Indian Airways aircraft descended through slate-grey rolling clouds, touching down at Hanna-wora airport just after lunchtime the following day. John had packed very little luggage, assuming that the weather would be hot. Instead he had found himself arriving in the middle of a spectacular thunderstorm. Rain blasted across the tarmac as the craft taxied to a halt. Beyond the airport lay emerald hills, backlit by lightning.

The taxi ride to Castries was slow and halting, the aged Mercedes skirting ruts and potholes as it made its way across the island, heavy raindrops slapping the leathery leaves of the banana plants which surrounded them.

'You picked a heck of a time for a holiday, mister,' said

the driver, who looked about sixteen years old and had a radiant, unavoidable smile. 'Forecast says we're in for the tail of a hurricane.' He rolled down his window and waved on a truck laden with guavas and yams. Cinnamon-scented air filled the car. Warm rain splashed on to the immaculate plastic-covered seats.

'I'm not here on vacation,' said John, 'I'm looking for someone. Can you recommend a place to stay?'

'You want a big American hotel or something local?'

'Local will be fine.'

'I'm your man.' The driver turned and offered his hand. 'Marcellus is the name. We'll get you fixed up, no problem.' The car tilted sharply to one side in a spray of pale mud. 'This is a beautiful island, but the roads take a little gettin' used to.' They had reached the far side of the land, the road folding through the palm-dotted hills in a series of breath-taking hairpin bends.

The pale Caribbean shelved gently away from the shore. Beyond the harbour low waves formed, their crests as livid as sapphires. Houses could be glimpsed within the hillside vegetation, villas of stone or wooden slats, painted in startling shades of aquamarine and lime, rust red and canary yellow. Families sat on their verandahs watching the rain. A child on a pink and green bicycle overtook the taxi.

Castries proved to be a low, stone town with a smart formal square, a blue and yellow fountain, and run-down factories of pockmarked brick. Everywhere people were sheltering under store canopies and trees, watching the rain, chattering and arguing. A handful of forlorn tourists waited for their coach, white knees thrusting from pastel shorts, cameras sheathed across sodden shirts.

'This is the place,' said Marcellus, pulling up before a dirty pink two-storey building. 'A good place to stay.'

'How do you know?'

'My mama does the cooking here.' Offering his broadest smile yet, he held open the door.

The rooms were plain and uncluttered. The mother of Marcellus was called Catherine. A pleasant, softly spoken woman half the height of her son, she had settled John in the room and explained the house rules. After she had closed the door, he stood at the balcony watching a pair of small, highly coloured birds — petites chittes, she had called them — drinking from the rainbloated drainpipe which passed his unshuttered window.

In the street below, a pale-skinned girl with dark hair ran across the road with a newspaper held above her head. For the briefest of moments he wondered — but no, her legs were too short, the body language wrong.

He checked his watch and saw that it was only 2.15 p.m. There was still time to locate the first of the addresses in Ixora's diary, the De Corizo family house. Showing Catherine the address, he thought he saw a flicker of recognition in her eyes. Grass Street proved to be within walking distance. Catherine gave him a clear set of directions.

If someone had lived there once, they did so no longer. Around the boarded-up house the sweet smell of rotting vegetables hung in the air. Planks had been hammered across the doors and windows, and a burden of weeds threatened to bring down the cracked wooden verandah. Once the property had been painted a smart pink, along with the rest of the street. Now most of the paint had been peeled away by successive seasons of sun and rain. Judging by the black soot-streaks above the upper storey windows, there had been a fire at some time.

As he stood looking up, an elderly woman stopped before him in the street and began to shout, her toothless gums mouthing words in a patois he could not understand. Finally she spat angrily at the door of the building and shambled on her way, oblivious to the pelting rain.

John checked the next address on his list and began to search for a cab.

The church proved less easy to reach. It was situated beyond a winding dirt track on top of a hill, and the car repeatedly slid across the road, its engine screaming in protest. The owner of the vehicle clearly thought him mad to be visiting such an out-of-the-way place.

St Mark's was a plain rectangle of unpainted stone, with a low square belfry and a crowded graveyard overrun with creepers and surrounded by Saman trees. The parish pastor, a small black man with wire-rimmed glasses, seemed amazed to be receiving a visitor at all, and asked in clipped British tones how he could possibly help.

John introduced himself and fished the diary from his pocket, opening it at the flyleaf. The pastor held the pages close to his face and read. Above them, rain filtered heavily through the trees to pound on the roof of the deserted church hall.

'Did you know this girl?' asked the pastor, pre-empting John's own question.

'I know her very well.'

The pastor gave him a wary look. 'Then you know that her parents are buried here.'

'Your administrator told me,' he admitted.

'It was all very tragic. Not just for them, but for the daughter. Are you familiar with the story?'

'Not really. Do you know what happened?'

'Well, I don't suppose it will hurt to tell it now,' he said finally. 'It was quite a time ago, although the people here have long memories. Come with me, I'll show you.'

The pastor hoisted a battered black umbrella and led the way into the overgrown cemetery. On the far side he stopped before a broad stone bier, half hidden by vines. Above them came the leathery sound of smacking wings as small bats dropped from the trees. He reached down and pulled away a handful of sucker-like weeds, revealing the inscription on a plaque which had been shattered into two large halves.

In Loving Memory
Of
Clarissa And Jack De Corizo
Taken By Our Lord
Through The Forces Of Nature
In The Year Of
1979
'There Is A Calm Harbour In
The Bosom Of The Saviour'

'What does it mean, "taken by nature"?' asked John. 'Did they die together?'

'Come back to the refectory and take tea with me. I'll explain.'

The room was small and dark, and smelled richly of wood, nutmeg and coffee. The pastor filled two cups and placed them on a bamboo table, indicating a pair of deep armchairs.

'Like so many tales of the Caribbean, it involves a hurricane,' said the pastor. 'Jack De Corizo married a European girl. I think Clarissa was French, or perhaps she was Spanish — I can't be sure. But she was happy to settle here, to give up the city and live a simple life.

'Jack owned a fleet of fishing boats. He was very fair with his men, and everyone liked him. On a small island like this, that is a very important thing. Ixora was his only child, the light of his life. She was born in the middle of a fierce hurricane, and the story goes that the shutters in the hospital room had blown in, and the air was filled with swirling flower blossoms — so they named the child Ixora.

'Like most of us who live on the coast she grew up in the water, and could swim like a fish. She was a very happy girl, and she soon became very beautiful. By the time she was fifteen the men had taken to following her around, sitting outside the family house waiting to catch sight of her. But she would have nothing to do with them. Ixora said she didn't want to marry a fisherman. Many of her friends were leaving school to work in the big new hotels that were springing up along the coast. Now, this part of the story may just be a rumour,' warned the little pastor. 'I am unable to vouch for it myself. Although I saw her at church every Sunday, she never spoke to me of such things. Ixora met a man, a travelling businessman who visited the islands throughout the winter, selling to the department stores. He was full of tales about the places he'd been, and she fell in love with him. She talked about him to her parents, and Jack and Clarissa insisted on meeting this paragon of virtue, so they invited him to dinner.

'There was a wind blowing up and the forecasts had been bad, but someone — whether it was Jack or Ixora I don't know — suggested taking the boat out to catch some special fish for the occasion. All three of them went — Clarissa after much protesting. She had never taken much to the sea, but Ixora insisted. They were sailing out off the point when the wind changed direction and a terrible storm sprang up, the tail of a passing hurricane that wasn't supposed to come within a hundred miles of the shore. But the forecast was wrong and it came inland, just like it is today. Their boat was shattered into matchwood against the rocks and sank instantly. Some men on the headland saw it riding the waves for a moment. Then it vanished from sight.

'Two days later the bodies were washed up on the shore. They'd received such a pounding on the rocks that they were barely identifiable. Ixora's travelling man was heart-broken.'

'I don't understand,' said John. 'Ixora survived somehow.'

'The bodies that washed up belonged to Jack and Clarissa, true. At first everyone thought that Ixora had somehow lived, because she was such a good swimmer.' The pastor lowered his head sadly. 'But soon they realised that she must have drowned with them. No one could have survived in a sea like that. The undercurrents can suck a man down in seconds. Although there was no body, her death was recorded in the parish register alongside those of her parents.'

'You're wrong, Father. I know that she lives.'

The pastor pressed his arm lightly. 'I remember those rumours, too. A few days after their boat sank, a girl appeared in town claiming to be Ixora, but of course she couldn't have been. There was some kind of argument over the matter. Then one night some young tearaways set fire to the De Corizo house.'

'If the family was so respected, why would anyone want to burn the house down?'

'I'm as unlikely to find out the answer to that as you are,' replied the pastor. 'These are people who take their secrets to the grave.'

That night he lay on top of the bed, listening to the slow swish of the ceiling fan as it stirred the humid air. Outside, the rain continued to fall lightly on the rooftops. Tinny calypso music played faintly in the distance.

'Where are you, Ixora?' he asked the shadows. 'Why are you hiding from me?'

CHAPTER
38
Joyous Occasion

John awoke from a shallow, fitful sleep and lay listening to the wind moaning forlornly through the shutters of his room. At 8.00 a.m. the clouds above the town were as black as night. He ate a breakfast of saltfish, eggs and fried bananas, a dish that Catherine said she usually only prepared on Sundays for privileged guests, then ventured out onto the street.

For the rest of the morning he searched aimlessly through the town, visiting the place names he had found in Ixora's diary. He did not know if he would find her. He only knew what to do if he did. At noon he stopped by one of the large American hotels and placed two telephone calls, one local and one to London. Then he headed back into the centre of Castries.

The dark sky had forced an eerie light on to the buildings, causing colours to jump out in sharp relief. The fruit and vegetable market at the end of town was a riot of unfamiliar shapes and tones. Christophenes, artichokes and okras were displayed beside yams, eddoes and sweet potatoes, all of them stacked in neat piles on mats and blankets.

The incessant wind had dried the morning rain from the streets, although the gutters still splashed with rushing water. Felled palm fronds, many of them taller than a man, had been blown across the side roads. Everyone seemed to be moving with a purpose, as if the populace was anxious to be indoors before the winds became too much to stand.

He found himself in front of the sealed-up house on Grass Street once more, looking up at the charcoaled shutters of the upper floor. The slats nailed over the front door had rotted through, and proved easy to remove. Behind them, though, was a heavy steel lock which prevented any further advance. As the rain returned with renewed vigour, he peered in through the boards which covered the single ground floor window, his vision thwarted by darkness.

Stepping over the rotting rubbish which filled the alleyway at the side of the house, he found a window at the rear which looked as if it would allow him admittance. Behind these boards the shutters were forced back from their hooks and lay twisted on the floor. Climbing inside proved easy enough, but the sponginess of the floor within told him that it would be dangerous to stray very far from the edges of the room.

As his eyes slowly adjusted, he saw that the room was bare but for a stack of high-backed velvet covered chairs in one corner. Striations of dim light crossed the walls and reflected dully from the remains of an iron chandelier hanging from the high wooden ceiling. There was a feeling of faded grandeur here, of a life once comfortably led. An intricately carved balustrade, part of the now collapsed staircase, had pulled away and lay sunken in the rotten boards. Light seeped through the gaps in the floor above and partly lit the landing. Perhaps the roof had fallen in.

As he approached the stairs, rats paused in their search for food and wriggled off, their claws rattling across the boards. He tested each step as he climbed, listening for creaks above the sound of the falling rain.

Something scraped against the wall above his head. He froze on the fourth stair, listening. The temperature had fallen steadily since the start of the storm, and now his breath clouded before him in the dark. Perhaps a bird had flown in through a gap in the shutters and had become trapped. His pulse picked up its pace as he climbed towards the landing. He could see the corner of the room above, a whorl of settling dust marking the recently disturbed air. Suddenly a section of shadow divorced itself from the wall and came at him, broadening into a human figure, a wailing scream rising in its throat as he found his own voice, shouting in fright.

The figure nearly toppled him through the brittle banisters as it fell against him. Ixora stared up, her body in darkness, her emerald eyes flashing wildly in a single sidelong strip of daylight. Her cry fell to a racking sob as she clutched at his body, and he sank down with her, supporting her weight as she crumpled to the floor.

The cool rain revived her, washing the streaks of dirt from her face, staining her crimson dress, muddying her sore bare feet. Together they looked up at the house as lightning flashed softly out to sea.

'Why did you come here?' she cried, pushing the wet strands of hair from her eyes.

He had planned the words for this moment, should he find her. Now they had deserted him. 'I had to find you,

Ixora,' he explained. 'I needed to know where you'd gone.'

Although she tried to free herself, he held tightly on to her left wrist. Nothing could make him let go now.

'I love you,' he said simply. 'I can't live without you. I want to marry you. Not just words. I mean it.'

Realising that he would not free her arm, she stopped trying to pull away and angrily turned to him. 'Why do you think I ran away, John? It wasn't because you wouldn't trust me, it's because I finally knew that you would.'

'You're not making sense. It was what you wanted all along.'

'It's all gone so wrong. It wasn't supposed to happen like this.'

'What do you mean?'

She did not reply, but looked away to the dark hills, wiping her eyes with the back of her hand. John reached his decision. He steered her along the pavement, forcing her to keep pace with him.

'Where are we going?'

'You'll see when we get there.'

As they reached the rainswept marketplace he called to an elderly driver who was sheltering under a store awning, and aimed Ixora in the direction of the taxi. 'I have a lot of questions I have to ask you,' he said, opening the rear door of the Ford and pushing her inside, 'but first just answer me one thing.' The driver slipped into his seat and watched him, waiting for directions. 'Just one truthful answer, yes or no.'

'What?'

'Do you love me?'

'Yes, I do, John, with all my heart.'

'That settles it.'

The taxi took off and drove back through the town, past a harbour filled with thrashing boats. Rain squalls rippled across the main thoroughfare which ran beside the dark-ened sea, buffeting the side of the car. Ahead rose the pale concrete towers of the American hotels. As they drew into the Hyatt Regency, John spoke with the driver, then gave him a handful of bills. The old man jumped from his seat and ran into the foyer of the hotel.

'John, what's going on? Where is he going?'

'He'll be back in a minute.' He raised himself from the seat and drew a small box from his trouser pocket, passing it to her. 'This is for you.' She studied the object in the palm of her hand, as if afraid of it.

'Well, go on, open it. You look like I've asked you to defuse a bomb.'

She prised open the lid and withdrew a slim diamond ring. He didn't dare to tell her how much he had paid for it.

'Well, go on, put it on.'

It fitted perfectly. She was still nervously admiring it when the driver returned. 'All set,' he said, holding open the passenger door. 'Just go right through.'

John took Ixora's hand and gently led her from the car.

'Congratulations,' called the driver.

Suddenly Ixora realised what was going on. 'Oh no,' she said quietly, then louder, 'no, John!' She removed the ring and shoved it back at him.

'It's just a short service,' he said, tightening his grip on her wrist.

'But you're still married!'

'Oh no, I'm not. My divorce became official two days ago. Helen couldn't wait to get shot of me. I spoke to the solicitors this morning.'

'But not this — this is wrong.'

'The vicar even comes with his own witnesses. The maids here are hardened professionals, they help out like this all the time.'

The idea had come to him when he had spoken to the travel agent. It was all the rage, he had been told, very romantic. And with a current drop in clientele due to the unseasonal weather they were having at the moment, it would also be inexpensive. John was more concerned with maintaining discretion. The travel agent had coughed into his hand. That, he had admitted, would cost a little more.

The pink marble reception area was a monument to the vulgarity of mass tourism. It was fitted with large brass sharks and starfish, and was open on two sides. There was no point in having large panels of glass fitted to West Indian hotels. The foyer and the manicured gardens beyond were windswept and deserted. Ixora's bare feet slipped on the wet floor as she tried to pull herself free, but John merely tightened his grip. On the stairs, a pair of whey-faced tourists in banana-leaf hats watched as they passed.

'I'm not going to let you do this, John,' she warned, close to tears now. 'I'll scream.'

'You can scream all you like,' he replied evenly. 'The amount of money this guy's being paid, you can slash your wrists and he'll carry on with the service.'

'Why are you doing this?' she screamed. 'Why can't you just stay away from me?'

'You say you love me, then you beg me to leave. You don't know what you want, Ixora, so I'm deciding for you. You demanded proof of my love, total commitment, that's what you're getting.'

'I don't want it any more!'

Ixora made a monumental effort to stand her ground, but slipped over. As he pulled her to his feet she managed to slide her wrist free of his fingers. His nails had cut purple crescents deep into her flesh. As she scrambled from his reach, he seized her around the waist and pulled her back to him.

They reached a half-flooded stone walkway at the rear of the hotel. The heavy white breakers which pounded the beach sounded like distant gunfire. Within an arbour of windlashed bushes they found a tall pink pagoda of scrolled baroque ironwork, like a prop from some forgotten musical. Beneath it, sheltering from the rain, stood an old white man dressed in a black suit and dog collar, and two bemused teenage housemaids, still in their uniforms.

'I won't go through with this, John.'

He shoved his fist in her face. 'We're getting married whether you're conscious for the ceremony or not.' He jerked Ixora in front of him, presenting her to the vicar, who had clearly been drinking. He scratched the patchy grey stubble on his chin and held out an unsteady hand.

'Congratulations, young lady. What a shame we couldn't have had better weather for you.'

'Help me, I'm being kidnapped.' She ignored his hand and turned to John. 'You're crazy if you think I'm getting married.'

The vicar smiled vaguely, ignoring her pleas. He reached down to turn on a small cassette player and nearly failed to make it back up. Then he turned to the groom, his eyes distantly focused. 'Do you have the ring?'

Ixora had dropped it into his top pocket, tearing his shirt in the process. He fished it out and presented it. The witnesses smiled. At last here was something they could identify with a normal wedding. Ixora batted the ring from his hand, and it fell with a ping into the surrounding flowerbed. One of the maids retrieved it. In the background, church bells had begun to peel wonkily from the tape deck.

'Let's get on with it,' said John, tightening his grip on Ixora's arm as she began to cry again. He watched her from the corner of his eye, wishing he could simply take

her in his arms and rest her head on his chest, telling her
that everything would be fine, but he didn't dare release
her until after the service.

'Dearly beloved, we are gathered today in the sight of
God ...'

'Is everybody around here crazy?' Ixora screamed, 'I'm
not getting married, for Christ's sake!'

'Is she all right?' asked the vicar, concerned.

John nodded and revolved his right hand, indicating a
faster pace. A fresh squall of rain hit the side of the pagoda.

'I'm not marrying you, John,' Ixora whispered, 'not like
this. Please don't make me.' For a moment when she
looked at him he saw the agony in her eyes, and his resolve
wavered. Then he forced himself to remember how their
life together had been in London.

'I'm doing this for both of us, Ixora. Trust me, it will
change everything. There'll be no more dark men in your
dreams. I'll always be there to protect you.'

'I can't let you do that.' She turned to the vicar. 'Please,
stop the ceremony.'

'It's no good,' said John apologetically. 'He's stone
deaf.'

'If there is anyone who knows of any just reason why
this couple should not be joined in holy wedlock,' intoned
the vicar, not bothering to glance at his prayerbook, 'let
them speak now or forever hold their peace!'

'I object!' said Ixora, John tightened his grip on her arm
until she cried out.

'He doesn't mean you,' he said. Behind them the wind
split a bough from tree with a sharp crack. The witnesses
looked up, frightened. On the concrete deck beside the
pool, metal sunchairs cartwheeled over each other.

'I now pronounce you man and wife.' The vicar was
forced to shout above the wind. 'You may *kiss the bride*!'
One of the maids threw confetti, but the wind whipped it

away. Then the three of them were off, running across the ravaged garden, propelled by the gale as thunder rent the air with an ear-splitting bang and the storm broke all around them.

The groom remained hanging on to the canopy railing, his face smeared with dirt, his shirt torn and flapping. Slowly, he released his grip on his brand new bride, who fell to her knees in her tattered crimson dress and began to sob with all her heart.

CHAPTER
39
Sea

Ixora remained silent as they drove back to the lodging house in Castries. She hugged herself, sniffing from time to time, and tried to catch his eye. John was careful not to look at her, and stared silently from the window as their driver negotiated the rain-filled potholes in the road.

Catherine doubtfully puckered her lips when she saw the bedraggled red-eyed woman he ushered into her hallway, but her good nature got the better of her when she saw how badly Ixora was shivering.

'Catherine, I'd like you to meet my wife,' said John proudly. 'We got caught in the storm. She lost her shoes.'

'What size you take, honey? Dainty little feet, about a five?' Ixora nodded miserably. 'I got a daughter takes a five,' said Catherine, pushing John to the stairs. 'Go and run the poor thing a tub, I'll bring her towels and some dry clothes.'

He sat her on the edge of the deep ceramic bath and pulled the torn red dress over her head. Without helping or hindering, she allowed herself to be placed in the steaming water.

'Is that where you've been staying, in your family's old house?' he asked, filling a sponge with water and squeezing it across her pale back.

'There was nowhere else I could stay.'

'Why not?'

She did not reply.

'How long were you there?'

'I don't know. A week or so.'

As he washed the streaked dirt from her face, he wondered if she had suffered some kind of breakdown. After all, she had been through so much in the last few weeks. He wanted to ask her so many things, but was wary of frightening her any more than he had already. 'I visited the church in the hills,' he said. 'I saw where your parents were buried. The pastor seemed to think that you had died with them.'

She looked at him and seemed about to speak, then changed her mind.

'Tell me, Ixora. Whatever happened back then, it can't hurt you now.' He filled the sponge once more and squeezed it gently against her neck. There were livid bruises on her wrists where he had gripped her. 'While you were in the boat a terrible storm rose up,' he said. 'No one had expected it . . .'

With her chin resting on her drawn-up knees, she began to speak. 'We're married now,' she said, 'so you may as well know the truth.' I was born here in St Lucia. And I grew up here. I knew nothing except life on this island.' She studied the muddy water between her legs. 'I know the power of the hurricanes. One moment the world is the brightest of blues, then suddenly it's dark, as if someone had drawn a shroud across the sky. The sea becomes dull, a sickly grey. Then the wind rises, and the swell begins. Mother wasn't frightened. Father earned his living from the sea. He knew what to do. The boat was small, but it was sturdy. We weren't even very far out when the storm came.

'I helped Father bring in the sail, and we started the outboard engine. We were cutting back through the waves towards the shore when we heard Mother call out. There were flying fish all around us, heading into shore. It was then that I turned and saw it. A wall of dark water, approaching our port side at an incredible speed. A freak wave which pulled the boat into the sky, held it there for a sickening moment which seemed to last forever, then dropped it.

'The trough behind the wave was so deep that it had exposed the rocks beneath. We landed hard and the wood beneath our feet just flew apart, shattering into staves. In the next moment the sea had closed back over us with a crash. But this time it was red, great clouds of blood blossoming upwards, rising around me, staining my body. In that second I knew they were dead, and that I was about to join them. The current flexed around me like a living muscle, pulling me under once more. I lost consciousness …'

There were goose pimples on her breasts and shoulders as she lay back in the water. 'The next thing I remember is waking to find myself still in the sea. I could taste sharp water in my lungs and nostrils, but I could breathe. And there was sand beneath my feet. The hurricane had died away. The sky had cleared. I walked to the shore, thankful to be alive, unable to understand how. There was a strange stillness in the air. I recall thinking that I had to be home soon or Mother would be angry at me for missing supper.

Then I must have collapsed at the shoreline. I remember hands carrying me. I awoke in hospital.'

She closed her eyes and folded her arms across her breasts, as if she had reached the end of her story. John lifted her from the bath and wrapped a towel around her shoulders. He didn't understand. It must have been terrible for her, losing both parents so tragically, but why bother to lie about where she was born? Why make everything such a mystery?

'That was when the trouble began,' she said, sensing his thoughts. 'The doctors said something had happened to me in the water. They came out with some long medical term, I forget. They said my balance was affected, my mental perception of distances, some other things. They couldn't understand it. I explained to them what had happened, and they told me that the bodies of my parents had been washed on to the shore that morning, three days after the hurricane. That meant I had been in the water for three whole days.

'Well, to survive so long while unconscious was impossible. I discharged myself and returned home, against everyone's advice. I was terrified. My mother, as I told you, was a very religious woman. I could not understand why I had been spared and they had not. I spoke to no one, staying in the house with the shutters closed.

'It was then that the taunts began. It started with the local boys, the ones I had been too proud to go out with. "Ixora," they would call up at the windows, "She's the Devil-Woman who lives in the sea." I knew it was childish. Of course I ignored them. Then the rumours started spreading. If I went to the market they would whisper behind my back. She rose from the waves, they would say; while the hurricane took her family she lived on in the sea. The Devil spared her because of her beauty. She's the Devil's bride now.'

'But this was just gossip, jealousy from the people you'd shunned,' said John. 'Don't you see that?'

'That's what I thought at first. There are many intelligent, enlightened people here, but ours was a community of simple fishermen. Soon I could only go out at night, and even then they would follow behind me. Satan's bride was washed back from the sea to tempt the men of the land, to betray them. That was the deal she struck with the Devil in exchange for her life. Wherever she goes, her beauty will lure men to their deaths. That's the bargain she must keep forever …'

'But it's absurd,' he said, holding her to him. 'You didn't believe it, did you?'

'Not at first, no.'

'What do you mean, not at first?'

'The taunting grew worse until he arrived …'

'Who?'

'I had fallen in love — or so I thought — with a man who travelled the islands …'

'The pastor told me.'

'The night he arrived back in town, he came to see me. I thought he would save me by taking me away with him. Instead he told me that he was sorry for what had happened to my parents, but he could only remain in Castries for a week. I begged him to let me return with him, but when he refused I demanded to know why his attitude towards me had changed. He told me he was soon to be married, somewhere far away. He would never see me again. I screamed at him, and threw him into the street. I couldn't believe what I had heard. He had been my last chance to escape. That night he went drinking with my father's friends, and soon he was behaving just like them.

'They arrived at the house after midnight, he and the others. They were singing, being cruel, calling to me. Do a spell, Ixora, perform a Devil-dance for us. One of them, a man who had once been my father's most trusted friend, climbed on to the verandah and pulled himself in through the window, offering to cure my "curse". He grabbed at my dress and ripped it open. As he reached to unbuckle his trouser belt, I picked up the oil lamp beside the bed and broke it over his head. He tore off his shirt where the oil had spilled and managed to save himself, but the flames spread, destroying the upper floor of the house. I had nowhere to go …'

'So how did you come to Europe?'

'There was some money left from my father's business. They hated me even more for selling his boats, but I had to get away.'

'Everything that has happened since must have reminded you of this terrible "curse" …'

'I thought I could come home, but I saw so many familiar faces in the streets that I didn't dare go out during the day. I'm sure someone will recognise me.'

'Well, you're safe here. Catherine and her family arrived from Trinidad just two years ago. They don't know you.'

He hugged her hard and kissed her neck. No wonder she'd lied when so many terrible things had started happening all around her. No wonder Dominguez and Saunders had thought her crazy, if she had told them anything of what she believed to be true! He had come to believe in her guilt, just as she had convinced herself. Now he understood Ixora's strange reaction on the day they had worked in Feldman's studio, when she had been told to lower herself into a pool of clouded crimson water.

Every incident which had occurred must have served to convince her more than ever of her terrible role. Her new life in London had become tainted with the deaths of adoring males. How easy it must have been for her to see herself playing the part of the evil temptress, sent back to the land to destroy the lives of men. And the dark man who had stood behind her in so many feverish dreams, the one who always sought to hurt her and steal away her lovers, could only have been the human form of the Devil himself.

CHAPTER
40
Religion

The operations room at Bow Street was buzzing with activity. At 11.00 p.m. the previous night, the area's largest ever drugs raid had accidentally netted two of the men who had set up the Strand mugging operation. Sergeant Longbright had spent most of the night attempting to unravel their conflicting statements, every phrase of which had been siphoned through a pair of obstructive lawyers in halting Maltese. By 7.00 a.m. the sergeant was exhausted. She was preparing to sign out for the night when Hargreave walked into her office. He was about to kiss her on the back of the neck when one of the desk-clerks passed in the corridor outside.

Longbright knew that Hargreave had stolen up behind her. He was not exactly light on his feet. 'You could have kissed me, you know,' she said. 'They must all have some inkling about us by now.'

'You're joking,' said Hargreave, returning to his side of the desk. 'None of them has the faintest idea.'

She decided not to spoil his dream. 'I'm just coming off-duty. It's been a hell of a night.' She gave him a tired smile. His heart soared out to her. She looked exhausted.

'You look terrific,' he said, 'I thought you must have just arrived.'

'Liar.' She swung a rucksack on to her shoulder. 'Will I see you later?'

'You bet. I've got my final session with Wingate this morning.'

'You mean that's it? No more after this?'

'Nope. But for my signature, the case is in place. We've got forensic matches, masses of circumstantial material and a detailed confession. The motive they're going with — Wingate's murderous jealousy of the man who slept with "his girls" — is admittedly dodgy, but then of course there are the psychiatric reports. According to Land, who has naturally read them from cover to cover, these detail enough abnormalities to lock him away even without evidence of murder. Look at this.' He withdrew a thick file and opened it at a random page. 'Chemical imbalance, suicidal depression, disrupted thought patterns, chronic isolation, neurological impairment, egocentricity, inadequacy … the man's a walking medical text book. When he dies they'll probably put his brain in a jar, like they did with Oliver Cromwell.'

'Why bother to see him today, then?'

'Good question,' he said, lighting the stub of a cigar. 'I guess it's in the forlorn hope that he might say something — anything — that he hasn't said sixty times before. That's the thing, you see. He never deviates. He uses the same phrases, the same sentence constructions, over and over. It's as if he learnt it all by rote. Or as if someone taught it to him.' He drew hard on the cigar. 'But no.

The doctor says it's quite common. In fact, it fits the pattern for this type of obsessive. So I continue to clutch at straws.'

'Good for you,' said Longbright, giving his backside a sly squeeze as she left the room. 'Sometimes straws can pull you out of a hole.'

Hargreave gathered his files and headed for the observation chamber. He had only just been relocated to a plush new office in Mornington Crescent when Sullivan died. The case had propelled him back to a makeshift bay at Bow Street. Although his stay would probably be over by this evening, it had least allowed him to see more of his lady sergeant.

He took his seat in the darkened monitoring room and watched the constable load a fresh cassette into his recorder.

'Sir, I'm afraid you'll have to …'

'I know,' said Hargreave, stubbing out the freshly lit cigar with a sigh of irritation, 'we don't want to glow in the mirror.' On the other side of the glass, Wingate was led in and shackled in the usual manner. As they settled down, the psychologist ran him through a series of basic test questions pertaining to his age, date of birth and current whereabouts. Wingate seemed as fresh as when he had first started answering questions, but his enthusiastic replies were now edged with anger. The medics always tired before he did. Each interrogation seemed to be conducted by somebody different. This one seemed to be barely out of college. There were a lot of people waiting to get a crack at a case like this.

'Dial the doctor, will you?' asked Hargreave. 'Get her in here.' He watched as the telephone rang in the room next door. Moments later the psychologist excused herself and entered the observation chamber. Her nametag read: Dr Maria Dallow.

'We haven't met,' said Hargreave, introducing himself. Dallow looked unhappy about being interrupted. 'I'm sure you're anxious to get started. There's one thing I feel I should warn you about. Owing to the extremely personal sexual nature of Wingate's occasional outbursts, we try to discourage young female doctors from conducting the Q and A sessions.'

'You don't need to warn me,' said Dallow testily. 'I do have professional training in this kind of situation. I'm not easily disturbed by what I hear.'

'I'm not worried about you,' explained Hargreave. 'I'm worried about him. He gets very steamed up if you mention sex, and you will; he'll see to that. You can conduct the interview by all means, but keep someone in there with you.'

Dallow returned to the interview room and the session began. Hargreave was pleased to watch the young psychologist take charge of the proceedings with authority and efficiency. Patients like Wingate were only dangerous when they sensed a weakness in their interrogator, a weakness which they could then exploit.

'Donald, let's go back if we may to the scene of your first murder.' Dallow consulted the forensic reports. 'Vincent Brady, of 16 New Church Street, Vauxhall. Do you recall why you — hurt — him in the neck?'

'"He deserved to die,"' recited Hargreave.

'He deserved to die,' said Wingate. 'And why was that?'

'"He had polluted the earth with his semen,"' said Hargreave.

'He had polluted the earth with his semen,' said Wingate.

'What do you mean?'

'"There shall be no whore of the daughters of Israel,"' said Hargreave, growing bored.

'There shall be no whore of the daughters of Israel,' said Wingate.

There was a pause. 'That's a Bible quote, isn't it?' said Dallow. 'Deuteronomy twenty-three, if I'm not mistaken.'

Hargreave sat up, surprised. At this point the doctors usually moved on to motivational questions.

'I'm sure it is,' Dallow was saying. She completed the verse. '... Nor shall there be a sodomite of the sons of Israel.'

'My God,' said Hargreave, suddenly standing. Why had it not occurred to him before? He left the room and walked briskly back to his office. Janice answered his call on the third ring.

'I hope you're not calling me back in,' she said sleepily. 'I've only just got home.'

'All you have to do is listen for a moment.'

'Fire away.'

'According to his statements, Wingate worshipped beautiful women. The photographs and news clippings he had saved featured half a dozen different female models, including Ixora de Corizo.'

'Ian, I know all this ...'

'He supposedly killed his victims because he had concrete proof that they had each slept with one of his love-objects, right?'

'Right.'

'But the first death doesn't fit. Vincent Brady was homosexual. The key murder in the case, the one which established Wingate's modus operandi, doesn't have the motive.'

'Tell me more.'

'Suppose the real killer found a scapegoat, someone else to take the rap. He provided Wingate with all the physical details of the murders, everything he needed to get himself locked away for life. He described room layouts, dates, weapons, how much time it took for each death to occur and the way it happened, drummed them into Wingate over and over until he was word perfect and ready to assume responsibility. He gave Wingate the same motive for all the victims: sexual obsession. But he made one mistake.'

'He didn't know that Vincent Brady was gay.'

'Precisely. If it could be proven in court that Wingate never witnessed a liaison between the victim and any of the models, it would be much harder to establish the case.'

'It sounds like you've got something, but it'll take more than that to get him off the hook.'

'There's something else. Remember I asked you why anyone would want to shoot at Santa Claus? Do you recall your reply?'

'Ian, right now I can barely remember what day it is.'

'You said, "Killing an ordinary person wouldn't have drawn so much attention." You were right. The murderer had finished what he set out to do. It was important that the police picked up the right suspect, the one that had been specially prepared for them. Hence, a showy display in a public place. Shooting Selfridge's Santa, for God's sake. Even we weren't able to screw up Wingate's "capture". This whole thing is starting to crack. I can feel it.'

'Sometimes you're as excitable as a schoolkid,' she said sleepily. 'I love it.'

'I just need one more break,' said Hargreave.

It came just after lunch, when Raymond Land entered his office with the updated notes from the forensic lab. 'I'm not supposed to do this,' he explained, 'but I thought you'd want to see them before they went into the system for collating.' He dropped the notes on to Hargreave's desk. The chief inspector was agreeably surprised. Land was obviously making a genuine effort to relax his adherence to the system.

'The high-kilovolt radiograph equipment couldn't identify the red flakes found in Feldman's studio and on Dominguez's body, although it showed that the substance was non-metallic, and both samples matched.' High-level, so-called 'hard' X-rays were normally used to identify car parts, guns and other non-fragile items requiring forensic investigation. Low-level X-rays handled the delicate task of checking counterfeit notes and forged letters. 'So they tested it with very low levels and eventually identified it. Take a look.' Land tapped the bottom of a typed page with his index finger. Hargreave's eyebrows rose.

'Brand name Liquid Beauty,' he read, looking up. 'It's nail varnish.'

The transverse arches of the church rose to become lost in gathering shadow. Helen checked her watch and absently genuflected towards the figure of Christ as she crossed the dimly lit nave and settled herself in a pew. Most nights at this time she came to church to pray for the deliverance of her husband's soul. There was no doubt in her mind now that he had been tempted along this path by the woman Ixora, who had filled his mind with the most base sexual desire.

After the accident on Christmas Eve, Helen was half convinced that the woman was an agent of Satan himself. There was no doubt in her mind that Ixora had used some kind of negative influence to turn John from her. As Helen had told the sergeant, she was a believer in evil. If you trusted in God, you had to believe in the Devil. It was no accident that she had lost the baby, and that the divorce had gone through.

Since then she had remained vigilant, watching for omens that would offer proof of the Devil at work. Last night she had attempted to discuss the problem with one of the priests, but he had refused to listen to her.

'You must help me devise a plan, Father,' she had pleaded, grabbing at his sleeve. 'I know my husband is in terrible danger. This woman means to take his soul.'

'Then I would suggest you arrange for her to take confession,' said the priest tersely, pulling his sleeve free and retreating to the transept.

Now she was alone with Joshua. Her son was the only one she could rely on, and he was too young to fully understand. For Helen, the solid world of cooking and cleaning and shopping no longer held any meaning, and instead of independence and liberation, there was nothing there to replace it. She wandered from one spotless room to the next desperate for something to do, the thought of her new-found freedom filling her with dread. She avoided the neighbours, whose pitying glances were all too easy to comprehend. Instead, she embraced the church, its scourging power to redeem and condemn. She could not understand why its agents were so reluctant to help her win what was obviously an outright battle between good and evil.

So be it, she decided, raising her tear-filled eyes to the tortured figure of the Lord. If no one else would help her, she would do it alone. She would confront the source of the corruption by herself. And if necessary, she would find a way to destroy it.

CHAPTER
41
Deadline

The Diamond Mineral Baths at Soufriere were constructed in 1785 by order of King Louis XVI. Across the centuries, the mineral deposits built up to form a glittering amber cascade, discernible through the orchids and ferns of the botanical gardens. Here the piercing sunlight had difficulty penetrating the creeper-clad trees of the park. The hurricane had passed by. The island had become a radiant emerald, and with it had come a change of mood. Now they were honeymooners, subdued by the memories of the recent past, certainly, but rediscovering the pleasure of being together.

In the last two days John had allowed Ixora to take him from one end of the island to the other. She was as she had been when they had first met, her misgivings about the marriage completely forgotten. He watched her as she stepped from the gravel path and walked into the forest, her footsteps lost in the sound of the waterfall.

'Come over here,' she called, pulling her T-shirt over her head, revealing pale taut breasts against a freshly tanned body. 'There's no one around.'

'What about insects?' he called back, laughing.

'Lizards and centipedes, big deal.' She was hopping on one foot, removing a sandal. 'If you get bitten by anything bigger, I promise to suck out the poison.' She wriggled out of her shorts and dropped down into the ferns.

He ran into the undergrowth and fell by her side, unbuckling his jeans as he went. They made love frantically, aggressively, the way they had a lifetime ago, one sunlit afternoon by the window in Hazlitt's Soho hotel. He saw her with fresh eyes, rediscovering her body as he ran his fingers over her thighs, her breasts, listened to the feline sounds of pleasure she made as he stroked her hair.

After, they rose and buttoned their clothes to find a group of elderly Canadian tourists staring at them in horror. Ixora was unable to contain her laughter for the rest of the afternoon.

'We have to go home some time, you know,' he said as they took Marcellus' taxi back to town.

'I know,' said Ixora, suddenly sobering. 'I'd forgotten how much I love it here. At first it was awful, going back to the house, punishing myself with all the old memories. I was terrified that someone would recognise me even in the dark, that the whole nightmare would start all over again.'

'Then why did you come back?'

'I had nowhere else to go. There's no one in London except you.'

'I've been thinking. Perhaps you should see a therapist when we return. Someone who could help you to forget the past.'

'I don't think I could ever forget, John.' She threw her arms around his neck. 'Thank you for looking for me. Thank you for finding me, and making me realise what an idiot I'd been to run away. Thank you for making me realise that this was meant to be.'

'I had no choice in the matter.'

She fell back against the seat. 'I'm going to make you happy for the rest of your life. That's a promise. First of all, we'll renovate the house.'

'What with?' He had not yet told her how heavily he had fallen into debt, or what it would cost to get back out.

'I'll do another film and become a famous international model. You'll get another job, just to maintain your ego while I make you a kept man, and then' — she turned to face him — 'then we'll have a baby.'

'You're serious?'

'Never been more so.'

'A baby.' The thought made him feel like a teenager again, but this time, without the attendant anxiety. 'We'll celebrate tonight. I'll take you anywhere you want to go.' After he'd paid for Ixora's return fare to England there would be little money left from the loan. If they didn't make the most of it tonight, he knew that they would not get another chance.

'It's Friday, isn't it?' said Ixora excitedly. 'We can go to the Street Jump at Gros Islet. The whole town turns into a party, nobody cares who you are.'

'Good idea,' said Marcellus, enthusiastically. 'I'll come.'

'But we'll go for dinner first. Just you and I,' John said quietly. 'Somewhere intimate.'

'I know just the place, a table for two beside tall shuttered windows overlooking the bay.' She laid her head on his shoulder. 'I love you very much. It makes me shudder to think I nearly threw it all away.'

You and me both, thought John.

They dined high above the harbour at the San Antoine, on delicate white fish baked *en papillote* in lime and ginger. They drank too much wine and planned too far into the future. Throughout the meal, John had to remind himself that they were now man and wife, that no matter how unorthodox the wedding ceremony had been, this incredible, beautiful woman was bound to him by the laws of holy matrimony. His problems of mounting debts and unemployment seemed as far away as London itself, lost in the bitter mists of a British winter.

'How long had you planned to stay here?' asked John.

Ixora settled back in her chair, her eyes fixed on the swaying lights of the harbour boats. 'I had no plan,' she said. 'I just wanted to come home. The house is still in my name, but it can't be sold until the debts which have accrued on the property have been cleared, and I don't have the money to fix the place up.'

'Then let's go back to London,' said John. Somehow he would find a way to straighten out their financial situation. 'No more living in the past.'

'The past is something you carry around with you. It can't be shaken off that easily.'

John drained his coffee cup and set it down. 'We'll see about that,' he said.

The lower half of Sloane Crescent was flooded. London had been in the grip of torrential rainstorms. He lifted Ixora across the muddy lake of the garden, then set her down while he unlocked the front door. Water lapped against the porch. Inside, the house seemed darker and damper than ever before. He tried the light switch a few times but nothing happened.

'What's wrong?'

John pulled out a lighter and flicked it. 'The rain's probably got into the wiring and caused a short-circuit.' He stood on a chair and checked the fuse box while Ixora waited at the foot of the stairs. 'It's serious,' he said, returning from the kitchen with a pair of lighted candles. 'Looks like the whole system's burned out. We're lucky the house didn't burn down. It'll be expensive to fix but the insurance should cover it.' He remembered their conversation about the roof. 'You *do* have insurance for something like this?'

'I think the policies may have lapsed,' said Ixora, worrying a nail between her teeth. In the flickering light she might have passed for a Pre-Raphaelite heroine, Ophelia with a suntan. He wanted to ask her how the hell she could allow something as important as a policy to lapse, but he knew if he did they would be returning to the old ways. Now that they were man and wife, that was not allowed.

'We'll work something out,' he said, taking the case from her hand and arming her with a candlestick. 'Do you have any more of these?'

'Maybe upstairs. I'll have a look. There's a stack of mail on the mat.'

'It's probably all bills. Let's wait until daylight to open them. Things will look better in the morning.'

They were able to find over a dozen candles, which they set in saucers and placed around the corridors and bedrooms of the first floor. The house seemed suited to these low, swaying pools of light, as if it had finally managed to overcome the impertinent glare of electricity and return to the decorous shadows of the past.

John stood a pair of brass candlesticks beside the bath. Shaving would have to wait until the morning. Somewhere above, water dripped steadily. 'You can go first,' he called. There was no reply. 'Ixora?' He raised one of the candlesticks and returned to the bedroom, where he had left her a few moments ago.

The bedspread was disturbed where she had sat to remove her shoes, but the room was empty. In the corridor outside, the candles flickered violently, as if someone had left a door open. 'Ixora, where are you?'

He listened for a moment. Something clattered on the tiled kitchen floor below. A chair scraped. He guided his way to the stairs and descended into the hall, pausing to listen again. Something was wrong.

There was a cold draught blowing from somewhere. A candle set on the hall table had been knocked to the floor, red wax splattering the wall like a bloodstain. Without knowing why, he found himself running towards the kitchen.

As he burst through the door, someone grabbed him around the throat and threw him back against the wall. He tried to stand, and saw Ixora on the far side of the room. She was being held down in a chair, a broad hand spread tight across her mouth. Something sharp was sticking into the back of his shirt. He tried to turn around, but the knife jabbed forward, piercing his skin.

'Welcome back, Chapel.' The voice was classless and flat, unidentifiably suburban. He had heard it before, the night of the drinking spree. The night he had borrowed money.

'Save us all some embarrassment and keep your mouth shut. Just answer the question: do you have it or not?'

John's eyes never left Ixora's terrified face. 'I can get it in a matter of—' The knife shoved itself deeper into the flesh of his back. He cried out, trying to twist away.

'Let's try again. Do you have it, right now?'

'Let me—' The knife slipped across his skin. This time he screamed.

'It's not that fucking difficult to understand. Yes or no?'

'No.' The knife eased back slightly.

'Now we're getting somewhere. Today is Monday. You're over a week late. We call to see you in all good faith, and find you've skipped off. Who's in the wrong, you or us?' Strong hands turned him around. He found himself facing Mancuso, the man who had agreed his loan in the casino.

Mancuso reached into his shirt and pulled out a laser-printed sheet of paper. 'Your bill, sir,' he said, passing it across.

John read the base figure. £4,240.00. Blood was seeping into the waistband of his trousers. 'That's — more than we agreed,' he gasped.

'You have to pay extra for housecalls. When will you have it?' John looked at Ixora again. The man holding her down was staring distractedly at the wall, as if he hated his job.

'Friday,' he said blindly.

'Friday,' repeated Mancuso. 'A full working week away. That doesn't sound very reasonable. Let's say Wednesday.' He removed the knife, wiped its blade and folded it away. 'Remember in future. Don't go past your payment date without telling someone. It's only fair.' He looked up at the light fixture in the ceiling. 'It's like the electricity board. If you don't pay your bills, you get cut off.'

He gestured to his partner to release his captive. Ixora came running from the chair into John's arms.

One of the men turned in the hallway. 'Wednesday evening, shall we say six o'clock, here?'

'Yes, yes.' Right now he felt capable of saying anything, just to get them out of the house. Especially as there was no money to give them, not a single penny.

'The full amount,' reminded Mancuso with a smile. 'If you don't have it, you'd better remember to cancel your milk.'

CHAPTER
42
The Key

The pale January sunlight glistened on the wet pavements, and fell weakly through the rain-grimed hall windows. Even the morning's pots of boiling coffee had failed to erase the pungent smell of candle wax from the house. Ixora collected the mail from the hall table and sorted it as she headed for the kitchen. John emerged tucking his shirt in over his bandaged back. Although the wound was severe enough to require some stitches, he refused to call a doctor. He was anxious to see his run of bad luck through to its conclusion, and he was determined to do it without anyone else's help.

He watched Ixora carefully cutting open her letters and setting the contents aside, and wondered if their life together would ever settle to an even keel. Since he had met her, he'd been threatened, shot at, stabbed twice, and accused of murder. And all because his wish had come true.

It was time to tackle the problem neither of them knew how to solve: raising the money to pay Mancuso.

'I don't understand it,' said John. 'They act like it's not the money; it's as if they're holding a personal grudge. I've never borrowed before in my life. Threatening to kill me is something from an old gangster movie.'

'There's no point in trying to understand people like that,' said Ixora, reading.

'Maybe I could arrange a second mortgage on my house.'

'No, John. You got yourself in debt because of me. I'll find a way to get us out of it. The paintings will have to go, for a start. Didn't you once tell me you knew someone at Sotheby's?'

'I went to school with him. I still have his number somewhere.'

'I know they're worth something. My mother told me she had them valued before she went to St Lucia. They must be worth a lot more now. Surely I'll be able to get an advance on them.'

'Ixora, the pictures are all you have left.'

'No,' she corrected, 'you are all I have left. Leave it to me. We'll have the money in time. We should even have enough left over to clear some of these bills.' She fanned the letters in her hand. The writing on one of the envelopes looked familiar.

'Who's that one from?' he asked, pointing.

'Oh, just another final demand,' she said hurriedly, tucking it to the bottom of the pile. 'Take a look at this.' Instead she waved two gilt-edged cards before his eyes. 'We came back just in time. The tickets must have been here for at least a week.'

Two invitations to the premiere of *Playing With Fire*, to

take place on Wednesday evening at 7.30 p.m. at the Odeon, Leicester Square, in the presence of the Duke and Duchess of York.

'We have to go,' said Ixora. 'But what about paying back the money?'

'I'll call Mancuso and tell him I'm coming by the casino afterwards. It's essential for you to be seen at the premiere. It's bound to be televised, and you need the contacts. Call your agent right now. She has to let the palace representative know in advance if you're going to be presented.'

Diana Morrison released a theatrical squeal that sounded like someone killing a pig. John heard it clear across the kitchen.

'*Daaarling*,' she was saying, 'where on *earth* have you been? We've been going simply *fraaantic* with worry.'

'I had some personal problems I had to sort out. I'm sorry, I know I should have called …'

'No matter, you're back now and that's the main thing. You're down for meeting Andy and Fergie at the premmy, of course. It's the royal B-team, I know, but we have to look on the bright side. It could have been Princess Michael of Kent. Everyone's going to be there. The distributors are too cheap to throw a decent party afterwards so we're all going to throw buns at each other in Langan's instead. Also, someone from Columbia Tri-Star has been frantically trying to get hold of you but I can't remember who it was. Hold on.'

Ixora cupped her hand over the phone. 'Sounds like I've got an audition,' she said, raising her eyebrows at him.

'Here it is. I can't remember, dear — can you sing? No matter, they're after a Look rather than a Voice. It's a modern day remake of *The Beggar's Opera*, and it occurred to me that you have the perfect hair for Lucy Lockit. They want you to read for the part of Samantha — that's the update. Brett Michaels from Tri-Star will be there on

Wednesday, so you can talk to him about it. Don't hold your breath about the final cut of *Fire* by the way. We had the Cast and Crew screening while you were away. Everyone filed out looking as if they'd lost relatives in an air crash. You made it through half a dozen edits without losing your lines, although I can't remember if they finally went with your voice, but Scott's performance is mostly on the cutting room floor, which is just as well. You couldn't get a more wooden performance from a roll-top desk. I must dash, good to have you back in the land of the living, see you at the bash.' There was a sharp click and the line went dead.

'She didn't even ask me where I'd been,' said Ixora. 'Write down the number of your friend at Sotheby's. I've got a lot of work to do before tomorrow.'

'I hope I still have it.' John rose from the table and went upstairs. As soon as he had left the room, Ixora shuffled back through the envelopes on the table and withdrew the one at the bottom. She had recognised the handwriting immediately. Turning it over, she tore open the flap.

John,
I must see you. It concerns your lady friend.
    You are in terrible danger.
    Please don't ignore this. I couldn't bear to see you hurt.
    Call me at home daytime or at St Anne's Church in Soho evenings.
    Don't show her this letter.
Helen

This was perfect. Everything would be solved in the space of a single evening. This time it would all work out. She would wear a dress of pure white silk. There would be no more red. Ever.

*

Hargreave turned back to Sullivan's notes and began again from the top. It was 2.15 on Tuesday morning. Janice was still handling the night shift, so the house was empty. He had planned to work in the new operations room at Mornington Crescent, but the constant interruptions had broken his train of thought once too often.

Here in his study, he had been able to lay out all the available information about the case. A pair of IBM diskettes contained the accumulated forensic and medical evidence on the murders. Sullivan's notebooks had been carefully annotated by Janice, who had worked on them in her free time. There were the psychiatric reports on Wingate and the transcripts of conversations with various witnesses and suspects. There was an electronic dossier culled from the LAN network which contained details of every known offender currently at large in the United Kingdom. There was also a terse but annoyingly vague note from Her Majesty's Inspectorate of Constabulary, a group appointed by the Home Secretary from the ranks of Chief Constables, concerning the urgency of apprehending a culprit, (any reasonably appropriate culprit, it implied) and publicly closing the case.

Somewhere here on the desk in front of him were the answers to all his questions. He felt that he now had the key which would unlock the case completely.

The key was Vincent Brady.

The evidence of the first case had been ignored in the headlong rush that had followed. Vincent Brady was West Indian, born in Antigua, resident in London for just three years. Friends said he'd left his homeland to escape the island's oppressive attitude towards homosexuality. Statements from friends indicated that he was well adjusted, and intelligent beyond the limitations of his job. So barwork was filling in until — what? A career in photography?

The camera equipment in his apartment was of high quality ...

No. In the rush to link Brady into subsequent deaths, Sergeant Sullivan had assumed that photography was the link in three of the murders. His assumptions had subsequently remained unquestioned.

But suppose photography had played no part in it? Brady's flat had not been broken into. He had admitted a friend. The chips of nail varnish indicated a woman. For once, sex was not a relevant factor. Assume she had come to kill him. Why? What had he done to hurt her? His movements during the days immediately prior to his murder had yielded no surprises, nothing of interest at all. So what about his pre-London past? He had asked Janice that question earlier tonight. Hopefully she was checking out the answer right now.

Time to look at it from another perspective. Hargreave laid out the files of the victims, omitting Sullivan's, whose death he considered circumstantial. Brady. Feldman. Dominguez. Saunders. Howard. Five men with nothing but their fatal ends in common. Five religious artefacts immersed in water. Five extremely brutal deaths, all by impalement of some kind or other ...

Hargreave tapped his teeth and looked from one photograph to the next. From somewhere in the garden came the scream of a cat, as human and as anguished as a baby's. He was still watching the window when the clock in the hall chimed three.

Five men with nothing in common.

Four men with something — some *one* in common. Ixora De Corizo. Feldman had photographed her. Dominguez had dated her. Saunders had worshipped her. Howard had worked with her. But there was nothing to suggest that Vincent Brady had even heard of the damned woman.

Suppose he had. How many other elements would fit?

The lingering, powerful aftershave at the crime scenes — could it have been a brand of perfume? Did she possess the sheer physical strength to kill someone? And what was her motive?

The jangling of the telephone made him start. Janice had known he would still be working.

'Ian, I've got something which will interest you.'

'God knows I need a break. What is it?'

'Before he lived in England, Vincent Brady sold timeshare apartments in the West Indies. I've just been speaking with his former employer. While he was visiting St Lucia, he met Ixora De Corizo. By all accounts, he dated her for a couple of years.'

'How long ago would this have been?'

'Late seventies. They were both very young.'

'So what happened?'

'He suddenly ended the relationship.'

'He realised he was gay.'

'That's what I'm thinking.'

'Janice, you're an angel.'

He was beginning to sense some underlying structure to the case. Five dead males, all involved in some capacity with one woman. A sixth, more involved than any of the others, who continued to survive. It was time he stopped thinking of John Chapel as a suspect, and started considering him as the motive.

CHAPTER
43
Playing With Fire

Janice set down her coffee and checked her watch. She hated the night shift at Bow Street. 3.00 a.m. was the witching hour, time of drunks and crazies as the clubs discharged their clientele. At least her office at the back of the building was quiet. The silence was marred only by the electric heater beneath her desk ticking as the bars cooled.

She thought of Ian, surrounded by his criminal text-books, working beneath the glow of the green desk lamp in his study. He'd be drinking cold coffee, swearing under his breath, making crabbed illegible notes on sheets of lined notepaper.

She wished he would understand that it didn't matter if the station staff knew they were having an affair — no, not an affair, a relationship. Though neither of them were married, an affair was what it felt like, skulking around pretending they barely knew each other, then spending three nights a week in each other's arms.

Tonight, the only thing that mattered to Ian was concluding the case. She wished she could be of more help, but right now he was in sole possession of all material relating to the murders.

Ian had wondered if Ixora could somehow be the culprit. At first glance, the idea seemed ridiculous. Violent predatory attacks were the province of the male. Janice sat back and checked the grips in her hair, pinning them back in place.

Strangely enough, she felt a common bond with the model. They were both ambitious and independent. They kept their private lives separate from their public behaviour. And they had both, in a way, stolen their men from a marriage. Although it was admittedly an unhappy union, Ian had still been wed when she had come to work for him.

She tried to see inside Ixora's mind, tried to imagine the men in her life. Jealous admirers, spurned lovers. Men who worshipped, doe-eyed and desperate. Ego freaks, swaggering in sports cars. That was why she stayed with Ian; the macho bullshit was all behind him. Perhaps that was what had drawn Ixora to John Chapel.

Chapel. The name suited him. Plain and sturdy, with religious connotations. She could definitely see the attraction. He was a straight arrow, born with a frank look on his face that suggested he was permanently surprised by the wiles of the world. Ian was more cynical, and that made him more annoying. His distance was infuriating. Sometimes he seemed to be barely in the same room with her, and she felt like hitting him with anything that came to hand, just to get a reaction.

Surely Ixora sometimes felt like that.

But what would make either of them kill?

Ian said that murder was particularly associated with two emotions: anger and fear. Anger was felt by those seeking revenge on someone. Fear was felt by those fighting to protect themselves or their loved ones.

Protecting their loved ones.

Janice lifted the scab from her coffee with the end of a pencil, and took a sip. Ixora's loved one was John Chapel. Suppose she killed to protect him. But if Ixora was the guilty party — then the one she was trying to protect Chapel from was — herself.

She grabbed the telephone receiver and quickly dialled Ian Hargreave's home number.

'Thank God you're back,' said John, throwing open the door. He had started to worry. It was the second day that Ixora had left the house early to try to raise money on the paintings. Now it was almost 6.00 p.m., the car booked to take them to the premiere was due at 6.30 p.m., and Ixora still had to change from her sweater and jeans.

John had spent the day attempting to arrange a legitimate loan via his bank and building society, with little success. He had no collateral, no job, nothing in the way of security to offer beyond the house his wife and son were occupying, and he was not prepared to put their welfare at risk.

'How did you get on?'

'Disastrously. Six months ago I was their golden boy. They were throwing platinum credit cards at me. Now I couldn't raise the cash for a sandwich. How'd it go with you?'

'All right.' She removed her cap and threw it on the table, shaking her hair loose. 'The provenance of the pictures is undisputed, but they've got to check the authenticity of the Holman-Hunt and the little Wright study.'

'Is there any doubt about them?' he asked, helping her out of her overcoat.

'Only on two of the four. They want to run some tests. I spoke to the bank, and they said they were willing to advance the money on written receipt from the auctioneer. To avoid the delay of exchanging letters I made them fax all the paperwork with the exception of the signed documentation, which I had to ferry back and forth. The problem is, I still couldn't get hard cash because by this time the banks were shut.'

'But you have a written guarantee that the money will be in the account?'

'Yes, it'll be in there tomorrow. That should be all right, shouldn't it?'

'It'll have to be. I'll phone Mancuso now and explain the situation. If he'll play ball, I'll withdraw the full amount first thing in the morning.'

'Great. We can go to the movie with an easy mind.' He made to kiss her, but she slipped past him, running to the stairs and kicking off her shoes.

'We can get the electrics fixed. I love candlelight, but this is ridiculous. Leave me alone for half an hour. I'm wearing something special, so it'll take some major refurbishment. You'd better get your dinner jacket on.'

While the hot water pipes gurgled and clanged in the ceiling above, John called the casino. Mancuso was not on the floor, or in his office. At John's insistence, his assistant eventually tracked him down. Although he expressed his displeasure at being disturbed he grudgingly conceded to John's request, on the condition that he brought the bank's letter of confirmation by the casino later that night.

John reluctantly agreed, knowing that they would be in the area following the premiere. At precisely 6.30 p.m., the doorbell rang.

A black Mercedes waited in the street, its engine purring.

'It's here,' John called to the landing above, 'the cab's here!'

He waited a moment, watching the top of the stairs. The chauffeur was still standing in the doorway. He gave John a 'Bloody-women-always-late-but-you-can't-help-loving-them' look, and smiled. Suddenly he was staring past him with his mouth hanging slack, as if he'd just been knifed in the back.

John turned around.

Ixora stood on the stair in a strapless dress of glittering frost, an ivory version of the dress she had worn on the night he thought he had first seen her at Waterloo Station. Her hair fell in a glossy black fringe above her eyes. Only the rope of pearls was missing from her throat.

The fluidity of movement as she descended the staircase in flickering candlelight, the way she slowly raised her hand to her forehead, returned the feeling that time itself had slowed to allow an appreciation of her beauty. He took her hand as she reached the bottom step. He could feel her pulse tapping hard inside her wrist.

'You look like a movie star,' he whispered, 'and in a couple of hours you'll be one.'

'I'm nervous. No, I'm fine,' she said with a paralysed smile.

'Let's go.'

The crowds in Leicester Square were packed from the walls of the buildings to the yellow steel barriers that police had erected from Charing Cross Road to the cinema. A large square pass had been taped to the wind-screen of the Mercedes, allowing it through the police cordon. As the car ahead pulled up, Scott Tyron and his new girlfriend alighted to a roar of approval from the crowd. A firestorm of flashlights illuminated their path along the red carpet to the reception area. The film's distributors and the cinema manager were to accompany them on a series of brief interviews while they were waiting for the arrival of the royal entourage.

The chauffeur drove to a halt beside the carpeted kerb, then alighted to open the passenger door. Ixora swallowed hard and gave him her gloved hand, glancing back at John with a nervous smile. Immediately there were cameras firing everywhere as a battery of reporters clustered about her. John guided her into the foyer as the crowd noisily voiced their admiration. Much to his surprise, Scott Tyron smiled across and shoved his way clear of a BBC film crew to join them. He was sporting freshly tanned skin and newly bleached hair for the occasion, and had dressed in a black suede cowboy jacket with sleeve fringes and silver cacti on each lapel, presumably so that no one could miss who they were dealing with.

'Hey, how *are* you guys?' he cried in a voice that succeeded in cutting through the deafeningly false *bon-homie* around them. Several of those attending the premiere turned to watch a real film star having an honest-to-goodness conversation, just like ordinary common people. He kissed Ixora a little too warmly on the mouth, then pumped John's hand.

'Where do you think they found these so-called celebrity guests?' he asked before either of them had managed to speak. 'It looks like the Night Of The Living Career-Dead. I guess you didn't make it to the Cast and Crew screening, huh?'

Ixora shook her head. 'No, I didn't.'

'Well, neither did the script. At least you're still in it, although that's a mixed blessing. Remember the restaurant scene? The old guy who played the waiter had a heart attack at Christmas and died. Good career move.' He looked around and waved at Diana Morrison, who was leaning on the arm of an attractive young Italian.

'I have to catch Diana,' said Scott, squeezing their arms. 'She's either brought her grandson along or she went out for a pasta last night. See you guys at Langan's.' He shoved his way back into the throng, the cinema guests switching their attention from one star to the next like Wimbledon spectators.

'*There* you are!' Park Manton, the producer, appeared between them. 'Are you being presented?'

'I suppose someone will tell us what to do,' said Ixora.

'Oh, it's easy. You go and stand in that little roped-off section of the foyer between those huge flower arrangements, then the royal couple walk slowly past and shake your hand, and ask you something inconsequential, like did you enjoy making the film, then you lie and say yes, then they move on. I'm sure they genuinely believe that all London cinemas are filled with fresh flowers for each performance. Have you got any coke on you?'

'No,' said Ixora. 'I have an addictive personality.'

'Give me a break,' said Manton, screwing up his face. 'It's not addictive. I should know, I've been doing it for years. Don't be too disappointed when you see the film. The Cast and Crew went badly, but then they saw it under adverse conditions: the projector was plugged in. Everyone's blaming the director, poor love. Scott's been going around telling people that when the rabbi circumcised Farley he threw away the wrong piece. You can't trust anyone in this industry, it's a snakepit. See you in the lineup, gorgeous.' He coasted off across the foyer like a breaker parting pack-ice.

Ten minutes later, the crowd outside began cheering as the royal limousine arrived. The audience had been sent to their seats. Spotlights were heating the waiting area to an unbearable degree. John had been allowed to remain beside Ixora in the lineup, although he knew that he would not be formally introduced. While her husband talked with the chairman of the film's British distributors, the Duchess of York paused briefly before each cast member and moved on. It was odd, John thought, that such a friendly gesture should be so invested in nervous tension. As soon as the royal couple had been directed to their seats, the members of the lineup took their places amid much sighing of relief. The lights faded, and the film began to roll.

One hour and fifty-five minutes later, as the end credits rose across the screen and the auditorium was filled with deafening spontaneous applause, John turned to Ixora and squeezed her gloved hand.

'My God, Ixora, you're on your way. You're really on your way. You were brilliant.' She looked back at him in the darkness, her eyes glittering wetly. She seemed unable to speak. The film was really very good. Much of the original script had been lost in favour of stylish visuals set to music, but Ixora was sensational. Perhaps she had been lucky in finding a part that matched her natural personality, but it seemed that in spite of what everyone had thought, she really could act. Her screen time amounted to not much more than fifteen minutes, but she was by far the most memorable character in the entire film, outshining Scott Tyron with absurd ease. No wonder he had been so friendly to her in the foyer. He had seen her performance at the Cast and Crew and had presumably decided that it would be better to make an ally of her than an enemy.

'They used my real voice!' said Ixora excitedly.

As the lights went up, John took her hands in his. 'Listen, you're going to be mobbed any second now, so I just want to say that — whatever happens to us in the years ahead — I will always, always love you, Ixora. You have my total trust and my undying love.'

'Oh, John, don't say that, please.' She suddenly began to cry. He tugged out a handkerchief and passed it to her.

'What's the matter?'

'It's just — I wish to God I didn't love you so much—'

'Why?' He didn't understand what she was trying to say.

'It's so hard for me—'

'Ixora, *daaarling*, you were magnificent!'

Suddenly there were people all around her, desperate to bestow praise, longing to be seen with her and recognised, anxious to be touched in some way by this new phenomenon. John rose from his seat and stood back, allowing her the freedom of her new-found fame.

He felt sure now that he would lose her, that he had already lost some indefinable part of her that was bound up in her reticence, her mystery. After tonight there could be no more mystery. Her private life would become public knowledge. Her private thoughts would be made available in magazine articles. Her films would eventually be released on videocassette, where her electronic image could be reduced in speed, the slow motion cadence of her limbs wheeling across the screen at the whim of each enthralled viewer. This was what he had helped to create and shape. He was happy for her, but the moment was tinged with the sadness of loss.

Perhaps somehow he sensed the truth; that it was to be the last night of happiness they would ever have together in their lives.

CHAPTER
44
Hypnosis

At 8.15 on Wednesday evening, Hargreave caught up with Raymond Land just as he was locking his office door. For the staff of the constabulary below it was the lull before the storm, which began in three hours time when the pubs turned out. Above, the detectives were hitting a shift change, and Land made sure that he always left on time. Hargreave was determined that tonight would be different.

'Raymond, wait up, I need to talk to you.' He arrived beside the exasperated doctor just as he was putting his keys away. 'What do you know about hypnosis?'

'Ian, I'm a forensic scientist. It's hardly my field.'

'Don't give me that.' It was common knowledge that Land had run a medical practice before turning his considerable talents to criminal investigation. 'I need some information urgently and you're the only one around who's familiar with the case. Can we go inside?'

With a sigh of irritation, Land unlocked the door and flicked on the overhead striplights.

'It's too late to do anything about Wingate, if that's what you're thinking,' he said. 'They're taking him back to Wandsworth Psychiatric Centre tonight.'

'I know. That's why I need your help. Can hypnosis be performed against your will?'

Land looked at him suspiciously. 'Wingate wasn't hypnotised into killing people, if that's what you're thinking. You can't talk someone into becoming a murderer.'

'I was thinking more of getting him to accept responsibility for the deaths.'

'Unlikely. It goes against the grain of basic human instinct. Although I should think there are plenty of ways to get around that.'

'What do you mean?'

'You can focus on a patient's weaknesses, use subterfuge.'

'Give me an example.'

'All right, suppose your man is a stickler for law and order. You tell him he's been instrumental in removing a menace to decent society, and it's something he can be proud of. If the patient loves kids, you tell him he's helped to destroy a child molester.'

'What about hypnotising someone with abnormal mental processes, like Wingate?'

'Patients with fully developed psychoses are often extremely susceptible to certain forms of suggestion.'

'How long does it last? Could he still be under hypnosis?'

'It's possible. There's a theory that hypnosis inhibits the higher cortical centres and narrows the sensory channels so that a psychological process can take place through transference. The perceptions and feelings of the patient are altered. His critical faculties are suspended ...'

'Could Wingate's own past history be replaced with a false one, or someone else's?'

'So long as he wanted to believe in it, yes. There's a famous case of an American actress who was cast in a stage role at very short notice. She was hypnotised into learning her part in the play, and astounded the cast by knowing everyone else's lines. While she was on stage at night, she actually became the character she was portraying.'

'If Wingate's "confession" is the product of hypnotic suggestion, he could see it as some kind of performing role, couldn't he?'

'One of the classic signs of psychological illness is a tendency towards exhibitionism,' said Land. 'Yes, it would suit an overdeveloped ego like Wingate's.'

'Could the command be removed?'

'I don't know.'

'More to the point, could *you* remove it?'

'That's out of the question. I'd have to understand the scenario that was implanted in Wingate's mind. I'd also need to know something about the character of the person who implanted it.'

'I can give you that on the way,' said Hargreave, heading for the door.

'But I can't come now!' cried Land. 'I have a dinner date!'

'Break it. Wingate is taking the rap for something he didn't do, and if we don't move quickly it could start all over again.'

'What's the theory behind all this?' asked Land as he led the way downstairs.

'We're supposed to believe that Wingate killed for the sake of his girls. But if you accept that he's a scapegoat, then one of those girls is the true culprit. The murderer is a woman.'

'I thought you'd already eliminated De Corizo.'

'She's back at the top of the list.'

'But even assuming that she could physically manage it, what's her motivation?'

'That's what I couldn't figure out. I sat there all night with the casebooks spread out in front of me and I just couldn't see it. Then Longbright called me. We tried to imagine every possible scenario, no matter how absurd, and we realised that it was John. John Chapel was the motive. Everything has been done for the love of him. Think about it: what had the victims done to harm her? True, Brady had dated her long before, then ditched her when he realised he was gay. Perhaps his murder was pure revenge. But each of the other victims had somehow tarnished her reputation. Feldman, cheapening her in his photographs. Saunders and Dominguez, always warning John away. Howard, telling John that Ixora had slept her way to the top. The assistant, Paula, heard them shouting clear through the office wall.'

'I don't understand,' said Land. 'It's an odd motive for murder. Why would it be so important for John's opinion of his girlfriend not to be damaged?'

'I have no answer to that.' Hargreave keyed in his personal ID code and pushed open the hallway door. 'It's as if she has to remain pure in his eyes. It'd be ironic if the theory proves to be true. Chapel was the PR man employed to create an image for her, and instead she's been building an image of her own to sell to him.'

They turned a corner and found themselves in the austere green and white corridors of the basement.

'Christ, we're dealing with a psychologically damaged man, and they've left him in the *morgue*?'

'It's not a morgue, Ian, it's a temporary holding bay.'

'You still keep bodies in there.'

'They're taking him out through the rear of the building in less than an hour,' said Land. 'There was nowhere else near the loading dock.' They paused before the door of the morgue, and Hargreave peered in through a small window covered with wire-meshed glass. Wingate was seated on the far side of the room, his arms and legs strapped to a heavy steal chair. He appeared to be asleep. Nearby, one of the doctors sat scanning a magazine, impatient to be relieved from his shift. He looked none too happy about being left alone with only cadavers and a possibly deranged murderer for company.

Hargreave and Land entered and introduced themselves to the doctor. Wingate did not stir, but remained with his fleshy head lolling on his chest.

'What have you given him?' asked Hargreave, indicating their patient.

The doctor checked Wingate's medical sheet. 'A mild sedative to keep him calm during the transfer. He's awake, he's just on "down-time". He does this whenever nobody's paying him any attention.'

'We need to talk to him for a few minutes. Will he be able to understand us?'

'Sure.' He looked wary. 'What kind of questions? Dr Dallow left instructions not to disturb him.'

'I'm overriding her orders,' said Hargreave. 'If you want to go and get clearance from her, be my guest.' He pulled up a pair of chairs and seated himself astride one of them. 'Raymond, can you make a start?'

Land shrugged helplessly. 'I'll try. I need to think of an angle. Just don't expect too much.' He seated himself before the sleeping giant. While the doctor called his superior, Land began speaking to his patient in a soft, soothing monotone.

'I'm glad you're relaxed, because this is how you should

be, relaxed and calm, sitting comfortably with the palms of your hands resting lightly on your thighs. You're sleeping lightly, very lightly …'

Hargreave watched the subtle changes in Wingate's posture and realised that they were dealing with a highly susceptible patient.

'We can't tell him that what he believes to be true is wrong,' whispered Land. 'As far as Wingate is concerned, he really did kill those people. I need to introduce a paradoxical situation into his mind, something which will confuse his feelings about the past. There's a very real danger here that by disturbing his illusions, we'll be causing further psychological damage.'

'That's a risk I have to take.'

Land turned back to Wingate, whose head remained on his chest, eyes closed. 'I want you to cast your mind back, not to the murders now, but to the young woman you did so much for. Her name is Ixora De Corizo, and she is the reason why you committed these crimes.' Wingate shifted in his seat, growing visibly agitated.

'That is correct, isn't it?'

'No,' grunted the patient.

'It's not Ixora?'

'No.'

'Have you ever met a woman named Ixora De Corizo?'

'Never met.'

Land shot Hargreave a look of concern. 'She could have used another name,' said Hargreave. 'Show him this.' He withdrew Ixora's model card from his pocket.

'When you open your eyes, Donald, you will see a picture of a woman. I want you to tell me if it's the woman who spoke to you. Do you understand?'

'Yes.'

As Land held up the card, Wingate slowly raised his head. His eyes flickered open.

'Is this the woman?'

'Yes. Alice.'

'Do you think she's pleased with what you did?'

'Pleased.'

'How do you know? Suppose she wasn't? Suppose she wasn't at all pleased, but very, very angry with you.'

Wingate gave no reply. His eyes remained open, eerily staring. The veins in his neck had bunched up, as though he was straining.

'If she was angry with you, she'd never love you.'

There was no reply.

'And she said she would always love you, so she couldn't be angry with you, could she?'

'No.'

'Because you have her blessing. Because she told you to do these things.'

No reply.

'To do these things, and then she would love you.'

Wingate was turning red in the face.

'You wouldn't even have to do these things. Just to say that you did them. Isn't that right?'

'No. Yes.'

'And to fire your gun in the department store so that it looked as if you really were a murderer. So that you would be caught by the police, and would tell your story to them.'

'Told me they were blanks.'

'But they weren't blanks. You really killed someone. She lied to you, Donald. She betrayed you.'

Dark blood began to drip from Wingate's nose.

'Jesus, bring him out, Raymond,' cried Hargreave, searching for a cloth.'

The doctor changed the tone of his voice. 'When I count to five you will feel your body growing lighter and your eyes will open. Then I will click my fingers, and you will become awake and alert. Five … four … three … two … one …'

Wingate suddenly snapped to attention, his eyes wide with panic.

'What in hell's name is going on here?' called a female voice from the doorway. Dr Maria Dallow was followed by the guard who had come to lead Wingate to the transfer vehicle.

'I'm sorry, Dr Dallow,' said Hargreave. 'It was something I had to try. I don't mean to sound melodramatic when I say that people's lives are at stake.'

Behind them, the guard was already removing Wingate's restraining straps.

'I really think you should have consulted me before trying something like this. What on earth were you doing, hypnotising him?'

'Quite the reverse,' said Land. 'He's showing all the signs of already being under hypnosis.'

'That's impossible.'

Wingate suddenly screamed, spraying blood over them. He had one leg and one arm free from the chair. 'Betrayer of men!' he shouted frantically. It was Hargreave's guess that Land had managed to break through the illusion in Wingate's mind, causing the reality of innocence to reveal itself. 'She fornicates with the Devil to condemn the living!' he bellowed. 'Eater of men's souls! On the night men come to worship her, she will claim her unholy inheritance!'

Dallow dived into her case and began loading medication into a syringe as Hargreave, Land and the guard wrestled with their patient. Wingate threw back his arm, slamming Land against the drawer racks. He punched the guard hard in the face and lunged for Hargreave, who jumped back out of the way.

A dissecting scalpel blade had been overlooked by the

cleaners when the stainless steel trays were washed out for the night. The glint of the edge in the drainage gutter must have caught Wingate's eye. Before anyone could move an inch he had lunged towards it, shoving it into his fist and puncturing his unshaven throat, dragging the blade deep across.

'Bride of the Devil!' he gurgled. 'At midnight she will tear out the heart of her husband and feed it to Satan's jackals!'

Then his words were lost in the froth of red bubbles that exploded from his torn trachyea.

CHAPTER
45
The Letter

The cinema foyer was a turbulent sea of talking heads, with camera lights and microphone booms swaying back and forth like the masts of yachts. The royals had been the first to leave, drifting out through the awe-struck populace, and then the media mob had descended, presenters calling to their camera crews, ready to process the key elements of the occasion into something digestible for the masses.

On one side of the foyer, Farley Dell was growing annoyed with a *Guardian* journalist who had just informed him that *Playing With Fire* should revive his flagging career. Further back, near the toilets, Scott Tyron was becoming infuriated with tabloid hacks who were more interested in photographing his new girlfriend than hearing him talk about the challenge of his film role.

But the star of the show was Ixora. She stood in the centre of the floodlit foyer, the hub of the media universe, demurely replying to each fired question, the reporters around her falling respectfully silent as she quietly spoke. For John, this was a sure sign that she was destined for greatness. Tyron's star was now quite suddenly and unexpectedly in the descendant. Ixora was the name on everyone's lips. Who was she, what was she, where had she been all this time? If only Howard could have seen her now, thought John.

He made his way to one of the side doors and slipped out. The crowds were thinning from the barriers, having achieved their aim of glimpsing royalty. Since they had entered the cinema, the temperature outside had fallen close to freezing point. John pulled the lapels of his dinner jacket a little tighter to him and set off to the north side of Leicester Square. He patted his breast pocket to make sure that it still contained the promissory note from the bank.

He wondered what Helen would say when she discovered that he and Ixora were married. Diana Morrison would probably ask them to hide the fact, in order to capitalise on Ixora's new status both as a sex symbol and a serious actress. He knew it would be easy now to find another job as a publicist, but he was no longer sure that that was what he wanted to do. He was starting to think of a career beyond the media world, something with less duplicity involved. After all, Helen and Josh would still need to be provided for.

He was still considering his future when he reached the Windmill Casino, a sleazy fifties gaming house that had somehow been bypassed in the Soho clean-up campaigns. As he descended the neon tube-lined staircase, he knew he should have expected trouble from a club whose reception area was in the basement. A young girl in heavy makeup and a red nylon teddy sat hunched over the signing-in book.

'Could you print your name please,' she said, giving an involuntary shiver. 'I'm supposed to be sitting up straight but the radiator's under the desk. Is it still cold out?'

John nodded sympathetically.

'Thought so.' She gritted her teeth. 'My tits are dropping off.'

He entered the club, passing between a brace of battered gaming tables where the punters, mostly foreign businessmen, were losing money in a perfunctory, disinterested manner. Reproduction tiffany lamps jutted from ruched clusters of red velvet curtains in a half-hearted attempt to conjure an atmosphere of glamour. It was hard to imagine anything less stylish. The circumstances of his earlier visit returned to him now like a half-remembered dream.

How could he have allowed himself to be conned so easily? Surely this dismal, damp-smelling hall filled with menopausal lotharios drinking watered brandies should have set off some kind of alarm bell in his brain, no matter how drunk he had been? For a moment he considered leaving to inform the police of a clear case of extortion. Then he recalled that the stakes were raised by Ixora's new-found fame. He could not afford to have her name associated with any kind of scandal at the most crucial point in her career. These people knew where she lived. There was no telling what they might do.

At the bar sat half a dozen girls dressed in schoolboy-fantasy outfits, mail-order versions of the real thing. They seemed neither happy nor sad, merely vacant, like patients in a waiting room. He asked the barman to direct him to Mancuso's office, and was escorted to a small room at the rear within auditory range of the toilet.

Mancuso rose and shook his hand, ushering him into a seat on the other side of the desk. One wall of the office was stacked from floor to ceiling with accounting folders. Computers, a printer and a fax machine stood against a bricked-up window. Only the sexual crudity of the pin-up calendars behind Mancuso's desk gave any indication that they were not conducting an interview in a chartered accountant's office.

Mancuso murmured appreciatively as he studied John's evening attire. 'You're a very smart dresser, Mr Chapel. I wish more of our customers had your class. Confidentially, business is bad. We can't compete with the hotels. They've got all the big spenders. That's why we're forced to diversify.'

'Things are tough all over,' said John. He removed the envelope from his pocket. He thought: let's get this over with quickly. Let me get away from here and nothing like this will ever happen again. In half an hour's time he would have joined the group at Langan's, ordered himself a drink and washed the taint of this place out of his mouth forever. The last of the loose ends would have been tied up. Now they could start to live.

'That's for me, I take it.' Mancuso reached across with an outstretched hand. 'I would have preferred cash, as we specified. There will be a surcharge on cheques. I'll have my man work it out for you.'

John was not about to argue. He'd pay the additional amount, whatever it was. Mancuso tore open the envelope and unfolded a sheet of paper. As he did so, the smile slowly faded from his face.

'The trouble with people like you,' he said quietly, barely able to control the anger in his voice, 'is that you have no respect for the working classes. You look down on us. You consider us useful. Then, as soon as you no longer require our services, you forget all about us.'

He leaned his elbows on the desk and turned over the paper, holding it aloft. The page was completely blank.

'Well, Mr Chapel,' he said. 'I promise you'll never forget us after tonight.

CHAPTER
46
Crucifix

Helen stood back from the crucifix and tipped the spot-light in its direction. The cracked gilt paint around its base glittered, casting diamonds of light against the wall. The rest of the team had gone home hours ago, but how could she leave when there was still so much to do? Helping to rebuild the church had become her new passion in life. Beside the pleasure she derived from this, her own problems paled into insignificance.

St Anne's in Wardour Street had been built in the last quarter of the seventeenth century, probably to a Wren design. The chapel had been destroyed during an air raid in 1940, and now only the tower survived, but in 1976 an appeal had been launched to restore at least part of its former glory.

Helen stepped back over the rubble, shifting the

workman's tools and setting down her lantern. Above her the tower rose in darkness, home to hundreds of shuffling pigeons. Sleet had begun to patter faintly against the slats of the turret. Here, where George II had once worshipped, William Hazlitt, Dorothy L. Sayers and the King of Corsica were buried. The small church gardens had been raised six feet above the pavement in order to house the corpses of over ten thousand parishoners. As she worked with the others, mostly students, she felt she was sharing part of their history.

The three-foot wooden crucifix was on loan, a premature installation arranged as a gesture to restore a sense of holiness to the gloomy shell. Around the church tower new offices were springing up. There was a sense of regeneration here ...

She looked up when she heard the street door open, automatically wiping her hands on her dungarees. The *diamanté*-clad vision which stepped into the dim circle of light was an absurd offence to their surroundings.

'So this is where you work,' said Ixora, eyeing the unplastered walls with distaste. 'Among the God-fearing folk.'

'What are you doing here?' asked Helen, momentarily thrown off her guard.

'I read your letter. My husband was too busy to come.' She stepped over a pile of splintered rafters and continued forward, her sparkling white dress and jacket seemingly parodying the design of a traditional wedding dress.

'Your husband?'

'We were legally married within a day or so of your divorce. As John was tied up on business, I thought I could help you with your problem instead.'

'My business is with John.' She looked around for a suitable escape route and found none. The rest of the tower was in darkness. The only door faced on to the street, from which Ixora had just appeared.

'You have no business with John any more. We are now man and wife. For richer, for poorer. In sickness, and in death. What you have to say to him can be said to me.' The top half of her face was in shadow. Her green eyes glittered in the dark like fiery emeralds.

Helen tried to speak but found she had lost her voice. She cleared her throat and backed up against an iron water-tank propped against the wall. The brackish liquid within clonged dully against the sides.

'If you must know,' she said, 'I wanted to warn John away from you.'

'Dear Helen, why would you want to do that?'

'I've spent enough time at church to recognise evil. I know you mean to hurt him. I don't know why. He's a good man. Anyway, I doubt John would have paid any attention to me. He seems totally besotted.' She studied Ixora's dress. 'I assume it was the premiere of your film tonight.'

'It was. I was sensational. Even you would have liked me.'

'I don't like films,' said Helen, playing for time. She was sure now that Ixora meant her some kind of harm. 'It's all just acting.'

'Isn't everything?' Ixora circled at the edge of the light. 'How do you tell what's real and what's not these days?'

'You trust your instincts. I felt there was something bad about you, right from the start. That's natural. After all, you stole my husband. But there was something deeper that disturbed me. The first night he saw you, at Waterloo Station, he talked in his sleep. Something about you being dressed in red, or white; I can't remember the details. Later that week I read about a man who'd been found dead in his flat — murdered on the same night that John first saw you. He lived in Vauxhall, very near the station.'

Helen moved to the base of the crucifix and sat, folding her arms. Ixora stopped pacing and watched her. She seemed deterred by the giant sign of the cross.

'Some time after John moved out, I got this foolish notion in my head that you had killed that poor man, that John had seen you running away, and that you had decided to seduce him because you wanted to know what he'd seen.'

She blew a wisp of hair from her eyes. 'I mean, given my near-hysterical state at the time, it seemed like a plausible theory. I had no real reason to think such a thing, of course. Why should I have? I was just sitting at home, turning thoughts over, reading detective stories. But the link was made, and it stayed. I remembered I was watching TV when John came home that first night. There was a programme on about conceptual art, people hurling great splashes of paint at canvasses. Then, the night he first talked to you, he came home full of this glamorous new world of his, and there I was, watching TV again, only this time it was a nature thing about spiders, something about the diadem spider killing its mate after intercourse. It's funny how the mind works. Flashing images, strung together. You running on the stairs. The splashes of paint. John describing your dress as red, then white ...'

'Poor Vincent. He bled so much,' said Ixora, her voice free of all emotion. 'I was dressed to the nines, returning from a photographic session. I knew where Vincent lived, and went to see him. We got into a fight and I cut him with a kitchen knife. I must have hit an artery, because the blood sprayed everywhere. It wouldn't stop. He grabbed at me as he fell, covering my dress in the process. My hands, my shoulders, everything was smeared with blood. I turned and fled, running and running until I reached the station. I suppose the downpour must have evened out the stain. The back of the dress was still white. John never quite understood what he'd seen that night. He kept asking me about it, but I denied I was ever there. He'd seen part of a scene I had filmed for *Playing With Fire*, where I ran up a flight of stairs. I felt sure he would make the connection then, but no. My secret stayed safe.'

'You killed all of them, didn't you?' asked Helen, shaking now with cold and fright. 'John thought I knew nothing of what was happening, but I followed the investigation every step of the way. I even hinted at the truth when the police visited me. How could you cause all of this, Ixora?'

'No one can ever know the answer to that except John,' replied Ixora. 'And even he will never be able to fully understand.'

'Why can't you let him be?'

'Because he is the chosen one. Because this must be seen through to the end, no matter how painful it is for both of us.'

'I don't understand,' said Helen. 'You are his wife!'

'I am John's bride,' agreed Ixora, 'but I am the Devil's mistress.'

'It was you who attacked us on Christmas Eve! You tried to harm us then. I lost the baby because you caused the power lines to fall ...'

'I don't know what you're talking about. I am in His thrall, but I have no supernatural abilities. Nobody does. The naïvety of people like you makes me sick. Do you honestly think the Devil would share his power with mortals?' She released a bitter laugh.

'Nobody at the top gives away anything that is still of value to themselves. They merely grant enough power to enslave. Do you think I would be doing all this if there was any way that I could stop it?' Her pale, sweating face was taut with strain, her eyes gelatinous with withheld tears. 'Don't you know how much easier it would have been if I hadn't fallen in love with him?' She wiped her eyes with the heel of her hand.

'I can't understand unless you tell me everything, Ixora,' said Helen, stepping forward.

'But I'm not allowed to tell anyone,' she cried. 'Damned if I do. Damned if I don't.'

'Then I must save you from this madness.'

'I wish you hadn't said that.'

Searching about her, she saw what she was looking for and suddenly hoisted the workman's axe by its handle. Helen screamed and jumped clear from its path as Ixora swung at the wooden crucifix. The metal blade chunked into the gilt wood, toppling the cross so that it swung upside down before falling with a splash into the water-tank. Ixora bared her teeth in a helpless vulpine grin. In the flickering lamp light she looked different now, possessed, distorted, her eyes hidden in bottomless hollows of shadow.

As Helen turned and ran, Ixora stepped forward with the raised axe and swung it with all her might, the head clanging and scattering a stack of pipes. With a scream Helen darted behind the pile, and found herself up against the rear wall of the tower.

She watched helplessly as Ixora hauled the shaft back and upward, swinging it high above her head, then allowing it to fall by its own weight. The flight of the blade came to a sudden jarring halt as it buried itself deep in the top of her victim's skull with a sickening crack.

'The final obstacle removed,' said Ixora, standing up straight and smoothing the creases from her dress as Helen slid down the wall and fell into the rubble.

'For what John is about to receive,' she said, 'may the Lord forgive me.'

CHAPTER
47
Renunciation

Hargreave threw open the door of his sergeant's office to find the lights off and her desk clear. He grabbed a passing clerk by the lapel. 'Where's Sergeant Longbright? She's supposed to be here.'

'She might have gone for something to eat,' suggested the startled junior. 'She was trying to find you.'

'And I was in the bloody basement.' He released the boy's lapel. 'If you see her, tell her to meet me at the Odeon Leicester Square as soon as ...'

'Ian! He's not there.' Janice came running along the corridor. 'I just spoke to the manager. The film finished half an hour ago. They're all en route to Langan's Brasserie.'

'Let's find my car.' They ran for the stairs at the rear exit.

'I've already put someone at the door of the restaurant,' said Janice. 'They'll call us the moment either of them turn up.'

'How did you—'

'I just saw Maria Dallow. She told me what happened. She's filing an official complaint against you.'

'That's understandable. Wingate said Ixora would kill her husband "on the night men come to worship her". She'd given him a false name, but she couldn't resist telling him when her film premiered. Poor old Wingate may have been psychotic, but he remembered his dates.'

'Apparently she was mobbed as she left the cinema. The manager was calling her a star.'

They left the building and ran for Ian's car.

'At least we know when she's going to do it,' he said, unlocking the door, 'even if it's not clear why. It's my guess that they won't go straight to the restaurant.'

'She has to be seen there. Everyone will notice her absence.'

'But their tables are booked for 11.30 p.m. By midnight she and John will be surrounded by people. They'll stop off somewhere quiet on the way, then she'll go to the restaurant alone. She could still be less than an hour late. Call in and have them dig out Chapel's car registration.'

'What about us?' asked Janice as they swung out of the car park.

'We have to check every building on the route between the cinema and the restaurant.'

'But that covers Leicester Square, the Haymarket, Piccadilly, and virtually the whole of Mayfair!'

'We have no choice,' said Hargreave. 'If Wingate is to be believed — and I am loath to ignore the words of a dying man — John Chapel has less than an hour to live.'

*

John stared back at the blank page and tried to rationalise his thoughts. Obviously a mistake had been made; Ixora had handed him the wrong envelope, or she had simply failed to include the promissory note.

'Believe me, I am not trying to make a fool of you,' he said carefully. 'I'm every bit as surprised as you. There has to be a simple explanation.'

'Oh, there's an explanation, all right,' said Mancuso. 'Gamblers are born liars, and bad gamblers are the worst.' He turned to the door. 'Jim, Danny, get in here.'

Two sizeable young men entered the room, City wide-boys in shiny suits and matching haircuts. Hauling John from his seat, they walked him out, their hands gently but firmly wedged beneath his arms. He saw at once that there was no point in arguing. He was facing some kind of painful physical rebuke, presumably a standard punishment meted out to debtors. Surely first offenders were merely given a good frightening, then released?

They climbed a narrow stairway single file, with John in the middle. At the top they crossed a small landing and climbed a second staircase, then a third and fourth. The floor above them opened out across the whole of the building in a wide loft, bare boards and angled panels of dirty glass, an area which had once been a milliner's sweat-shop. At the end of the room, snow drifted in through an open skylight. Presumably nobody downstairs would be able to hear him cry out.

He was led to a chair which stood alone in the middle of the floor beneath a single neon striplight. Dark stains on the boards around the chair legs confirmed his worst fears.

'Just sit there for a moment, will you?' Mancuso had followed his boys to the top of the stairs. Now he spoke to one of them, who nodded and left the room.

'I know you don't believe me, but this is a genuine mistake,' said John. 'It can be put right very easily.' He knew that Mancuso's main concern would be to recover his loan.

'So I let you leave, and you skip the country again. Where is the money, Chapel?'

'At the bank.'

'In your account?'

'No, in my wife's.'

'You told me you'd left your wife.'

'That's right. I left her but I married someone else.'

'When?'

'Just recently.'

'You married someone else while you were out of the country.' Mancuso considered the facts for a moment, then shook his head. 'No, it won't do.' He pointed a finger at Danny. 'Hit him.'

Danny withdrew what looked like a grey, flexible club from his pocket and hefted it in his hand. Suddenly he lashed it across the bridge of John's nose. There was a sharp crack, and blood spurted hotly across his face. He fell forward, gasping. Fingers slipped into his hair and pulled his head upright. A fist punched at his throat. Mottled darkness, like clouds of ink, blossomed before his eyes.

When his vision cleared, he found Ixora standing before him.

'Why is she here?' Mancuso was asking his other lieutenant, who had suddenly returned.

'She ran up the stairs before I could stop her,' said Jim.

John tried to speak, but his throat was full of blood. Ixora's hands had flown to her face. She was still dressed in her premiere gown, but now it looked as it had on the night he had first laid eyes on her. Deep red splashes covered the bodice.

'Ixora,' he managed to say finally. 'Don't let them hurt

you.' He hawked and spat a bloody chunk of gristle on to the floorboards.

'They won't hurt me, John.'

She sounded strange, as if she was fighting to control herself.

'Tell them this is all wrong.' He pointed to where the sheet of blank paper had fallen. 'For God's sake, explain.'

Before anyone else could speak, Mancuso gave another wave of his hand. Danny punched John squarely in the stomach. He cried out and doubled over, falling to the floor and retching. Ixora gave a small scream and ran forward.

'For Christ's sake, tell them!' said John. 'Tell them it's all a mistake!'

'I can't, John. There's been no mistake.'

It was a minute before he could regain enough breath to speak. 'You gave me — wrong envelope—'

Ixora walked forward until her legs were within his vision. Her stilettos were spotted with blood. 'No, John, I've betrayed you.' It sounded as if she was trying not to cry. 'I've betrayed you, and they are going to kill you. Please don't make it any harder than it already is.'

He tried to sit up, but Danny kicked him in the chest, then the stomach. Fresh spasms of pain started him coughing. Blood filled his mouth. 'No,' he whispered, 'you don't understand — the letter from the bank—'

'There was no letter, John. I never went to the bank.'

' — no—'

'I've lied to you all along …'

' — no—'

'From the moment we met …'

' — no — I love you—'

'I'm guilty, guilty of everything.'

' — I love you, Ixora—'

'You must believe it. You cannot trust me. You never could.'

' — but I do trust you. Isn't that what you always wanted?'

He sat up against the chair as Danny looked to Mancuso for instructions. 'You're just blaming yourself — I know that you're innocent — I know it in my heart.'

'Take him up on the roof,' said Mancuso finally. 'I've heard enough of this.'

As Danny pulled him upright, the sharp pain in his side told him he had a broken rib. There was a bang and a blast of cold air as the steel roof hatch was thrown back. The room tipped as he was thrown across Danny's shoulder and hauled on to the tiles. Outside, the bitter wind sharpened his senses, the disorientation within him settling.

The gable roof sloped away to a brick parapet and a five storey drop into the market streets of Soho. They climbed above the skylight on a wooden walkway to the peak, where a row of ancient chimneypots ran along one side of the roof. It was snowing hard, luminescent flecks falling from a slate-grey sky as the city lit the clouds. Danny pushed him back against the stack and held him there. The proliferation of cigarette packs and beer cans suggested that this spot was used on a regular basis.

Blood was leaking from John's mouth, reappearing as fast as he wiped it away with the back of his hand. He wondered if he'd been damaged internally.

Mancuso dismissed his henchmen and stood before him, alone. The light from the streets below formed a grey haze of snow around him as he stood back, balancing on the angled walkway. As John watched, trying to understand what was happening so that he could plan an appropriate course of action, Ixora appeared at the hatch. She climbed out on to the roof and tapped Mancuso on the shoulder, reaching up to whisper in his ear. They seemed very familiar with each other. Finally, after listening to her, he nodded his assent and walked down the parapet at the end of the roof. Ixora came over and stood before John.

'He's going to kill you,' she said angrily, 'don't you understand?'

'Why would he kill me? He'll never see his money then.'

'It's not about money. I told you I was … cursed.'

'You explained all that and we agreed—'

'Listen to me! He thinks you killed one of his best men. Matteo Dominguez worked for him.'

'Matteo? But why would he think I killed him?'

'Because that's what I told him.'

'Ixora, nothing you say makes any sense. This is all in your mind. You've just convinced yourself that these crazy things are true. I love you. I can't—' A wave of nausea passed over him. He held out his arm, trying to steady himself as Mancuso came back across the roof.

'Okay, Mr Chapel, you have to go now,' he said, looking towards the parapet. He seized John's arm and marched them both down to the edge of the roof. John slipped and fell in a welter of broken tiles, sliding the last few feet, his head thudding against the angled parapet. Mancuso began to pull John's body upright and bind his hands with cord.

'No,' cried Ixora, 'I need more time with him.' She pushed Mancuso out of the way and turned to John.

'Now listen,' said Mancuso, 'we had an agreement. You turned this asshole over to me, remember?'

'Then let me do it.'

'Wait a minute.' He grabbed John under the arms and hauled him on top of the sloping brick parapet. 'You want to talk to him, talk all you like. I reckon you've got three minutes before he slides off. Try to aim him between the trucks. That way my man can get the body off the street before anyone sees.' He rose and dusted down his trousers. 'I'll be downstairs. If we don't hear the thud, I'll be back up.'

Ixora fell to John's side. He was half-conscious, slipping slowly toward the edge of the parapet.

'You can't love me any more, do you see that now?' she cried. There was something pleading in her voice that suggested she was trying to extract a particular reply from him.

'I'll always love you,' he said. 'I don't believe you're guilty. I used to, but you taught me how to trust. Don't you see, Ixora? There's nothing you can say or do that will ever convince me of your guilt.'

'No, John—'

'You can tell me anything. Show me your hands covered in blood. Let me see the knife go in. It won't make any difference. I know that you're innocent in your heart. I know.' He tasted blood and coughed, crimson splashing the shattered tiles. He knew he was losing blood fast, and would soon lose consciousness. Ixora was crying now, hard angry tears.

'You fool!' she screamed at him. 'Don't you understand, even now? It's only when you fully believe in me that I can destroy you! I can't do it until I have your total trust!' She grabbed his shoulders and shook him. 'I tried to warn you. I tried to tell you the truth. This is my hell, John, my penance for being saved from the storm! He appeared to me, he appeared in the water and told me I would live, that my beauty was too great to be lost to the world forever. I agreed to his bargain. He would save me and make me his. I would live in his service, and my beauty would be worshipped by the world. But the penance for my life and success — the penance—' her words were released in ragged sobs — 'was to make men fall in love with me, to betray them only when they became convinced of my innocence. But at that moment in the swirling sea, I had no inkling of the awful deal I had struck. To be adored forever, and forever alone.' She fell back on the tiles, sobbing. John wanted to reach out and hold her, but he dared not shift his weight any closer to the edge.

'It should have been so easy,' she said. 'You weren't the first. And you were so naïve. It was me who spoiled everything.'

'— Why —?'

The light was fading now. He could barely discern her outline, his vision tipping as he slithered on the snow-slick brickwork.

'Because I fell in love with you!' She leaned forward and he saw her eyes, filled with the pain and horror of loving him, and he knew she was speaking the truth.

'I love you, and by loving you I am damned for all eternity. John, listen to me.' She grabbed at his neck, trying to pull him back as first one leg, then the other slid out over the edge. A tile cracked and fell to the pavement below. 'You still have a chance. Renounce your love for me. You can at least save yourself.'

' — can't hurt you, Ixora—' His words were slurring now. He was fading fast. The lower half of his body was swinging out over the street.

'Renounce it!' she screamed, clutching at his clothes as he slipped faster.

'No,' he said. 'I can't.' He studied her smeared face and tear-swollen eyes as she pleaded with him, knowing that his last sight would be of her, and he drew warmth from the thought. She twined her hands tightly in his, desperate to prevent his fall.

'You said you'd never leave me. John, don't leave me alone!'

'I won't, Ixora.'

'Then say the words! Say you no longer love me!'

As the darkness closed over him and he felt himself torn from the warmth of her embrace, he cried into the sky:

'*Never.*'

CHAPTER
48
Epiphany

'The nurse told me you were awake. I brought you some vegetable soup. Sergeant Longbright, remember?' She pulled at her sweater. 'I don't go on duty for another hour. Nobody ever recognises me out of uniform.'

John tried to sit up, but the pain in his chest made him wince and fall back to the pillow. He was wearing a neck brace. Soft sunlight fell through the slatted blinds, striping the cream counterpane of the bed. There were flowers and a Get Well card on the nearby cabinet, he couldn't tell who had sent them.

'I wouldn't try to move,' she said, setting the soup bowl in front of him. 'You've a lot of healing to do.' Longbright was right. He would never have recognised her.

'How did I get here?' he asked, surprised by a fiery pain in his throat as he spoke.

'You have Chief Inspector Hargreave to thank for that,' said the sergeant. 'We were searching the streets and he spotted you just a few moments before you fell. We managed to break the worst of your fall with a tarpaulin from one of the market stalls, but you still hit the ground very hard. You broke your leg and two toes as you landed. You have a shattered nose, which is why you sound funny, three broken ribs and some internal tearing. You've also broken one of the tiny bones in your neck, a *plexus brachialis*, which will be painful for a while. They gave you a transfusion, but you've been unconscious for nearly a week. I thought you'd prefer me tell you what happened rather than start again with a stranger. Not today, though. We'll wait until you've fully recovered.'

'You saved my life.'

'Part of the job, as they say.' She filled a spoon with soup and raised it. 'This is quite cool, so it shouldn't hurt your throat.'

'What about—' He had opened his mouth to speak, and found a spoon in it.

'I think that can wait until you're up and about,' said Longbright, extracting the spoon. 'Your son has been to see you every day. The card and the flowers are from him.' She passed him the card. 'He's a nice boy. You must be proud.'

As Longbright rose to leave, she tapped a large envelope which lay on the bed. 'I'm leaving this with you. It's a photocopy, I'm afraid. We had to retain the master for fingerprinting. It was left at your house.'

After the sergeant had gone, he tore open the brown paper flap of the envelope and extracted a handful of lined sheets. The jagged edges along one side told him that they were the missing pages from Ixora's diary. Some of the notes appeared to be more recent, and had been written over the top of existing entries.

john.

if you are reading this, it is because our life together has reached an end. i have told you so many lies. i have to confess my sins and i will never be able to do it to you in person. i hope this will explain everything.

i suppose you could say that ixora de corizo died when she drowned in the storm that terrible day off the coast of st lucia. in her place was a creature men could only see with lust in their eyes, a woman destined to destroy all who dared to love her.

they say the devil cries each time he steals a soul, because it takes him one step further from the love of god. i suppose the devil is in a special hell of his own, always having to tempt mankind, knowing that he can only be redeemed if man resists.

so it is with the devil's woman. as i descended in that terrifying maelstrom of sea and blood, feeling my last breath torn from my lungs, i heard his voice booming in the water all around me, and understood the nature of his offer. there was a way to cheat my tragic end. and i wanted so to live and love! is there a woman alive who would not have agreed to his terms, as i did?

but as i waded towards the shore, i had no idea of the terrible price i would have to pay for my redeemed life. i swear to you that i tried to resist my fate. but the devil has the wiles of a man. he tricked me. when i emerged from the sea that day i was transformed into a vessel for his use, a creature with a destructive carnality as natural as the pulse of the tide.

slowly i grew to understand what i had become. he taught me blood-lust. first, he made me take revenge on the one man i had known in my old life, my travelling man, the man who had deserted me without explanation, vincent brady. i knew where he lived, but i resisted for a long time. finally i was forced to go there and confront him.

as i progressed, i discovered the rules of my contract. i could harm no one wearing the symbol of their religion. it had to be removed and immersed in fresh water in order to be robbed of its protective power. when i killed vincent brady it was as if an exhilarating force entered me, some mighty power that cocooned me and took away the horror. i gained strength when i killed. i recognised the terrible potency that grew within me as the power of the devil himself, entering his mistress to achieve his climax in a purifying act of violence.

after, as he withdrew from my body and the power faded, the full force of what i had done overcame me, and i fled from vincent brady's flat in terror.

and then you saw me on the steps of the station. i was covered in blood, but the rain and the light must have hidden this from you. our meeting at the party was sheer coincidence. nothing might have happened, but then i saw the way you looked at me and i knew you wanted me, and our fates were tied together.

the scene in the film where i ran on the steps made you think of that night at the station. i suppose i subconsciously performed the same movements. i had to lie to you, of course, and then i couldn't stop.

i set out to make you love me and trust me so that i could destroy you. but then i learned another rule of the contract. if you lost faith in me, or saw through me, i would lose everything.

the first thing that went wrong was the photographic session. when dickie feldman made me wear the clothes of a whore, he didn't know that i saw him shoot a roll of film without telling you.

i was sure that if you saw the photographs you would discover my deception. killing feldman was a genuine pleasure. filled with satan's cleansing power i returned to the studio and rammed the film down his filthy throat.

i refined my art. it was easier to influence you when we were in a place associated with death. that part was easy. london is a city built on the dead. waterloo station once had daily funeral trains collecting corpses from their necropolis. its building is topped with the roll-calls of the slain. i met you in the crypt at st martin's, surrounded by corpses. and so it went, death helping us to love.

i first met matteo dominguez in st lucia. he took some pictures of me with vincent. innocent snaps, the three of us at dinner. when we saw each other again in london i went to bed with him. matteo never trusted me from the start, so the contract was void. we could have become friends, but instead he jeopardised my relationship with you.

matteo recognised vincent's picture in the newspapers. i knew it was only a matter of time before he used his knowledge. i tried not to kill him. instead, knowing he was dealing drugs for mancuso i had him framed. he came to me desperate for money, but his clumsy attempt at blackmail failed, and he beat me.

even so, i would have let him live, but then he tried the same route with you, and i was forced to act. ironically, sergeant sullivan showed you matteo's photographs on the night of the wrap party, but neither he nor you spotted vincent brady in them.

at that time i had not yet fallen in love with you. even so, something made me want to set you free.

when you began asking questions about dominguez it sealed his fate, and yours. i had to chase him to the fountain near the palace, so that i could place his crucifix in water. i put his body high on the railings to make it look like the act of a man.

the afternoon when we visited the river, and you quoted poetry, you said you had no knowledge of the verse. but i knew; it was the pact-sealing scene from goethe's faust. at first i thought you were taunting me. when i realised you had no idea of the truth, i saw that my sins were starting to reflect on you.

soon there were so many lies i couldn't remember what i had told you about my past, my family. one thing was sure; i knew i could act. i was so good that sometimes i had to fake bad acting for the cameras. otherwise you might have guessed the truth.

the last thing i needed was for tony saunders to reappear in my life. yes, we really had been married, but we divorced after two years, when he discovered my secret. his survival after that depended on his silence. when he began to pester me again, i set out to make him fearful for his life.

several times i waited for him in the dark outside his house, the spirit of my master filling me with avenging strength. but each time i resisted the killing urge. it was you he sent the marriage certificate to, not me. he was trying to warn you away. as a doctor, he was dedicated to saving life.

luckily i intercepted the mail. when i showed you the envelope later, i kept my hand over the address. tony realised the certificate had been diverted, and tried to get it back. it was the only way he could prove to you that i was lying. he was sure that i would get to him first. that was why he carried a weapon. he was in daily fear of his life.

i learned another rule of the contract. as long as tony still loved me, i could extend the time limit on his death. i decided to deal with him after you.

and you, john, *you* were the problem. i procrastinated. you left your wife for me. some days i felt so sorry for you i looked for ways to break the contract. and the more time that passed, the more i fell in love with you.

then tony saunders showed up and tried to poison you against me. i was forced to do something about him quickly. i arranged to meet him on the bridge. i even drugged your cocoa to keep you asleep that night. but tony had a trick up his sleeve. on his way to the rendezvous, he came to the house and knocked you unconscious. no doubt he thought it would keep you out of the picture while he dealt with me.

i was desperate. i relocked the front door so it looked like you'd imagined the attack. i had no real gun, so i took the speargun i used to fish with. but i was late arriving, and tony had been arrested in my place, so i was forced to kill the policeman.

helen found out you were having an affair because i called her. i even gave her your new address. remember you wondered how she'd got it?

i left false clues. at each murder site i sprinkled aftershave i had stolen from tony's bathroom. i even impersonated him when i left vincent brady's flat. i made sure the shopkeeper opposite saw me. i think that particular subtlety was wasted on the police.

i could see that my growing infatuation with you could only destroy us both. i tried to pull myself together, to harden myself against you. i knew that if i didn't, all was lost.

i told scott tyron i was sleeping with you to have you thrown off the account. i had sex with howard to get you fired, did you know that? but howard turned on me. it occurred to me that i could get rid of him and have you blamed.

i was just another made-up model entering the club that night. i knew no one would ever remember seeing me in the crowd. i took my revenge on howard. i used the sword that hangs in the downstairs lounge. i actually wore it into the club. one slip-up though. i had no idea he was carrying my ring.

so there you were, out of a job, detained by the police — and i saved you, bailing you out. but thanks to that damned ring i had left beside howard's bed, you still didn't believe in me.

i had to have that declaration of trust to fulfil the contract, but you were more suspicious than ever. i deliberately smashed up your car, hid interview letters from you, did everything i could to break your will, to force you to rely on me. but still you held out. and the worst thing was, the more you held out the more i loved you for it, because my darling it meant that you were safe from me.

there was another bright lie. the one about my father trying to assault me. i thought it would give you a hook on which to hang your understanding of my problems.

by this time there were so many deaths surrounding us i needed a scapegoat to take the pressure off. i found wingate walking the streets in camden town, a vagrant with a history of mental problems. he was perfect. he and tony saunders even shared similar backgrounds.

i learned how to hypnotise from a book, although you might say i had a head start. on the right person, it was easy. i told wingate that i was his key to fame. i planted my story in his mind, then made him to go into the department store and do something stupid to get arrested. i suggested stealing a gun and firing blanks. i didn't think he'd kill someone.

just to make sure, i well and truly framed my poor mr wingate. i put fibres on his trousers, and left a sliver of matteo's skin beneath his fingernails.

so an innocent man confessed to my crimes, and i thought that was the end of it. but you and i were at an impasse. i had fallen in love with you. you still didn't trust me. what happened next was unexpected for both of us.

i had a moment of weakness. after all the planning, and all the hard work, i acted according to my heart.

i ran away to protect you, and to save helen. i knew if i stayed she would have to die, and you would soon trust me enough to be damned. i took your money to escape. when you discovered it was missing, i lied to you. then i fled.

but you tracked me down and forced me to marry you. and the moment i said 'i do', i sealed our fates forever.

i prevented the reconciliation with your wife. i frightened her at the house. you have no idea of the pains i went to. i stopped your calls connecting by tampering with the line. i even had your gifts sent back.

but you still felt for each other. i had to remove the final thorn in my side. i had to kill helen. and, with the film premiere — my deadline — approaching, it was time to betray you.

you presented me with the method, getting yourself into debt with the company matteo had been working for. it was a simple matter to turn them against you.

all the time, i searched for a way to beat the

contract. and then i found it. it was so simple. i would break your trust in me, and i would trade your escape for the future deaths of many others — even the devil could see the logic in losing one soul to gain ten. i would seduce only those who deserved to die. we would lose each other, but at least you would be allowed to live.

scott tyron was friendly to me at the premiere because i had begun to seduce him. i was grooming him as my next victim, the first instalment of my debt for your release.

there was just one fatal flaw in the plan.

i'd done my job on you too well. you really did trust me, and nothing i could do would break it. do you understand why my moods changed so? i was being torn apart inside, loving you and hating you. desperately trying to set you free, knowing you had to die otherwise. unable to hurt you, unable to have you.

so now you know the truth about me. i don't expect or deserve any sympathy, but try to remember what i was, a child who begged for her life to be saved and unfortunately got her wish. evil against my will, held somewhere between life and death, terrified of both. but john, you know that if there is any truth in this insanity, it is that i love you with all my heart, and always will until my dying day.

how i wish i could die, a real final death! i do not know what will happen to me now. he has not told me the punishment for disobedience. but i am ready. i will not cry. just remember the afternoon when we first made love, the golden quilt, the sun in the trees.

pray for me.

ixora

SPRING

CHAPTER
49
Sleeping Beauty

At this time of the morning, the residents' wing of the hospital was still quiet. He had become a familiar sight in the ward. Nobody stopped him to check his identity card any more. He passed a solitary nurse in the corridor, then arrived at the room.

The strong spring sun was trying to bleach its way through the blinds, so he opened them a foot or so. The band of light fell across the bed just above her waist, illuminating part of a pale shoulder. As always, he changed the flowers in the vase beside her bed, dropping the old stems into a plastic carrier bag. If it wasn't for the intravenous drip suspended from her arm, she might merely have been asleep, waiting to be woken with a kiss.

One of the nurses regularly combed her hair when they turned her, arranging it neatly on the pillow. Lately it had lost its lustre, and Ixora's face had grown more sallow, but the doctor assured him that she was still maintaining a sufficient level of health. Was she dreaming, he wondered? Her smooth features betrayed nothing. Perhaps she was in her own hell now, the reigning bride of a far-off place, safe where no mortal could ever reach her. Behind him, the door opened and closed.

Inspector Hargreave gave a tentative smile and held out his hand. John reciprocated. The detective looked down at the immobile bed. Ixora's breathing had become so shallow as to be imperceptible. 'I was in the next ward on a case,' explained Hargreave. 'I thought I might find you in here. Are you all right?'

'Yes,' said John, 'fine. How is your lady friend?'

'Er, um ...' Colour flooded to Hargreave's face. 'Janice is fine.' He turned back to face the bed. 'The doctor tells me the charts are a little down this week.'

'I know. He said if they get below a certain level she'd suffer brain damage, and they'd have to consider turning her off.'

Hargreave sighed sadly. 'She's been here for over four months, John. There's been no flicker of life since the night we found her on the roof. She's experienced some form of catatonia. Given her anguished mental state at the time, the emotional tug-of-war she says she was going through in those diary notes, perhaps it's not so surprising. If she had undergone intense therapy before this happened, she might have broken the hold this thing had on her mind.'

'It wasn't in her mind,' said John. 'She wasn't crazy.'

'You can't honestly think she'd signed a pact with the Devil,' said Hargreave.

'There was no piece of paper, just a voice that called to her at the height of the storm. Why must the Devil perform parlour tricks to prove his existence? He simply invades our minds and bends us to his will.' He sat beside her, studying Ixora's waxen face, and reached for her hand. 'There's no magic to good and evil, just people and power.'

'She killed your wife,' said Hargreave.

'And I still love her. I guess that's pretty sick, isn't it? She really tried to save us both.' He rose from the bedside. 'Next week the graph will have slipped a little farther down the paper, and they'll want to shut her down. And part of me will die with her.'

There was a knock at the door, and a large constable with cropped blond hair stuck his head in. 'There you are, sir,' he said loudly. 'You're wanted back down the hall.' He noticed the body in the bed. 'Blimey, is that the actress that murdered all them people? What a bitch! Women, eh? You can't trust 'em.'

'Get out, Bimsley,' said Hargreave. He turned to John and placed his arm on his shoulder. 'Did they tell you Mancuso was found guilty? Thirty years, more for the drugs than murder. You know, it's not my business, but if I were you I'd leave this place. Spend the time with your son.'

'I have to be here,' said John. 'I brought this on us both. I had everything a man could possibly want, but I looked at Ixora and for the briefest of moments I wanted more.'

'That's understandable,' said Hargreave with a gentle smile. 'I guess we should all be careful what we wish for, just in case we actually get it.'

He closed the door quietly behind him. John stood for a moment at the head of the bed, watching the inert figure, then bowed his head in silent prayer.

'It wasn't my responsibility to check!' cried the staff nurse. 'I'm not even due on the ward until three!' Everyone began talking at once. A number of orderlies and nurses were milling around the outpatients' reception desk, where the matron stood with a telephone receiver in her hand.

'Don't worry,' she said threateningly. 'I'll soon find out who's responsible for this. It's a criminal offence. I'm on the phone to the police this minute.'

'What's going on here?' said one of the doctors.

'It's the patient in 122,' said the staff nurse. 'She's disappeared.'

'She couldn't move of her own volition. Somebody must have abducted her.'

'How do you know?' asked the matron, holding her hand over the mouthpiece. 'She might have made a sudden recovery and become disoriented. She could be wandering around somewhere, lost and frightened.'

The doctor peered at her above his spectacles. 'My dear woman,' he said, 'that's quite impossible. At 2.00 p.m. this afternoon she was declared clinically brain dead, and the support system was turned off. You're talking about a corpse walking out of the hospital. They might have already removed her to the morgue. Have you checked with the orderlies?'

'Of course,' she said angrily. 'The clearance order for 122 hasn't even come up on the computer yet.' The receiver crackled beneath her chin. 'Hello? I'd like to speak to Detective Chief Inspector Ian Hargreave, please.'

CHAPTER
50
Last Kiss

It was dark by the time the taxi turned into Sloane Crescent, and rain was falling lightly. John absently checked his watch. He would call Cesar's mother and make sure that Josh had been settled for the night. As today was a special one, his son had arranged to stay over with his school friend.

At the final moment, John had been unable to remain in the room. He could not bear to watch Ixora's heartbeat fade to a flat line as the doctor disconnected her support system. Instead he had waited in the corridor, feeling as though part of his life had been cut away. He needed to return to the house and sit alone in the dusty bedroom, as if his presence there would somehow bring her spirit home to rest.

He paid the cab driver and alighted, studying the darkened house where they had spent so much of their time together. Spring had dishevelled the garden into a tangle of unruly dark foliage. He looked up to the dripping eaves and saw that one of the bedroom windows had been shattered. While the lawyers squabbled over property rights, the building was deteriorating. Soon it would resemble the house on Grass Street.

He hadn't expected the hall lights to work, even though he had paid the electricity bills. It had been important to keep the house alive for her, in case she had awoken and wished to return. In his heart he had known that she would never do so. The torment which held her in its thrall would not release her until death, perhaps not even then.

The smell of damp was all-pervading now. Even here, in the temperate comfort of an English city, mould and decay were fast to set in at the first sign of neglect. At least the house had not been broken into. The lights on the landing crackled and fluctuated as he passed. Mottled patches now marred the wallpaper below them. This would be his final visit to Sloane Crescent. Soon the house would be locked up, the victim of looming financial disputes. But for these few last melancholy moments, the place was his.

The golden counterpane still lay on her bed, covered in dust. The lustre of its densely stitched design had dimmed to a dull glimmer. Combs and brushes were neatly aligned on the dressing table, and a nightdress still lay folded on a chair, as if the house had readied itself for her return.

The ridged metal casing of the light switch tingled uncomfortably beneath his fingertips as he switched on the bedroom lamps. He opened one side of the heavy oak wardrobe and saw that her modelling outfits still hung in plastic bags, like absurdly patterned butterflies in transparent cocoons. Could their life together have taken any other course, he wondered, unfolding a sweater which still retained faint traces of her scent, Atar of Roses.

The sound on the stair scarcely surprised him. The floorboard outside the bedroom door had aways creaked. With a pounding heart he closed the wardrobe and stepped out into the hall.

The Persian cat stared up at him and hissed, its eyes no more than emerald slits. Its hair was filthy and matted, revealing its skeletal form. So rarely had he ever seen the damned thing that he had completely forgotten about its welfare. Somehow it had survived, probably living on scraps thrown out in the affluent neighbourhood.

He took a step forward, but it shot between his legs and dashed off into the darkness of the corridor.

And then he saw the human form beneath him, at the foot of the stairs. In the buzzing, flickering lamplight it shifted slowly from one foot to the other, rising step by step, limbs creaking drily, its shadow casting darkness across the ceiling. The hospital gown trailed from shoulder to ground, adding height to the apparition. John stepped back, the hairs on his neck rising. As it moved within the cone of light on the landing, its visage was revealed.

Ixora was paler than she had ever been in life. Her black, flattened hair stood out in shocking contrast to her face. He knew that the power which had kept her alive for these four long months had been withdrawn, and that now another force controlled her physical form.

Her eyes, pale and sad, seemed focused on some distant point. As she moved awkwardly towards him he backed against the landing wall, unable to tear his eyes away from her.

She came to a halt two feet in front of him. Her left hand, its wrist still encircled with a plastic patients' bracelet, clenched and unclenched as if in the grip of a surviving nerve. As she opened her mouth to speak, one eyelid drooped low across her pupil.

'He let me come.'

The sound escaped from her throat in a sigh, as if the air in her lungs had been forced through her vocal chords like a breeze through a harp.

'Do you know what happened today, Ixora?' He found himself wanting to talk to her as though she was still alive.

'Today.'

She slowly turned her head from side to side.

'Today, I was released from the pain. The — terrible — pain.'

'He has you now, Ixora. You are dead.'

'I know. You still love me — don't you?'

She raised her left hand and held it before her.

'Yes,' said John, shrinking from the touch of her searching fingers. 'Yes, I still love you.'

'Then — kiss me.'

John found the corridor at his back and moved slowly into it.

'You knew I would come, John.'

'Yes, I knew.' He realised that this had been his intention, to see her once more. It was conceivable that she had not died in her room, that the shock had somehow revived her and that in the darkness she had walked from the hospital. But one look at the muscles protesting beneath her dead, desiccated flesh told him the terrible truth.

'He let me come to you, John. To say goodbye.'

In the sputtering lamplight he could see that her eyes were wet. A single tear broke and rolled down her cheek. Against his will, he found himself moving forward, into her waiting arms.

Kissing her was not so terrible, merely passionless, like brushing one's lips against cold vinyl. Her dry tongue absorbed warmth and moisture from his. Her left arm gripped his back, its hand grasping and unclenching. As she spoke, the cool air emerging from her mouth smelled of hospital chemicals.

'Such a cruel taskmaster. He would not let me see you — without something in return.'

'What does he want?' John pushed away from her cold body, but the arm at his back kept him in place.

'You, John. He wants you.'

And now for the first time he saw her right arm rise from the gown, its hand withdrawing the sword that had killed Howard, the light shining across its razor edge as it curved high above him. He pushed back hard, but her left arm stayed in place across his back like an iron bar.

'You're not doing this, Ixora, he's forcing you! You never wanted to hurt me.'

For a second it seemed that her eyes still held him in focus.

'You said you loved me. I still love you, Ixora. Even beyond death. Do you understand?'

' — John—?' Like a child, frightened in the dark.

Tears were rolling down her cheeks now. Part of her was still fighting to release them both.

'You're finally dead, Ixora. Your body is just an empty vessel now, that's all he can control. He can never touch your soul again. You can find peace. *He cannot hurt you any more.*'

' — oh John—'

Her hold gave, and he fell back from her, landing hard on the floor. A great ragged sob escaped from her body. He thought for a moment that she would collapse, but suddenly she stiffened as if whipped. As she raised the sword once more and moved towards him, he knew that her spirit had finally been released, that he had lost her forever. Only flesh and bones remained.

She swung the blade and he stumbled back to the door of the disused upstairs lounge, fumbling for the light switch.

Steel hit the wall somewhere to the left of his head. He could no longer see her at this end of the corridor. He listened for her breathing, but no sound came. Instead he heard the sword pulled free of plaster and wiring, and for the first time it occurred to him that he might be destined to die in this house. There was nowhere left to go.

Behind him, the lounge, a single room with bolted, shuttered windows. In front, the dead end of the corridor. No furniture between, no fixtures that could provide a makeshift defence. Ixora stood before the only escape route, armed with a weapon that had killed before and powered with the strength of ten . . .

He had not been concentrating. The blade swung again and found contact with his skin. A stinging flame burst across his left arm. As he cried out and clutched his shoulder, he was aware of an instant deadening that warned him of some major damage to his body. The sound of blood pouring onto the floorboards was like the drip of a fast-running tap.

Wincing painfully, he twisted his body into the lounge. His fingers found the light switch and flicked it. In the room beyond, a dirt-encrusted chandelier briefly burst into life before the electrical circuits overloaded. And in that moment of illumination he saw her coming for him, her mouth widened in a scream, eyes blazing, sword raised, and he knew this was the sight that had confronted each of Ixora's victims a split-second before they had met their deaths.

The smell of burning filled his nostrils. There was a crackling beneath his feet as the ancient electrics burned out, an angry spatter of sparks, a low explosion beneath the boards that burst a ball of flame around the trailing hospital gown. The sword was falling, then spinning from Ixora's hands as she turned around and the flames swept up the back of her dry linen gown, engulfing her entire body.

She screamed and fell against the wall, thumping showers of sparks all around. Within seconds the carpet at his feet was alight. She fell on to the landing with a brittle crash as flames scattered everywhere, and the fire was transformed into a conflagration.

Dazed, he sidestepped her body and ran to the top of the banisters. From the strength of the roaring heat at his back, he could tell that the house was ready for destruction. He ran down the stairs to the hallway and peered back up at the landing, but Ixora's crumpled form was lost within the escalating inferno.

His contract with Ixora was complete. The legacy of their life together had been fulfilled. Was it possible that now her physical form was destroyed she would be left to lie in peace? He lost all sense of time watching the blaze. Nothing of Ixora existed outside of this house. He was still staring up at the flames when a section of dry-rotted ceiling broke away and fell onto him.

Above, the sound of exploding glass could be heard over the roar. He opened his eyes and saw smoke, darkly poisonous, rolling down the stairs towards him. His legs had become pinned in place by the smouldering raft of planks. The air around him had grown hot and heavy. He wanted to sleep, and to forget. In the dim distance he could hear hammering. Someone was at the door ...

'I'm not making a habit of this,' said Ian Hargreave, as two of his officers heaved the burning wood from John's trapped legs. The chief inspector reached down and hauled him to his feet. 'Anything broken?'

'I — don't think so.'

'Then let's get out of here.'

He pushed through the front door and they walked into the garden towards the crowd that had gathered on the pavement.

'I must admit,' said Hargreave, 'I really thought it was all in her mind. But she really did come back for you.' He noticed John's arm. 'Let's get you some medical attention for that, old son.'

At the corner they turned and looked back at the house. John could hear the heat collapsing the roof, and wondered if it was right that he had been spared. Helen was gone. Then he thought of his son, and set off in the direction of the waiting ambulance.

Behind him, luminous embers from the blazing building rose in the night sky, to become lost among the stars like a thousand departing spirits of the dead.